SHERBURNE

SHERBURNE

stories

R.T. SMITH

STEPHEN F. AUSTIN STATE UNIVERSITY PRESS
NACOGDOCHES, TX

SHERBURNE. Copyright © 2012 by R.T. Smith.
All rights reserved. Printed in the United States of America.
No part of this book may be used or reproduced in any manner whatsoever without written permission except in the case of brief quotations embodied in critical articles or reviews.
For more information, address SFA Press, 1936 North Street, LAN 203, Nacogdoches, TX 75962
sfapress.sfasu.edu

Distributed by Texas A&M Consortium
www.tamupress.com

LIBRARY OF CONGRESS CATALOGING-IN-PUBLICATION DATA

Smith, R.T., 1947-
Sherburne : stories / R.T. Smith.—1st ed.

p. cm.

ISBN-13: 978-1-936205-44-8

I. Title

To Sarah

. . . this thing of darkness

I acknowledge mine.

– Prospero

I could 'a' stayed if I wanted to but I didn't want to.

– Huckleberry Finn

CONTENTS

ACKNOWLEDGMENTS

The author wishes to thank the editors of the following periodicals in which some of these stories first appeared:

Ellery Queen's Mystery Magazine : "Thurston"
Grist : "Maggard"
Louisiana Literature : "Rose-Handled Pistol"
Missouri Review : "Cooper's"
Virginia Quarterly Review : "Ina Grove" and "Wretch Like Me"

"Ina Grove" was reprinted in *Best American Mystery Stories*, and both "Maggard" and "Rose-Handled Pistol" were cited as Notable Stories in other editions of that annual. "Wretch Like Me" was reprinted in *New Stories from the South: The Year's Best*, and "Ina Grove" received the 2006 National Magazine Award in Fiction.

Many thanks also go to ZZ Packer, Ron Rash, Scott Turow, Charles Frazier, the Virginia Commission for the Arts, the Virginia Center for the Creative Arts, Donald Secreast, who said exactly what I needed to hear, and to Uncle Clark's red mare who brought me home through the dark.

Finally, I wish to acknowledge my indebtedness to Ryunosuke Akutagawa and Akira Kurosawa, the former for his stories "Rashomon" and "In a Grove," the latter for his film "Rashomon."

THADDEUS

Wretch Like Me

The soldier kneeling in the wet gully has ceased his rocking and sobbing, though the claw-formed limb reaching over him keeps trembling in the breeze, its shadow shaking. It's an oak branch, and its wet-gold leaves are among the first to burnish with the season. The man is grime-faced and hatless, no more beard than a peach, his eyes gray and stunned nearly silver. His blue tunic is soiled and torn at the shoulder, where Du Pre's saber kissed him in the fray. We have watched over this New Yorker since last night, and a weary-faced Garland says the man's collarbone is broken. He's a buck private green as creek moss who just followed orders, factory-like, but he is one of Kilpatrick's new Shadows. His saddle-mates have killed too many of my friends, and he knows the musketoon poised at his ear is cocked, the trigger finger eager to be finished with all this.

We are traveling too light to accommodate a prisoner, and we don't feel kindly toward any of these Yankee mudsills, no matter how addled or inept they seem up close. We've seen their deeds. The sky is rank and smudged with their aftermath. Pure demons, and they drive us to acts of shame.

Last night the prisoner opined to Garland how he found in singed weeds a shell-shot Rebel drummer not more than a dozen years on this earth with his front blown open like a butcher's display. The soldier said he could see the red beating heart as the boy whispered Lordy God and died. Our captive claimed he tried to ease the boy over. Suffer the little children. Everybody gets baptized in the blood. It's out of my hands.

The morning's first rays are spangling, and the wheeling birds have found our handiwork again. They get bolder with each feast, their featherless heads red as the raw wounds they delve. We splash the dregs of what we call coffee on the embers as the sun clears the rise where we can make out ruins of a torched plantation, the big house, sheds and barns all rubbled. The chimneys dark as pillars of ash. Time to shadow off ourselves and seek the column. It's a suffering world. "This flesh and heart shall fail," the grace song says, and I repeat it in a whisper as I sling my kit over the makeshift pommel. The camp apostle would say it's all a veil of tears.

I am in the saddle and out of the ravine, ready to hunt where Wheeler and his staff broke their fast, when I hear the roar of the muskatoon. Eye for an eye, but it is not Christian business, none of it. What could we do but embrace their ways? The horse snorts and champs. He doesn't care for the slaughter smell trailing behind us like spoor.

This is a place where deer would nuzzle and browse at a kinder time, where rabbits would slumber and hungers of the spirit might be fed. A vee of geese is arrowing eastward in the clabbered sky. How fine it would be to rise and flee with them. How splendid to be delivered and redeemed. Best to stifle that, though. Best to heel my mount and leave the misgivings behind, mourn my companions at the gallop. If somebody has to beg mercy for all this at the Last Reckoning, his name in Hell is Sherman.

DREAMING BACK NOW, I could almost believe it was the horrors I beheld, rather than a lead pellet, that knocked my left eye into darkness. In the fall of sixty-four the rivers were burning, rails snarled around pine trunks, homes and barns and churches black as Christy's Minstrels, the burdened people streaming pathetic along the roads. Torched bales and gangrene gave off a stench like the pit of Gehenna. Who were the monsters behind it -- the laws of nature repealed, milk of kindness spoiled, even warfare a set of ruined rules? Stirrup jerky and biscuit, skillygalee and hominy, reloading on the run. The smell of horse sweat and smoke kept us dizzy, a poor excuse for righteous avengers. Our only hymns were rackety bugles or cannon blasts. Sortie and demonstrate, raid and rebuke.

We were keeping owl hours, saddle sleep if any. Maps and the long glass, scouts in and out, always somebody coughing hard or falling behind with the scours. Any hickory might shield a sniper. Any knoll could conceal a score of horsemen. Caution and dispatch, hide and seek. Outside Fentry we halted at a sweet spring. Fighting Joe Wheeler spat his plug and turned to offer me the gourd: "Bible Job had no more reason to grumble than us, Goddamn it, Major, but at least we've got powder and chuck and a barrel of hard spirits. Any well-versed God must take up our side." A dedicated honey man, he was ever seeking after bee signs – some said because his beloved was called "Deborah" – but by then the flowers were long gone. Need be, he could live without sweetness or bacon. He was just sixteen hands high and weighing one twenty, hair ever-tousled, the boy general, a saucy talker, thrice shot, over a dozen horses gone to meet their maker under his saddle. "Damn this" and "shit on that." He was a terror, our best thing left.

We had hit Kilpatrick's mob near Sylvan Grove at dawn. A quick breech. We exploited it full force. It was "Let her go, Gallagher," and the pukes showed their backsides. Kils escaped, but we captured his braided hat and camp kit. A day and a night. At Waynesboro we fought the Federals' barn fires and their repeating Spencers till dark. Our dozen bugle boys went down, every one. Kils torched the bridge over Buckhead Creek, but we patched it with church pews and pushed hard till the niddering buttermilk rangers stampeded headlong into their own infantry. Other days went their way. Sharp work, flummoxed fury. We rode on.

Atlanta was two hundred acres of ash behind us. Wick-black chimneys at every turn. Georgia was already howling, as Lazarus and his wolves headed to the sea. He chewed a cigar even in his sleep, Dame Rumor sang, the bastard who once had claimed to love the South. Lazarus to us, risen from the insane. They had sent him home to Ohio as mad but summoned him back, madness being much the fashion. Now he was blindered as a mill mule, pushing his horde east, muttering, "Salt water, salt water." Nothing to stop him now but pitiful militia and us, Wheeler's Desperates. Thin as crickets, mean as hornets but twice as busy, we had flanked him at Dalton, stood our ground in Kennesaw's inferno. We learned from lightning how to strike and leave only singe and sorrow. Hit and run, harry and sting. Our numbers were not great. Garland Rutledge was still with me, Marichal Wilkes, Big Buck Cooperman, Champs Du Pre, but we lost the Soames boys at Griffin in one volley. A ball cut my collar there. John Sparrow lost an ear. Dozens of horses went down wailing like the damned, thrashing and blood spray everywhere. We buried the Soamses at the depot with hardtack lids to mark their rest, names and dates carved on the front, "Pilot Bread" stamped on the back. Lean times, desperate measures, the season turned frosty and bleak.

GARLAND WAS PRACTICAL, the first to shred the pages of *Cooke's Cavalry Tactics* for tinder. He had been with Wheeler since Chickamauga, but he was reared up in Spalding County, so this was his ground. He had purpose. The blue demons thought themselves Thrones and Seraphs. They were setting the Lost Tribes free, their tabloids boasted, and we were no more than Satan's spawn, soiled knights for The Kingdom of Chains.

"We'll teach them manners," said Garland. "Reap evil will they? We'll put a nick in the scythe."

A slashed country, braised and gloomed. In the railroad beds, they'd prised up the irons, heated and bent them like hairpins around jack pines. "Where's your Jesus now, Taddy Sherburne?" Garland was fuming. "Where's your sword of the Lord? Trust Fighting Joe, dry powder and Mr. Sharps, but Sweet Jesus is obsolete or sleeping. Let's be Hell." He spurred his Tennessee and galloped toward the stench.

IT WAS A CAMP REVIVAL that sparked my appetite for scripture and incited the wags to snipe at me with rough humor. If we'd had a graceful God back in Carolina, my folks had scarce been acquainted with His ways. There was a Bible in the pantry and one dinner blessing: "Keep the plow wing sharp and the mule safe from snakes, our Father. Amen." But they say the whiz of Minié balls can teach you devotion. When Cam Hatley fell at Peachtree Creek, I was altered. On picket before dusk, just lighting our pipes, he was bragging on a jug of molasses he'd scrounged. Then I heard the howl of a shell, felt gust, and nearly half Cam was gone. I was talking to a belt buckle and bloodspray. I didn't talk long.

That night the End of Time Man showed up in a caravan, bone-colored Testament in his fist. He was no agent for the gold road of Heaven. Raw-ribbed, tall, rough as a cob. "The Whirlwind is near," he shouted from the wagon tongue, "Get ready, get ready!" He balanced easy as a bird. "Prepare your eternal soul for the pain and the glory." In the flicker of a brazier, he gave rant and brimstone a flavor even Sherman's butchers hadn't summoned, but he promised solace, and I needed some. I let him wet my head with spring water the horses had likely pissed in, let him bless my sinful hands. He said, "Praise be. You're safe now, boy" and winked. Since then, I'd tried to "Lord-is-my-shepherd" on the march and read the tracts by firelight. Many of the hymns in "The Times in Which We Live" I studied till I'd got them by heart and worn the booklet almost to shreds. Garland showed me no mercy. Marichal was worse.

"Joe Wheeler's fool, Jeff Davis's fool and now Jehovah's. Parson Parsnips! You'll be a man of the cloth before we know it, Sherburne. And won't your little wifey be proud. Now pray me up some sheep stew and a glass of nockum stiff. A warm wench from the flesh farm. Pray us fresh horses, old son. Put your faith to use." I took it in the spirit of my new-found humility, rank aside. We all had more than enough paradox already, trying to get a mind around loving neighbors while hating the Yankees enough to gut them, and I was desperate to preserve some of the man Maggie had pledged *yes* to under the arbor just after Manassas.

Two nights later big Buck invented the cowbell ruse, and I was up to my wrists in eye-for-an-eye again, hoping Jesus would set aside "Thou Shalt Not" and excuse my occupation, though I knew I'd be too ashamed ever to tell it back home.

We'd get close enough to smell their hish and hash, a few of us bellying through the bramble, and when we found a sweet spot, the decoy would clang the bell gentle till some of Lazarus's jackass foragers could start to picture ribs sizzling. They'd dispatch a pilgrim or two to come seeking the stray offering, and we'd hold the Arkansas toothpick up before a man's eyes just after we showed it to his throat, his own breath rasp the last note he heard. Thou Shalt Not, I know, but think of Joshua and young David. The ruse worked four times before word rippled through their ranks. Soon they were shooting at any bovine sound.

WHEN LAZARUS TURNED HIS EYE on Savannah, still prosperous as a wedding cake on the coast, Jeff Davis in his wisdom announced the whole Union force would flounder like Napoleon in Russian winter. They'd starve and freeze, suffer and limpdick it home just like the French fools, but Lazarus sent Jeff a note on Yankee wiping paper, just the two words: "No snow."

Both sides needed to believe they were fighting God's ordained war. We were protecting native ground – corn fields, sisterly virtue and the right to say, "We step out of your Union." The Lincolnites were wiping away an abomination, enslavement of a stolen people. By '64 I'd sure seen enough lashed backs and shackled urchins to know they had an argument, but back in Buncombe County the only slave I knew up close was Aeneas Beedle, and he always sported horehound sticks in his pocket and a big-foot dobbin to run errands for Doctor West. By the time I saw cotton bottoms and regiments of sad stoop-overs aching in the autumn rows, Lincoln had sent his saviors over our threshold. My personal heart's opinion was, "Go home, mill monkeys, and then we'll discuss this other matter." Three years of blaze should have been enough to educate any imbecile. Hell, three months would more than teach a man.

The Soames brothers had come to Bragg's muster with a body servant all shuffle-step and *yassuh, boss.* They loved him like a whipped dog, but no better. Cam had confessed his own family had a dozen and treated them "decent," but he said slaving was a rewardless practice, so they hired smallholders to sucker their tobacco and shell their corn. Results about the same. Out in the world there is no end of questions and ample evil for both sides. What happened to the twelve I never asked.

We fought the blue jackets because they were our enemy and because Lazarus meant to burn a rift in Georgia. His rear guard cut the well ropes and stole the buckets, pissed on the salt licks and shit in the weirs. No more conscience than a crow. His bummers murdered every stock animal they couldn't wolf down and nailed silver services to trees for target practice, poured sorghum in pipe organs. They shot anything resembling a dog for being kin to slave hounds. Here is what Back-from-the-Grave told the papers: "I will scorch this land till its residents feel a permanent night has fallen upon the ground and clung to it." I dreamed him with a bottle of cask-aged how-come-you-so? and a cigar glowing and smoking like a brand.

AS SANDY CHAVIS LESSONED ME over one breakfast of guineas, it was easy to believe whatever favored the coloreds cursed us directly. After all, Lazarus had arrived to raise them and flail us down. *Set my people free* was his command and provided excuse for rampage, though even before the Ebenezer Creek confusion, I could see the way truth was all stewed up with fraud, the Devil's work. Some Yankees just came south for a big Barnum show, the swag and permission to relish arson. "The goose question," as parlor society named slavery, well, it wasn't what made factory minions take up arms. As I saw it, they came foremost to seize our land, so I donated a small plot to each hoplite I could fell and prayed forgiveness.

One evening Captain Wilkes and I were on vidette outside

Macon, and we happened upon a yellow-toned wench sitting by a willow spring at twilight, dressed as fetching as Lola Montez herself, her hair in an apple-hued rigolette, a flowery umbrella in her hands. When we came rattling up, rifles and tack banging the saddletree, she didn't raise a glance to see if we were blue or butternuts.

"Gal," called Marichal. "You, nigger gal." She finally issued just a sigh, but she was so don't-carish in her finery, we might as well of been squirrels. I leaned hard into her face and said, "What ails you, Liza?"

"Well. . . ." But when she dropped back to a mutter, I sharpened up my voice.

"Well, young marsters, ain't no profit to try twisting it all into sense. Don't sort out straight no more than a red snake."

"Speak plain, gal."

Then she stuck out her feet, bare and bleeding. "Jubilo come. Horns a-blasting, big men with killing swords and feathers in they hats, they come march on through like a blue-sky storm with wagon guns and colors in the wind, cast out the marster's old ways, give us the freedom and set us to dancing a Jordan reel. Two days they roast hog, prance about, promise us pretties and snuggle us gals in the hay, then the whole bunch button up and head on toward the sun's come-rise. Next day, they dirty drag-tail buckra spill into our camp, haul off the free nigra men to use they shovels. Last one come through the farm steal my field hat and shoes, then ride off whistling that 'Dixie' with Missy's peacock slung over the mule back."

She had set out after her footwear, but being a house gal she lacked the soles for such a trek, and now her feet were raw as steak shambles. I thought it a woeful tale and wished for solutions, a pair of charity boots, but we had a rendezvous to keep.

Marichal spat dry and said we should put them out of their misery, all Ham's issue, but I answered she had not invaded us, just another weed in the sickle's path, little different from ourselves. He had a blindness of his own woven deep into the otherwise fine instincts of a golden soul.

KILPATRICK AND WHEELER had dueled for half a year from Tennessee on down till Kils had taken a ball at Resaca and was packed back home, but they couldn't hold him from the grand farce. He'd long been a gaslights man for the sham pleasure of it and liked to strike poses, take curtain calls and curse Lee and Lincoln in one windy speech, theatrical fashion. Now he was the prompter for a swarm of locusts. "I am pure Harry on a raid," he boasted to *Harper's Weekly*. To break the Confederacy's back, they would not leave chick nor child unmolested. It was his men who'd broken into the playhouse in Atlanta and looted off the costumes. They cut the fool at Cassville in pantaloons, capes and helmets, as on a lark.

That Cassville fight was the first day I ever glassed him up, despite the covey of white-glove staff trying to shield him. They were dolled up as Turks and queens and such theater exotics, but I spied him in those mutton whiskers and a frogged coat with more braid than wool. Joe Wheeler hated the man, his brags and lies, and when I directed the general to their command position, he ordered up our jackass gun to loft a shell in that vicinity. The two had been at West Point, and General Joe said in the case of that tuck-tail son of a bitch chivalry did not apply. "That pig pizzle wouldn't have the sense to rub down a frothy mule nor piss with the wind. It's a long taw, but give that barrel full elevation, kiss it for distance and see if we can break his frolic." If the Yankee thought this was all a fox hunt, we'd show him teeth, give him a snarl. Shortfall, somewhat, but their horses reared and startled. We saw them shit and scamper.

RUNNING RECONNAISSANCE after the Yanks hunkered down in Atlanta, the Soames boys and I had come on a file of civilians pulling their goods on Indian-style travois. A pert young woman with too many freckles was swearing with every step, so Garland hove to and asked could he be of service.

"They are turning out our dead in the cemetery," she answered, "tossing blessed bones to make room for their own fallen. It is sacrilege." This through rillets of tears.

The Soames boys worked themselves into a frenzy, cussing Lazarus and pledging to go on private raid that night. Even their servant John was wild with it by darkfall. He doted on those boys, and when the one barrage took them both, I offered him their personals and said, "Go home or go north, John. Likely you're free. Thank Jesus." He joined the shovel brigade instead, throwing up works, and I never saw him after that to find out exactly why. But Sherman, the resurrection man, the grave robber: now he was primed to lick our skillet clean. God forgive me, but I would sink to anything to stop him.

Before long, I was dreaming him as a game rooster, all spurred and cockerel-surly, his head a flame that raged across the state, like he was dreaming back at me, all waste work and incendiary. I could picture him strutting under bloody clouds, his boots turning frost to cinders as he strode. He was waving a map of Carolina big as a bed sheet, and I was crawling through an endless woods to warn my Maggie. I could feel the pressure of his mind. Then I would wake in a sweat, the taste of ditch water on my tongue. It was all turning personal.

Wheeler said to hurt him, to clip his wings. Every time, whether with Garland or Zeke Mapple, I volunteered for advance guard, against Jesus' rules or not. I thought I was learning how the righteous are meant to smite. The Assyrian had fallen wolfish on the fold and should be thrashed and rendered sightless. Sometimes, we'd come on a Yank just sent to his Maker, somebody's darling, his face all ghast and nasty, and Wheeler's orderly Stowbridge would put another shot up his ass, to sign the message, so to speak. It wasn't Christian, but I started to reckon it wasn't altogether wrong.

WE HAD OUR OWN DISPUTES, as if invaders weren't ordeal enough. On bivouac, those rare evenings out of the saddle, we'd debate customs of engagement and the war's mainspring and cause.

One evening Marichal advanced the idea we were justified in any act designed to rid our rightful land of trespassers. If you could think it, he said, the Almighty had lent His stamp. "Assassination of generals, poisoned wells, snakes flung into their camp. Delilah spies or playing scorn songs at them like an Irish harper rhyming rats to death. Anything. And don't go righteous. Your God, Taddy, comprehends our plight and licenses whatever we can conjure."

He was a lean, straw-headed Alabamian with a brow like a russet potato. You couldn't help but like him for his shroudless spirit and craving for jest, though he was the most bloody-minded. He would cut you half his plug, though, or take blame for others' errors, Samaritan-like. He'd come back for me when my horse stumbled at the scurry by Harris's gin, the lead hot and hailing. I was so mommocked, I didn't know hith from yon and stumbled about like a child. Out of the smoke he came of a sudden on that ghost horse, his open hand reaching out and my name on his tongue. That act alone purchased him my tolerance and admiration, though I saw his scapegoating of coloreds as half-sighted, at best.

Garland picked his teeth with a twig and praised all partisan procedures. "What I hold most high, gentlemen, is the boy who will force slow toxin down his pet duck when the foragers come close, or Zora Fair of Oxford, who blacked her face and lurked into Atlanta to map Sherman's works. She is a paragon, sirs. We should all be so zealous."

"But what of the wounded, Lieutenant? Surely you sponsor mercy there. You know of Jesus in the garden and that Roman's ear." I couldn't resist.

But Garland was adamant. He tossed a pebble off into the dark, and his face was serious as canister. "They don't want the inconveniences we provide, they should not wander down here, Parson. We are not obliged to be hospitable, and we will give their injured quarter when it is offered to our women and children. Our by-God dogs. This Lazarus wants to put the living under the earth and spill out the buried. I say, the man commits to swapping the dead and the quick about like chess pieces, let him brace for all havoc. Every plague we can muster. Woe betide." He hawked and spat a bloody missile into the flames.

As always, Marichal had to introduce the slaves. He lit an old turd of a cigar and jabbed it into his mouth, an organ we scarce had ever seen, due to his thicket of whiskers.

"As I see it, it is your son of Ham who introduced savagery into this whole damned matter. Once we seen what the Nat Turners and their ilk enacted up in Virginia, the whole ante was raised. Lacking that, us whites might have arrived at a compromise." He went back to whittling slivers into the fire, his anger transferred to his wrist.

Du Pre laughed like a jackal, his big shoulders shaking. "It's always the niggers for you, Wilkes. I speck you'll soon inform us that John Brown himself was truly a brown man bleached off to pass scrutiny and buy those rifles folks call "Beecher's Bibles." Beecher a dark man as well, I assume?"

"If not brown, then black to the heart, anyways."

"And what of you, Parson Sherburne? Do you also take mutinous slaves for your models and conduct yourself a notch more brutal to follow their example?" Du Pre, playing with me again.

I needn't answer, as Garland would not let the rein fall slack. He leaned close, nearly touching brows with Du Pre. "Some men are inclined to depravity by misbirth or Yankee raising, but most of us have the aptitude but lack the appetite. We act the fiend out of responsibility, Wilkes, to avenge our damaged nation, our honor, our bottomland and orchards, our sovereign God-given rights."

"Here, here," added Wilkes. "Duty. And to reclaim our chattel, but you, Reverend Sherburne, can you with your new-got religion be fierce for the sake of Georgia?"

I had only time to mutter, more at the dying cookfire than my companions, "I reckon." Little did I know how in two days time circumstance would provide ample answer, but the horn blared "Boots and Saddles," saving us from further disputation. Cursing and kicking, we debouched, and when I gave my new horse the quirt and spur, he leapt across the trickling branch. He was a spirited Irish Draught I called Festus at the suggestion of the End-of-Time apostle. "One of the judges," he said, "a right-thinker." A strong haunch and lean gaskin, a thinking animal. He had a white hourglass feathering his breast, but his hide was black as a Bible.

THE NEXT AFTERNOON Garland and I were deployed as skirmishers, our end of the line wending through a scorched peach orchard. On a northward ridge I saw a lone figure at the quick march and motioned Sandy to bring up the glass. A fine mist was blowing too hard to make out details through the scarified lens, so we thought it best to investigate and put the heel to our mounts. Up close, we found an old colored man in deaconish habiliments, a grain sack over his shoulder.

"Captains."

"Uncle. You from nearbouts?"

"Nassir. I was of the Joliets up by Madison. Them Gen'l Baird and Sherman come through a-burning, and the everywhich of us scampered hither and skither. Come morning, I was discombobbed and lost, so all I knowed to do was follow em, they smell."

"So you're an emancipated?"

"Just unattached, I speck."

Garland stood in his stirrups and surveyed the landscape. We could see a few of our advance down by the stream, but no blue ahead. Even the sky seemed uniform gray, but in the distance, no matter which way you turned, smoketrees rose.

"What's in the poke, uncle?"

"Just my pones of cornbread. Seemed like the kitchen door the best one to skitter out." I counted just three dark teeth in his smile.

"Pass on."

As we rode along, I remembered aloud. "Lazarus said he'd scalp this swath so bad a crow passing would have to tote his own provisions. Likely that uncle is one of those he meant."

"If he was the genuine article I'd shoot him and start a pie. Wilkes might do it anyway."

"We've already had a-plenty of those, and why any nursery rhyme king would order up crow pie lies beyond my reckoning, unless he was King of Georgia."

"That would mean Joe Brown, if a governor is akin to a king."

"No, that would refer to Lazarus, and he's crowned himself king of the Dead Land. I expect Wheeler means to let him sample the taste of blood and grue before this week concludes."

The dust of our column to the north was sharpening the sunset, so we turned our nags and cantered back toward our own kind.

Next night, we would truly cut loose from the civilized for the first time since the cowbell ruse, and I had to image myself as Gideon to forge an effective outlook. Marichal had set the pace, for I figured that he'd met the old refugee when he winked and offered us extra rations: "Cornbread all around."

Recognizing the poke dangling from his saddle tree, I stepped up to speak, but Garland touched my arm and shook his head.

"Fortunes of war, Taddy. Let it be."

THE NEXT MORNING Sergeant Zeke, galloping pell-mell back from a scout, caught me filling my drum canteen from the first wet well in days. He swung off without pulling his gelding to a stop. I'd ridden with him in the actions at Lovejoy and Rough-and-Ready, and I knew from his red face he was in full pique. His usual forage hat was missing, his scabbard empty and eyes big as a horse's.

"Rape and murder, Major. Lazarus has got no shame. It ain't quadrilles and reels no more, I'll tell you. You'uns got any quinine left? I'm feeling swimmy." His eyes seemed not working as a team.

"Take a deep pull of air," I said, though that always meant the smell of burning, "and you can quaff some of this sweet water. So Lazarus has snaked back and struck out again?"

"You've hit the bull by the eye, son. Howard, you know, but most specific Kils' First Division. They swept some of Joe's infantry he'd put on commandeered swaybacks, but later a few of our run-offs found a little farm nestled secret-like in a vale. A couple of old non-slavers had held three sons back from this nasty business, but they were quick to offer Joe's lads aid and comfort, two daughters swabbing wounds with benzene and wrapping bandages, the mama beating biscuit, boys tending the horses. A nice little spread, pigs and chickens, a couple Dutch milkers. I don't know how the blue columns missed them, but our boys found it a haven. They were lollygagging half a day, not even bothering with pickets. I guess everybody's desperate for a spell of relief.

"An hour after they traipsed off, Kils' First came on in force, rushing the farm from all sides, barrels blazing. Not a question, not a by-your-leave. They locked the women in the smokehouse and strung the men up in an apple tree. Apple fruit falling down while the men rose, drums and fife driving 'The Dead March' to a jig."

"Hanged them, Zeke?"

"Sure enough. Tongues dangling out, faces blue as damsons. Strangled sons and sire, milked the cows, filled a wagon with chickens and loot, then shut the razorbacks into the house and burned it."

Worse than Herod's minions prowling for firstborns. "And?"

"The officers went off with the wagon and the cows, the one girl says."

"Which girl?"

"Onliest one left. Louandy, they say." Other died, and the mother was shot when she tried to stop the raping. Taddy, it was awful to hear: wolves had the gals spraddled-tied on wagon wheels, treading them like brood hens, one and then the other."

Trying not to think of Maggie, I slung the canteens over my pommel as I mounted. "How much lead have they, Zeke? Can we catch up before they re-join their column?"

"If'n we don't spare the spur."

"Company's over yonder bluff. Let's ride."

We called that kind Shadows because they were kin to the night. We didn't know whose license they carried – Kils or Hitchcock or Lazarus himself – but they were no more soldiers than wild curs. Faces painted demon-like, one old darkie told us, they were showing us the savage path. Keen to overtake them, we drove our mounts to a lather.

At the farm, the bodies were laid out with arms crossed, except the old daddy, who was a hunchback and wouldn't straighten. The one young woman was weeping in torrents, her mother and sister covered with horse blankets. I left a grave detail. How could God allow it? How might a man ever make his wife understand what he'd seen? I wondered. Jesus wept. We dashed on till dusk.

"They're fifty," Du Pre reported back, "having an evening feed by a quick little river. Pickets out, but no sharp guard. I do believe they've been sipping some strong wet goods, as they're lax and boistery. Moonlight coming and going through clouds. They've staked their horses and spitted chickens. Muskets stacked. Some still in the face paint. Two miles. I love it when idiots travel in a pack."

We were just over twenty strong – Sharps, three repeaters, pistols and steel. Mustering all the reserve I could to cloak my rage, I said we could pick at them, cut and run, or just swarm in direct at all hazards. Not thinking military or Christian, I had seen Wheeler race into such a fight yelling, "Kill the scabby-tongued whoremongers," and I'd watched the End-of-Time rise to full fury when scolding drunks for scorning the Gospel. Borders blur. I was champing at the bit, not hearing anything inside me saying "No."

"I'd wager we'll take the bushwhackers in a sweep," said Garland.

Wilkes had blood fire in his eyes, no restraint. "Liberators my ass. Desecrators, Taddy. Criminals. This is bigger than war, and numbers hardly matter. It's End Time now and you know we can fight like bull dogs when it comes to scratch. Avenge those gals. You know God wants us to set things right." Looking at his face, no man would doubt it.

I had orders to monitor Kils' forage parties and harry them but not to open a pitched fight that would cost more than we could afford. All at my discretion. But I was losing the mood to be discrete by quarts and gallons.

John Scott and I went in with Du Pre, cat-walking, then on our bellies to the top of the bluff. The sky had cleared off and the rain had ceased. We were inside their pickets and could only whisper, but the camp we saw downslope was without discipline, their fires high and racket higher, boots off and jugs passing. The moon hadn't showed itself for a spell, but there were stars in the sky and in the river, which rushed on like hot black glass across the cold night.

Scott was a good scout with sharpshooter's gray eyes and cold blood. He reached out his hand to indicate their deployment.

"Mighty damn sure of theyselves, Major. Like a picnic."

"A picnic with Spencers. No telling what's in the wagons."

"Ripe, Major. Lax and napping." And he was on the mark. An owl whooed from a treeline. I didn't know if it was courting or hunting, but I whispered back, "It's our omen, John. Let's mischief their festivities."

Scott placed the three troopers with repeaters to the south. The river would block the east, and we'd come in the other two ways. Already we'd worked quittance on a pair of their pickets and gained two more Spencers. We'd have surprise, position and vinegar. I thought, "The sword of the Lord and Gideon."

When we were deployed, shucked of anything but killing implements, Wilkes asked the honor of going in first, quiet-like, in one of their uniform coats. He and Harold Leary in full masquerade, laughing like the other Yankee tipplers, swinging a jorum and bluffing the sentry's challenge. I told the cadre, "These raiders are not soldiers. Send them straight to Canaan."

A battle is all whirl and hot breath like the weather in Hell. Even a skirmish. Anybody with sense will reel against it and be hang-back at first, but you get used to the music quick. When the puzzle starts to fit, you learn to lose yourself. At night, though, it's worse. You can't be sure how long it will be all a-swirl. As we eased in, a big picket smoking a pipe said, "What the Samuel Hell?" and one of our riders shot him through the middle. I hardly recollect the next details. Whirligig and scramble. Wilkes and Leary slung some stacked carbines into the water and commenced to shoot. Some of the Yanks recovered quick, and it was hot work. We yelled like gamecocks, then bore down in a file, and I never thought again of Gideon till a big blur knocked me from my horse. Festus rushed on, and both pistols went flying into the dark, so I was on the ground, rolling. Rocks and roots. I had naught but my little belly gun to face the fray.

As I righted myself, running and stumbling were general amid the smoke and river mist. I could hear our new Spencers raking them where the waters forked. One wagon was ablaze, and I figured everybody on a horse was ours, but the cookfires and flashes from weapons were too unsteady to judge, and what moon showed was slight and cloud-scumped. The general blur came at me again, and I could see a big Yankee in a coat emerging from the fracas. He had a farrier's hammer in one hand, a pistol in the other. Tall as a cornstalk, beard red as pepper, swatches of white and yellow painting his brow like some Chickasaw. Then an officer drew alongside him, and I saw them both looking straight into my eyes, but just as I figured this my faretheewell, I saw the outlines of a gang of plunging horses over their shoulders, their teeth gleaming and hide sheen picking up whatever light would flare like lantern beams striking a stack of anvils. Somebody behind them was driving the Federal mounts right at their masters, and they were coming as demons, bucking and snorting. The pair demonstrating against me sensed it, too. As they cut and ran, the sudden smell said one of them had shit, and I could see Wilkes waving a blanket to encourage the stampede. The hammer man had dodged left, and he got off a hasty shot that passed my ear like a hornet, but I saw the blanket swoop over him, and when Wilkes turned his big horse, he had the saber out, and then it was wet and the Yank was on all fours like a hog.

I have seen men perform prodigies in the heat of the hunt, but nothing to match Wilkes. He galloped the officer to the ground and, ignoring the dropped weapons and surrendering arms, shot the man through the neck with his boot gun, then caught a horse by the bridle and led it over. I loved him most at that juncture.

"Climb on, Taddy. The assholes are scrambling. They're ours." So a second time this poor gump was lifted from the fray by an angel.

About the time I got a leg over the horse, a wagon with Hale rockets caught fire and sent missiles whizzing, and by their light we could see the remaining Yankees making a stand in a runoff ditch. Garland held our riders at bay and said, "Let the fireworks die off. We know how to pick blackberries in the dark."

In a few minutes the Yanks were crying for quarter in general alarm as balls rattled through the brush and found them, but our boys had no interest in recess. One soldier was whimpering as he handed his Spencer to John Scott, who turned it about and shot the man full in the face. I was glad it was still too dreamy-gloamy to register the details. Blindness has its virtues.

What I could see and hear were the dead and injured horses all about, heads and legs thrusting skyways with the fires agleam behind them. The Yankees had fired into the stampede and found the panicked animals easier to hit than us. No doubt we shot some, too, and I saw one muley-looking brown struggle to its feet, shaking like a wet terrier, but then its legs spraddled, and it collapsed in a braying heap. I looked for Zeke to put them from their misery, but he was down. And Harold. Scott carried out the order, but I knew we'd suffered bad losses. I didn't want to hear the count.

The camp was ours for the ransacking, but we couldn't be sure how long before the commotion would bring a relief squadron, so we heaped up what we couldn't carry quick and put the torch to it, the flames licking higher than the riverside willows, while Munce Bratton's squad salvaged some of the roasted chickens. When I saw them, I realized how scratchy my belly was with hunger, and my lips were dry as bark. One cart turned out to be full of leathered books, and though you can't eat them, I ordered the crates separated. Before anybody could follow up a stray spark caught purchase on the paper, and they went up as well, just more waste. I was finally asking after our casualties when Marichal touched my shoulder.

"A decent prize, Taddy. They had a brigadier. Didn't get his name."

In the shine of the fire and the half moon now out of the clouds, I saw him raise his hand, which was holding by the hair a mangled head, beard all matted with blood and soil. Even in the dark, I saw as much detail as I wanted, like some picture of Goliath.

"Like I said, didn't receive a proper introduction. I hoped it might be Smith Atkins."

"Burn it," I said. "Burn it all."

I couldn't but wonder was this the "fountain filled with blood" our column's apostle loved to fill his cool tenor voice with.

The men were still racing about, seeking the last skulkers along the river, and two of them were using horses to drag bodies about the bonfire. I had never seen my veterans so taken with the fever, but it seemed in that strange light in the wake of the owl's call and the Yankees' crimes as just as any decree ever handed down. I had but one concern: we had to ghost off by cockcrow. If we were to steal a moment's rest, it had to be far from this position, or we would all be crow food.

"Du Pre," I sang out, "find us a ford."

Breaking out of the woods and onto a farm road an hour later, we headed east, dripping wet, squinting at a red moon low in the soapy sky.

THREE DAYS LATER our Joe Johnston's sappers had hacked and blazed the bridge over Ebenezer Creek to fluster Lazarus, but Buell's Jersey engineers strung quick pontoons, while their General Hawkface Davis strung a cordon to detain on the near side the great multitude of displaced coloreds trailing their saviors. Our scouts had seen the to-do, and John Scott said the tag-alongs were massing on the west bank, mostly old folks, gals and young uns pacing around scared or just hunched in the icy squall while their liberators crossed over, Ohio conscripts looking hard over their shoulders, skittish, nearing panic themselves, wary of our ruthless ways. When our vanguard snaked through the cypress swamps to the bridge site, we saw hundreds of coloreds milling about and the last of the Federals holding back the mob with bayonets fixed. "Aha," said Du Pre, his arm sweeping in grand presentation, "Behold the true face of manumission."

Wilkes grinned like a sheep-killing dog around his dead cigar: "On occasion, I applaud the suitably cruel." Sensing his blood was up, I shook my head and wondered "What next?" as I muttered a prayer for guidance: "Lead us not into temptation."

I could see our horses' wet breath in the drizzle, mist billows from their nostrils like cannon smoke, their fetlocks clotted with dried mud. Festus gave a shiver to shake off the water, then pranced a bit sideways. The rain kept raining. Even this far from any recent sparkfest, the taint of old smoke was conspicuous and charnel amid the first smells of autumn. Every man jack of us was sodden and desperate for rest, but this was not the time for such wishes.

Riverside sycamores stood leafless and ghost-like, peeled to their winter bones, and the live oaks hung with ringlets of Spanish moss like manacles. Not exactly our native ground. Gnarled cypress, cedar, palmettos and salty cordgrass testified we were nearing the sea Lazarus lusted for. The throng of abandoned vagrants gathered in their calico and sacking gave off their own smell I could just catch from the bluff: it was a battle smell, an old familiar, the sweet stink of fear. A fair few wore coats of Federal issue blue, trousers of kersey, but not a one was a soldier. The rabblement was milling more animated, confused, and fog off the rain-swollen water lent its own haunted flavor. Despite sunrise, the place was silver and black – skeleton trees, char – and the shimmer of the water was like new tack leather that's been spat on.

We were under a dozen at the vanguard, but the coloreds must have reckoned our whole column was close enough to mount an assault, and here they were, hemmed up, liberated but wholly unprotected. Valley of the Shadow. For them, we might as well be bonafide demons. For me, they were the darkness of smoke upon the land. They were ghosts shaped from night's deepest hours, and I wanted them to cross and get out of our business. Was this throng the cause of it all? I thought "stamp Thy image on my heart" and wanted to muster charity, but my heart would render only ashes. I intended no harm but could not cease being anxious to have them permanently gone. Equal in God's sight, maybe, but still somehow at the genesis of things, the bone of contention. Gone, that's all I wanted.

Directly, the Federal engineers got nervous and strutted about howling orders. When they cut their pontoons free to haul them over, the contrabands, realizing they were to be stranded, let loose high panic, as if Moses had come to the Red Sea and left a tribe behind to deal with angry Egypt. Whatever they screamed or begged separate, the one shrill of their predicament rose like a choir of the damned. For agony, I have never heard it exceeded.

One granny in her rocking chair atop a plunder wagon turned west and pointed hard in my direction. I could see how large her eyes were gaped open, and her mouth as she hollered, "Dez dare, de Reb sojurs. Mercy Jesus."

From the rise where I leaned forward on my saddle, I could detect them edging toward the swift water, beckoning to the last blue coats beyond the deep, their gestures frantic, their words unanswered. From where I sat they might have been dolls or even some midnight phantasm. It was mid-December, their number in the hundreds, and as the bluebellies began to turn away and enter the trees, one by one, the howling coloreds started to abandon dry land.

At first, they eased or leaped into the current, old men and women, gals with their babes in arms. You could see they knew little of swimming, but the crowd at the back was pushing, not able to reckon what was the hold up, and those up front were trying to enlist logs and even slight limbs for floating. Some few were decked out in fine rummage, probably snatched from attics or chiffarobes, but most were in blue rags with hats like something off scarecrows. They were weighted down with bundles, and the lion's share that went into the river struggled with the rush and swirl but were pulled under. A child in a daffodil frock, a woman whose gingham was green as leafing laurel, a grandpappy in a livery coat red as blood. "At Hell's dark door we lay." The notes of that song climbed through me, and I nearabout said them aloud. Maybe I did, and I felt the heart go out of me. The daffodil child bobbed up once more and was gone.

Then it came over me that it was likely the simple sight of us setting the match to their fright, and I was ashamed. There I sat on Festus, leg cocked over the saddle now, wind tickling the turkey feather in my hat band, my hilt and bridle and gun trimmings flashing in the dim light as murderous metal. What was I but Nightmare poised for their destruction? What were we all but Revelation horsemen, locked in the center of their eyes and champing to rampage down? In terror, the mob pushed up to the banks and by ones and pairs into the cold water, which splashed silvery where they entered but quickly closed.

"Colonel Goode," I called back, "Sir, might we withdraw and lend some calm to this scene? We are like unto ghouls as they see us. The contrabands will not be crossing today at any event. No use in us roosting here, now that the Lazarus legion has slipped us."

He leaned to the right and cocked his head, as he did when

pondering, then removed his slouch hat and pulled a sleeve across his brow.

"Yes, Major Sherburne, call in the point riders. We mean no slaughter to even the lackeys that worship Lazarus. I would prefer to engage instead with the shitpoke soldiers who marooned them there. Hell of a note. Not our trumpet. Pull back. We will renew our discourse with those blue scoundrels on the other shore."

Du Pre was reined in beside me, and as I swiveled to pass the order, I caught the shock in his eyes, then turned in time to see Marichal's red face, merry and wild. He had wheeled about and was facing me, his horse rearing as he whipped his saber from its scabbard and shouted, "Kill the niggers. What a chance. Kill them all." Again he wheeled his roan toward the river and gave it the spur. He was hatless, his flaxen curls flying behind like a dancer's ribbands. I felt a twine tighten on my heart.

"No." My voice was weak with the moment and the damp, so I forced a second try, "Marichal, no." I was too stunned to do aught else but draw my Colt and raise it, as I shouted – "Wilkes, you Wilkes" – but he heeded me no more than a lark. He had executed a perfect moulinet and was leaning steep, as if the naked blade pulled him toward the melee ahead, and I could see the contraband had glimpsed him, as their ant-like movements suddenly increased and more rushed straight into the river. I reached with my thumb to cock the pistol, thinking "no, no, no," but my whole hand was trembling, and I discharged high into the pelting rain.

Then I saw his head snap back and bloom like a rose, even before I heard the cracking rifles and saw smoke puffs rising across the river. Kilpatrick's rear guard had swung to action. True to discipline, we swiftly dismounted and made answer with our Sharps, while cries of dire agony rose from the shore below, and more coloreds – dozens now, a hundred – entered the water snarling between the banks.

We could see some Yanks had dropped their muskets and were trying to pull swimmers to safety. They reached in branches and threw ropes. Some felled saplings to provide a ladder over the rapids, and we did not aim at them. Most of the coloreds who entered just threw themselves in, though, trusting to Providence, but no divine mercy was granted, and you could see their heads bobbling in the water still tack-brown and silvery with some trick of shadowed light and deluge. It was all chaos and scramble, and nothing we yearned to touch. I tried not to picture old Aeneas Beadle in the bunch, but his face kept ghosting up before my eyes.

Billy Goode said, "Pull back" and waved his plumed white hat, but even as we left the wraiths to die or prosper, I could still hear Marichal's "Kill all," and – much as I had seen and even acted myself since Chattanooga and Atlanta – I was unsteady in my saddle and tasted the vomit as it rose.

In an hour we went back in force, flanks covered, skirmishers out in a fan, half dismounted, mountain howitzers unlimbered, the rest ready to surround or engage. The Yankees were gone. Some coloreds had skedaddled into the swamp, but most were huddled about their wagons and pelf, ignoring the rain, resigned, eager to plead for our mercy. I found Wilkes' body undisturbed, our only casualty, and while our companions herded slaves off or fished out some of the drowned, we spaded a grave in sandy earth and placed him down at a distance from the dead coloreds he so despised. Garland and I piled a cairn of stones licked clean as cobbles, though the woods were so hunted out no rooters were likely to probe. I said some scripture over him, trying to find the right tone, words like "Well in the house of the Lord forever," but they felt empty, coming from me.

"Ebenezer." It means "stone of help" in the Hebrew tongue, and Marichal's end was the stone I carried badly. Wheeler, with his boastful notion of arithmetic, claimed we corralled two thousand runaways that evening and returned them to rightful owners, but who believed that? The country was waste and rife with decay. Planters were dispersed or too meagerly supplied to tend to themselves, and did we have time to perform escort duty with Lazarus in full frenzy and hammering the gates of Zion? Their General Davis was said to guarantee we'd butcher our captives, but mostly we just turned them about face and scolded, "Get you gone. Beg forgiveness of your masters, Judas." We'd seen how their train could slow a column, and now they were so pitiful, we could scarce accommodate such an anchor. I handed out two boxes of hardtack and gave a sobbing pappy Marichal's blanket, but nothing more. Leading my companion's roan away from the catastrophe, I felt no trace of God in me and wondered if I could manage to re-light the wet wick of Christian charity the preacher had once kindled. I reckoned his End-of-time warnings had come too late to save one such as myself.

SOON WE WERE SWEPT BACK into the big tempest. Millen, Bristow, along the Ogeechee. Savannah fell, while a night ruse permitted Hardee with his now-mongrel command to escape north toward Lee. So Lincoln received that year his sweet Christmas gift from Lazarus. As for us, we limped northward, riding jockey weight, still fit and feisty, despite all accidents of battle, most of us hoping to meet Lee and make another stand, but Johnston used the cavalry mostly as file closers sweeping our rear ranks to discourage or shoot skulkers. It had come to that shameful duty. At times, I was thankful Marichal was not present to endure it.

The heart for it was out of me by then, which is why I let my guard down outside Bentonville where a Yankee sniper up in a young sweetgum like some Nicodemus opened up with a scatter charge, and I went down. Mostly I was scarred about the face and neck, but of course that left eye would be dark forever. When I finally walked out of the hospital, the whole circus was ended, Kirby Smith the only big Reb still in the field. A bald doctor nearly short as a circus midget handed me my boots and explained how to clean the socket and why I should keep it patched against the elements. Crossing the empty street toward the corral, it struck me like a slap in the face: I had been on a camp bed for some forty bleak days, and not one prayer had risen on my lips or in my heart, no matter how often I thought of home or the general horrors or the melee at Ebenezer. There's a song hung on that word, too: "Here I raise my Ebenezer." A stone, yes, but it also means your standard, but I didn't have so much as a scrap of flag left to fly. I would have to find Him all over again, I thought, but this time delving with just the one eye.

I soon ran into Garland who was headed west, and he said Du Pre was gone back to New Orleans to marry a cousin. We three had been scorched but not consumed like the Hebrew boys in the furnace, though I couldn't cite a reason for us to be spared. Garland had seen Wheeler, too, shackled and cussing. Surrender didn't much alter his vocabulary. Fighting Joe. His story was just starting, if you follow events. He'd wind up in Congress.

I straggled on home slowly and saw more waste and sorrow than even the one eye could stand, but Maggie was safe, our acres untouched by the war. We made our crop and I built a cradle, so we were looking forward and hopeful. Maybe I thought it was over, but it comes back baleful at night. It takes me by the scruff and hauls me limp and will-less to a particular November ravine.

IT'S THE MORNING AFTER a wild fight, and the men are finishing with the fresh graves. The clang of spades on stones, the smell of clay, that other smell. We are still licking our wounds and winding our watches, and the buzzards have come for their rations. They circle and light and sup on the fallen Yankees as if they thought themselves the chosen tribe. That boy with the shoulder, with no hat and the fish-silver eyes has pissed himself, and I am the ranking officer in the squadron. I could say just leave him, but four of our own have fallen, and the turned dirt is mounding up as sorrow's souvenirs. I could say just bind him on an extra horse and we'll bequeath him to the column by noon. Not practical, I know. I could at least pronounce "forgive our trespasses" over him or "bright shining as the sun" and order them to dig another hole. He keeps shaking like a colt, his eagle buttons catching the first sprays of light. He keeps whining, "his heart beating, I tried to help," but I've given the order only I can alter and am riding off. Let the cup pass from me. Sunshafts in the pine needles, the report of the weapon, wind whipping the cold trees, gallop sound of my horse's hooves. I give him the spur.

I can still see the boy's face, hear his damp breath. Small scar over his nose. Silvery pupils. His features give way to the floating daffodil frock in Ebenezer Creek, the empty face of a child pointed toward heaven, the screams like Hell's choir. And Wilkes' accusing eyes.

I should want to go back and reverse it, save the boy, pass on the mercy of Jesus my Shepherd, but hard as I try, lying there in the still bedroom with enough floor space to fit eight rough coffins, I come up empty, unforgiving, unwilling even in the heart to change my command. And now I have become that shapeless cry in the wilderness, though my mind labors to summon the song: Dangers, toils and snares. Blind but now I see. Just words now, just animal murmurs as they issue from me, the milk of pity soured. And there's also the other voice: Spur the Irish horse till his flanks bleed. Do your duty: red thoughts, red deeds. Wolf back at the wolves till blood is the general weather we tenant. The voice I've come to know as mine. Lamb of Jesus, revenant avenger. Poor Marichal, poor pitiful savage human race. And alone in darkness, sinner cold in his own bedclothes, wretch like me.

BLAINE

Ina Grove

***The Rockbridge County Gazette*, June 28, 1904**
PAINTER, THE IRISH CREEK DESPERADO, ARRAIGNED
by Reese Prescott

Lexington: After two hours of deliberation, a panel of magistrates today in the circuit court of Rockbridge turned in an indictment in the rape and murder case of Brodie Painter, the so-called Irish Creek Desperado. The crime, which raised a significant stir hereabouts, involved felonious assault on a fourteen-year-old girl named Ina Grove, and the prosecutor, Captain Stansfield, now has plans to petition Judge Armbruster for the gallows in light of both the harm done the girl and the savagery with which her uncle Leaf Pogue was stabbed to his death.

According to testimony, Painter, a robust man of 35 years and uncertain race, has scaped the ministrations of the law on several previous occasions. Something more than a year ago he killed a neighbor, Cash, in a fracas on the headwaters of Pedlar Creek and eluded punishment when arraigned at Amherst Courthouse, due to a dearth of witnesses. His latest crime was committed in South Mountain on Irish Creek in the county. He had been acknowledged a desperate miscreant and was for some time variously reported either to have fled to territories unknown or to be at large in the dense recesses of South Mountain. Commonwealth's Attorney Moore entreated Governor Montague to levy a reward for Painter's capture, and Richmond offered up a replevin of $100.

This turn of events was kept in camera that Sheriff B. R. Sherburne might initiate proceedings without raising general alarm or alerting the fugitive to the actions of his pursuers. Local enforcement had previously been frustrated on learning that Painter had left the settlement, probably by way of the Norfolk and Western Railroad, his one-time employer. To run his man to ground, the sheriff enlisted the services of Constable John Pink of Buffalo District, a man known in these quarters for his taste for the dangerous.

Pink was himself reared in the Blue Ridge on the Amherst side, often called "The Free State" for its hospitality to fugitives, and is familiar with the locals and all the paths through Pedlar River Country. It was Pink who cast a quiet net and finally located Painter in the environs of his brother Darl, and upon his intelligence Sheriff Sherburne convened his posse comitatus and despite wet weather took the White's Gap Road up into the Blue Ridge.

In what will no doubt be acclaimed the model of corpus juris efficiency, the trap was laid and sprung. The lawmen and their deputies rode through rough mountains. After two days traveling against heavy impairment of weather, they reached an abandoned farm in the precincts of the Painter homestead and there without leave or license secreted their horses in the empty stable. After miles of difficult travel through mud and dense brush, the officers spied the brother and several womenfolk of the Painter clan moving about the place and so deployed sentries. The sheriff kept vigil behind the house, while his subordinates took to the laurel and rocks on foot. All caution was exercised with weapons at the ready, as Painter is a veteran of the Spanish War and numerous violent scrapes and disturbances in the region. Shortly, Police Chief Hazelwood of the party surprised Darl Painter, who had surmised the presence of the lawmen, climbing out a window with intentions of signaling his brother.

It was then felt that the house must at once be searched, and though none of the runagate's kit was discovered, it was determined that Pink's intelligence had been essentially correct, so the posse mounted a hushed ambush about the Painter house. Approaching sunset, according to Sheriff Sherburne, Brodie Painter appeared with a Colt's Navy dangling from his hand, at which time Hazelwood showed his shotgun, and as the sheriff reported, the arrest was effected without further incident. The party quickly retraced their steps to their concealed horses and obtained some supper at a house in the mountains before making their way back to Lexington.

Throughout the hearing, attorney Spencer argued that his client had been treated with malice and hard measures, but the examiners pressed vigorously for the facts in the case. The prisoner promptly admitted to the likelihood that his blow had killed Leaf Pogue, albeit in defense of his own life and limb, but he contended in unpopular testimony that no rape had taken place.

Before the bench the accused was shouted down until Judge Armbruster ordered the courtroom cleared of all but the principals. Reading of an affidavit submitted by the alleged victim quickly gave the lie to Painter's desperate strategy. Although not present herself, Miss Grove recorded under licit seal that her uncle, who had acted as her guardian since her father's demise, her mother having died in childbirth, was about to serve supper when a man scarcely known to them burst through the door waving a butcher knife. Her account described the accused in many particulars, including the dark hue of his skin and the blue serpent tattoo on his arm, and outlined a bloody scuffle, followed by reference to unspeakable acts. Injured and in shock, the unfortunate received assistance from a passerby, the widow Kate Fell, the next morning, but it is feared she will be forever damaged by the atrocity.

The sitting panel, including one veteran of the Confederacy and others known to be distinguished citizens of our community, indicted Painter on charges of rape and capital murder, and as many of his other actions came to light during the testimony, his conviction is expected, which many surmise will produce a calm on Irish Creek in the aftermath of his little reign of terror.

The trial, which is expected to draw extensive public interest due to long-standing disputes over property rights and livestock among the denizens of Irish Creek, has been scheduled for August tenth. Although no trouble from the Painter kin is expected, Jailer Lisha Jackson says a double guard will be kept posted around the clock, and no chances will be taken with the outlaw.

Sheriff Blaine Sherburne, His Log, Excerpted: 1904

<u>April 13</u>

A chilly evening and still raining. I have been struck with the Arkansas travels and could scarce stir from the office this day, but legal business will not desist on sole account of my bowels' inconvenience. This morning I was informed by Bill Brewster of another killing up on Irish Creek. They are a rough bunch up there and prone to scrap, which I understand is common to such woodloafers and rullions as dwell thereabouts, but I wish those bravos would fashion their own law, however perverse, and stick by it. This new instance is dire, as there is rape of a young girl involved, and I am somewhat acquainted with the supposed killer, one Brodie Painter who slew his neighbor Sink Cash last autumn but was not testified against and walked scot-free. Tomorrow I will be obliged to ride out beyond the pale and snoop into it, as this rash of misdeed must be stomped out.

The events appear to have unfolded yesterday or the day before, and the victims Ina Grove and her uncle Leaf Pogue have little kin up that way, so at least the lynch talk, according to Brewster, is but a whisper so far. I knew Painter in the Spanish war, and he has ever proved to be a blacksnake who could not keep his hands in his own pockets or his Jemison in his trousers. Of late, by what I hear, he has taken to quarrel and plunder whenever he inclines, showing blade or barrel if opposed. As the region is rife with Ramps, Melungeons and of recent a swarm of Mormon Saints, reports from the place read like from the cockpit.

This will be the fourth time already I have had to seek copias on one of those Irish Creek rabbit twisters, and I am inclining to fall in with that faction of the Gentleman's Club that says they should be rousted and shot like so many mad dogs, their sorry cabins blazed and the whole of South Mountain and Whetstone Ridge sowed with salt. It grows more difficult being the officiary voice in light of such widespread evidence of devilment. With each page of the calendar Adair's father's entreaty that I serve out only my current term and relinquish the star to share his livery concern grows more alluring, though to work daily with a man who incessantly recites from Mrs. Browning is not my aim in life, and I suspect his desire for a grandchild is fueling his offer.

If this rain will let off, we will likely get some warming and I will pack angling gear and strive to at least turn the junket into a couple of trout. Now the wick is raising more smudge in the lamp flute than glow, so I will risk another swallow of Tut's Pellets and try not to wake my sweet Adair when I slip into the covers. I must not propose to excurse to Irish Creek without the pump gun and must never think to foray to such treacherous haunts without full vigilance. For the time, God save the Commonwealth of Virginia and so good-night.

<u>April 22</u>

Granny Kate Fell brought the unfortunate orphan by the house this morning when she delivered our butter. We had talked two days previous, at which time she put forth that the child would be less skittish if we could conduct the interview in a sitting parlor, instead of my office. Adair with her usual breakfast radiance poured us coffee and repaired to her sewing nook. The first thing I noticed was that Ina Grove is hardly a girl, though she claims she will not even reach fourteen till August. Her make is full womanly, and she has the sort of green cat's eyes that follow you without moving and hair of raven silk like mourning clothes, though she does comport herself in bashful manner and is slow to answer even the simplest questions. Probably a sense of shame influences this manner, and I briefly feared that she was as well somewhat slow as a result of the inturning bedlam mating up there on the thicket slopes, but later I came to appreciate that her shyness is not without device.

In the matter of her testimony, told in the minor key voice common to her stripe, she is consistent with what Granny Kate had previously conveyed. The man known as Brodie Painter, whom she had seen on various occasions but never truly met nor heard named, had on the day in question surprised herself and Pogue as they sat to a meal. Miss Grove steadfastly maintains that the accused rushed through the open door with not a word and knocked her uncle to the floor, then slit him twice with a big knife while she sat frozen and voiceless. Once the uncle was disabled though still breathing and moaning, the intruder threw her onto the floor, raised her skirts and ripped her undergarment. When I inquired if she did scream, she reckoned not and said she felt as one seeing actions unfold from outside her natural body. This could result, I suppose, from deep shock. What she remembered was Painter's muddy eyes and a blue or green snake drawn onto his dark arm.

This was, she said, her scandalous despoilment and had made her dirty, and she kept staring at a red knot in the floor, scuffing it with her brogan as if she might shove it aside could she only approach it in some yet-undiscovered fashion. I did not press her hard on any details but the man's build (which she puts at over six feet), his clothes and aspect, as well as the tattoo. On various occasions in our conversation, which filled only just more than a quarter of an hour, Miss Grove did interject that the man's skin was unusual in its color, and sometimes when she shut her eyes she saw him blue. Granny Fell then took her away, confiding that she prayed this child would not be called upon to appear in open court.

Though I would not agree that this girl is so much lacking in art nor such a wilder flower as others might perceive her, there is something of the deeply wounded in her look and the quaver of her voice. Her account having no inconsistencies nor inaccuracies according to my eventual search of the scene of those lamentable events, I find her a credible witness and am ready to sue for warrant, despite Adair's conviction the girl has something of the hussy in her comport.

Whether Painter will be susceptible to surprise or not is yet to be uncovered, but I remain suspicious that this situation will not resolve itself without extensive attention and no small expense. An owner of pasture, paddocks, hauling stock and Surrey carriages would be at liberty to turn a blind eye to such considerations and enjoy an afternoon glass of Goldbrau to the tune of the overzealous weather. In my position, however, no ostrich logic will suffice.

Adair wishes us to attend a performance of "Lovey Mary" at

the Buena Vista Opera House tonight, but I am resolved to plead paperwork concerning the recent embezzlement by Mr. Monroe of Jordan's Point, as some theatrical matters are best left unexplored.

<u>May 1</u>

I would like to boast it is time to soak the rope and stitch a new hood, but we are as far from snagging Brodie Painter as from catching a bingbuffer. I would as lief chase the latter, as their non-factual nature would excuse my empty-handedness, while Painter is as slippery as the painter cat that shares his name. He was ever known to be an able man in the wild, which is why we never hoped to collar him in casual patrol when he was no more than a fractious misdemeanor up there in the Free State stilling splo, playing the cunny hound and eye-gouging with his ilk. Now all evidence signifies him as the culprit in this dastardly affair of Leaf Pogue and the girl, and he must be delivered before the gavel. Nor will Cash's intimates in the township let that old matter rest.

Warrants aplenty today for non-payment, assault and petty pilfery, but they are the reason deputies are born and sworn. This morning's mail brought a sealed dispatch from the capital that reward will be paid out for leads to Painter's arrest. My own fear is that he has absquatulated, feeling things too hot in my bailiwick for his pleasure, but I will follow the creek again and discover what Nettle Mountain and Yankee Horse Ridge have yet to reveal. Last time I ventured up there to the catamount kingdom was pure snipe hunt, all the shiftless hill hawks mouthing out false information on everything from where the creek forks to if Painter did ever abide in the old bark mill said to be anent his brother's freehold. Although I know those people have been left scathed in the wake of the timber boom and bottom-out of the saltpeter wells, you've got to plant the seeds you're given and grind the corn they grow; whereas, these Cashes and Painters, Eisenhowers and Griffins turned to mischief natural and quick as a roused hornet stings. What I require to sweep this arena is a company of Rough Riders.

The sullen nature of the whole district not being enough, I was fair skunked under the lee of the crest and nearly thrown by Sylvester, whose nose took as much offense from the polecat as mine. You might expect the predictable showers to provide some relief from the insult, but that reasoning suffers defects, and back at the office Lish Jackson found it all a great rusty and howled till he near choked. I am now riled personally on this matter of the renegade and will balk at nothing to fetch him before the bar and thus to the gallows, God willing. If I come back empty this time, it will not be before I am assured of his exile to some place not on the charts.

Responsibility being a many-sleeved jacket, I must now ready myself for Preacher Rose and his pullet wife who come to take a cold bait with us this evening. Adair has been redding up the house all day, and I must make my manners and pretend interest in questions of new pews and robes for the choir. Will we dispatch a mission to the China, and who will mow the glebe? These are matters meant to keep us of sound mind and not over-trained on the Manchurian war and other major key troubles of the world, so I will endure as well another hour about the pianola, which Adair plays with great enthusiasm and virtue but little glory. It is her armor against tidings I bring home from the courthouse and cellblock. Bless her knack for conjuring such foils.

<u>May 6</u>
John Pink sauntered in today. A tanner by trade, he has been of use on occasion as a scout and knows the factions up on Irish Creek, where they call him "Constable Pink" in ridicule. Pink is a rough sort but of good and pliant purpose, and I am comforted to think him on the side of order. His tall size and beard shape him just like another tush hog from that neck of the woods, but he has even judgment, a flair for moderation and eyes the blue of cue chalk. I have come to abide him well, and he is a crack shot and not a man to chew his tobacco twice before moving.

We drank a full pot of coffee just slightly softened from the flask and scanned the survey map, touching on crossroads and granges where we can trust to what gossip he might assemble. I then walked him down to my father-in-law's stable and rented a good horse, a bay belonging to D. D. Moore himself. So many of our highborn neighbors trust their movements to haggard nags and intractable spavins, I was afforded pleasure to see him thus served. Pink has his own lever rifle, but I gave him a sack of cartridges and my good wishes, plus a dollar for grub. He will be up there mixing with the drovers and their feuds longer than I could stomach, but I trust he is the man for it.

Nothing much more to report but an afternoon on a stern courthouse chair giving testimony on civil matters, for which I again give thanks. Drone and drone. The tedious will weary you, but will not shoot from cover.

<u>May 9</u>

All morning at my paperwork, but crows continue to alight and debate on the backhouse roof. Up close they look as silk, but otherwise live in the sky, which on days like this occasions envy. A telephone message relayed from Pink asserts he has found one reliable spy amid the forked tongues. By general assent Painter is moving among his confederates, broguing it back and forth like a lostling, but never too far from a jug of busthead and a wench. It puts me in mind of Cuba again when we led Colonel Monocle, feather in his cap and pistol popping off to no particular effect, up San Juan Hill. It was a botched job with little of the tactical in it, nothing of the gallant, more blood than design. That such action put the subsidy of "soldier" on a no-count like Brodie Painter taints the whole *Maine* affair further, and what do we want from Cuba anyway, as we raise our own effective cigar burley right here on Commonwealth soil?

This black mood is no doubt come of my knowing I will soon have to jaunt back to Irish Creek and drag the grapple for our prey. It is no wonder legends and ballads rise up from that purlieu. The feel of rot and fester is general, the close-breeding mix little relieved by the influx of tin miners and other roughs. Knowing that Jackson came to these surrounds as a mine man and Pink as a hide hunter doesn't abridge the stench of bark mills and tanneries, and I have twice heard hushy mention of a second version of the Leaf murder which I am loathe to entertain. Either way, Leaf is dead and Painter is the killer, so I had best cease pollyfoxing and gird myself for a campaign. Daily some well-wisher like Turner or Dr. Cravits stops by the office to wish me luck in the matter, but I can read between the words.

Was ever a man less inclined to keep oiling a Webley and waxing the draw leather than me? The star I collect payment for sporting emits little light in such times. But the vote on which joiner will receive commission on the church pews looms heavy this week. Settle for that distraction and hope for the best. May the daily torrent at least rinse something clean. Now to split some nightwood and turn in. God bless and keep and so on.

<u>May 28</u>
Pouring-down rain, pouring-down rain. The Maury is at flood again and little chance to move about with dispatch. This wilderness business sits heavy on me. Today I have the chivaree of Bob Dove as accompaniment, as I was roused last night to attend his pranks at the Star Diner and subsequently had to take him into custody. He is most often an affable and harmless drunk, but something was stuck in his craw last night concerning the jibes of some cadets from the Institute, and he was busting glass and spreading threats like broadcasting so much wheat seed, though today his sole crime is that tuneless caterwauling.

I must plot this campaign anew, as the Irish Creek inmates seem little inclined to step forward for the reward, and Pink's agent, whom I know of only as Cratis, has turned in a blank book where details of the fugitive's habits and dens might be concerned. If you believe hearsay, the creature is at once everywhere and none, reeling at a party in Brownsburg and pistol-whipping a barber in Amherst ten minutes later. Pink further reports that Painter has posted in one tawing shop a notice of two dollars reward for the governor's own noble pelt. If there is comedy in this it is too rustic for my appetite.

I cannot strike from my mind today the first visit I made to the Pogue homestead last month. Granny Fell had already taken the assailed under her roof, and I expected to find the place empty but instead came up a draw on the morningside of the mountain, then over the ditch which resembles nothing so much as a siege moat, only to find myself facing a sallow girl sprite perched on the slanted porch of the shotgun house and plucking a white chicken in lazy and distracted fashion. The house was shabby with loose chinking, bullet scars and scorch marks where somebody had done mischief. It was just touching twilight, and though the ash and dogwood, the judas and earliest blackberries were showing bloom, the big rose oaks were limb-empty and clutching at the sky with many claws. The first night noises were tuning up. The rain djinns were resting a spell.

I tied Vester to a shrub and approached the urchin when she leveled at me the most unnatural and lifeless pink eyes and commenced to sing softly in a nonsense jargon. She was clad in a coarse sacking, and her one hand began to snatch at the feathers with vim, tossing them aside almost in rhythm with her crude lullaby. It is Bob Dove's infernal serenade that puts me in mind of the scene again, and when I made effort to speak to her as one would gentle a jumpy filly, she slung the corpse over her shoulder, sprang up and dashed through the gap and into the north room, the hen's red-combed head bouncing on her back as she ran, its dead eye squamous and weird.

When I mounted the scaffold steps and entered, the room was near empty, most likely already plundered by those who knew the place uninhabited. Beside the cookstove a plank table was tossed aside and a rent patch quilt on the floor, the windows glassless but for the front one, the place a general shambles. A few bent speckleware cups and pans about, empty cans and windblown woods-debris, a chipped slop bucket. A whet strop hung nailed to the wall with pellets of scuttling creatures here and there, the whole affair shoddy. Seeing no sign of the child and aware I was soaked to the skin, I paused to surmise the unfolding of the drama – the two victims settling toward dinner, early moon hanging, the alleged felon charging in from the rain with a blade in his hand. Here the two men tangled and fell, there the girl sat shaking. Then the girl grabbed by her garment and thrown, mounted and trod. I turned aside from it and walked through the open door.

The south room was smaller and more peculiar, as it had instead of door a curtain of loose-threaded feathers from various birds stitched to a hide. Two broken bedsteads with shuck sacking and a rocking chair not much bigger than a grown buck's rack were all the appointments, but the one wall where internal pine paneling had been raised was all scarred and painted in goggle-eye faces which appeared to pre-date the vacant state of the house. Now as I think back, I am sure there are many instances in which you can see what's not there as plain as Jacob's potatoes. Perhaps that was one such, and I have not thought to ask Granny Fell or Pink about the etchings, which no longer carry a stable shape in my mind.

Outside, an equally empty pig sty and back house, but no child, no sign or sound of company other than the poor-wills warming up, though I could see on the far peaks opposite thunderheads were mustering for storm. It was clear from first report that the remote location of the house would eliminate any opportunity to glean corroborations from the scene, and it seemed I could not now even keep hold of the one fleeting soul who had appeared and might be able to answer questions on the practices of the deceased. I shouted out a bold how-do to the general surround and raised no answer but the shadow of my own voice and wondered were the portraits inside a child's rendering of shoats and the old brindle boss Pogue was said to have owned. I had no doubt those beasts would be forever forfeit, melted away like spring ice.

Though there was no time to descend the mountain before full dark and hovering rain, I was disinclined to pass the night on the murder grounds, and as the cutthroat was intimate with the place, I preferred we might stumble upon one another under different circumstances and thus stirred with dispatch toward a homestead known to me just under the ridge where I was offered a good bait of supper and pallet, along with a gill of other refreshment and fine-strand tobacco for my briar. Sleep came easily but brought vexing dreams of the glimpsed child and the queer drawings, and I wished for the warmth of Adair's flank and the comfort of her steady breath. It is tempting enough to remember that another brand of life might proffer more explicit pleasures than quiet affection and trust, but in suchlike haunts and on such occasions, only a fool would fix merit on anything trimmed with risk or steeped in shadows.

My dark reverie, if that be the wordage for it, was brushed aside by the sound of Lish Jackson's voice declaiming an urgent message, which turned out to be no more than reminder from Adair of our invitation to a garden party at the manse. The commotion was enough to stir Bob's voice to new verses.

The fresh editor of *The Rockbridge County Gazette* is eager to announce the reward, so I must supply my consent. Before we are waded deep into June I hope to put this Brodie case behind me, if I have to posse up and send him and all the moonmen up there to Ujinctum. For the present, it is pressing to attire myself for the soiree. Therefore the thinking day is ended and finds me in dry clothes. For that much, thanks be.

<u>June 4</u>

Today as I loafed by the door of Brown's Forge, I saw the Irish Creek girl passing by, slogging through the mud gum, evidently toting milk for Granny Fell. She stopped full still before McCrum Drug on Nelson Street and gave me a hard look with those bitter eyes. I reckoned she was using jimson weed to darken her stare and berries on her mouth. The only sound discernible to me was Muse Brown's hammer ringing the iron for Vester's left hind shoe, and when she caught my gaze, Miss Grove resumed her stroll, swinging the rack of milk bottles till the sound of glass rattling liked to wash out the racket of metal. As she sashayed down the street, I saw the afternoon sky was gone to quicksilver and doubt not we'll see the resumption of the judgment rain that has baptised us all season. Oftimes, I almost sense connection between her disturbing aspect and the disrupted sky.

Queries from the citizenry persist. I must soon tighten the snare about Painter, whom we now learn has not been in the county at all but shammicking down in Roanoke where the spindle side of his clan was once known to squat. As soon as I can trust a sighting in this district, I will convene a committee of riders and make a sweep. No more stealth and half-measures in this, no more doodle-bug-come-out and hard wishing at prayer meeting. If I am to continue boring with a big auger in this town, results must swiftly unfold.

<u>June 15</u>

The train wreck toward Fairfield has brought news from a brakeman well known to Painter that the wanted man is surely now in the area, tidings that must not lie unemployed. An illusion master said to be able to glean thoughts from the air and to snake-shed his own skin unveils in Buena Vista tonight, and would that I could trust such wonders enough to query him about the slippery outlaw.

On the journey back from Fairfield, I yearned for time to pause by the old church at Gethsemane, where Mother and Father lie at rest, but the current urgencies allowed only a glance from the road. At least the field is well-scythed, and the yews shadow the slope with a feeling of peace. I must return with Adair on Decoration Day to set fresh flowers and clear the stones.

<u>June 20</u>

After several days of sog and commotion I am at last able to report the capture of the outlaw Painter, which went not so smoothly as we had hoped, but as he is the most public catch between Roanoke and Staunton, my relief is not paltry.

Word came the fugitive had phantomed in and out of our jurisdiction at will in the guise of a woman but was now bold enough to call on his brother Darl and move among other kindred, though always by stealth and moonlight, so I gathered a squad of willing men and headed for the steeps with a provisioned jack in tow. John Pink and his cousin Suttuck on the latter's apt-named gelding Mud were there, also Drennin, who is claimed able to track at a gallop, and two others. We met Chief Hazelwood aboard a dapple I do not know on the White Gap and swept watchfully in a long arc toward the Painter place. As per usual, the rain was our constant companion.

We assayed first the Blood Tavern where the accused is wont

to linger, and not finding him there put out word among the local hog rangers we would retire to Lexington in defeat, then feinted southwest before double-tracking. The first night found us in Turkey Hollow, confident in our ruse, but we kept a cold camp and slept in a tight of laurel to prevent detection, though our tenting provided inadequate comfort. Of all the wildcats I have pursued, this man cat was among the cagiest prey, and with all South Mountain's caves and hells offering refuge, we were far from assured of success.

Next noon found us circling slowly -- Dark Hollow and Big Dark, easing in on the base of Nettle Mountain where we were bound. The woods are lively there, glossy, and more than a few rudducks would break from cover flashing their red wings. This in full sunshine, to our amazement. Twice we spied scheming bell-tails coiled snug behind conchy logs, but we gave them wide berth. I can easily see how those briar hoppers escape accounting and rusticate while running laurel farms and bobcat herds, as the tales have it. This is not yet a tamed tract. Goat's beard and hellebore were common amid the itch ivy, and the footing treacherous over declines of slate waste. Though it was good to be in the saddle, not a soul we rousted could inform us of any events beyond their immediate sight. If the local denizens harbor any respect for the law, they are sworn to secrecy on the matter.

Vester issued his protest nicker and slung his mane about more than once in the hard going, and I hated to push him through such terrain, as he is no hog pony nor slink hound but a good horse for the chase. Still, there was nothing else for it, as we wished to close in on Painter's trail before he might again flee.

Being apprised of the partisan nature of the neighborhood, we were always on alert for bushwhackers, and the nervous result brought Suttock and Richard Travers near to blows over a trifle on one occasion. Not a little wind was spent on the rascality of Painter, his invisible nature and deep schemes, and I again remarked how he seemed a four-legged painter more than human. Not one man-jack among us doubted his culpability, so we moved through briar and blowdown with resolve, always singlefile, often leading our mounts over scabby ground. We also found that region much tangled in suckle vine, and despite the blossom waft, the Irish Creek area had about it some odor of decay and abandon throughout the ivy slick. The ceiling dropped low and threatening again, and the much-washed earth had sprung up every species of noxious toadstools as recompense. In one beat-down I took for bear wallow a great razorback tushed by and startled the entire party to snatch for weapons. The whole district exhales the hospitality of a grave.

There being no real path in the final mile along the bluff, we were obliged to conceal our horses in a barn and pioneer through dense green to achieve a vantage over what Pink claimed to be the seat of the clan. It was slow going, and the day a sweat bath with further showers impending, but we shuckled as best we could and just before dusk found our target. You could see the frames of drying pelts and a lot full of sorry-looking cull hogs. Critter traps, some bee gums, punky cordwood and divers trash cluttered the demesne, and from various trees hung a kind of bonechime – jaws, ribs, back knuckles and skulls still slick with gore, whether to lure ghosts or repel angels no man could have ventured. A slight worm of blue smoke rose from the flag chimney, but no soul moving, so we took to the rocks and laurels, deploying in skirmish fashion, waiting for life signs. Last daylight was a rouged edge through the foliage, but I found little of beauty in it. I checked my watch and my revolver over and again, reminding the Lord to keep a sharp eye, as I was entering danger, though ostensibly clothed in the power of the law.

Before twenty minutes had passed, the jar-flys humming up in their seventeen-year chirr, I could see a window opened in its sheath at the back of the dark house, and a dim figure appeared -- Darl, who having somehow surmised the besiegement of the house intended to make for the tree line and apprise his kin.

That was not allowed, as Chief Hazelwood surprised the brother with a Spencer rifle at the level, as he rounded a strawstack. As Haze marched him around to the front, Darl, who has much of the scarecrow about him, made to jackrabbit, and for his efforts received a blow from the gunstock behind his knees.

Sam Watts of our party then rushed into the house where the

distaff kin huddled and purported he would kill every man, woman and child if they issued a sound. He was snarling like a coon dog and they wolving back when I entered the fray and found a quartet of females, all with hacked hair and wearing frocks sewn from the same bolt. All were sparrow-eyed and snaggley, the least a mere imp and the eldest a crone of rawky voice, dugs scarce covered by her cloth, and her steady sneer evidenced she bore no respect for my badge or rabbit-eared two-barrel. Everything in the single-room cabin was ashed and scutty with a stink of fish and rancid lard, and I would have been much pleased to be in any other of the world's sculleries but that one. Soon our party were both in the reeking house and beyond it, a picket line of our deputies to let the fugitive pass through, and with lanterns lit inside, we impressed the women to make supper motions and stir the fire.

Before long, the object of our search emerged from a stand of scrub pine, his expression that of a preacher on a spree, an old Navy Colts dangling from his hand but his gait a carefree lope. Although he was much altered since his soldier days, I knew him at once. He is the blackest of the Painters, likely issued from different loins than Darl, and in that twilight one could indeed describe him as damson. At his approach Pink shouted his name, as in turn did we all to announce the full surround. The women, knowing Painter's indisposition to surrender and seeing so many firearms brandished, commenced to plead and keen for their beloved relative's life, and he raised his hands as if to come in peaceably, bringing me to a sigh of relief. Catching his face holding back all feeling, I had to think for one moment he was but little different from myself – worn out and edgy – and hoped he would yield easy.

But that was not to be. Haze strode forth with the irons in his hand, and just at that pass, Painter abandoned his ruse, roostered his hammer and dropped to his knee to fire a ball at the Chief. Would the result be the snap of a null chamber or the voice of fire? In truth, the miscreant was wobbly on his feet before Suttock feathered into the man with his Winchester, swatting as if he had an axe handle. Even stunned and bleeding from the temple, Painter, who is both stout and tall, was loathe to be manacled or handled roughly, and he thrashed about. I finally had to put on the quietus with a blow to his nape from my belt stick. Peeling back the sleeve of his dustcoat and shirt, I saw the viper drawn into his skin, though hardly visible against his own dark surface. He had affected a handlebar moustache and bore scars unknown to me, but this was surely our culprit.

Even after the man was cuffed and revived and I had served the papers, he was no more cooperative than a mad fox, snarling curses at us and kicking till I decided to hobble him as I would a headstrong colt. When he spat my name and called me a pussle-gutted son of Nick, I had heard enough and swatted him out again. All along Sam Watts held his weapon trained on the rest of the family, taunting them as they reined still enough to satisfy any portrait photographer. Darl was so flinchy-eyed I felt certain he was scouting for some edged tool to make an unwise demonstration, so I judged it best to cuff him as well.

Coming to all bound up, Painter heard Hazelwood to say we should best shoot him on the spot and sling him down the shaft of an old tin mine to save the county money and the poor victim much discomfort and trauma. This was laughed off by some of us, though Pink alleged as this was far the best suggestion of the campaign. For my part, I am sorry to say, the proposal seemed not without merit, but I registered at once we were too many eyes and tongues to keep such a course concealed. The banter seemed to have a sobering effect on the accused, however, who was thereafter compliant except on the matter of his army hat, which he insisted in vain we fetch from his camp among the hemlocks. Watching in lantern light his coiled hair as he sat the jack on our descent, I could not but think this was all a tainted business, neither clean nor worthy of our charge.

After the prisoner was delivered to Lexington the next day in sheveled and humbled state, the posse was dismissed, and the cost of this chapter of the manhunt to the county has been in excess of thirty dollars, including rations, grain for the horses and three dollars bounty for each volunteer. The distance covered in the hunt, much of it through rough mountain, could scarce be less than a hundred miles, though the map reckoning from Lexington to the headwaters of the Pedlar and back is but forty-two miles. I must continue to implore the county to ordain a constable to take jurisdiction in the Irish Creek region, as upheavals there are frequent and the labor and cost of enforcement from town prohibitive. Though yet a somewhat hale specimen, I do not possess the resources for many more such misadventures, and I relish them not at all.

Tonight I will cap my pen with some small satisfaction and truckle off to bed somewhat less burdened. If the trial unfolds as I foresee, I can either stay my current course or option for the stabling enterprise in the autumn with assurance of widespread support, not to mention Adair's delight, which is nearly enough to put the heart back in me.

Final Testament of Brodie Painter, September 7, 1906

copied and witnessed: Ella Ree Cutchins, notary

She said he would not be about, would be down in the levels to fetch a spool of wire and a rabbet saw. That is the story I opened to lawyer Spencer, but he allowed as how it would not wash in court. There was a prejudice against me among the hatefuls, and I'd have to make shift for myself. This being my last shot to spill the whole tale with noose-day just around the bend, Mr. Prescott, please be kindly to mark it all down, spike to scut.

As I was saying, Ina and me was no strangers one to the other. There's many a time we had spoke previous, and she had showed me her sweetmeats when I first chanced on her up in the orchard. We had enjoyed full congress every occasion afterwards, as I honed for her steady. Though I am an old hand at scamping about, swiving and giving moustache rides to loose gals from here to Christmas, she was the sort that put your sense away from you, made you give up all other donies and train your heart on her. I thought she seen it that way too, and when we twined, I law, it was like a fire on fire. She made my blood to sing.

I had been paying her that fashion of courtship for two months and had already gave her patent slippers and a red frock when Pogue discovered the pretties and wrenched the matter out of her, and what she pleaded to me was he was agreeable to my repeating so long as he reaped a full dollar each time I called, on account of her age. He would make hisself scarce off with the hogs or out after squirrel, except I could oftener hear him blowing that French harp up in the brush. Spook music is what he made, and it was no aid to love dealing and rankled me somewhat. Still and all, we had some merry times, and when I debouched, I would leave my dollar on the keghead.

That was the bargain, and it suited me well enough till she commenced to whisper that himself was rutting at her too, which was by my reckoning full tilt unnatural. A Pogue will do that, you know, will jape even his mother when in a needful state, and there's slathers of them down in southside who show the nasty fruit of it.

She asked would I spirit her off, as she knowed the whereabouts of his money poke and had some kin over to Kentucky we might veil with and farm moon till Pogue turned over a new leaf, which give her the giggles. You know, his name. Though I had done struck my bargain with him and spit over it, that was in ignorance, and I won't suffer nobody cutting my territory like that, won't tolerate it.

So that afternoon I come up the wash expecting nothing but a couple gills from the jug and needling her to the bone, which I done fine and fancy. She has all the buck and moan of a Cuban washwoman, you know. It was a mighty tussle. Later, whilst we was laying up in the shucks listening to the quillerees high in the oak woods, she was snuggling while I stroked her slow along the moosey. As she is honey-voiced, she commenced to croon a little infare, and then we fashioned out our plan to make tracks off for the blue grass in just a week when Pogue would be off trading his angel's teat whiskey. I knowed well my brother Darl would help smuggle us out in a freight wagon, then onto a slow train and no man be the wiser where she was gone. It was a sweet thought, and whilst I savored it, my heed was down. I was a mooncalf in full daze.

I know you have cause to judge me on further accounts, the killing of Cash and more trifling matters. If ever a man needed a view window in him, Cash was it. He had cleaned my brother's plow twice over the matter of one sorry salt lick, and had once slandered my mama to boot, so his calendar was out of pages. He gloried in everybody's miseries. I admit to plugging him with my daddy's pitted old 32.20, but don't be forgetting he had a rifle gun hisself.

There's always those who put the stain on ridgers like me just to even things. I can shoot sharp and ride like a demon and cipher faster than a storm bolt. My whiskey is always silver bead, and I can ringer a horseshoe most every time. I can shear muttons, skin and stalk and witch wells. I have always been a step ahead of others, and the snake-faced bastards didn't savor it.

Much accused meanness I am lamb-innocent of, but I have drawn slurs like a gutted cur draws flies. I law it is surely the Melungeon in my blood that makes me the blame goat for so much, and even in the

Spanish war I found charges heaped against me before ever I could kick off the blanket of a morning. If I am guilty of half what they have laid to my door, let my spirit take flame in hell's hottest stall. I have stilled and scrapped and raised my voice against the heel of lily-white men who wish to scoundrelize us of color. I have thumped those who come up against me and swapped rich people's cattle for binge money, but I never raped at that girl or any other, nor needed to, and what Pogue got he requisitioned on his own account. He will be little missed, especially among those who relish real music.

He come stomping up the porch afore I knew he was on the mountain a-tall, and he called out her name like a he-bear roaring. Ina run out the room with the quilt wrapping her while I snatched my trousers up and legged in. He was storming at her, and when the smack of his hand on her face sounded, I run out the feather curtain and into the kitchen room with my boots in my hand. He saw me then and slung her aside like a poppet. I could see his face was the hue of lean meat, and he shouted out, Painter of the painter cats, you have brought your prides out into the open in my house onct too often. That was when he snapped the twine round his neck and drew the straight razor from his shirt front. I could see it was a nicked and ugly thing, rusty and long unused for shaving, as Pogue's whiskers were end-of-winter.

He started circling and me circling backwards till I spied the meat knife amongst the dishes, so I seized it up and took a crouch to fend him off. He jumped and I jumped, and it was arms and legs a-tangle for a minute there, me not sure where he left off and myself started, but for his teeth in my neck. Then in a quick jab I drew blood from his belly, and when he staggered back, I went slashing random-like and got the throat, I reckon. I was right drunk, but I am not a man to mess with. If you have seen a pig cut you have seen that much spray, but if not, you can't even speculate, so I must of got him square. He went to knees, then face forward, and the girl was screaming like a wildcat till something over her head seemed to catch her voice and bandy it back down. That was when she went dark and dropped to a heap on the floor.

The boards was loose fitted, and I could see young shoots prying green underneath and thought I might be sniffing the tang of new-sprouted mint. When I leant over to stir Ina that we might scape the place together, I slicked on what must have been his blood leak and fell on my backsides hard, for which there was nothing but to laugh it. All the bouts and skirmish I had been through, and never before ripped a man's life out of him, excepting Cuba and also Cash, but the court quit me on the Cash matter. It takes a part out of you, killing a man. It sucks you down like a water whirl. Now here I was over a crow-haired, scarce-hipped girlchild all trussed up in the kind of trouble that won't rub off with neither words nor worry, and here I am now about to climb my last stairs.

Laying there, she was blue in the face as a possum's cods, and tossing dung and dogwood on the coals in the stove box, I kettled water and thrashed about for some mixings. I was still blurred in my sight with the whiskey and having some trouble sorting things. What I found was a honey jar with a mouse drowned under the comb, but I poured off the top and tippled a dad of blockade in to stiffen it. That and the cooked water I brought to her lips with honest regard, but once I roused her, she right off started to take Pogue's part, weeping and carrying on like I was the varlet, and I couldn't wedge in so much as a squawk but what she would scrowl out again. I never known the beat of it, and seeing no hope of our traveling plan coming to bloom at that point, I reckoned such as me had best be scarce when the world come to know whatever story she was fixing to tell. Couldn't no good come of it for me, that was a sure fact. It was a red business all around.

Riddle me how you would of acted in such a mangle. I could figure the law would be on me like ducks on a crippled june bug, so I rifled and skeltered the place till I found the wall board warped out from prizing. Back there was the money poke, sure as ramps root neigh creek, and I took half the eagles, thinking Ina would need some her own self. Then I lit out, not giving a back glance.

What come strange to my ears in the court was all these other tales spun concerning my rangering about in the weeks following.

What I really done was leg it down to Vesuvius and wait under Orion and the bears on a steep where the train would stop to take on water for steaming up the grade. Once on, I rode all about, hopping off for provender and some loft sleep, but high-tracking it from Green Cove to Damascus, Bansock to Luray, Lithia back up to Second Pigeon, steering clear of Lexington and its ward. I rode the Norfolk and Western back and fro all over the mountains, breathing in the smoke whilst it shadowed laundry on the line by daylight, laying on my back to watch it silvering against black night. All my running mates from the N & W I would surprise at their lunch pails or when they were frying up corn dodgers at railside. They credited the story I have rendered you and gave me forage, but I will not raise their names in this matter, as I know the law's grudges do not die off easy.

This is my honest story of how a misfortunate man come to be painted as desperado. They come after me in their black coats like corpse birds and sneaked up on me asleep by my fire. They beat me and give me the boot, called me nigger and spat in my face. They shoved and cuffed my whole family, too.

This is how a man with no evidence against him got hunted down by a pack of bounty hounds. Scribe this down right, lady, and you can show it to whosomever might have an eye for justice, cause the public needs knowing even too late to save my neck what manner of rascals run their statutes and how a man can suffer evil though he swore on the preacher book and let only unscutched truth cross his red tongue. I'll sing the devil this same tune tomorrow in his crowded coal hole, Miss Cutchins, Mr. Prescott. A man in the derbies and the scaffold's shadow has no call to throw the lie.

Oral History, Staunton, Virginia: Ina Grove Fell, 1964

When I came to a woman was screaming through the rain. That's what I thought. I didn't rightly understand where I was, the room blurry with a funny smell, but I could hear her voice, all fury. A light was coming through the apple tree and then the window, a green light, and I thought it was going to sift through me like some loose flour. Thirst was what I felt, almost that only. I thought the scream was going to shake me back to darkness, and I was shivering. Then I knew the woman was that blue jay nesting in the north haw. I smelled the hard smell and saw a rough face moving between me and the green light, and then I felt sore all over, a slow ache that went sharp in my fork. My knickers were gone entirely, and all my clothes. I was twisted in a robe like a Bible wife, but it was a quilt. Things started to remember. The face was moving, and something rusty was dried on my legs, and something else. This feeling had been upon me before, but never so severe. I thought I would die and I wanted to die. I wanted that jay woman to cease screaming, but I was crying to match her, and I thought another bird like some sparrow with purling notes should light in the apple tree any minute and trill out so its song might lift me or duck me under for good. I might just drink it and be drunk by it and rise up invisible as a ghost and shed all my troubles. Woe be.

That was a long time back, and I was only a girl who saw blackbirds in her mirror and eyes of a cat. Some things you misremember, and others shimmer and divide up. I think my daddy used to say we tell stories to forget what we need to get behind us, but I have never told this one, since I was spared most of court. What I swore then was what I thought, and though I had been something of a wild girl, nobody had the right to do me like that and go free. Since Uncle Leaf was dead, it was best to forgive him any trespass or unseemly doings and move on. I did. I moved on. I know that Painter pushed at me before and pushed till I gave in listening to the yellowjackets drilling windfalls, a red color like off the ripe fruit overhead. When he was done I felt different with a hard rank smell on my clothes and salt in my eyes, but he gave no gentleness, saying all woman folk are born with the round heels. Then he galloused up and said he'd see me again, not even looking back. I hoped he'd never.

When I saw Uncle Leaf sprawled in the blood, his eyes were open and baleful, glaring fierce, and I did not know if he was alive or dead. Stop hexing me, I shouted, and the other face was still moving around me, about the house, its voice saying calming things, but I was not calmed.

Some times you don't want to say a thing as it will loose a whole waterspill of words you can't bear to hear, the rushing of every fear you've ever had burning as it crossed your tongue. I was wracked and damaged and my only close kin looked dead, no matter how angry his eyes, no matter how little pity he'd showed in his life. The other thing in the room was gone then, but I could taste honey. The watchbird had screamed itself from blue to red, and then it fell off. I went swoony again and slid into the dark.

That night the Io moth came to my window like a mask, its buckeye eyes boring into me. I had been often accused of making flirtation and primping, but this was a new thing, and I did not take pleasure from any of it at all.

Those years I worked for Granny Kate with the stain on my name, most people showed kindness, and I learned the ways of her milk cows and how to churn. Flies would light in the cow pies and then on the bucket rim. People drank it anyway. They didn't see. She gave me Chichester's English Pennywort concoction with a paste of her own devising, and what made me swell seeped out one night, but not without pain of the damned. Granny taught me her potions and poisons and how to gather makings off in the forest. Also to read. Four years after the misdeeds I climbed up after a Christmas snow shower with a jug of coal oil and splashed it about inside the rubble of the old place. I set the match and stood back, shivering under a rind moon, watching the boards smoke and catch and blossom. It was time to sear the ghosts out, time to send my girlish wall etchings back to whence they came, though they had once been my only true friends. I knew the hive in the walls was still and the bees sleeping in their wax wouldn't feel a thing.

Only the spy apple tree by the window caught the fire, its limbs spidery against the winter air and then glowing. The house shouted and crashed, black clouds coaxing night to hurry on, and when the roof caved, something inside me lifted, delivered me, and I was no longer so lost.

I became a woodsweed girl with pestle and mill and steam kettles, a whole cellar of concoctions, but when Granny Fell foxed out that my mama had passed over birthing me, she said I could be a thrush witch, named after the bush bird, and that was my main call, blowing the sick color from the throat of a child. I cut bloodroot and pulled sang. I gathered in the galax. I was a cat keeper and nightwalker, a tender of gold bees, and I could sew and bantle, nurse and drive a nail straight to the heart. I was alone. I got by.

I won't say there was no other. In the doughboy times I slipped off some and had no regrets, but I had already shut my heart and shot the bolt. It was just a letting go here and there, then back to my pets, my own cow barn by then with peafowl strutting. I would lie under the rhododendrons and stare a lady slipper in the eye. I was comrade to orchids and a friend to owls.

It was the year that rain was raining all the time, and I recall Granny wet and cold when she found me, me cold and wet too by then, because the roof was not tight. It was the year the ferro beetles showed up for their seventeen- year courtship, and what I heard them saying, even in town, was spoiled, spoiled, spoiled. It was a question why my uncle and another with skin so blue he was a dark flower at first would pitch into killing rage over me, as not one seemed to want much to do with me most days. That is the limitation of a man.

It was a hard tramp down South Mountain to a road, but she propped me and kept shushing when I tried to say what all I reckoned had transpired. She named birds in the trees and flower bells by the pathway, keeping my mind from drifting back to that blood scene. It wasn't till I'd had a night sleep and bowls of broth and some dittany tea with hard brandy that she said, let's tell it now, and the whole swirling tussle came back before me, the blades in frailing light, some rutting and laughter, the red tide and apples, jay scream through green light and the hint of bee honey. Before long the pieces in my heart had commenced to come together like a puzzle, while the rain was drumming again, shaking me back to that day with its whirlwind and bloodshed, and then I knew what I knew.

The Account of a Baffling Spirit Appearance as Reported by Sister Sura Sawyer in *The Roanoke Alternative Magazine*, April 7, 1965

As I was about to release my familiar, Prince Akira, at the conclusion of a successful séance, a voice unknown to me interceded, and delivered a mysterious report which bore on none of the present circle but which seemed not of negligible import. As follows is my best recollection of the monologue spoken by a beard-faced essence hovering above the table but never fully in focus, as tormented spirits are wont to appear:

When my sister Sheila passed in child-birth, I swore to help her lawful husband hold the child precious, as the Irish Creek was rife with copperheads of both the crawling and walking kinds. Poor sister, who was smitten hard with Anders Grove and never recovered from lovewit before she met her end. She was fool for a fiddle, and he bowed string music all along the Peddlar at play parties and stump speeches, moving widows, wives and maids alike to sashay and smile. Even I took a shine to himself and pleasured at playing reel music to his devil's box. It's true enough he doted on her, but he had more eyes than the one, and they traveled, so even before Sheila was spent, I had concerns for her and the baby that he mightn't stay and provide. When Anders was done in by a broke shaft timber, I knowed the child would get her best raising from me alone. I might be prone to poach and loathe to till, but I had my own ways of bringing the specie in.

Why I come back to speak with the white tongue is to say I done her wrong, swapping care for neglect whilst I milked the worm and horsed barrels of apple pomace about when it was too wet for the wheeling barrow. Good shine kept a roof over us and vittles on the table, but she much growed up her own creature till something ugly in me started taking low notice.

In close quarters like ours, you can't miss seeing, and she bloomed like the may apple all creamy and soft. Seems one day she was a doll child herself scolding the rag baby. Next day I was chewing sweetgum sap to cure my breath for her and sprucing my hair, as she was a little woman with fair flesh to taunt the hungry. I was hungry. I partook.

To even talk moonlight with such close kin is a misdeed, I know, and I would wish for a hard brush to curry myself after we cuddled. I would speak to great God to stop me before hard harm grew to habit. I said Lord I would not wish to tread her, but I do, and nothing ever smote me.

There's another verse to that song. Ina was rambunctious and would always hide where I could find her. We kept up the tease game for a year, never fording the stream, but then Painter commenced skulking and watching. At first, I took him for a still spy seeking my trove and found relief over him just ogling the house from out in the rain. I figured him for a half-breed the John Laws kept in corn to scout us, knowing that'd peg him as lazy. He'd be all vine and no taters, and nobody's idle spy will find where I shift my mash nor cut my faggots on Whetstone. By dark, in case he was peering from some windbreak, I'd have Ina strike the wick of a grease lamp and venture out to the crib or muck house. Anybody taking notice would follow her, and I'd slip over the casement and to my works.

But then I seen he had other notions. She come back from the slope orchard with a ill smile and said, when I asked after the lurker, that she'd seen nothing but two yanks nesting in a white oak and a checkervest hammering his mattock after tree beetles. It was yet too airish for the birds to be stirring so, just Easter or thereabouts, and she had that grin like a doll's face stitched on. Jealousy is as bad to shake you as the preachers say, and if that Injun was to have zip on his stackcakes, it would not come from my ambry.

One afternoon I claimed to her I'd be off a whole day decanting my usquebaugh but circled back to catch them in the beast act, and sure enough they was raw and blushed when I come in, Eve and Adam, but him dark as the devil. It was rage, all I saw, and after I slapped her a strong one, I pulled the razor, so we went round, thrashing and panting like we was red-tails mating, but he got lucky and cut my breadbasket, which leached much of the fight out of me. Still I had the advantage, as I'd slung Ina about in my temper, and he went to tend her, then started heating up a pot of water, like he was to care for her, and I had forfeit all his attention on account of my weakness.

That was when I reached for my boot gun, as I should of done at the outset. I knowed it was closing in, the deep moment, and what I was fighting for might fall to me forever mine or never, so I stuck my hand down toward the pistol butt. Then it closed over me, something floating dark and silky as night wind, and I felt my throat tearing like a lamb's, the fountain flowing scarlet. The spray of my own life toward a sway of darkness was the last thing I could ever see, and I am signed to tell it whenever a listener heeds.

The News-Gazette, **March 4, 1968**

IRISH CREEK PROPERTY SOLD TO O'MALLEY LUMBER

-- The property previously known as the Pogue Homestead on Irish Creek has been sold by the County of Rockbridge to the O'Malley Lumber Company of Fairfield. The twenty-four acres of prime hardwoods had been held in trust by the county for three years against unpaid property taxes, and the commission voted Tuesday night last to approve the sale to Michael O'Malley.

The transaction would have proceeded with little notice but for Felton Newday's insistence that a brief history of the property be read into the record, as the Pogue place was the site of a vicious murder and rape of a young girl sixty-four years ago. It was also the known haunt of brigands and poachers, and the murdered Leaf Pogue himself was long a recognized trafficker in illegal whiskies. The taxes were for a time paid sub rosa by a Ms. Fell every spring from 1954 until 1976 on the supposed anniversary of the crime, for which one Brodie Painter was convicted and hanged. The felon had put the old Pogue home to the torch after the crimes, but the outbuildings persisted as ramshackle reminders until the late fifties, and excursionists and hunters often used them as shelter. Many local residents will also recollect childhood legends of a spectral "hen girl" haunting the region.

Mr. O'Malley plans to harvest the timber and eventually offer parcels of the land as multiple homesites in a division to be called Kissing Ridge. The area harbors some of the most majestic white oaks, locusts and hickories in proximity to Lexington, and it will be a shame to see them laid waste, but it was concluded the world must progress. The council decided unanimously that continued suspension of taxes would be a burden upon the community budget, and as Commissioner Lee Sherburne remarked, "The time of outlaws like Painter and Pogue has passed, and it would be a relief to see a commercial venture usher the infamous Irish Creek region into the twentieth century."

A small band of local citizens in attendance raised protest that the sale of that property would usher in an era of speculation and desecration of some of the county's wildest and most beautiful land. Chairman Mack Thaxton declared the issue closed when a Mrs. Cash accused him of taking money under the table to facilitate the rezoning. Her complaint was silenced by Thaxton's gavel and, the matter being concluded, the meeting was adjourned, followed by refreshments and the consensus that the timber money might help wash away the sins perpetrated in the past.

Maggard

At the head of the trail Byron's head seemed to be floating about five feet above the scruffy ground – its remaining skin ash-blue, eyes pecked empty, his face unrecognizable – and the wren perched on the boy's – the sheriff couldn't stop counting him a boy now – matted scalp was struggling to free a single black hair. When the strand snapped, the bird bobbed its russet head to shake off the shock of recoil, then recovered its balance, flexed its wings and darted into the thicket of sharp green pines.

This was what he saw through the rifle scope, and no other thing moving until a buck rabbit hopped out of a grass clump and proceeded to graze, almost in the shadow of the grisly totem. In another circumstance, the rabbit might as well have jumped directly into a stewpot, as Sherburne's skill with the Henry would have made him a good bet at this distance to clip the twitching head off the creature without marring the meat. This morning, however, he could not allow his mind to drift toward thoughts of tender game or the hot coffee his body was craving. He might wish for a banked fire to lean toward or a camp blanket over his shoulder to keep the morning chill off, but such thoughts were distractions, and seeing the boy's aspect thus rendered had already interfered with his breathing and concentration.

He needed a different kind of slaking, and he'd have to make due with the wool jacket – a touch small for him now – with so many moth holes it looked like an unlucky veteran of San Juan Hill. The campaign hat and trousers of old canvas, the holstered Colt and bandolier, the horn-handled knife. Hunting garb, and then some. Flexing his veined wrists and big-knuckled hands against the stiffness of the night before, he believed he could hear the red hand of his watch, snug in its pocket, slicing off the seconds.

He'd been at this work so long even his ambushes had taken on the feel of ceremony. He squinted and looked again. Down there in the swale, Byron's mouth was wide open, almost a yawn. Some of the teeth had been smashed out, and the blood Sherburne could see looked black. Someday soon, he had promised his wife, he'd retire this jacket and let her order a new one from the Sears and Roebuck. But not yet; he still depended upon it for luck. Following an armed and fugitive Melungeon around the countryside was the kind of exercise in which luck would help but would not be enough.

"Doodle-bug, come out," he thought.

HE'D HAD TO COME in light and quiet, had stalked slowly the evening before, picketed his black horse with the one white sock far back down the slope, then ape-walked and eventually crawled to this position with its lethal alley through the brush and saw-toothed outcrops. His father had been adept at finding such sight lines through the foliage, but it was less a family trait than an acquired skill much dependent upon practice. He also knew he could stand, if he had to, take a position against the hemlock behind him and cover a wide killing zone of scrub and sedge to the west, between the high path and any possible escape. The east sheered up quickly, and nobody was going out that way.

Training the sight on Byron again, he thought of the boy grinning across the cluttered desk when he'd been told that not even the prisoners appreciated his attempts to master "Turkey in the Straw" on his penny whistle. Sherburne winced at his miscalculation: The boy had not been ready to confront anyone with violent possibilities. It was his error, his job. Then his eyes and barrel swept toward the timber line. If the trophy Byron had become was bait, maybe he had been lured into something he couldn't yet unriddle, but he'd been following this trail for four days now and didn't see another option. Right now, speculation would serve no purpose, just muddy his mind. And anger was no better. He was paid to work cold and achieve simple, lasting results, but right now he just wanted to damage the man and see him flinch in pain. Even if others never witnessed it, he was sure this kind of impulse tarnished the star in his pocket.

He'd ALMOST SURPRISED MAGGARD on Monday, early in the afternoon when the fugitive had paused, mixed with touring strangers gawking at the high arch of the Natural Bridge, complicating his trail, buying supplies and swapping his spavined mule for a stout work horse. From what the sheriff was about to see, it might have been a Belgian – right head, right ears, eyes far apart – but that was at distance and no time to be playing at breed recognition.

The grounds were teeming with scenery gawkers, as well as the predictable buskers and acrobats, the souvenir hawkers and shills and pocket artists, and Sherburne was afoot, far from his own mount when he saw his quarry ascending the Buchanan Road with full panniers and that dark sack slung from the pommel. He hadn't yet known what it held.

The sheriff cupped his hands and shouted out, "Maggard, stop under authority of the law." The festive and noisy visitors in their holiday finery froze and fell silent around this tall man, who looked like a refugee from Buffalo Bill's extravaganza. When some followed his gaze up the rough heights, they screamed and ran or fell to the ground. The whole plaza quickly became a swirl of color and various outcries of fear. One woman in a plumed yellow hat and heavily-ruffed dress stumbled and fell right at his feet. A goggled motorcar driver ducked, and his ridiculous vehicle smashed into the corner of a store, shattering window glass but missing the organ grinder and his rebel-uniformed monkey.

In plain view Maggard sat his horse on the bluff and was pointing the Sharps down into the street, directly at his pursuer.

"For God's sake, man, give this up. Come on down, and I'll treat you fair, hear your story. I've talked to the girl." He couldn't be certain his words were clear at this distance, but he could almost feel the pressure of the wide-bore barrel against his chest, as if they were no further apart than arm's length. Maggard could have pulled the trigger right then and had a chance to eliminate his nemesis, probably the only man he was aware of with both the skills and the grit to run him to ground. From such a height and with only a notch sight, it would be a considerable shot, and the stakes were certainly high, but he chose instead to give his requisitioned horse the heel and galloped on up the grade, around the bend and out of sight, leaving the sheriff with the afterimage of a horse's hindquarters and dark tail, and an acid taste in his mouth.

Sherburne was left to wend his way through the shoving, panicked crowd and back to where he'd looped his reins around a rail. Everyone scrambling to get out of his way just amplified the chaos and slowed his passage. A spooked carriage horse almost dragged its rig over him, and a foolish-looking imp of a man in a white suit and spats waved his cane and shouted questions at the sheriff's back as he passed. He knew his suspect would quickly hit the coach road and mingle his tracks with hundreds of others, then probably loop back to enter Cedar Creek and use it to conceal his next veering into cover. The sheriff had no way to guess which direction his journey would turn next, and he didn't have a moment to spare. He pulled his coat open to show his badge, turned a full circle to display it and swung into the saddle. "Make a path," he shouted, and they did, as if his words cast a spell.

Now, AFTER THREE DAYS of trailing Maggard from Panther Falls – where luckily a logging crew had spotted him and one of their number had even spoken with him – over ridge and through thicket, Sherburne had seen more of Brown Mountain and Staton's Creek, Grapevine Bluff and the Piney River than he ever wanted to. And he was disappointed in himself again. The first time Maggard cut east into Amherst County, he had to know his pursuer would ignore all jurisdictions and keep coming. So the fugitive must have decided to set a more private rendezvous, to cut back toward Whetstone and his own stomping grounds, the safety of the familiar, the way a bull in the ring will return to his chosen charging station. The sheriff should have tasted that in the wind. It had been a ragged, exhausting three-day circuit, with Sherburne constantly swiveling in the saddle, glassing the horizon and riding little crochet figures through the woods in fear of some circle-back strategy in Maggard's mind.

His horse Bishop had been steady and patient and at first seemed to enjoy the stop-go of tracking in the refreshing weather, the nights on the trail, the sweet unbrowsed grass at the scut end of autumn. He was a well-mannered horse now, though wall-eyed and just a touch coon-footed. A serviceably sound Chickasaw mix, despite the martingale Sherburne still used to keep him from throwing his head back. One broken nose was all the lesson his master had needed, and now with his prominent withers and deep shoulders Bishop had developed into a valuable companion with keen trail sense. He usually moved at a good daisy-clipping pace and was at ease on any incline, but now Sherburne could sense that the animal was giving him quizzical looks as they scrabbled up and down these hills of scree and mazed through the understory with even less apparent destination than usual.

What this promontory he had nestled into this morning provided were ample cover and a sweeping perspective, though he hated having to leave the horse so far behind, even with good grazing. If anything or anyone came down that old washout and through the busted gate which marked the verge of Maggard's kingdom, if so much as a rodent approached the staked remains of Byron, Sherburne would see it from here and draw his bead in complete secret. The sun would be behind him and would not show the glass of his scope. He would come out of the sun as he had been instructed first by his father, then by Colonel Wood in the Spanish War, and the matter would be decided with one even squeeze of the trigger. If Maggard were as set on forcing a conclusion as the trophy staked near his own haunts announced. . . if Maggard were just one step slower and one guess less canny than the sheriff. . . and if his luck held. . . . If not, the sheriff would never even hear the roar of Maggard's Big-Fifty Sharps nor know the answers to a dozen questions that pulled on him like a calf on a wet teat. Why kill the deputy? Why take his head like some demented souvenir hunter? Why not pull the trigger back at Natural Bridge? Why not just come in meek to begin with and let the law uncover the real story or light out to hide in the hells of West Virginia? Why, even stranger, hem himself in now with his back to a steep drop-off, even if it was his home? And he knew already the only crucial question left was: Will I have to go in after him?

He shifted his weight and swept the barrel along the draw, then up the defile and along the ridgeline. No use expecting anything from that precinct. The rhododendron and laurel on the incline were so thick, nothing but a copperhead or a spirit could move through them easily. Mysterious as the Melungeon was, and much as some townbodies claimed he had reptile in his family, he was no more spirit than Sherburne, though some accounts of the sheriff's history suggested that was considerable.

NOBODY KNEW WHERE they came from. Or everybody did, as any hill dweller old enough to whirl a bullroarer harbored a theory. Melungeons. They were Spanish, Turks, Jews, a mix of free blacks, Indians and rogue whites. They sprang fully grown from a gap in the earth down in east Tennessee where the clay was cupric and blue, which gave their skins an indigo tint. Demon spawn. They were gypsies or half castes or creatures born of the dark courtship between renegade Cherokee and razorback hogs. Some said they were hatched from leathery eggs and could see perfectly by moonlight. Amanda Jewett vowed she had seen one walk across a lake. They were known to cast spells with roots and chicken blood. They had two sets of genitals. They had none. The speculative volley went back and forth about origin and nature and what habits and crimes they were born to. Charley Munger said they were the beings the Old Testament scorned as the children of Cain or Ham. "Portuguese," corrected Tom Sloat. The mongrel element was the most common belief, inbreeding some and then crossbreeding of a hazardous and unsavory sort. They were said to have six fingers on one hand and shovel teeth, as they were inclined toward cannibalism. Lincoln, Coburn swore, had been one of them. "One look," said the old Rebel, "and you'd know right away and forever. He had the spare finger sawed off in secret over in Kentucky, but his tribe's bloodthirst was a cinder glowing deep inside. Just look at the war, how he ran it, all that God-forsaken slaughter." They had butte-like bumps, even the women, in their scalp, and all of them, even the women, were huge.

Clearly, Melungeons were not town people nor much schooled, ordinarily, yet a couple the sheriff had met in passing had been canny and adept and possessed of a quiet wit. He'd also known a family of them – the Painters – ferocious as pit dogs. Though many of the theory mongers swore their skin had the bluish tint, the race looked to him simply like mestizos and jungle Spanish he had met during his own war. The Neversweats jawing and slivering up sticks in front of the courthouse said they were savage to a fault but could work forever without water or lift a full-grown hog and toss it over a five-rail. One thing everyone agreed upon: They were undesirable and to be shunned. If they were often surly or savage in contact with whites, Sherburne figured, it was likely a response to such unconcealed scorn they faced wherever in the mountains they surfaced. He wasn't sure they could be blamed.

This one, Fox Maggard, had thick ringlets of dark hair and pale blue eyes. Just four fingers and one thumb per hand, a lopey, unhurried way of walking. Tall. His skin was a deep, bruisey black in the summer light, his look raw-boned and hungry. When

Sherburne, who was unaccustomed to looking up at a man, went out to the Haunts along Whetstone to ask him some questions on another matter, he had seemed indisposed to offer more words than absolutely necessary. They had locked eyes, and the sheriff had needed to say, "Don't gaze me, son, or I'll blackjack and shackle you on general principle." That broke the look, but the man's mind was still staring hard into Sherburne's.

"I SHOULD HAVE KNOWN BETTER than send Byron when his name came up again," he thought. "A deputy isn't a sheriff. Poor kid. Young judgment, scant experience . . . ," but the shadows near the gate darkened, and a gleam of light appeared, then vanished. He pivoted his wrist, moving the barrel a few degrees this way and that, covering the adjacent ground in every direction. Nothing, really. He was dying for one of those fine black cigars Adair never approved of, but he would settle for a chew. Gnawing off a corner, he thought, "If she knew I resorted to quid, she'd pitch a hissy." For a moment he pictured his wife at the parlor spinet, playing "Listen to the Mockingbird," "Annie Laurie" or one of those indistinguishable hymns. The way she never missed a note but never quite seemed to keep the cadence steady amused him. No, it touched him, made her all the more endearing, as it was about the only thing she wasn't adept at. She was his treasure and his fire. "Put that aside," he thought, then peered through the scope again, convinced he was not alone, as he'd been in the world long enough to know you're almost never alone when you think you are.

FOR SOME LAWMEN, such a vigil as this was the shiniest lure of the occupation: to perform as the community's appointed avenger, to mete out punishment to the transgressors and scofflaws, the felons who had hopped right off of society's carousel for the sake of contraband and blood, or the misfits and outliers who had never been sewed into the civilized fabric, who scrimmaged among themselves outside the pale until occasionally their disputes and tangles tumbled them into jurisdiction and jeopardy and custody.

Such lawmen as relished these hunts and vigils, the smell of gun oil and leather, sweat, then the sudden whirlwinds that usually marked the conclusion . . . they were themselves men of the margin, those who had tasted the fruit of violence and found it fulfilling, despite the small wages and attendant hardship. They were not men of hearth and hall, feather mattresses and the scent of a woman. Though he had long ago entertained the notion of himself as such an unshorn Sampson swinging that mule's jawbone on behalf of law and order, Sherburne no longer resembled such a being. Not for a long time. At first it had seemed the cost of winning Adair, but now it seemed one of the rewards.

OF COURSE, WHAT RANKLED MOST on this occasion was the knowledge that Fox Maggard had turned out to be innocent of the original accusation. When Bee had handed him the telephone receiver down at the slaughterhouse and said, "Mollie Burish looking for you," he'd blinked, as Elsie the cross-eyed switchboard girl seldom went to the trouble to track him down. "This might be bad," he thought.

And it was. Bee's voice was hardly audible, not uncommon since some fool – one of the Kolly tribe, most likely – had built the telephone office behind the train station, and the clamor of railroad activity punctuated and blurred every conversation. What he could make out was that the Burish girl needed to see him, and since she was the one who accused Maggard, her every word right now carried the urgency of a dispatch from the front. "I'll be there directly," he said, and turned back to finish his conversation with Bee about the coming frost, then hog slaughtering and its offensive stench so close to the Washington Street merchants and the college.

"I can't control the wind," said Bee. "And you ain't got a smell law on the books."

But Sherburne had responded, "No telling what manner of law I can turn up, I forage those old books hard enough, Mister Kline. Some of it's printed so fine, you need special-order spectacles. You don't want to squander my time that way, now do you?"

It might almost have been an omen that he took the call at the abattoir, which his wife still referred to as "the blood house." Most farmers around Lexington did their own killing and cutting, but Bee Kline was a master butcher who kept his knives bright with whetting and knew exactly where the tendons turned and the meat sweetened, even if he was generally a fractious and blustery man. He called the little platform the cattle, sheep and pigs crossed to their destiny "The Bridge of Sighs," and if he liked anything as much as neatly killing animals by the dozens, it was the feel of money, even if it was damp with blood. Sherburne looked at the peeled and marbled red slabs on their hooks, the clever pulley system that moved them toward the cool room, the new delivery wagons in the yard and the telephone itself, all efficient and modern, expensive and ridiculous, all of them the kinds of things that convinced Adair that relocating to a real city would no longer be necessary; Lexington itself was so prosperous, it would soon be an important port-of-call. The fancy resorts booming nearby provided all the confirmation she needed.

Sherburne had also lived here long enough to see the weave in life's fabric alter entirely. Brave new world, he thought, to have such creatures in it. He was amused at his own bookishness and hawked, then spat right on the toe of Bee's mucking boot. "Sorry," he said, giving Kline his official constabulary gaze, which was withering. "I'm sure this will all work out fine. I'm convinced you'll find a way to make me happy. I know you don't care to spend your precious days producing records or napping and collecting cobwebs on a courthouse pew waiting for your case to be called."

Then he had struck out for his office, stepping carefully across the blood-slick boards. Even a newcomer could find the telephone shack, he thought, by following the overhead line. Then they could trace it on to the jail. Remembering with pleasure that the livery was still a refuge from the voice instrument, he made a note to stop by later in the afternoon and see how things were going with the Andalusian mare Gertrude, who should drop her foal before the next day dawned. Looking up again, he wondered if the starlings filed up on the wires like pickets could feel anything of the voices that ran under their feet, urgent with information, usually of the trivial sort. A modern woman, Adair had already recognized the device's potential for spreading the latest news, but he was loathe to dismiss her chatter as glibness. She was forever planning something to rescue the misfortunate or organizing a shindig to do with church, and her schemes inevitably bore fruit. A generous woman, and he was glad she put up with him.

Blaine Sherburne's appreciation for his job no longer resided in the manhunts and watchdog duties so much as everything implied in the term "peace officer," and he almost smiled to remember episodes where just the sight of a tall and weathered man with a badge on his parson-looking frock coat would make passers-by stride a little more calmly before the grocer's stall or adjust their posture to coincide with the notion of "upstanding," even as they sauntered out of Grace Church. He had always been satisfied that his presence was indeed a deterrent, and when his appearance was not itself adequate, he was still pleased to restore order at a betting parlor or race course, an election yard or college shindig, even a Methodist social, just by the application of the right words, soothing at first like you would address to a ructious pony, but ending in well-tempered steel. The still eye of the storm, the slight reminder of borders and boundaries, policies and procedures: That was what he desired to embody and to move through the eddies and scrapes of the town, the disputes and frictions like a calming and unexcitable force. Now he had ample deputies, and the place was tame enough that he seldom stepped out with the Webley visible at his hip. If his constituents didn't know about the short .32 with a bird head grip under his left armpit, they were no worse for the illusion of a town so safe its sheriff went abroad unarmed.

DURING HIS FIRST BRIEF eye-to-eye meeting with the coaly-skinned Melungeon, Sherburne had, uncharacteristically, sized him up wrong. It was over a year ago, but he could still recall it. Maggard's people up on Whetstone Ridge were said to be fiddlers, poachers and downright thieves, but the sheriff sensed a lurking softness in the man's eyes and thought, "He should turn shepherd. Running a flock over the hills would suit this man more than the hand-to-mouth survival and rowdiness that usually accompanied living by your wits with woods skills and a wide-bore rifle."

The exchange had been about a flock of buzzards that was plaguing Widow Proffitt's spread, roosting in her locusts and fruit trees, the filth and reek of their shit and vomit crazing her bees and ruining any hopes of a honey harvest. The sheriff, talking mostly with Miz Proffitt, had granted Maggard permission to use surplus Hale rockets and a shotgun to free the widow and her daughter from the siege. That was his first error, the one all the other mistakes were built on. Whenever he thought about that day, he cursed himself for not looking deeper, and he felt a wave of shame.

The man had been wearing green trousers dark as a fly's back, a narrow-brimmed black hat and a coat made from a black-and-white cowskin. He wore an oddly-carved wooden charm around his neck, and three jay-blue feathers dangled from it. Sherburne thought he cut something of a figure.

"Where'd you get the rockets, Fox?'

"Daddy's, I reckon. They's in his things."

"And you know how to handle them so that the widow's house and livestock are safe. They're bad to stray and misfire. Do you know what war they're left over from?"

"Can't say. I've studied them. Ye got to fiddle with the fuses some, see that the powder load is laid in even so mis-weight won't wander them."

The unsightly birds were occupying a pecan tree and a white oak like black candles. He could smell their mess and hoped the widow could be relieved soon. And though Maggard clearly had some idea what was involved, the sheriff still pressed the matter.

"And you know to have the house back of you, definitely full to the rear. I've heard of a pair going sidewind back in the Spanish War and hitting a hospital tent. Fire broke out. People died."

"Maybe the widow should take a day in town whilst I work the cure."

"Would be best if you had a light rain. Maybe I should dispatch a deputy to lend a hand."

"I can guarantee the rain – kill some blacksnakes and drape em over that high rail yonder, but not with no deputy gawking me."

"You got something to hide, boy?"

Maggard had winced visibly, and the sheriff saw his eyes go hard. He was clenching his mouth to keep from saying something, but then he seemed to relax, and his face went slack, as if a storm cloud had passed across his visage, then moved on.

"I'll fill the stock troughs and barrels. My brother Erm, he'll stand with me. No cause to worry yeself, sheriff. I'll shoot straight and clean, rockets and bird shot. Got to quietus this here shit. I like to do a right job."

The smile on his face had seemed genuine, truceful, and he scuffled his feet about like a boy, though Sherburne was aware he was talking to a full-grown man who stood surely four inches over six feet. His big hands were calloused, eyes crow's-footing, and his cheek carried a long new-moon scar that probably came from a knife. "How'd the other fellow look," Sherburne wondered, sizing up the fellow's wide shoulders and bull neck. He thought better of it before he asked.

That had been pretty much it, a little fencing of wills, the Melungeon offering token resistance, probably as a matter of habit, then accepting instructions. Nothing personal. Certainly nothing feral or perverse or demonic, as many in town would have predicted. Sherburne was convinced nothing ill would result for anybody but the vultures, and he had been right: Maggard was a man with neither ill intentions nor peculiar pedigree to twist his soul. And in a week, the dark birds were nowhere to be seen.

FOR TWELVE YEARS NOW, since he returned from Cuba, Sherburne had been charged with upholding law in Rockbridge County. He had purchased Dominion Livery in Lexington, married Adair Cosley despite her social circle's unanimous disapproval and settled in, extending the powers of his office and eventually coordinating with various constables, marshals, committees and prosecutors, as well as special deputies from Richmond. He had recently sworn in a fourth lieutenant and kept a jailer, Byron Rainwater, the newest of the crew. And his sobriety and gallant demeanor had eventually won over Adair's lady friends. It was a quiet community, despite its proximity to the unruly Irish Creek region and beyond that the wilds of Amherst County, where more stilling and scuffling went on than any two accountants could have tallied or regiments quelled. But the colleges in town and the whole strange reverence for Robert E. Lee, who had spent his last years generaling Washington College, exerted a soothing influence, mostly, as if a benign ghost moved about the town dispensing blessings. When the jail was empty, a white flag flew from its roof above the street, and Sherburne kept a count of how many consecutive days that piece of cloth signaled that the citizens were obviously in good hands. The banner was exposed out in the elements enough that no flag had yet lasted a whole year. Whenever he had to ask Adair to hem up a new one, they celebrated like Christmas, with the deputies over for dinner, carefully censored stories, beer and a tipple of whiskey all around.

THE DAY'S HEAT was beginning to muster, and looking at the clouds over South Mountain, he guessed it would be hotter than necessary by noon. The rifle was beginning to grow heavy in his hands, and for a moment, his mind drifted toward the peaches he'd enjoyed down in Florida. That was hot duty, and headed for hotter, but he still relished those days of training with the Rough Riders, old four-eyes always grinning and quoting Jefferson and Herodotus. Sherburne had taught the green men plenty about horses – how to keep one collected while you fired a rifle from the saddle, the importance of good grooming, water and salt, how to head off brucellosis and strangles, the best way to wheel on the run and exert control with the minimum gestures. Despite the range of breeds and tack and foolish theories, he'd taught everyone from sailors to football players where the hock becomes the cannon, how to settle a saddle to prevent galling of withers, how to post and save the horse labor. Of course there were polo boys and vaqueros he didn't have to show a trick, but he had turned out a cadre of serviceable jockeys, though a fat lot of good it did them, as most of the regiment spent the whole Spanish War slogging the swamps as infantry.

He was lucky to have been too useful to be denied a mount when they hit Cuba, and once he proved his value as a sniper, he enjoyed many of the privileges normally accorded an officer. What he missed most from that time, however, had little to do with horses and less to do with shooting at strangers. The eastern boys were always full of clever monologues, accounts of exotic places and cagey chess moves around the campfire as the brash-colored parrots and Lord God birds went rackety in the trees. The Cubanos – many of them dark-skinned as Ibos, or so he'd been told – were a cagey and soulful lot, more reliable than reputed and as eager for freedom as any of Sherburne's own kin. Adair had not yet consented to bestow her hand, and even in his thirties he was fond of the rough conversation and bawdy stories about camp. In Cuba he had read *Monte Cristo* for the first time and learned about truly fine cigars. And the peaches, which were sweet as a sunset in heaven, were as splendid to behold as they were to consume. He could sure stand one now. And a cup or two of that native coffee.

HE'D FOUND MOLLIE sitting in his rocker by the empty woodstove, swaying slowly and staring into the grate, as if some revelation might be coaxed forth by her scrupulous attention. She was wearing a cornflower-blue house frock and a plain ribboned bonnet. Her high button shoes were coated in mud. She was not lovely, her hair mouse-colored and face blemished from chicken pox. Nor had she a fair figure, as she was in the sheriff's mind too plump too soon. "A pullet already," he had thought. When he entered and took her in – the way her muscles were clenched tight but breathing deep and unrhythmic – even before he took off his hat and hung it, he spoke her name and asked how she was faring.

"I got a thing to tell you." Her eyes remained locked on the feathery ash gathered in the stove.

"I see." He tried to keep his voice soothy and open, "preacher-like," he thought. "Another one? You know I have sent Byron out to Whetstone to look into what you told two days back." He looked about for Monocle, his sentry, but it was about the time Seth would have leashed him and started his rounds.

"It wasn't like that. Wasn't like I said." Her stare at the stove was so hard that, beyond his understanding why, Sherburne used his boot toe to swing the door of the fire box shut.

"He never . . . it wasn't. . . ." She looked up at Sherburne, but above his eyes, along the hairline. "Here it is."

She had removed a creased paper from the folds of her skirt and was not simply offering it to the sheriff so much as thrusting it at him.

Opening the sheet of plain stationary, he began to read.

Dear Sheriff Sherbern and Daddy,

I have made an awful mistake and blamed where it wasn't due. That Melungon I said was hanging about when it went missing – he wasn't. I saw him downtown that morning or maybe another one and when Richard said he would sell them and we could run off we plotted out who to point to – and the Melungon came to mind as we know of them stealing things from people's back lots and in other troubles.

Sense daddy –you won't let me have anything to do with Richard now, we have decided to run off and we didn't take all of Mama's jewelstones and trinkets but left you her favorites. I don't wan't to be crass daddy but Mama always said she looked to the day she would see them on me and even if she's gone to her Reward of the influensa I think her wish should be honord. Richard and me planed to go to Washington where he has good prospeck of imployment and those jewels was how we planed to make our way and set up house keeping. You will ask why I am saying this now, but my consciens won't bare it when I think of that man who might be a scoundrel anyway but hasn't got any busyness baring the blame for my act of desperateness. I just wanted to get free of your chains and fare with the man I love. Now I see this can't work out right for anybody if another shoulders the fault so this is my confession. I have led Richard to this it was not his doing. The jewels are back now at the house. I hope its not to late the prevent the wrong things from happening. Sheriff can you help me make this right please.

Your daughter (daddy)and citizen (Mr. Sherbrn),
Mollie Mabry

The Koontz boy was actually a recent graduate of Washington and Lee College who could gabble in Latin and had stayed in town, working at various jobs, including a stint at the livery, all the while attesting that he soon intended to get a place to read for the law. His background wasn't much known, but he was hard-working and clever, and Sherburne could not for the life of him imagine what Richard wanted with a dollop of a girl like this.

So it was as simple and cockeyed as that, and he had tried immediately to picture Byron climbing the ridge to stand on the stoop everybody had heard was all spookied up with its antlered skulls, drying pelts, charm glass, snake hides and assorted bones. It was said to be painted in two shades of red. Then Byron rapping his knuckles on the doorframe, as the actual door was a deerskin flap, and when Maggard or perhaps even one of his kinsmen pulled the skin back and gazed into the boy's eyes, Byron stammering out "Sheriff Sherburne" and "just to answer some questions" and "missing jewelry." Had he remembered to warn Byron of the man's height and the force of his gaze? Whatever he had omitted to explain, likely somebody would have to pay. He hoped it was not too late to keep this whole business from yanking further awry.

What was it about taking off heads? Even in Cuba he'd never seen evidence of such wolfish behavior, yet he knew his father's stories from that earlier war, not to mention old Goliath of Gath after he took the stone. But up here in Virginia, the practice seemed, if not widespread, not uncommon. As if he had come to the end of a vine swing's pendulum across a swimming hole, he felt his mind arcing backward, right back to the atrocities he'd encountered under Harbor Mountain when he'd first journeyed up here to bargain for horses – a whole family wiped out and savaged, and the culprits just some local roughs who'd whispered each other too many scare stories and swilled too much bad splo. Judge Crispin had told him people had always done it to cheat their enemies of a happy afterlife and to terrify anybody left standing. Heads, hearts. Trophies, he supposed, and the boast that you'd do anything and best be proffered a wide path.

Now he was thinking about justice and revenge. Clearly they could converge in the world of actions, but he wondered if they could sit the same saddle at once in a man's mind without becoming braided up forever. His mind said, "I am out here for the law and to perform my sworn duties, and it wouldn't matter if the man was green-and-pink tartan or had six eyes," but his heart was telling him that, given Byron's fate, nothing but the Melungeon's death would meet his present needs. It would be akin to bringing down a rabid animal, but more personal. This was one of those few thoughts, those rare conundrums Adair never needed to hear. Which meant he'd keep hearing its echo inside his head long after the world had again circled the sun.

To free himself from the uneasiness stirred by self-examination, he began to look carefully across the range of possibilities before him, where his quarry might appear, what mischief he might be staging now, but before long he noticed a more subtle tension infusing this little cantle of land. The wrens and finches that had been darting about were gone, seemingly vanished but probably scuttled into cover. A shadow wheeled over them, and he knew something else had discovered this grisly tableau, maybe something drawn by the blood. What he saw above, however, was no carrion bird but a hunter, a hawk circling easily, always ready to plummet, but meticulous and in no hurry. This was not a time to be bird watching or even bird dreaming, but the hawk – a cooper's by its underfeathers – was difficult to dismiss. Doubtless its keen eye, its own sniper's equipment, had detected the same rabbit Sherburne had seen, which unlike the little scavengers, had moved now further from its concealing meaze and into easier view, probably frozen with the illusion that stillness was akin to invisibility. It wasn't.

It occurred to him, as the bird circled in the thermals, how much of his job – which was protecting people who chose to live in close proximity to one another and away from the wilds – was spent alone and on the peaks or back in the holler where patches of snow lingered into May. Much as he might prefer to be jawing with deputies and citizens with complaints, on the long bench whittling and swapping yarns with the Neversweats, again and again he found himself in the saddle or occupying some lethal perch like this one, hoping that he would not have to kill the next man he met.

He knew the hawk saw him but seemed untroubled by his presence. As he wondered if it felt the same kinship he did, the hawk dropped, screeching, and the rabbit shrieked as it was borne aloft.

HE DIDN'T WANT TO SPECULATE any further on exactly how it had all come to pass once he'd taken Byron by the shoulders back at the office and looked into his eyes.

"We don't know he's done a thing wrong, so don't try to badge him. Just act the friendly neighbor bearing a message, inviting him in to clear up what's probably a misunderstanding."

"Don't I wear my star?" The boy was proud of the five-pointed figure inside it's wheel inscribed *Rockbridge County Sheriff's Office*. It was the circumference of a bean tin lid and not much thicker.

"You do and you don't. It'll be on your coat where he'll see it, but don't act like you're standing behind it. If you hold yourself like it's just lit there by accident but somehow belongs, it will be man to man, and people respect that."

Sherburne liked to keep his own hardware in the dark beneath the coat during the daylight hours. That way he could seem little more than a liveryman, husband, Methodist and war veteran whom people granted respect and were inclined to hear out just out of his natural gravity. And that, too, had been on his father's advice: "The badge won't make you right or strong. Not that you won't be. And it won't even mean the voters back your play or sing in your key. Beat tin has no power to stop an argument and isn't stout enough to turn away more than a bird pellet. But you've got the stare, the size and the quickness when you have to. God knows you're tall enough to make any man-jack think twice, and you know how to wait. Nossir, don't rely on that trinket to do anything but steal a moment's notice and leave pinholes to foul up the weave of your clothes."

Years had proven the truth of it, and he wished, checking the ridgeline again, he had said all that to Byron. And said to be certain he did not address Maggard the way some were still prone to discourse with the few former slaves in the county. Now, he surveyed the still brush along the path and listened, sniffed, tasted the slight breeze, not allowing his crosshairs to pause on the boy's head again. Speaking to Grice at the logging site, Maggard had said something like, "A damn deputy come up on my stoop with a gun out and said I was to shuckle down to town because somebody stole some diamond stones from a girl and hurt her. He allowed I could just come along gentle and they wouldn't be no need of irons nor cords. When I said to send the real shurf, he pointed the little gun at my belly, so I took it and whipped him about the face." Maggard had said he supposed Byron was dead before he hit the floorboards, and then he knew it didn't matter what he'd not stolen or who he'd never hurt or even clapped eyes upon: Sherburne would be coming. But, he'd said, he'd already figured Sherburne would be coming.

Maggard hadn't mentioned anything to the lumberman about the decapitation, except that he had a "keepsake" in the obviously-bloody croaker sack, or where the rest of the body was now. To keep himself from worrying that question Sherburne hoped that Bishop was tied secure, though the horse knew to stay where he'd been stationed and probably wouldn't wander far, even if the knot slipped. He wasn't the kind to gnaw a rope. And Adair – he thought about her hacking down the stalks in her kitchen garden, cutting pages on a new novel or peeling apples over a basin. One evening just a week back, though it certainly seemed longer now, he'd surprised her at the counter with the room full of fresh-sliced apples, and he was so overwhelmed by the aroma that he began kissing her neck and lifting her skirts. Later, he was relieved to notice that the kitchen windows were shut and curtains drawn, so their congress was probably unnoticed, unless one of the Sults had gone to their shed and heard the pleasured sounds. In the heat of the hunt, however, neither had given propriety or privacy the least thought.

Then he did smell something. Not apples. The sky behind the rise where the Melungeon's cabin sat was wisped with dark smoke where there had been none before, and he thought for the first time, "What if his people have met him up there or are just now heading to him? Aiming to lend comfort and advice, maybe firepower. They're clannish, and though some might scatter at the first sign of law trouble, others might rally to his cause." They could discover Bishop and come up the same knoll he'd climbed, could track him as he'd tracked their brethren, and that would leave him between the sledge and the spike. He would need to move. Sweet spot for an ambush or not, he'd have to leave this place and take the lair, so he might as well start calculating how to cross the open ground and then approach the house, which he was not much familiar with, though he recalled the red stoop and that it was situated near a drop-off. That briar-hopper could be up there eating ashcake and sidemeat with a telescope in one hand, the Sharps across his lap and an abiding familiarity with every inch of the ground. But that didn't matter now. This was not one of those times to practice waiting.

The birds seemed to have appreciated his stillness, as they foraged and flitted about with cheery sounds, but as soon as he moved, up suddenly and zigzagging at a dead run, they went silent and hurtled off.

WHEN IT CAME TO ACTION, a man's feelings about a thing like this could aid or hinder him . . . unless they were mixed, in which case they could only water down his resolve, delay his reactions. As he passed what had been Byron, Sherburne felt his trajectory steady. It didn't matter how the story had unfolded, who said what, who did which. Melungeon, white man, officer of the law – no matter. Even the lily-white girl's false witness against a man who likely had enough trouble on account of his skin color. No matter: The boy was dead and defiled. Law, revenge, any combination would serve: He swore Fox Maggard would not witness that night's moonrise.

He was rushing north, roughly, over brown brush and fallen logs, some of them hemlock, patches of what people called laurel. A few junipers about man-height, forming what might have been a neat fenceline, though they were more likely seeded there by passing birds in too much hurry for a resting shit. He crossed the path here and there, dash and bound, practicing evasive motion, though he knew it could all be for naught. He kept an eye out for man pits and barb wire, snare and pointed stakes smeared with shit. How would a man capable of cutting off a head set up his defenses? And would there be a dog? He thought about Monocle usually dozing beside his desk, gun slots in the jail's outer door and shutters, the sniper's boxes atop the Alexander-Withrow house and the courthouse itself. What he called "the disappear passage" led from the cellar and under the street to emerge in the Dodd Building basement behind a tall cannery rack. If it seemed like he kept a fortress, these were all civilized defenses, as were the covered carriage house where one could mount out of sight, the jail's portcullis, all in the service of the body politic.

As these images rushed through him, he realized he was trying to distinguish himself from Maggard – different tactics, different beliefs, two wholly separate ways of being in the world. But was that honest? Whatever had driven the Melungeon, it must have been raw and undiluted, something to do with anger and his reputation, nothing to do with his color. No time for that equation to cut in. The man had felt unjustly called out, like things had lost all proportion and consideration. And he'd been right. He'd responded in exaggerated fashion according to what the survival animal in him demanded. Sherburne could understand that, and if he was doing the same thing now, then they were two of a kind, locked in this dance.

But they couldn't be one, for he had the badge and the judge's warrant, the whole force of the orderly world behind him. And they couldn't be one because suddenly they were facing one another, mirror-imaged almost, scarcely fifty feet apart on the trail, Maggard in the blotched hide coat that made him look almost comical. He wore a forage cap, and the sheriff thought he could see the bluejay feathers on their cord. Both were moving fast and pulled up as if they'd collided with something invisible, but habit cut in for Sherburne as his voice rose without his willing it.

"Halt now, Maggard, and toss aside that piece."

Instead, the man was raising it to his shoulder, and the sheriff was still mouthing "in the name of the law" as he sprang, rolled and came to his knees behind a rotten stump. He had not heard the expected report of the Sharps, and this stump would afford no protection when it spoke. He launched and rolled again, this time almost stunned by the volume of the shot when it came. "Damn cannon," he thought. "Always louder if you're on this end." He felt a trickle of blood down his face from a cut on some rock or snagroot. This was not good. It was going to get worse.

He hardly registered that he had lost his hat during the rolling tactic, but when he came up he needed to be shooting and couldn't. The rifle had knocked free on the rough ground. "Too much mind in it," he muttered but went instinctively for the Webley. He had cleared the holster but had not yet leveled the barrel when he saw Maggard steadied against a dead poplar ten strides away. Since the Sharps was a breechloader, he could be pretty certain it was ready to go again, and at this distance, well, a blind granny might be able to bring the matter to a close. He dropped the pistol to the ground. Nothing else to do. And immediately he thought he'd lost his best chance.

"If y'uns don't think I'll kill y'uns because yer handy gun's down there in the dirt, y'ain't give much thought to my situation." Sherburne remembered seeing the kind look in the man's eyes on that occasion of the vultures. "A natural shepherd," he'd thought, "no trouble-maker. Bull shit." And now the eyes and voice were cold, and he was just another rullion with a gun.

"No, but I've given considerations. Maybe there's some things need to be said."

"Like why'd y'uns send a armed policeman, a foolish boy, up on my peazzer to accuse me of shit I didn't never have even a knowing of. It was wrong-headed, probably just deciding to throw some blame on my kind. Not the first time, shurf."

"He was just meant to request that you come by the office and give your testimony. Hell, we already know now who did the stealing and where the trinkets are. If you'd just been biddable . . . ."

The sun was beginning its descent, and over the quaver of jar flies the morning's hawk shrieked somewhere in the distance, out of sight. His eyes cut off that way, then returned to Maggard's, which had paid no notice to the noise. Although he could see Maggard's muscles relax some, the big barrel was still aimed right at his breastbone.

"If y'uns had done yer job proper and not hopped on the stupid wagon."

"I know. I know." He shook his head and pushed away the lick of graying hair that had fallen across his brow.

"Look, I understand why you didn't come in, but why kill the boy?"

"Just a happenstance. I meant to whoop him off, but he went down like a sack of nailing hammers, and I knowed right then he was likely gone."

"Keep him talking," Sherburne thought. "Every word is a chance." His mind did not stray to Adair, Thaddeus, or his long-dead brother or any of his habitual touchstones.

"Then why not absquatulate? You could have run clear to West Virginia or Kentucky, back to Tennessee even, far outside my jurisdiction. You know how to disappear into the woods, no trail, not even a rumor. Why this circle down to the Bridge and back, toting a damn bloody head? Jesus wept."

"Put yeself in my boots. I knowed y'uns wouldn't of quit. It ain't the kind you are."

There was not a hint of admiration in his voice, and the sheriff knew this was all about to wind down. He had his hole ace, but he had to find a way to get an edge.

Maggard wasn't done, though.

"Where's the place I could of lit on where y'uns wouldn't been on my tail? I know law, and I read y'uns the first time we crossed. Y'uns is bigger'n courts. Y'uns is the king man, the man what holds the words, and to keep it, I had to be brung in."

So he had been outreckoned from the first. Any desire Maggard might have felt to cling to the borders and deep woods was fuelled by contempt, not by some pastoral appetite. That had been Sherburne's romantic invention. Fantasy. If you let your mind into that, you always had to pay.

Last ditch effort now: "Why his head? Why cut off . . . ?"

"You ain't stupid. I had to be sure y'uns wouldn't be shuffling about to figger me. Planning a posse and a big stalk. Needed y'uns to come up arter me single before I even started off west, so wouldn't nobody have a notion whichaway I lit out. Onct y'uns heard about the head, hell, I knew ye'd be coming hard."

"But you're not the killing kind, and if it was self defense, there'd be considerations. . . ."

"Kind of fool y'uns take me for? Killing kind, hell. Ye lay one brick, don't make you a brickmason, but fuck one dog. . . kill one lawman . . . ye never be anything else again. Never again won't change it."

And then he thought, "It makes no sense. The man knows he needs to kill me and get on, but he's not doing it. He's not reluctant or two-minded, not mulling something over. There's a problem. He's got a problem, and it could be the gun. It could be the Sharps. He didn't take the first shot he had when I rolled, and there was that stand-off down at the resort. It wasn't the crowd or the demanding shot. He's been trying to draw me close. It has to be the gun. It's all I've got. It has to be."

It was a risk he had to accept, so he reached his left hand into the side pocket of his coat, where his black quid was. Maggard's face tightened, and he lay his cheek against the stock, as if ready to squeeze the arc of the trigger.

"If I'm wrong, dear Jesus, forgive and don't forget me." He hadn't quite said it aloud.

"Just a last chew? Custom, isn't it, me being the condemned man?"

"Y'uns put yerself in it when some town fool took me for a thief. Yeah, we'uns all condemned, but bite ye shag and say ye last save-me-jesus."

When he'd ripped off a corner with his teeth, Sherburne gestured the quid at Maggard, then tossed it softly underhanded toward the big man, and as he did so, he dropped to his knee and the right hand went fast to the little pistol under his arm. Though it was a cross draw, he had practiced it so many times it was like the strike of a coiled snake, and the blued piece seemed to come out faster for the flash of its metal in the sunlight. In a way it didn't matter, as Maggard had dropped the weapon and was rushing at Sherburne like a bear.

The first time the .32 spat, it left the Melungeon one-eared with blood running down his cheek and neck, but that didn't slow him. He kept coming at a crouch with the big butch in his hand gleaming along its edge brighter than the Sheriff's pistol. Holding his kneeling position he fired deliberately, at regular intervals, like a soldier on the firing line. Each step forward brought another shot, but the cylinder held only five, and the rounds were small for such a large man who seemed to absorb the slugs. Sherburne aimed the last one right at the center of his face, and just as he let fly, Maggard tilted his head to the side. But not enough. The round went into his mouth, taking flesh and some teeth with it and ripped through, splintering jawbone and slamming his head back, as if he'd been poleaxed. With an animal scream he dropped the knife and fell to his knees, hands over his face. He was six feet in front of the sheriff, who was still on his knee, had already dropped the spent shells out the gate and thumbed in three fresh bullets. Now he rose and took two steps backward.

"Fox Maggard," he said, "you're under arrest for the murder of deputy Byron Wilcox." His voice was trembling, covering nearly an octave, and he knew it, but his hand was steady, the pistol pointed right at his prisoner's throat.

"I'll not do it!" He stood up, spun about and lumbered back toward his cabin, which stood just beyond a clump of blue spruce trees.

Sherburne didn't know what to think, unless he was headed after some other weapon. In cautious pursuit, he leaned over to grab the Henry and rounded the bend in time to see Maggard pass the stoop and step out onto the rocks. He was leaving blood on everything he touched, but Sherburne was almost certain he hadn't delivered a lethal shot, so he levered a shell into the receiver, ejecting the unspent one he had forgotten he'd never fired.

Maggard was at the edge of the rocks when Sherburne understood what was about to transpire. The big man turned and dropped his hands from his face. What Sherburne saw resembled an aspect little more human-looking than poor Byron's staked one out on the trailhead. Maggard's language was not easy to make out, but the bullet had evidently done little damage to his tongue. Still, his words sounded like some child with a cleft palate. The thought flared through Sherburne's mind that if there was a Melungeon language, it might resemble this babble.

"I rather be dead," he could make out and "jail" and some tangle of sobbed words, then "God damn me for an innocent," and he stepped off the ledge. By the time the sheriff got there, everything was still but for a few pebbles skipping and bouncing down amid the rubble, half a dozen rock wrens darting away from the disturbance. Maggard's body lay in an impossible contortion amid loose rocks, its piebald coat vivid on a black shelf well over a hundred feet below. The sky was brutally blue, and Sherburne peered hard, trying unsuccessfully to believe he saw a blue tint in Maggard's face and hands.

He was still trembling and looked down to make certain his trousers weren't damp. Then he looked up to thank somebody, but the sun was so strong he was forced to drop his eyes again. "Okay, luck. . . and God's favor, I suppose." The broken man could lie there until he sent some people up with ropes and a mule and time on their side.

"I expect we are all pretty much condemned," he thought, turning away, "just a matter of time and place, and likely none of us old enough to talk is innocent." You could slip from innocence to not-innocent so quickly, and the way was so steep, so slick, well, there was no going back. Not for Maggard or Byron, not for himself.

"Maggard was at least not guilty of filching, and then he was guilty by accident, made guiltier still by his idea that a boy's head would be a good lure, and more by his acting on such a damn fool idea, but he was right, and if it hadn't been for his ordnance problem, I'd be down there and he'd be off to the high nowheres on Bishop."

And he thought how much of this one he could tell Adair. He'd have to say that he'd erred to send the boy up and that he bore as much of the burden in the large court of common wisdom as anybody else – the boy too excited to just ask, the half-caste or whatever he was too jumpy to believe anything when a pistol was pointed at him, a girl who said "that one" because she was in love or wanted to be. His wife would be soothy and merciful; he could count on that. It might be enough to staunch the wound inside. That would truly be lucky.

And though Byron's mother already knew, no question, he'd have to face her and explain his part, and the words would not ease much or excuse anybody, and she'd have every right. But first he'd have to poke around this place – split-log cabin with its animal remnants pegged to the walls, horse barn, fold and ramshackle outsheds – to see if he might turn up the rest of the boy's body. It might be far down the Cliffside, like Maggard's, or under some dirt or just anywhere, but the mother would want all of him she could get, and it might ease her some if he was already entirely found.

But then he wondered, "If I can find it, maybe I could burn the whole thing and say Maggard did it, save her from knowing the head and the rest had separated." Burning it would not be honest, but maybe honesty wasn't the best course. Having done so much, erred so wide, one more lie would likely damage his tally significantly.

But before he gave any more thought to other people's ease and other people's deaths, he needed to locate that Sharps. He had to understand Maggard's options and find out why for the moment he was safe from the great nothing. Retracing his steps, he could imagine funeral flames rising. Poor Byron, poor Maggard. Who would call this justice? He would fetch his horse soon and gather wood for the fire.

Rose-Handled Pistol

1.

When Tarvis found me I was in the back stall shaving soap into a bucket to wash down Vester. I could of let the night boy at the livery attend to it, but I was easy in Vester's company, and I'd rather Bobby Dean spend his time slathering axles and dressing carriage tops to a good gloss. I also wanted to brush the hooves on the tantrum gelding I was trying to tame up and give them a once-over in case they needed me to swab on some Gladdings. He was a crow-hopper, and I knew I'd likely be frazzled before I won. But I would win.

Rounding the corner fast, Tarvis said, "Thanks to either hell or the other place for your lantern light, boss. I thought as I'd never find you. We got a mess out at Lily's, a cut fight that got worse. It's all mommicked."

Tarvis knew I hated being called boss, but he'd been my deputy long enough to figure when pressing matters might interfere with my scolding on him. I also railed against him smoking those Mereweather's denicitized cigars around the barn, but I supposed his mischief was on the large more entertaining to me than vexing. He was jimber-jawed and green-eyed, born and reared in Rockbridge and a fair hand at most chores, though sometimes not brisk, as he had a cautiousness around animals leftover from a horse with a bad plan of side-spraddling and rolling to shuck him off.

"You have a way of catching me just at the start of something." I picked up the bristle brush and pointed at the horse.

"Ain't that what you pay me for, to thwart and hinder, clog the works like a coon in the stovepipe? Ain't it why a body takes up lawing, Boss, to keep your own self from tending to horse business so's you could enjoy complaining about they never being enough time?"

If that was my mission, sometimes it seemed I had more helpers in it than Judge Gideon on his night attack in the Bible.

"I like to think of you as my chimney sweep, Tarvis, brushing and swabbing so I can tend to the actual fire." I winked at him, and he tried to return it, but as usual, both his lids flicked together, and he removed his Derby hat and slapped his thigh.

This could be the kind of night, I thought, when Adair's plans for me sounded better than my own. "Just give up the badge while you're ahead and devote yourself to leasing horses, counting money and keeping your wife amused," she'd say. In fact, she'd said it a bunch lately, but there wasn't time to ponder it just now.

Sylvester nickered and scraped a hoof like he was counting, like he knew his day wasn't over yet.

That was when Tarvis raised his left hand with my service rig, the buckle and brass trim of the big-bore Webley catching the light.

"Over those yellow crib girls again?"

"Don't know. The Harrison boy that brooms up for Lily called it in. He couldn't hardly get it out and breathe without busting a gut. I started a-hunting you from Henry Street to the Grand, figured you to be walking the rounds."

Lily's place, in the books "The Falls Tavern," was in North Lex, just across the river, maybe a mile from where we stood. When I first came to Lexington nearly twenty years back, it was just a rude monkey rum parlor and fell outside the sheriff's bailiwick, but over time this and that owner had built on and grown greedy, and the town had pushed out its borders, planked the road, widened the bridge. Now it was still the favorite late spot for the tanners, trappers and roughnecks that seeped out after dark from the region called The Squabbles, and there they met up with the town's stop-over drovers, passing packetmen and general excessives. The boys from the college and cadets from the Institute were not welcome there, and they knew it.

For the first decade Lily had run it, I'd personally never seen another female face under her roof, not that it was on my regular social calendar, but about six months ago she'd brought in two Chinese girls and the redhead. "Bit of sport never hurt nobody," she'd claimed, but their presence had raised the steady simmer of the place to a blaze. Just like my wife augured, it was but a matter of time before the bloodletting commenced. I knew right off she was right, but I hated to lock horns with Lily. Now somebody else had paid for my mistake.

"Get your horse and meet me down yonder at the bridge, Tarvis. And bring the two-barrel." I'd pulled on my coat, buckled the gunbelt and had the blue blanket in one hand and the saddle in the other. A shiver of excitement ran through the muscles under Vester's hide.

2.

ANY TIME AT ALL SPENT SOLDIERING, a man will either take a shine to uniforms or start despising them in a way that lasts till he stops breathing. I was the second kind, even though I'd scarce had to priss around in full dress gear during my short hitch. The outfits the Volunteers wore in Cuba were khaki and blue, good Stetsons, kerchiefs, leggings. A bunch us shed the braces before we left

Florida, and the heat on the island argued strong for comfort over regulations. Captain Pendleton told me early, "Sergeant Sherburne, just keep em drilled and don't let em run about jaybird nekkid. But see to it the Krag bores are clean as a captain's whistle, bolts oiled and ready for action. Doesn't matter how sweet the boys look on parade, long as they shoot straight and don't die." Given the fever and the Spanish Mausers, there was no way I could guarantee success, hard as I strove.

Right now, though, I was content I'd made my regular black getup a sort of law uniform. Most gents in town would go to light cloth in the mosquito months, wear white hats or none, sheepskin or fur in winter. I'd settled on black trousers and vest, long coat, black hat, boots, all matching my hair, which had so far shown only scant signs of frost. Mine was the kind of outfit you'd reckon for an undertaker or, according to my dear wife, a circuit rider. It set the star off right nicely, and it meant business.

When my daddy came home from his war, he'd made a fire in a pit and thrown in every stitch he wore home but the greatcoat, which was civilian in cut and not gray. Even the good brim hat, mama said, right into the flames with a nickel's worth of coal oil. "Put that mistake behind us," he'd said, and you didn't get much by way of Confederate stories out of him. Where he kept the brace of navy Colts I wasn't sure; I only saw them a few times when he fetched one out and stuck it in his belt on the way to town.

Despite his service record, Thaddeus wasn't all that pleased when I signed up to fight the Spanish. He called them "Hozeys" and said, "Another fool war, and this time us not so much as attacked. We don't even know what those people are saying. An army of Hozeys out there and one more Tom Fool who wants to fight for the Yankees. I be damn."

I pledged my only plan was to teach the volunteers horsecraft, how to sit a mount and worm and curry, how to ford and when to cinch tight. There's the fool for you. Half those boys were cattle workers from the Arizona who could piss from a stirrup or sleep at a trot, and anyway, most of our mounts never even made it on the boat in Tampa. The only time we weren't walking across Cuba we were running. Or crawling. Laying up with heaves and fever. My real purpose for going was more private and involved a woman. Two, truth to tell. Whatever else the Spanish War did, it occupied my mind.

I KNEW I'D BE WALKING through Lily's door as the only man jack without a few drinks in his belly, and they'd be couraged up and feisty, dressed in all manner of rough gear, catch-as-can, dirty and rank, all manner of sheaths and pouches for toting dangerous implements. But I was tall enough to turn heads on size alone, no need for swagger, and as soon as a man's eyes fell on me, he'd see the scar running like a creek gully down my jaw. By then the clean blackness of my getup would make its sober point, my face divided in two by the full cavalry mustache. I trusted it all said "No nonsense." If I needed to shout, there was the Webley.

It was one of those ghosty nights, light fog, but you could gaze out a few stars. The last jar flies in the pine trees were still racketing, and the scabby sycamores bleached along the banks added to the hauntiness of the Maury River, but it was the kind of night I usually doted on. If I was to ease out into my own garden to savor it, I'd end up dawdling, trying to make out the peaks off to the north, till Adair would come to the doorway with the hand lamp, a shawl pulled tight, and say, "Blaine, you'll catch your death. What can a girl like me do to encourage you back in?" Then she'd shoot me that come-hither smile. I wouldn't tarry long. But tonight had a different feel, and I wasn't enjoying it, couldn't imagine so much as a grin.

Halfway across the bridge, holding to a quick trot, I heard the second set of shoes clattering over the boards. Tarvis was on Bishop, and he was galloping, nobody else about. Drawing even, he swept off his hat and popped Remus's right flank with it as he showed his teeth. I knew he was likely arching his eyebrows to pull a face at me in the dark. When I gave Sylvester the slight nudge and leaned forward, he put his own head down and ran. The river was fast between the banks after nearly a week of September rain. A nip in the air, loose planks rattling. We didn't pay the noise or anything else much mind.

The horses laid their ears back, and in a minute we were there.

3.

SOME FOLKS THOUGHT I had history with Miss Lily, but that was off the mark. We had some business understandings and swapped respect, that's all. It was her sister Rosette I'd been snarled up with back before the war. Rosette Collins. That was before Adair said yes and my name got painted over the star on the big glass window, before my share in the livery commenced putting folding money in my Rio Coffee can every week. Before I could say I'd prospered. Back then, Rose and me'd gotten frisky enough behind closed doors to start taking daylight buggy rides down Main Street, eating at the Easy T on Jefferson or visiting over to one of the mineral spas for cards and beer. She wasn't my dream gal, but she wasn't a bad second. Picnics, barn dances. Rose was a wild thing thin as a whippet who liked to wear a purple ribbon about her little neck or in her blackbird hair. So far as she was concerned, it went well with any frock or was just fine on its own. I couldn't disagree.

Rosette had grown up on the ridges and wasn't the sort to blend in with Lexington society – the professors' wives, preacher's wives, gussied women of the big landers, the rich types who came to visit the health springs and claimed to be sinking roots – and it wasn't long before she got close to scuffles and spit-fights with the quality. After a serious row with Miz Covington over nothing but a stub-tailed cat ended up in a milk flinging incident, she elected to turn her back on what she called "this narrow-hearted town," her sister's lodging business and one deputy soon to be headed for Mr. Hearst's Cuban adventure. It was all sudden, but I shouldn't have tried to stop her. Some things won't reverse, especially with a woman, and woe to him who tries it. I missed her, but I recovered.

A SCORE OF HORSES STOMPED and whickered or just dozed where they were hitched, and the whole yard smelled of new shit. I recognized John Pink's knuckleheaded old Morgan, two standard breeds with near-matching blazes that belonged to a couple of hunters. I couldn't call their names. Anthym McClung's nag was there, too. Beside Swan Brotherton's scabby mule a light gig's blanket Appaloosa was still harnessed in the limbs but happy with a feedbag. I wondered what idiot was using such a rare animal to cart with and stepped over to stroke her flank.

When I noticed Corvis's blue roan with the taped pastern and badly-clipped coat, I stopped taking roll. Corvis had been the mayor for three terms until the last election, but I'd never found him much use. His wife had died of a cancer not long after they jumped the broom, and he'd grown fond of cards, white whisky and pullet widows. Not a small man, and not soft. He had gangly wrists and was bald but for a circle of fringe the color of a soddy Irish potato skin. He wore it long, looking to my mind ridiculous, and despite the arms ordinance, I knew he carried a pocket pistol in his fancy coat. I'd decided to allow blades in town and just deal with it, long guns too, but I can't abide every man-shaped bundle of tinder strutting about heeled under his coat tails and waiting for a spark. I knew I could take that piss-gun from him anytime I liked, had done it once, but a repeat of that night and I'd have to hire a back-scout to cover for me. Or kill him. He was that uncouth.

There was more to it. It was Corvis who'd already been keen on Adair when I first showed up in Rockbridge County on a horse-buying sortie for my father. I was wet behind the ears, but back in the Smokies I'd learned stock and hunting, scratch-ankle farming and a fair number of books Mama insisted on my nosing into. It was my nose that got me into that tracking party sleuthing down the three who did the Haven Mountain murders. Killed a whole family and made sport of the bodies in the snow, then arsoned up the farm and traipsed off. When the posse formed up, we didn't have a bird's notion three of our number were the culprits. I don't even like to think of how low a varminty man can stoop.

I'd shot deer and squirrels, possum, coon, bear and wolf, even a few painters, and I'd wrung off enough chicken heads to fill a hogshead, but it was on that search party I was truly and forever blooded. Blooded and bloody, and in the aftermath Adair had been the one to nurse me. First time I fought through the fever haze to see her like a healing angel hovering, I was smitten from ears to socks, and it never wavered, but it looked like I was riding single on a double buggy, herself keeping aloof, and her father all the while shoving her at King Corvis – that was his actual name – with his emporium and pasture land. He was "a pillar" and had a house six normal humans could live in without crossing paths.

His store dealt general merchandise on the square, including yard goods, and he added leather to his store to lure her along. Adair had a shoe fancy, and leather worked by little Popish men in the mountains of Italy drew her eye. The slippers could be sturdy but smooth as butter, fit snug, she later told me, but make your feet feel free as if bare. And he squired her over to the Opera House in Buena Vista and out to reels and balls at the Homestead and Forest Inn down at the Natural Bridge. Fancied himself a stylish dancer. Teas, speeches and waffle parties, too. He favored licorice whips and would offer them about like some cure, and he was skilled at the tennis and lawn croquet. For the most part, Corvis cut a spruce figure in the merchant ranks and had all the right words, but I expect on the sly he was already up to his elbows in dark business, smuggling and such. Adair was a touch honeyfuggled, I'd wager, and she didn't want to cross her pa, so she couldn't yet see Corvis with a clear eye.

I pitched my woo, though, and I'll say it turned her head some, even if Corvis was running on the rail and not sparing whip nor spur. If he thought he hated me when I was the swoony puppy his feet kept stumbling on, he was dead sure of it when my rushing to the colors perked up her attention. He had likely been some relieved that winter when I took up with Rose, and he most likely hoped I'd find a way to die in the war. When I mustered out and came home the hero (hurt again, arm slung, but my step more stylish and sure) he started whetting the tongue and jabbing. I recall they were there together to meet the train, not for me personally but for all the hoopla over three survivors and two coffins. Miles of bunting, a little band, all the whoops and hollers. Tiny flags on sticks and the smell of treacle and popped corn. I was about to pass them on the platform when she stepped near about into my path, pointing to my bandaged arm.

"It seems you don't know how to look after yourself, Sergeant Sherburne."

"No safety in soldiering, Miss Adair," I said, tipping my Stetson. I gave her the wink, and you could see she was remembering when we met. Corvis in his silky gold vest and spats was about to blow steam like the B & O engine huffing behind me.

"We missed you, Mr. Corvis. Cuba was the Grand Cotillion, and that anjeho rum was special. Hope to see you again, Ma'am." When she smiled and nodded deep enough to jiggle the ostrich feather on her hat, I knew my luck was back.

I'd been the low-rung deputy before I left, and more than once Corvis had tried to get me ousted for snooping about, especially up on Irish Creek, where he had some dealings with Eisenhowers and the like. I knew he had a hand in the whiskey trade and more than a passing interest in who paid what to get bateaux through the Maury's locks, but I also had a slight whiff of him being involved in some white slaving, scullions and the like being trained up to crib girls and sold around like so many guinea hens. No proof, though, much as I want it to be so.

When the Spanish threw down the sword and I came home a decorated hero, the earth had shifted: Sheriff O'Malley was ailing, one deputy was too old to grapple the cadets from the Institute when they got raucousy and the other's wife was after him to take up barbering at the New Health Hotel down at Rockbridge Springs. And by then I had seen enough to know the world will pass you by if you wait for the brass ring to hook into your hands.

In short, there was an election, and I got the circled star, so Corvis lost some ground. There's not much doubt he's the one put out the ambush on me just after the century turned, but I couldn't get the goods on him. Not that it mattered. He was showing his true nature clear enough for even a school boy to see, and Adair was not moonstruck. It didn't hurt that I had been gallivanting about with Rose just before the *Maine* business. Such a show will catch another woman's eye and stay there, despite that my Rose fascination was scarce a strategy. I can't say that woman ever had my heart, but flesh has its power, too, not to be made light of.

Shortly after Adair and I announced our troth, Corvis came after me in the Grand one night. He was drunk and grabbling about in his pocket for that gun he toted, all the while putting his tongue to my name like a blacksnake whip. I grabbed him by the belt and snatched upwise till his eyes told me the crotch of his britches had more than snugged him at the fork. Then I spun him and pulled the coat down over his arms to bind them, removed the pistol and hauled him off to jail, all the while him shouting things like, "You're done for, hayseed. Your day is over. You're gonna taste crow. You'll regret . . . ." It was good sport for all in attendance, but it was the first time he openly promised to be the agent of my demise, a vow he renewed on various occasions when we met without audience. I'd usually answer, "Here I am, Corvis, right here. Start killing," which just fuelled the deeper fire. After he married up with Liz Bayne, it all seemed to flicker out, though. He kept his darker business outside my jurisdiction, and we learned to nod, tip the hat, speak civil on the street and in town council. It was best for everybody that we arrived at a truce.

He was far from a poor man, though, and many a ridge ranger around here is needful enough to sell whatever skill he owns, including shootmanship, so it's a wonder I'm still casting a shadow. But now he was in there with the others, no telling what commotion in store for me. And the rifle scabbard under his saddle, I noticed, was empty. Maybe he'd just left it back home.

4.

WE TIED UP TO A PIECE OF DRIFTWOOD left over from the spring freshet. Nearbout a flood, truth told, and you could hear the falls upstream. I stepped through a patch of jellico weed and surveyed the brush. The bank beyond Lily's back verandah was willowy, the ramshackle pier sturdied with new pylons and braces. She could afford it.

I could just make out the river talking to itself. Or maybe it was muttering to me that I should of taken all this in hand sooner. A skiff was moored to a moss-slicked piling that picked up a scab of moonlight. Amidst the ribs and spines of smashed rowboats, an upturned old bateau lay along the shore to act as a table when the meat pit was fired up and the spit turning, and just beyond that, out in the flow, the outline of a heron on a silt bar was stabbing something. He knew his business and didn't miss. I scanned the scrubby yard carefully and even looked to the roof. The house was in dire need of a painting, and some warped boards had prized their nails right out. Shutters sigodlin, roof shakes loose or already on the ground, panes cracked. It had once been a respectable house, but now in the dark it seemed to bear witness to some twisted idea or lost world. Two stories, four high gables with tight-draped windows. I was thinking, "No surprises tonight. This hour, this place – it's a full skirmish or I'd be done with the horse now and plumping my pillow. Be ready for anything."

"A body needs to know the plan, boss. Where you want me?"

"Hell's cellar, eventually, Tarvis, and it's Sheriff Boss, if you must take my name in vain. In a minute I'd enjoy for you and the ten-gauge to slip in right behind me and step lively along the left wall, over toward the raised pulpit Lily's gun guard's cage sets on. Klute's to know he's been trumped from the minute he glimpses iron. See to it. Just keep the muzzle pointed over his head. He'll read the meaning."

"Maybe he'll give me excuse to change his face. He had to've been made on God's nap hour, and he's mean to boot. They's a right smart of his ilk inside there, too, not worth a smooth nickel. You know I've been wanting to scour out this den of drunks and rattlers. I've been saying . . . ."

"What kind of shot have you got loaded?"

"Brass buck."

"Always the pricey stuff. Tarvis, you are ever a burden. But it'll serve."

"Let's Injun-up on em. I'm ripe."

The heavy door was rounded at the top, thick oak with t-hinges, simple but sizeable. If not for all the scars, the sharded off spots and lead shot dug into the wood, it might call to mind a church door. Shut snug and with the thick log walls, it kept the devil den's business inside. I knew there was a stable lock, two slide bolts forged by Hank Simpson and a hickory bar in there where the sporting went on. If the door would open for me, it meant nobody was trying to keep the night's mischief private. That could be welcome news. . . , but I wasn't counting on it.

An oil lamp over the arch flickered and gave the whole scene a wavery feel, like everything was drunk as the millers flitting about it. So much whiskey in that building, you could nearly believe that the case. A couple of horses shuffled their feet and neighed. Likely just dreaming. I used the light to check my chambers. Five full, the one under the hammer free. Knowing what was to come might not be a cakewalk, I pinched a sixth cartridge from my belt and thumbed it through the Peacemaker's loading gate, then wrapped my fingers around the bull nose ring that served for a handle and pulled the door open, thinking, "Welcome, mayhap, to hell."

5.

THE ROOM WAS DIM-LIT and right quiet. You expect it to be ratty, but the circles of candles hanging overhead threw their light on heavy playhouse curtains and photographs of bare-knucklers and Rebel heroes, a couple of half-naked women painted mural-style, sporting signs of bullet holes and repair. Through the wraithy tobacco smoke you could see the walls themselves were painted dark but not able to hide the stains and nicks of hard use. Tables and cane-bottom chairs were scattered about, and candle light caught the spittoons and foot rail along the serving bar, which was littered with various beer mugs, one-shots, bottles and a handle jug the color of a spring river in flood. Somebody had stuck yellow wildflowers in the mouth of the jug, but they were drooping, losing petals and making no difference.

Lily had some fancy glass lamps on the walls. They mostly didn't work but were still pretty with their bangles, though you had the impression the room needed their light something desperate. The big mirror behind the bar was losing silver, and from a flaw in the glass it bent people's likenesses to a specter look. The east wall held some posted notices, but it was too dark to read them. A piano against that wall, guard perch on the west and the gun bin beside that. You could see a couple of long barrels sticking out, but you just knew the collection hadn't been thorough. The sign overhead couldn't of been simpler:

*Girls
*Whiskey
*Beer
*Cards
NO GUNS
NO CREDIT
Tomorrow is just a rumor

Beside the bar was Lily's throne, a fancy high-back armchair with blue velvet cushion held on by brass tacks, behind it a skeleton stairway with no handrail leading up to the next floor, which the customers called "dear heaven" and where there was a dark narrow loft with red doors to three rooms. Not a window in sight. I knew from past visits it wasn't the roughest looking roadhouse in the county, but it was no church.

The smells of sweat and whiskey were equally strong and sour, but there was a sharper scent running underneath, and I knew it was blood. Maybe twenty souls, most of them customers, filled the room, which was the size of a middling feed lot, and they made a shabby klavern, but before I could start to pick faces out of the puzzle and check Tarvis's flanking move, I saw a blur in the mirror and the big Ramp was on me from behind, his arms wrapping mine and stealing my breath. I could take air in just enough to know I didn't care for his smell, and since I couldn't see the advantage of this waltz, I found his right moccasin between my feet and raked the heel of my boot down shin and ankle till it was planted right on the bone. I'm no lady-weight, and I know how to stomp. When all the brunt went through that steel-shod heel, he let go quick, and he gave out a sound that made you doubt the room could of ever been silent.

When I spun, it was with the Webley out, and I brought the

barrel strong on his collar bone. I scarce had ample time to notice his face had the tint of an eggplant skin. Another howl, and he went down, wiggling like a halved blacksnake.

Nobody can say what a Ramp is. "Melungeon" most call them. I didn't know many, as they chose to lurk away from town. Fine by me. It's said they can shoot you the evil eye and give you the withers or drown you in plain air. This one was a Mullins, almost dark as Africa but his long hair fine and straight as a Cherokee's. Portugee, they claim. No horns that I could see, though, no extra thumb. He wasn't out of any ogre book, just a mongrel, like most of us. But a big one. I'd seen him once or twice before at a distance, but his jumping me made no more sense than whiskers on a chicken.

If he was big, Klute was bigger, looming from his crow's nest, but Tarvis had gone my plan one better and had the shotgun's mouths pushed against his Adam's apple. Klute's own gun was on the floor already and his fingers close to touching the ceiling. I could see by his face he was surprised and riled. Tarvis was smiling and saying, "Kitty, kitty, kitty."

"What the fuck?" I said.

I don't much hold with such language, but cursing's a tool like any other. You're not too quick to spend it, its value grows. I said it again as I swept my aim across the room at face level and saw every eye widen, each man bending at the knee a mite, trying to sneak shorter, but that only put my sight notch on their brows. Slowly, a couple garbed in whitetail skins stepped to the side so I could see the body and the blood pool. It had stopped spreading and was losing luster, seeping between and into the boards. It was oozed from the heap I could just tell was the red-headed doxy called Marge by some, Rusty by others. If she wasn't stone-cold dead, she was the best actress I'd seen.

"Razor. Throat. Look for yourself." It was Lily's voice, toad-husky from years of sucking the pipe that stuck out of her mouth, but no smoke was rising now. She was the only one to look me in the eye, and I could feel her stare. She was squinting, and the look had something of the reptile in it, like I was the one responsible for the red pond and the slow-down in her spree night business. It was beginning to seem like blame was falling to me, and that had me puzzled.

"What's he to do with it?" I cocked my head back at the Ramp.

"I can say what jumped and when, Sherburne, even some of how, but I can't read what any of these edjits is trying to think."

Corvis was slinking in the corner, a mug of beer in the hand I could see. Every time I happened on him outside the civic eye, I'd recollect how most men who bury the hatchet don't dig it under so deep they can't get back at it.

"Evening, mayor," said Tarvis. "You looking in fine fiddle on this happy occasion."

"Maybe he knows the guts of it, boss."

"Whose razor?"

Tarvis and I were scanning the room, probably both thinking of the Corvis rifle, which I would bet against finding in Klute's bin. I wanted to keep everybody's mind on the present matters.

John Pink, who I had used as a scout and find-em spy a few times, stepped forward, offering the razor, the blade folded shut in its sunset mother-of-pearl handle.

"Howdy, Sherburne. This trinket belongs to God's servant."

"Saying what?"

He pointed with his boot toe to a dirk on the floor about the right size for skinning squirrels. "Appears that one belonged to poor Rusty here, though I don't know it for hers." At that point, it seemed half the men in the room undertook to volunteer their accounts, but Pink jerked his thumb toward the half-open door behind the beer kegs.

"She's back there, the evangelist gal. In the counting room."

It was Tarvis's turn to pinch his face up and be surprised: "Evangelist? What the fiddle- fart?"

That was when Lily stepped up to hook my left arm. She had on her green dress with the shine of a June bug in its cloth, and the two dead foxes wrapped over her shoulders were staring at me with dead glass eyes. Pistol barrel pointed to the ceiling, I wheeled back to the drinkers.

"You ridge runners just hold your biscuits right here whilst I untie this. Tarvis, no more drinks, nobody goes out that door. They can sit, if it pleases them. They can sing hymns, chew cud or blow snot. But no shuffling about.

"Y'all just hold tight with us, boys. If this is not your cut job, you got nothing to fear from me but a little intermission. We'll see you all have another taste before we piss the fire out and send you to your horses. Lily, where are those yellow gals?"

The back room was lit with a banquet lamp, and I could see a tumble of barrels and cases, baskets full up with laundry, bundles of handbills, Lily's big desk and some trunks. It was the belly of the place, and not in much order. I figured it was enough mess to set Adair to tisking and rolling up her sleeves. Across the room Lily's house girl Idean was kneeling in front of a chair where a thin woman with white-streaked black hair was slumped over. Idean was wrapping the woman's right forearm with bandage, and she had a couple of nicks about her wrist that were cleaned but still slightly seeping. I could see she was thin but not soft.

"It weren't her fault, sheriff. Rusty asked for it sure as a bear wants berries."

I couldn't make fast sense of Lily taking a stranger's part over her own employee, but before I could ask, she answered.

"A Burning Worder, from what I could hear of it, come in here all preachy with her white Testament and cat-scratch voice. She was scolding about the whiskey and bad women, but the boys took a shine to her, kept spending hard and drinking harder. I got no complaint about any speech that sharpens a body's thirst. I was back yonder bunging a keg, but before I knowed it, Soo and Sung was in here jabbering half in Chinee speak that the woman was spoiling their take. Didn't nobody want to slip upstairs for a slice when they was all this free entertainment."

"What you're leaving out is what I need to know." The deeper this got, the more regret I had that I'd let the skin trade get a toehold in Lexington.

Lily conjured a stick match from somewhere, thumbnailed it and commenced to draw on her pipe.

"Rusty ain't the kind to complain. Weren't, I mean, poor soul. She had her own ways of settling up, direct like. When things went wrong, I seen it too late to cross the room from back there at the river stud game. What with that pack of yahoos out there clutching around not to miss the scuffle, a body could scarce get a glimpse."

"What do you suppose brought a damned evangelizer in here, anyway?"

"Rumor's out I'm running the worst Gomorrah in the county spoiling souls right and left. It's good for trade. I started it myself."

The tall woman on the chair was still slumped over, breathing but almost in a slumber. Her bonnet was askew and nearly covering her face, and she wore a high-necked riding dress in bulky layers, about a whole bolt of shimmery black cloth, maybe velvet. I could see sticking out from under her skirts the calfskin boots, long lace-up things with more eyes than a peacock. I could guess Adair would appreciate them. They whispered *money*, despite being on one with her sights on the Better Place.

"And where have you got the Chinese now?"

"They upstairs behind lock and key. I don't want no more confusion."

Lily was a sensible woman, cooperative when necessary, though seldom pleased to be, but as she spooled out her details of the cut fight, I reckoned this was near to gospel. She told how Rusty commenced to raise a rucket, catching the evangelist woman by the skirt in mid-testimony, which wasn't much understood above the commotion anyway. She jerked the new woman off the chair, hissing something about selling her moosey from behind the bar like the rest or getting her damned goods off the market. Idean said the ringlets of red hair were jouncing about and Rusty's eyes flashy as she circled the woman kneeled on the floor, and they seemed to produce sharp instruments as if at a signal.

"You could'a heard a dozen pair of skivvies sucking air when them roughs saw the preacher woman had a straight razor, and she got low and scampy real quick like it wadn't no first time for her.

They done ring-a-rounded, slashing out an spitting, little strikes here an there bringing some blood, but I even from the back could guess Rusty wadn't about to quit till something dire come on one of em. She was fast as a snake, but this here one was faster."

I kept looking back and forth between Idean's patient and Lily's face with smoke pouring from her mouth and piggy nostrils.

"Now exactly why didn't you put a stop to it?"

"Corvis. He done held me back. Hell, I couldn't hardly see a thing. He said it'd all come out as God willed it without no interference. I couldn't wrench myself free till too late."

I wanted to hear Corvis's story, too, and what Pink had to add, not to mention something about the Melungeon's reasons, but about that time the Burning Worder seemed to come back into the world of the living. She sighed real deep, sat up straight and pulled the bonnet off, looking up from two cindery eyes. Just as I saw the purple ribbon at her throat, she said, "Evening, Blaine." I reached up and ran my fingers across the scar over my left cheekbone. It felt almost fresh.

Lily said, "I be dim-damned," and rared back to laugh.

I couldn't help smile. "Evening, Rose."

6.

I WAS THINKING THE YEARS had been hard on her, given her the look of a weary spirit, but maybe it could have been a civil enough reunion, if the shot hadn't boomed on the other side of the door. I was moving fast, saying "Tarvis" under my breath, hoping it was just a warning blast through the ceiling. Come to pass, it was Klute instead of the ceiling laths, and he fell over the pulpit, still writhing, head a mess with blood gushing in a way I wished not to see again after Cuba. But if wishes was horses wouldn't anybody walk. Klute's pistol had clattered to the puncheon, so he'd made the play, the hostage part not setting well with him, and the room's other occupants were all scuttling for the door when the next shot roared. It was a rifle, and I was just in time to see Tarvis slam back against the wall and slide to the floor, a blood smear on the plaster where his shadow had been.

The room was a full scramble then, everybody making like Rough

Riders under the barrel of a Maxim gun. I'll give them this much, for drunks, they were quick to grasp a situation. Then the overhead candle ring somehow came crashing down, and I saw the first up-rush of flame just before the slit-nose Lungeon's unbroken shoulder walloped into me again.

"Hell bastard!" Then I felt the air leave me for the second time since I walked through that church-looking door.

The next thing I saw was the back room's scabby ceiling. What I felt was hands on my neck, getting tighter, one thumb over my apple. What I heard above my own gasping was a craze of shouts, and then I knew there was no longer a revolver in my palm, though I heard one pop. Mullins was still burdening my chest but not moving, the pressure off my windpipe, and when I twisted to the side, the Ramp rolled off limp. Men were scuttling hither and thither, and I figured right away Tarvis wasn't wounded so nasty as I'd thought and had plugged the big man just in time.

Turns out Tarvis was hit bad, but through the shoulder, which would render that arm little use to him all his days, as a Winchester cuts a big tunnel. He'd live to learn a thousand ways to cuss that night. But it was not the Ivor from his belt that kept the Melungeon from strangling the life right out of me.

"Blaine," she said again, and I saw her standing then, the bright little pistol in her hand, a wisp of smoke from cheap powder snaking out.

"I see you've still got the Smith."

"Some gifts last a lifetime. You remember the handle?"

"Your name, yes. Carved for you." I know I said something else, but I don't recollect it. The room rushed about in a whirl, and a black ink washed it all away.

I couldn't figure how there could be so much light in that darkness. I must have been a fish down in a brackish backwash pool, and there were rounded off shapes of light that appeared here and there, over shadowy shoals or stones or something, but would go off to nowhere whenever I tried to swim up through one of them. The breathing came hard, and all the sounds I could hear were like animals off in the woods somewhere. Then I heard a voice, quavery at first, but when it came clear, it was Corvis's, and then I saw his face, that fringe of hair hanging down, his eyes tight and cold. He was holding the butt end of the rifle over me like, and I almost knew what had happened. I could feel a spot on my skull throbbing.

"It's like the past has come back, Mr. Sheriff."

He kicked the door to the big room shut with his heel, but I could see the rowdies had all tucked tail and run. Even Idean was gone. Despite the dim light, I saw Lily and Rose standing against a row of casks against the far wall, and the Melungeon lay where he had rolled. I blinked several times and shook my head hard to buy some time. My gun was on the floor behind him where he'd likely kicked it. I couldn't see other weapons of any sort, and I knew Lily had never toted a firearm, but the Rose pistol still had to be somewhere in that room.

"Much as I appreciate you looking up at me, Colonel, why don't you try out your legs, see if you can't unwobble them? I always knew you had a hard head, so you'll shake it off."

This was one of those times when you want to keep hearing a voice you hate. If he clammed up, no telling what would follow. Thinking Tarvis dead, I couldn't see hope in this for Corvis unless he put Rockbridge behind him forever. Too many men, even if most of them rogues, had seen him shoot my deputy. And he'd know I wouldn't balk at tossing the county star on the table to come after him to Georgia or Gehenna. He'd never be able to sleep with both eyes shut again. No, if he had any hope of freedom, he'd have to kill me. That was what I was worried about when he spoke again, a mocking wheedle in his voice like a cur.

"Adair, the widow Sherburne, might enjoy to see this, you and Miss Rose together out in a roadhouse on a Saturday night. Or to just hear it from others. She's smart enough to add things up. Easy now, hero, just hold easy."

He had a dead smile, but his eyes were lively, evil. I was getting to my feet in stages, holding my hands out like everything was a blur. Rose and Lily both made to help me up, but he stopped them.

"Ladies, if I can use that word here and not stain it forever, let him be. You don't want to come between this Winchester and our friend the colonel. He's got some destiny to reckon with.

"It did work out nicely, didn't it? Soon as she stepped up on that chair, I thought, 'Now here's Sherburne's flown bird from ancient history.' I figured you wouldn't want harm to befall her, and when I saw the gals start in to swear and simmer, I thought here was a way to put the quietus on your old spark and have no hand in it myself, so I slipped over to Rusty and allowed as how I wouldn't stand by for somebody spoiling my hot night harvest. I even offered her loan of a knife, gallant that I am. When it went haywire, I sent Billy Harrison over to the telephone Willets had put in. Kind of doing my civic duty, you might say. They should have kept voting me in, giving me some stake in the law-and-order prospect. They really should."

Lily and Rose appeared to understand they were best silent, but I sort of stammered out, "What did the Melungeon have to do with it?"

"Old boy went into a rage when I told him you went to Cuba to kill dark people and were hatching a plan to burn out all the Ramps in Rockbridge. He took it for true and said you ought to be stopped, and when I told him you were on your way out to look into this cutting, he touched over his heart and said, 'That jack won't see morning.' Too bad about him. I admired his spunk. Miss Rose, this plays bad for you, too: he was an unarmed man."

I knew I had to locate that little pistol, and soon I caught it in my eye atop some ledgers on Lily's desk, five feet from me, twice as far from him. But his Winchester changed the proportions.

I held my head in my hands like a man still seeing fireworks in his brain, and when I felt the scar under my palm, I pulled the hand back.

When a woman sets her mind to leave, you might be able to stall her a while, but she's going. Try anything stronger than honey words, and you might see something to make you hanker for her to be gone sooner and forever. That was pretty much what befell that last night when I grabbed her by the arm and turned her to face me, saying,

"You can't go, Rose, not now, you can't." All she had to hand was a hat pin, but I like to lost an eye, and she managed to scrape a gash not even the undertaker's tricks will be able to hide. If I catch myself starting to wonder what might've happened had she been in reach of her pistol, I rein in and turn my mind elsewhere. When people asked, I always had a barbed wire story. Some believed.

I looked at Corvis's eyes and then measured distance to the pistol again. I was afraid he was getting tired of talking.

7.

THE HANDGUN WAS A SWEET little Smith & Wesson delivered to Ben Hankshaw's store by accident, but once he saw it held up to the light, he signed off anyway. It was a .32 five-shot made for a woman's hand and for her eye – high-shine nickel finish and the rosewood handle buffed and oiled with love. Three-inch barrel. The metal was like jewelry for some queen, and you'd be hard pressed to prove it was plate: it looked like solid silver. When Ben lifted it out of the plushy red case, Rose took it in her black riding glove, and a shiver ran down my spine.

"It's one of the original purse pistols with a cylinder to drop out the side so you could empty every chamber with one finger on the extractor. A fine piece of tooling, it is," Ben said. "Way it's milled and filed and fitted, you'd think to see it in a museum. Pawl and bushing, stirrup and struts – as fine a J-frame as you'll find. Listen to its clockwork when you cock it. The spring, the nocks: it's music. And light, perfect balance, likely no more recoil than a field hare's kick. The trigger pull is so easy, it can't need two pounds. A child could fire it. Easy to hide, simple to operate: a woman carrying this, she'd be safe as she wants to be." He flashed us that possum briar grin.

And hefting it, turning it in the light, you knew it wouldn't misfire, you believed it couldn't miss.

"Delicious," she said. "Doesn't it just beckon?"

The wide-spur hammer was the shape of a woodpecker crest, and the trigger was a new moon, but the man who made the grips – he had to be an artist from some old guild with rules and secrets – he had taken the word "rosewood" another way, too, and once he had carved the whorl-grained rosewood block into two grip pieces, he had scored into either side a blooming wild rose, both of them complete with swirling petals, stem and thorns. But they were different, too: one had two saw-toothed leaves, the other just one. The single-leaf rose had lost a petal, and it was etched in down near the butt.

It was the priciest thing I had ever bought shy of a horse, but from the moment Rose saw it, she wanted it, despite saying it was a death flower, and since wanting her was part of what I had taken as my occupation back then, I didn't resist. I still had a tender yearning for Adair, and strong, but she kept things cool between us, churchy and proper. I didn't see a hope there, but what I had for Rose was randy and fierce as red pepper, a wild fire. She would have the pistol and I would have her.

We made a wild night of it with the revolver still in its box on the settee, but what I couldn't see was she'd be gone in three months, and I'd be left with hundreds of bottle shards at the foot of my pasture gate, the leftovers from her learning to shoot. It was the east side of the house, and when the sun snuck up over the far pines, it would dash off that sharp glass, all diamondy and fit to break your heart. They were a danger all scattered about there, and I had to cut another gate and teach the horses to change their ways, but I couldn't raise the good sense to be rid of that heap. It wasn't till I was about to head west, to see the Alamo fort and meet Colonel Roosevelt and go on from there to free Cuba, that I finally dug a hole and raked all the chips and slivers in to say I was done with hungering for Rose.

8.

"WHAT TICKLED MY GIZZARD" said Corvis, "was seeing Her Roseness playing the saint, what with her history not being a secret. You've got to ask yourself what would turn the town jape-mare to Jesus. But I figure it had to be money, a taste that runs in the family, and you can see for yourself looks don't last."

She made a move at him, but Lily help her back.

"It wasn't money."

His face showed he'd just had a new thought.

"Money's going to be a problem for me, though, as I can't wait for the bank to open come Monday. Lily, I'm going to have to beg your pardon, but I'll be relieving you of tonight's take.

"You see, a man on the run needs the ready, especially a man on the run who'll be taking a charming lady along for company and comfort."

I saw in the corner of my eye that Lily and Rose looked at each other, but I kept my view trained on Corvis.

"No, no, no, no, no." He was laughing as he shook his head. "You ladies won't be going anywhere this night. You see, it's the lovely Mrs. Hero who'll be accompanying me. I'm sure she'll recognize the sheriff's horse, and I've always had something of a persuasive way with her. There's sure to be no trouble, once I get her properly mounted."

I hadn't previously realized a man that drunk could shoot straight. But if he was counting on me making a move, he wasn't wrong, though he hadn't counted on Rose moving first. I saw her shift her weight before he did, and when she lunged at him, I wasn't far behind, hauling for the desk where the little gun sparkled in the light.

Corvis swung the stock of the rifle like a scythe and cuffed Rose across the left ear. I knew that butt stroke from the army, but there was no time to think about its force or anything else. I was scrambling on the desktop with the little pistol in my hand when Corvis turned on me and pulled the trigger. There was no more space between us than the length of my body, and I was thinking "How did he miss?" as he worked the lever and jacked brass into the air.

He'd missed because Lily had kicked him, and he wheeled to smack her, then turned back but the time he needed to ready another round was not time he had. Lying on my side I shot twice, hitting him about the shoulders close to the neck both times. Knowing the caliber of the pistol, I was going for the throat, and I was starting to stumble circle-wise toward the door. He spun with me and got off another round, which went into my side just above the hip and stung like a company of yellowjackets.

The impact knocked me over, but I must have been going on nerve or bile. I came to a knee while he was cocking again. We were eight feet separate, and I heard him say, "I'll kill you, you dog fucker."

I squeezed and squeezed and squeezed. The gun felt like a toy after my forty-four, but it put out a roar twice, then a click, as it was a five, and Rose had already saved me once with its first. I recall feeling how perfect it was, though, toy-sized or not. No recoil, no slip in the action, the little trigger guard tight on my finger, the curved steel flexing almost on its own, almost like it had a mind to shoot, and I was nothing more than the mule it used to work its will.

The room was echoing like we were inside a barrel struck with a hoe handle, and I could hear Lily's voice higher and hurt and long.

Corvis dropped the rifle and flung his hands toward his face. His life was spraying out red and fierce from just under his chin and his cheek, which I'd nicked while taking out the eye. It didn't take him half a minute to kneel forward, slump and die, and I caught myself clicking the empty pistol at him as I stepped to hover right over him, blood still pumping, now painting my boots and trousers, mingling with my own. Then I felt swoony and turned to see that Lily had Rose's head in her lap and was rocking back and forth, but her sister's skull was smashed in, and there was no chance she was alive.

I went down then myself, sudden-like. And for all I knew, I was right behind Rose at the ford of Jordan.

9.

I WOKE COLD ON MY BACK in the wagon and felt every jostle of the wheels on bridge planks. Tarvis was conked out beside me, and I couldn't have said if he was dead or alive. When I heard Adair's voice saying, "Just lay still, honey. Doc Rayville has you stoppered up, which he says will last till he swings by after you've had some rest. Pink told me everything. It's sad, but it's done."

"Tarvis?"

"Unkillable, evidently, but mad as a wet cat. The doc's sent for Talitha, who is back there tweezing shirt bits out of his wound and cussing the limits of medical science. Tarvis will be singing for lye hominy and a swig of hootowl in a couple of days."

She was keeping the team on a tight rein, but it was no pleasure drive, and I wished she'd just use the whip and gallop us up the road and to our door. To stave off the pain, I breathed deep and looked at the lightening sky where the morning star was winking through the gap in the canopy over the river. The sun was just whispering red in the east, telling the night critters to den up in a safe place and warning livestock and farmers alike it was time to start shucking off their dreams and face the day. Then the whole sky was washed with a flash of rose color, and there was nothing on the earth I wanted more than sleep, to forget about being careless and putting off right action. I was about to utter "Poor Rose," but then I heard Vester snort in that quirky way he has and saw Bobby Dean was riding him alongside, slumped half dozing in the saddle, but his unmindful ways didn't matter, as the horse knew the way home.

Widow

A bird could arrow its way along that corridor through the curled and rusting leaves with no effort. A wren or scruffy quilleree darting out to find a renegade sunflower, brown and drooping, still stingily gripping a few nourishing kernels against the wind and frost of autumn. A bullet could make the same journey, but Sherburne was hoping that the eye of a catamount skulking toward the scent of fear would not detect the cleared line of sight leading back to his perch and that the burlap wrapping was sufficient to prevent his gun barrel from catching moonlight or the last rays of the sun.

Day fading, a cool breeze rising, so there should be moonlight soon, the bright rim following Venus above the limestone hogback into the sparsely clouded sky, and it would offer him the chance for a clean shot, if his eyes had remained as sharp and his hands as steady as he liked to imagine. Maybe even a swift series of shots, at once eliminating the menace and satisfying his own needs. Careful not to rattle the dry limbs of his blind, he swept the scrub and rimrock with his German field glasses, observed no movement, then hung them on a snag. He thumbed the old rifle's safety again to make certain the steel leaf was clicked left, disengaged, and the hammer in its half-cock notch. The stock was rough but familiar against his right cheek, the trigger housing cold as a casket handle. Shifting his weight in the creel he had constructed, he tried to ease the equally familiar pains along his spine and pressed his thighs together against the chill, then pulled the flaps of his Swiss wool cap over his ears and tilted the bill back.

For three days without his favorite racking horse or a decent campfire he had been broguing about, running figure eights, mapping the painter's plentiful tracks and scat, which revealed abundant scraps of bone and hair like a savage fetish. Across the sprawl of Hammer Mountain he had studied the strides, sometimes two feet long, and scratch marks along the wild cherry bark and chestnuts, trampled sarvis, scuffs in moss and litter where the cat had made his scrape and pissed his rank signature. Broken witch hazel canes, dust wallows, crushed toadstools. Occasionally, in stretches of soft dirt, he could see where the big animal had dragged its tail as it loped along. Traces of other life crossed and surrounded the trail – rabbit scat, a nibbled antler shed from last year, tufts of fox fluff in a bramble, a hole he stepped in and turned his ankle only slightly, as he was treading carefully.

"Judas Priest," he whispered. Bending to examine the depression, he found mangled grey yellowjacket comb strewn about. A hungry skunk had found good fare – one fellow seeker successful – but he was trying to clear his own mind of anything superfluous, straining to think as a panther, the way his father had back when they were plentiful – squinting his eyes, sniffing the wind, tasting it, canting his head to the left, breathing from the toes up, but slowly, wondering how the two sets of whiskers made feline navigation easier. Never mind squirrels racing overhead, faint birdsong, the scuttle of a startled woodchuck or the shadow of a hawk on the leaf litter, its sharp shin gliding off above. "Painter mind" was all.

Whenever he stumbled or was forced to rest a spell and swig from his canteen, he had to remind himself why he hadn't just announced a bounty and let the usual crew of Irish Creek hog rangers dog the animal up a tree, then swagger its bullet-riddled head and hide all over Lexington, if only to quiet the scoffers who swore the cats had all vanished, gone west as noisy humans invaded their range. Despite the general wisdom, three sheep and a prize ram had gone down in as many weeks, two yearling calves near Fairfield and a colt belonging to Riggy O'Neill. Such a predator could range twenty, twenty-five miles in a day, leaving victims hither and yon. Five days back a hart had run down Timber Ridge onto the Staunton road trailing blood from claw marks along his neck and shoulder. It had lumbered in front of a log dray, then into a scrub thicket where it had foundered and fallen, easy venison for the drayman, manna, but an alarm to the nearby families. It was the colt that did it for Sherburne, however, brought down within a hundred rods of the farmhouse but hardly tasted, just ripped and ravaged, its pitiful remains shat upon like some tribal taunt. And yet, that wasn't the whole story, either. Of course, no one had actually seen a lion cat, and the identity of the culprit was disputed from Doyle's Lunch to the high table at VMI, along Nelson Row and the courthouse steps. He'd like to settle it. And perhaps, he thought, he was also testing himself, trying to measure his age in something more fundamental than decades.

Above the logging road now reclaimed by haw and birdy-looking bracken, he had soon found a stone pool where the animal often drank and the ledge where the grisly remnant of its last kill – a full-grown doe – was cached and masked by an uprooted dwarf pine. The area offered plentiful mast to draw the ruminants, but the twigs and duff underfoot had still held the cat's musky scent, and the few remnant coral berries nearby seemed almost to announce the presence of blood. Looking at the dead deer, he had to admit that this phantom cat had made him angry in a way he had long been committed to resisting. The personal nature of his response was worrisome, but it did feel refreshing to sense his blood heating up even when the topic arose in casual conversation, to know his cheeks were flushing and his resolve turning to steel as everything else grew dim and he cut his eyes toward the slopes of Hammer Mountain.

With little comfort or embellishment beyond the heft of the rifle in his hands, the sheriff had weathered and established his bona fides for three days: he smelled like the mountain, looked like a shard of the autumnal landscape, absorbed and gave off its tannic flavor, became part of its nightly sound. But not without cost: his knees and elbows ached; one thigh muscle spasmed; when he flexed his fingers, the joints snagged and cracked sharply. The neck scar from the wound he'd received near the Natural Bridge so long ago seemed to tighten and throb to the left of his windpipe, while the damaged nerves from just below his ear, sweeping along the cheek to his jawbone, radiated their spooky half-numb distress. It could still be a sobering question: What if the bullet had struck a finger's width higher or an inch to his right? "Mighty lucky, son," Dr. McClung had announced back then, "Just grazed," and Sherburne in his near-delirium had thought of ponies grazing in a pasture. Tortured now by his body's history, he was at least able to salvage solace from the vista his current perch on the saddle afforded – rough terrain sweeping down to a calm bowl and the patchwork farms of Rockbridge County, fields of wet sedge the color of iodine, roads of all sizes, the Maury's meandering course, fences and streams, chimney smoke in the middle distance, the heights of House Mountain, then the hawk-colored woods below two rude and rugged knobs called The Skulls and the other summits and rims hazing on the horizon. Ground fog was beginning to rise in the cuts and hollows. "The gloaming," he thought, a silvering-over, then "master of all I survey, my bailiwick," and he almost chuckled, snugging his scarf against the gusts as the wind narrowed through rock rifts and even sang eerily across one shelf of riven shale. He was almost amused by the thought that, had he read the animal's mind as well as its trail, he could have skipped the meander and come straight up Hammer from the turnpike, saving himself two days. But that might not have given him time to adjust to the cat's way of thinking, to feel him on the wind and the ground. A ruffed grouse drumming beyond a stand of junipers startled him back into the moment.

He had to admit that, when he set the snare to catch a bait animal, the lariat's effectiveness had been half luck. The little spike whitetail that slunk in after his lure of sliced apple stumbled as the cord's slipknot tightened and had broken a foreleg when the trigger released the bowed sapling. After a brisk wrestle and hogtie-lashing, then still tighter binding with thongs, it had been manageable, though not easy, to portage the sixty pounds of wriggling, frightened deer across the crest, then hobble and tether him on the bald amid scragwood and cotton trees, a little sumac and the stripped tendrils of huge flame azalea bushes on the edge before the ground fell off westward where in summer the bear grass would dangle white bells from its stalks and the azaleas shake in scarlet when the wind shifted. Occasionally, the deer gave out a desperate bleat.

The heart of the big predator's current stamping ground was a desolate patch, much of it scorched black just four years before by a lightning fire. The surround had already been branded "haint ground" since a Carson woman from Goshen had disappeared thereabouts half a century before, and hunters sometimes claimed to hear her keen or see her wisping about at just this very hour. Recovering amid its hellish snags, the tract had become harsher than the neighboring terrain and spoke to Sherburne somehow of the bleakness of the unredeemed human soul. This was certainly a region where one could get thoroughly, irrecoverably lost. And in this hard, isolated place or any other, he wondered, what might constitute sin or error, and what might amount to redemption? Certainly not good intentions: he had rangered up here alone, despite his wife's plea, and kept this stark surveillance to rid Rockbridge's Delve Creek region of a livestock menace which might also be behind last month's disappearance of the Hostetter girl, but so far he had managed only to wear himself out, torture an unlucky deer and leave his wife with no company by the evening fire – and more than a little nettled.

He spat and knuckled at the corner of his itchy eye, which was dry from the wind. Noticing that in one severe rock niche a few chicory stalks still held their petals against the season, he thought, "Nobody wants to give up the ghost." He did not relish finding the remains of the missing Hostetter child – Beth Ann? – in his reconnaissance, but he knew it best in the long haul if he did, for he held out no hope of her survival. Bones, he thought, all over this mountain there were bones and remnants of bones from all manner of creatures not yet gnawed to dust for their minerals. But then, the whole world was a bonefield, if you but knew the stories.

He'd also constructed something of a shelter for himself about a dozen feet up and near the trunk where the wind could not carry his presence toward the bait. He'd lashed the broken limbs carefully to form a cradle in the hickory fork, braced the rifle rest and cut a passage through thinning foliage for the corridor of death. He had covered his signs below and trusted his scent was at a minimum, as this venture fell well within his experience at both tracking and ambush. In fact, even his freshest deputies might have accomplished it, but he had also come to the high, haggard ground to be alone for a spell. Two nights in different tree stands he had pulled the army blanket of smoke-colored wool about him and stared at the heavens, squandering much of his attention like some unlettered savage tracking Orion's journey along the south rim. But why was that word "savage" so convenient to his mind these days?

He had read that deep in European caves an ancient people once sketched Orion for magic, homage to the hunter in hopes he'd bless them with his art, guide them to a clean kill. He could still picture the glow from his father's face when he had talked of Orion, almost as if the constellation were a kind of woodsman's Christ. The figure etched in distant light on the surface of his own mind said simply *pursuit*, but world-weary as he had become, he now preferred ambush, cunning, the still and patient way. He was no longer spry and on such excursions missed his hearth – with its hounds, its books and sherry and the mime show of flames behind the screen – and most of all his wife, who even while working her ivory crochet needles in near-silence or turning the pages of an English novel, glancing at him over her wire spectacles only furtively, seemed in her contentment to be emitting a song. Despite its two gray streaks, her hair still caught the light and glowed like a girl's, and her laughter was the best sound he'd known in this mortal world. If she was a bit riled over his decision to come after the cat, he could hardly fault her.

Right now, though, he was blue-boned cold and wondering how things might have turned out had he stuck to the livery trade, hovered about town, supplied Adair with more fine things, and more of his attention. He did owe her a secret debt, but she'd never know. He didn't imagine a warehouse of luxuries or a trip up the Eiffel Tower could have rendered them fonder of one another, yet the wish to bestow grand splendors and marvelous journeys upon her was never wholly dispelled, and he was certain her usual acknowledgement that he could "fend for himself under even the most foolish circumstances" masked a constant concern, intensifying as the years accumulated. This time, when he said, "I have to go, Adair. It falls to me," with finality, she'd ventured to suggest he at least take along a deputy. "Train one up," she'd said. "You can't keep doing this forever."

This present task was, however, the least complicated kind of business he knew: sheriff serving as game warden once again. Stealth, thrift, dispatch – a discipline that now amounted to habit. That had been the plan, anyway: scout and shoot, skin it out and pack the trophy home with no political or ethical complications. That was the kind of public service he enjoyed, but for two of the last three days, amid the slanting afternoon light of early November, his field glasses had caught the Nevers widow from Bluebell Farm in her dark dress and shawl climbing – despite rumors of the fierce cat so near her fields – up the brushy slope to enter the dilapidated line shack where Victor Reevis would be waiting, usually sheltered inside the doorway from both wind and any wayward eyes, only the smoke from his roll-up visible through the long glasses most of the time, though occasionally he would step forth under a little bare persimmon tree to stretch and survey the inclining landscape. He figured they must tether their horses – the buttermilk mare and the paint – somewhere down in the deep ravine he could just see the edge of. Reevis was a tall man, rawboned and ruddy and hard with a patch of red hair and a broken nose, easy to identify at a distance, but hard to read up close. Unlike so many of his coloring, he had little to say in the public forums of mercantile, auction lot and tavern and seemed to live mostly for work and sleep. But you never know; maybe his restraint was a form of prayer for something or a scheming. As his predecessor behind the badge had warned, "There's nothing you can imagine so bad or odd that somebody somewhere ain't doing it or about to as we sit here." This case was not so extreme, but in any event, Sherburne found the rendezvous more than a touch puzzling. Brought near by the round lenses, she was, under her barn coat, still dressed in mourning. As he mulled it over, an arcing hawk abandoned its circuit and plummeted, shrilling, toward something stirring in a sparse meadow in the middle distance.

The pair met in shyness and, it seemed, hid their business in shame behind the shed's weather-worn planks with no tell-tale smoke rising from the leaning fieldstone chimney, no fire to comfort or betray them – but who would give it more than a passing tisk or titter to know the widow's public grief was not so simple as she pretended? Remembering Adair's warning that after a quarter of a century he was in danger of becoming pure sheriff, of narrowing down to a collection of theories and suspicions, he kept trying to convince himself the rendezvous on the laurelled shelf far beneath him was not his business.

Jim Nevers had been dead since late spring, and, he thought, a woman has necessities, even if they trespass on some people's notions of propriety, sufficient respect for the deceased, even loyalty. Selfish, some might say. But no, that was a harsh read, ungenerous. Susan was a tall, bright, buxom young woman with black hair that sparkled like a crow's and eyes not much lighter, a lilt in her step, over a hundred acres to manage now. And a deep-seeded, mysterious quality of sorrow that current circumstances had intensified till it probably couldn't ever be wiped away. It was not his business: Let her jape whoever she fancied. The lion, he thought: he's enough for this evening. So each previous glimpse of the couple had been drowned out by the requirements of his tracking. She was a free woman, after all.

STILL, HE REMEMBERED that Fool's Day cotillion at Jackson Hall, the gangly Nevers beating the tune on a dog-gnawed bull fiddle and encouraging every guest to drink up and dance. Laughter and whiskey improving his bland face, he bullyragged his wife to promenade with every man present, from preacher to layabout to the eight-year-old McCrowell boy shaking the tambourine. "Mississippi Flood," "Listen to the Mockingbird," "Blue-Tail Fly" – townspeople and farmers alike clapped their hands, raised a shout and followed the caller's figures, while Miz Nevers drank in the attention like lemon sling on a hot day while she galloped and pranced and reeled, her sadness seemingly overcome for a while. And Reevis, to Sherburne's surprise, had eventually abandoned the stag corner to become one of the dancers. "Leather Britches," "Virginia Rose." On "Queen Sallie" Dorsey Jerrold made the fiddle smoke, and the dancers whooped and clapped. When time came to taw up with Reevis, did she embrace his waist a little tighter, sway her hips with more zest, smile in a manner that wasn't appropriately shy? But, if she had, where was the fault in that? Had not Adair once cut a similar figure, belle of the ball, a lithe and handsome sprite with a white rose in her hair and a smile for every able man? Shouldn't hide your light under a bushel.

It was in this attempt at dismissal that the wide net of Sherburne's imagination snagged on something and drew it in. Any habit of keeping the assignation confidential at this point in the story might mean it was not fresh practice, and if their private meetings – even just one of them – went back to before the spring planting and the misplaced barn tool, it might warrant further speculation.

Common enough, really, for even a savvy farmer to run afoul of his own implements. Papers down in Roanoke or over in Staunton were full of such accounts. People were in jeopardy. Farmers, especially. Metal held points and edges and gears that spun and jabbed or just snatched in the wrong direction. Ropes broke, animals panicked, saws jumped and water took surprising turns. Scotched wheels skidded, trees toppled wrong. Anybody could be careless or unlucky, and if Jim Nevers fell through a weak board in his barn loft and found the hay fork neglected in the tangle of straw beneath him, the happenstance and any consequences that followed hardly invited suspicion. Sherburne had welcomed young Doctor Starling's explanation, which suggested no foul play was involved, no inquiry needed beyond the routine, two rusty tines angled through the right lung. "Impaled" was not a word he savored, but keeping strictly to the book he had ruled the matter settled, stamped and filed.

Now he was not so sure.

Something back in the shadows moved, or the shadows themselves shifted. He had arranged a brake of windfalls and beech limbs behind the young deer to simplify his shot, and the helpless thing wrestled with the tether tied to a red spruce trunk, but to no avail. Frantic, desperate, its hindquarters be-shat and muzzle frothy. This was unquestionable suffering, but Sherburne knew his was a necessary cruelty and hoped it would be brief. The little buck would flail and jerk, then buckle completely and rest on his side, panting, before half rising on his three good legs to resume the struggle when his breath evened out. And occasionally, that mournful bawl. Had the bait sensed a new presence, as well?

Less than comfortable himself, Sherburne stretched out in his tree stand, still and stern, not allowing himself coffee, tobacco or even a sip of the peach brandy in his flask. Focus was all. And even in this blustery hither-skither place the panther's keen nostrils deserved full respect. He rehearsed the heft of the old government Krag-Jorgensen, double-checked the tangent sight, white bead at the end of the barrel and the round in the chamber, glanced at the watch his father had left him and immediately forgot the time, his mind lurching back to the night he received the cable from his mother: "Thaddeus failing. Come quick as you can. Might have a week." He had not lasted that long, and Sherburne reached the farm down in Carolina the day after his father passed. He could never quite say why he carried such a heavy guilt over that, but he knew he should have gotten past it long ago.

Right now, he needed something to warm his body, which was

cocked like the rifle, and yet relaxed inside. Hot coffee would be the ticket, alright. Hoecake with a splash of zip, a steak off the yearling deer. He would say grace over it all and express appreciation for his own survival. Since Monday he'd been going on jerky and apples, cold beans, hard cheese with the remnant of what was now a three-day-old pone, and the trailing had been tiresome.

It was an active mountain cat, canny, much given to circling and backtracking, mazing, leaving so many prints as to baffle with abundance. But it was rash and ravenous, as well, and having operated in these parts with impunity so far, secure in its habits, it might do anything. The early frost might have driven him to a feeding frenzy. Four years old, maybe five, he guessed, but the signs were uneven and inconclusive. It might loll of a morning, catching sun, then rush about in a swivet, half hunting, half playing, just halt and bask again, licking its muzzle. Strange, Sherburne thought, that an animal and a gun both had a muzzle. He supposed you could say a man had one, as well. It was most likely a young rogue, probably solitary and scavenging pretty far from what would serve as his winter den. Just bad luck for the locals and inconvenience for himself, but that's what they paid a sheriff for – sharp eyes and decisive action, even if it meant lonesome vigils like this, endless inquiries and occasional bloodshed. It was all done on behalf of balance, safety. Who was it that had written, "If you want peace, prepare for war"?

It was all just familiar enough to recall his months with the First Volunteers the press had dubbed "Rough Riders," off to the tropics even without their drilled and valued mounts, marching into the heat waves and morass rife with snakes and tuskers. But this was not summer. It was the metallic hinge of the year, and as the grizzled ridgelines in the distance faded and blurred to a vague and soothing curvature, the wind cut under his hat and stung his ears red. He hoped the cat would be active early, while the moon was still emphatic and his mind remained alert. Below him, the little buck snorted and bawled.

It was dangerous to jump to conclusions on matters like this one concerning the Widow Nevers, but it was equally unwise to discount intuition or delay too long in following a thread, especially with such surprising information. Fresh trail, so to speak. And stalking was essential to his profession. Not the aspect he preferred, but perhaps the part he most excelled at. He believed the photographs adorning the office walls – Spanish War veteran in his peaked hat beside the jackass-grinning TR, incumbent public servant with the trussed outlaw named Brodie Painter, with an eye-shot black bear hanging like a transit plumb, astride Dandy with a pair of Kentucky arsonists shuffling ahead in their manacles and so on – amplified his reputation and made campaigning easier with the passing years. Perhaps his growing picture gallery had some crime deterrent effect, as well. More than once he had told his wife, "If I was to quit, no telling what manner of mischief the rascals will start believing they can get by with."

The cloudless air held insinuations of rain, and something in the way rain-breath and waiting sapped his energy brought back the Cuban campaign, the weevil-riddled hardtack, bad beans and worse fever. "Wouldn't they have to be fewer if they was any bigger?" Wallington had joked about the mosquitoes, just two days before a bullet caught up with him. But the sheriff – sergeant then – had his job to do and then, as now, ashed his face and shimmied up a hospitable tree with his rifle slung over his back. Once installed, he scanned the landscape and hoped for the moon to favor his mission.

"Sniper" some called him; it was not a pretty word, piercing with the long eye in the center. "Sharpshooter" suited him better, "marksman," which might betoken a craft, but then there were those said to yearn for the poetic – every company of soldiers had them – who wanted flamboyance and glamour in the sobriquet of a cold killer. He became in their stories – due to his reliance upon celestial illumination – the Honeymooner, and while the German-designed Mausers the volunteers called Spanish Hornets slung their lead overhead all day and stung more than a few men he had broken bread with, he regretted that the thumping howitzers and chattery coffee-grinder Gatlings were not enough to set the dons to flight. There were always mules dragging caissons about, men shouting, heliographs flashing in the hills. And there was always twilight work to do.

Gifted, he knew, with the hunter's eye, he accepted the avenger's role but never relished it. "Honeymooner." "The Last Word." "Goodnight, Irene." He would perch in a lush mangrove tree, sometimes with a spotter, usually solitary. He'd scan the enemy position and hope for a prime target, on the best occasions a quirt-switching horseman posting sentries or some other Garlic conspicuous with his flashy ornaments and the cockerel strut of an officer. At first, his work vacillated between ineffective and lucky, hit-or-miss, but at least a startling noise that kept the Spaniards guessing and slinking about behind knolls or their makeshift barricades. He figured he was at least providing their camp tarts a good reason to stay home. As he learned to allow for wind and the drop of bullets at five hundred yards or more over irregular terrain, he mastered the tight weave of stillness and motion and gradually became more than a rude gesture toward the enemy. Patience and precision became second nature to him, and in position above the ground, as now, wholly focused, he always felt on the threshold of something, an understanding, that almost but never quite clarified. As if he were almost allowed to glimpse the dark heart of life shining, but it evaded him each time, its secret safe.

Some of his men had claimed to keep count of his successes, but it was guesswork, at best. And even after he emerged as a valuable weapon, holding the Garlics low and skittish near sunset and even beyond, it afforded him little satisfaction, for though he knew even the preachers made wartime exceptions to the sixth "Thou Shalt Not," he was never quite certain his own spirit could be rescued after such a vocation. To bring sudden death to an officer was one thing, but a man who was running a message, setting a listening post, relieving himself or even bringing water to his wounded companions – what kind of calling was this? On whose behalf, really? Better to work at capture and prevention, to be the agent of order and an inspiration to good behavior. "Sheriff" – old Jay Johnson had told him it was originally "shire reeve," back in England, a kind of warden. But the long-time jailer had added, laughing, "Back then, folks from the village was called 'villains.' Fair measure of truth in that, but don't put it to the test."

Waiting for the cat to sense the baited snare, Sherburne allowed his mind to wander forward to next week, and he realized he could tell his wife about the assignations, and as Susan's church friend, Adair would no doubt express sympathy, defend her and offer alternative explanations. Perhaps she even knew the truth already and would start in on the damaging side-effects of his occupation. He didn't want to vex her any further and would at least hope for an obvious, blameless explanation to echo clear as a dinner bell in winter. Innocence, indecency – it could go either way, but his years behind the badge had taught him to expect the worst.

Despite his own professional reservations, he knew his wife shared valuable confidences with other women which the curious eye of the law was incapable of penetrating. Incapable and ineligible. Maybe he was growing blind to decency. And Adair had her own code of discretion, what she felt free to repeat and what not. Sometimes he wished he could see deeper into her purposes, her own secrets, but there were shadows there, too. For now, he only yearned to suspend speculation, just as he wished there had been no cold words between them before he tightened Vester's girth, swung into the saddle and called back, "Three days, at the worst."

What the field glasses had revealed was a curious regimen: two people meeting in secret for no obvious reason. It could not be mere discretion, he reckoned, but what his logic always narrowed to was the pointed question: "Since when?" The timing was awkward and looked bad. In a few days he might have to pound at the glass-paneled front door of Bluebell Farm, stand there pinching his hat brim and apologizing as he asked – through the transparent camouflage of official concern – personal questions, including testament and insurance inquiries, additional details of the unfortunate day. He certainly hoped he could avoid alluding to the clandestine meetings. And if he consulted Judge Eaton in confidence, he would likely shake his head and suggest that Sherburne wait, allow an appropriate interval for the orthodox commitment to grief, privacy, the solitary inventory of the soul. Although he understood such considerations, his badge did not always allow him to be civil. And the soul was not his responsibility, though it would not be denied, showing up even at the tag-end of capital sentences – "and may God have mercy on your soul." His right hand began to stiffen with the chill, and as he surveyed the thirty-five yards between his perch and the exhausted whitetail, he flexed each finger, considered slipping on the second glove, then tried to distract himself again with thoughts of setting ambushes in Cuba. Regrets, as well, even after two decades.

But his witnessing could not be denied or left unexplored. He must trace down the invisible strands before any open interrogation or, ultimately, maybe – though he hoped not – accusation. Meanwhile, other, less direct, less official inquiries would have to be pursued. There it was again – *pursuit*. But it was his livelihood and responsibility, and if he moved obliquely – in turning social conversations to the subject of Susan Nevers, feigning neighborly concern – he had better be right, as a general uneasiness could arise, and then rumor would ride the wind to her door and seep over the threshold with every gust. God help her if she was guilty or, almost worse, just unable to allay new suspicions with dispatch. And the liaison with Reevis, a man who never quite mixed and seemed to harbor secrets – that drew the bowstring even tighter.

His attention to the deer ruse had begun to flag, but then the animal grew once again agitated and renewed its panic bleat, as if the very air were tightening about it. He felt secure in his lethal perch, dressed mostly in skins himself and smelling of grass and earth, animal grease and stillness. He would be invisible to the big cat, obligated now only to silence and a steady aim. No judgment here, just mechanical elimination of an unquestionable threat. He could feel the approach, the prelude to those tight seconds a hunter would work for days to open the door for. And when it happened, even great noise would issue with a hush, like a whisper.

He fingered the magazine and receiver, knowing the flat-shooting Norwegian weapon was shunned by most hunters for its lack of punch. From all his arsenal, he had chosen it for the silky smooth action, as he might need to spend two rounds here, three. And maybe there was a tinge of nostalgia for youth and Cuba, the bright birds and unerring eyes. He adjusted the makeshift sling grapevined around his arm and steadied his grip.

And the lion would have a reek about it when it came, the result of wallowing in entrails, the unmistakable breath of the single-minded carnivore. The smell would perhaps serve advance notice, if Sherburne could stay alert, as the crisis approached, and he would have to sweep aside all speculation and soul-searching, narrow the world to one impulse, instinct, trajectory. And it would be as if he not so much launched the bullet, but released it from where his will was holding it in check. If he didn't err, the lead would veer just a little but end up exactly where it was meant to be. It was only in such simple deeds that you got anything resembling purity anymore, and he had long ago learned to embrace and savor the untarnished acts where you could find them.

As his kinsmen had for ages in wars and, word was, feuds, he had done this before, and on the Spanish island he had been an assassin operating with his regiment's communal endorsement. His commander's blessing had been conveyed directly by the chaplain, who mentioned the Spanish tyranny and their vicious attack on American sailors, saying that this kind of killing was a just retribution and would be forgiven. "Terrible swift sword." It was, he thought, war after all, even if a trumped-up one played out for the profiteers and thrill seekers like Hearst. More to the point, he was saving his messmates' lives. That did not prevent the faces of his victims – less remembered than imagined – from rising before him on the verge or from the depths of sleep, their faces torn and bleeding, their bloody mouths open as if to scream. More than once Adair had shaken him awake, saying something like, "Hush, Blaine, it's nothing, it's fine. You're home now. Sleep, my love."

Down in the swamps with the reptiles and fever, he had nothing to do with the financial barons who had worked up the populace with banners and headlines and "Remember the Maine," offering enlistment bounties, whipping on the throng, converting legions of previously-stolid Christian women to something akin to Valkyries. Young yet and smitten but rebuffed by a too-elusive Adair who still had not made up her mind about him, he had signed up for the volunteer cavalry in jet black ink and chased it with white whiskey. Back-slapping and "Good lad" all around, but blood had followed, including some of his own, and though he would eventually receive a medal, by the time they finished training and landed on the fragrant but desperate island, he had already been convinced the devil's hand was in it, and in this unfinished business below, as well. Shock would ripple through the Lexington sewing circles and ambeer spit seminars on the memorial park's long bench where the Neversweats yarned and analyzed and passed judgment like so many Solomons as they whittled. Tundridge and Munger, McClung, the Bristow twins, Barger. And in other venues, all their wives and daughters. After he killed the cat on the mountain, he might eventually have to encourage his deputies – both sworn and those others, unofficial and self-appointed – to lure anyone in town old enough to fasten their own buttons to exercise some thought: Why are those two up there amid the sheers and scree, the sleek widow and the rusty-haired foreman, meeting like spies or thieves on the very border of the tamed world? He would learn the answer, for if his methods were not always orthodox, they usually bore fruit.

It was the almost abrupt blooming of the moon that snapped him back when a cloud moved. A bright battered pan radiating its silver above the eastern outcrop, a common thing transforming the dying landscape. Sherburne had to smile, for he thought of old Don Quixote, the way that foolish Spanish errant saw the marvelous in the ordinary. The moon was as ordinary as spit, but still had the power to transform everything it touched. The landscape before him, despite his purpose there, was otherworldly and enchanting.

THE PANTHER CAME ON IN A RUSH, like some berserker, yowling huskier than the woman-scream people usually heard at a distance. Out of the dark, "out of nowhere," as the yarners would say, a storm of teeth and claws and sheer muscular bulk at first silvered in the full moon's radiance, all graceful lope and pounce, its weight surely the match of its hunter's, snowy muzzle black-splotched and whiskered, its ink-dipped tail fish-hooking behind. A whirlwind, it ripped the deer's throat away with harrow teeth and slapped the carcass to the ground amid the spraying blood, then mounted the animal and started disemboweling it with its claws like some deranged hunter trying to field-dress the carcass.

He held still and slowly took in a breath. Below was a shocking and haunting sight, the evening's now-bluish luminescence playing on the cat's electric fur, sheen of the spraying blood colorless in the half-light, the sheer skill of the killing, the feline savor of its achievement, almost now resembling play, but done for hunger, done out of necessity. No other reason. That was how Sherburne wanted to see it, and so efficient, it had been as if the cat were concerned that the deer not suffer, another tempting viewpoint his general experience – and the mangle of O'Neill's colt – would not confirm.

Necessity. He exhaled, relaxed, twitched his left eye, as his father had always done. He easily found his personal rhythm. Then the .30-.40 spoke with its old authority – once, twice, again, the bolt and trigger smooth as butter, recoil minimal, the *snicky-snick-snick* hardly audible – and the big problem was solved, question answered. More blood on his own personal account, of course, as the impact threw the panther against the brake in one startled writhe. The first round had struck forward of the near shoulder and would have punched a lung, but the second went through the neck, started tumbling and probably cut the spine, the third in close drill. The barrel scarcely bucked as forty grains of smokeless powder thrust each load forth, and as usual, he had achieved a tight group, even firing faster than most marksmen under range conditions. He still had the eye, the killing gift. When the body, once so lithe and lethal, hit the bark-and-needle-strewn ground, it wrenched in one mad spasm and did not stir again. He was reminded suddenly of his cramping position and the unseasonable cold not just because his blood was pumping more slowly now, but by the old nickname, "Honeymooner," which reached back from his past to send a shiver through his frame. He thought he could smell shit from one, perhaps both of the animals, but the familiar odor of blood thickened the air.

A shroud silence had replaced the brief savagery of the catamount's attack, the deer's final cry and the rifle report. He had not even been aware of the echoes ricocheting across the ridges, and what was left was a soughing wind across the entire landscape with its burn snags, weather-beaten trees and craggy surface. It might also serve as an expression of his gathering dread that the widow's recent behavior might cast shadows on the authenticity of her grief. He couldn't shake the thought. What if she were not akin to the widow in Lamentations who "weepeth sore in the night"? All the searches and deadly questions, a community returned to alarm and sorrow over Nevers, who had been a decent enough neighbor, he supposed, if given to tippling a bit too much on holidays and inflicting his political opinions on the willing and unwilling alike, a fair horseman, a provider, a faultless tenor over the hymn book, even if there had been a strange feel to him, an unnamable coolness behind his laughter. And that would shake into disorder the community, the little world he tried to hold straight and calm like a team in harness. He did not want to consider why this dalliance occupied him so, but no matter how Adair might feel about his peering and prying, there was no use wishing it was not his job to stir the embers. Wish in one hand . . . .

First, however, he had a proven killer to examine, perhaps dispatch, if there was breath or heartbeat. No need for the animal to suffer, as this was less revenge than a kind of husbandry. He smiled wryly at the thought of that word. His troubling anger had been wholly washed away. And a predator on display back in Lexington, perhaps hanging outside the office for a couple of days – if the cold snap deepened the way his read on the moon and the fast clouds suggested was likely – would indeed serve to remind the voters and gossips that their man Sherburne was vigilant and efficient and right there when they were threatened. How fortunate they were. And himself? The persistent speculation: Would he be more content hiring out horses and gigs full time, spending evenings closer to his own threshold? And with less blood on his hands? A gnawing question, but better held for a snowed-in afternoon over a pipe and cider.

The sheriff swung down from his perch and slowly approached the still form of his quarry. Unsnapping the holster, he drew the revolver for insurance, and for a moment he could smell the gun oil and leather as it cleared the holster. He could build a fire now, he thought, before he circled back to his shelter to huddle against the dropping temperature, could have at least the luxury of that venison steak and coffee before setting out in the morning to haul the cat's carcass back to his horse. He should reach the camp by mid-afternoon and hoped the Billford boys were still down there with old Vester, learning patience and how dollars don't just fall off trees, moving the horse to fresh grass each day and not blowing him up with sweet feed. Never mind the pelt and the rest of the meat. He would be wiser just to sever the cat's head, which was about the size of the globe map of earth back in his office, and leave the balance to the birds that would surely begin to circle and thirst by daybreak. Simplify his descent. "Savage," he thought again, remembering another time, another decapitated victim. He wiped that away.

The painter was still in the moonlight, its blunt muzzle now placid, one ear skewed, its dark markings elegant. A male, as he'd guessed, newly full grown, well fed, its palomino hide – just slightly more yellow than a May fawn's coat – mapped with black patches, like someone had tossed the inkpot on him, the chest fur whiter than any nightgown. Its pelage was just beginning to go shaggy with its winter coat, and despite the stench from natural musks and remnants of earlier feedings, anyone would be tempted to stroke it, to pet against the lay of the hair and then with it. Was there a connection, he wondered, between the beauty and menace? He removed his left glove and ran both palms along the bristly pelt, then deeper. It was stiffer than one would guess, but still plush. A tingling ran through his fingers and into his wrists. He could feel it also on the back of his neck. The muscles showed confirmation few horses could rival, the new-moon curve of each talon, the golden-eyed gaze, now frozen and fogging over and heart-stirring, as wild things are when the needs of men bring them to this final sleep. The color of new-cut cedar, the tongue was hanging out the side of its mouth which was filled with an arsenal of teeth white as Sunday china, and a big gout of blood.

He was kneeling, the Krag on a ledge beside him, the pistol on a flat stone within reach. After whacking up a deadfall hickory with his belt knife, he began whittling a dead pine limb for tinder. He was already thinking of tomorrow night, the warmth, fresh milk and peppery mutton, an inch or two of whiskey, the various comforts of Adair's presence. She was yet a handsome woman, angry or not, and so far, always forgiving. Even in his imagination, her countenance glowed and her words sparked. She would appreciate the beauty of the animal's hide but in her own half-secretive way would mourn it. He loved both her sensitive heart and her restraint, and performing his job well, even over her objections, seemed only a part of the way he worked to deserve her.

The knife along the dead bough whicked and whicked. The moon was higher still, its radiance muted by a cloud wisp, and owly sounds shivered up from the valley. He was satisfied at his accuracy and thrift, the converging threads of a careful plan, and as he began to feel a sense of completion and relief, his body's many mechanisms began to slow and settle, for he had not reckoned on, had somehow not even imagined the possibility of the other cat.

Returning the broad blade to its leather, he let his mind relax and wander to sketch a scene: Adair and the widow laughing as the women drank tea from the willowware service, their voices hushed, a tabby across the room batting its yarn ball on the peacock-print carpet. The Sherburnes had made that consolation visit right after the accident, and as the two women sat in the parlor where afternoon light played on the glass bangles of the table lamp, he had spoken briefly with Reevis. The man was not smooth or churchy, not prone to easy exchange, but they smoked together on the bench beside the stable while Reevis continued cleaning a shotgun with a practiced deftness.

"Nice piece."

"A Greener. Don't think it's been tended to regular. Thought I ought to swab it and find some slugs. The lion, you know." He jerked his head in the direction of the highlands where most of the killings had occurred.

Running a patch down one barrel, Reevis claimed he didn't know much about Nevers' fall. His eyes were the dark green of ivy. The smell of the gun oil was sharp and more welcoming to Sherburne than the widow's white china and the scent of oolong tea. He could hear a calf bawling in the byre beyond the rail fence.

"Mrs. Nevers found him, you know. Bad luck. I don't reckon she'll get past that sight for a while. Jeremy and me was up pasture with the cows, Tim and Sasha stretching fence down by the creek. Damn shame. He was a fair man, in his way, Nevers, soft-voiced, not greedy, easy enough to work for. Strange, though, not country at all. Flatlander, I figured, out of place."

Sherburne hadn't given the exchange much thought before. Reevis was the newest of five men who worked the large spread while their employer, who was no farmer by raising or inclination, spent most of his days with pen and blotter, tending merchants' accounts in a cramped office on Henry Street. A Methodist, hail fellow and supporter of orphans, as he had no children of his own. Like Sherburne in that single respect. Reevis was his opposite – rough, decisive, salty but civil, preferring his own company, silent on the subject of his past. He might have seen thirty-five years. The sheriff had from the beginning thought him a man to be trusted with even complicated work, but not one to be enjoyed or missed in his absence. Yet their conversation over the shotgun had left him uneasy in an indefinable way.

They spoke further, mostly about horses, the likelihood of using draft animals with trolleys, what the fall hay crop had been like.

HEARING THE RUSTLE AND SNARL, he whirled just in time to raise his free arm in front of his throat, and the she-cat was on him, his left forearm in the animal's maw, the fangs finding purchase as the powerful jaw began to tighten. He felt the teeth as flames, despite the protection afforded by his cowhide coat, wool sweater and union suit. He pitched over backwards, slinging the animal, slapping its nose while kicking out and doing some damage with the heavy boots, and as the cat spun loose, scrambling for traction, he felt his arm torn and knew the blood was coming. Surprised, all he had going now was the surge of adrenalin, the habit of combat and survival, decades of discipline settled into instinct. And the knife.

For a moment they were both crouching, glaring into each other's eyes. Even in the moonlight, Sherburne could see that one was the predictable yellow fire, while the other showed a cold silver, probably blind from some previous engagement, and he figured this was the mate, younger, sleeker, maybe a hundred pounds, half his own size. So much for his "painter mind." So much for his cunning and finesse. His hurt left arm again shielding his throat, he reached across his body and unsheathed the knife in one sweeping motion, rotating his wrist as he did so but knowing it didn't mean to an animal what it would to a man. The cat in a patch of dry guinea grass licked its chops, which were a touch wet with Sherburne's blood, then emitted a raspy hiss and gathered its force for another lunge, and the only thought Sherburne could muster that would abide words was "like the storybook's damn ape man himself." The black lips parted, and the thing seemed almost to be grinning.

He flourished his blade, feinted forward with the left side of his body, and as the cat brought forth a molten growl and leaped, he answered with a roar and pulled back in a pivot, sliding the left leg rearward, feeling not pain so much as blunt impact when the airborne panther's shoulder struck him, spun him almost off balance but swinging his body exactly where he wanted to be. He was astraddle the thing, managing to grip its left ear briefly with his hurt hand as he stabbed in a windmill motion with all the force of his right arm and shoulder, leaving the knife up to its hilt in the animal's neck as it bucked him off and whirled away.

It could have been a foolish choice, leaving the knife lodged in his attacker, as the animal was going now on its own surge of survival impulses, probably oblivious to pain, pulling out of its tumble just as it struck the trunk of a lone sweetgum sapling the sheriff had noticed earlier in the twilight, many of its limbs still ablaze with leaf sugars.

It might have been his farewell mistake, letting go the knife, except that he knew where the handgun lay and scrabbled the two yards toward it, rolling over roots and stones as he clutched for the plow grip, thumbing back the high spur hammer even before his finger was inside the trigger guard, and the cat was charging again, straight at him, all bound and fury, not even limping from the knife, which must, from the blood slobber, have struck its bellows. Despite that, it shrieked like a demon, and its open jaws showed teeth nature had perfected for one purpose.

Then the Peacemaker boomed and boomed just inches from Sherburne's ear, the barrel pointing vaguely at the blur, nothing he could call aim, and the roar of it was awful, but not disconcerting enough to keep him from rolling again, this time toward the Krag, or so he hoped. He didn't get there before the world became only that echo resounding off the surrounding rocks to thunder against his ear drums, and then there was nothing but moonglare followed by a rushing eclipse and then nothing at all, a kind of submarine, drifting nothingness articulated only by the taste of blood.

As he floated with the current, images formed and altered and vanished – the Lord God bird in a tropical tree with its beak racketing like a crank gun, pale blue walls ringed with other dancers as he whirled just inches away from Adair's face, the veil pulled back over her hair; then the ashen remains of the Bellew house and the figure of Red Coat leveling a lever gun at him across the frozen hillside. He felt himself trying to reach out to these, and to his father's living face, the rogue bear back in Carolina, the Melungeon's greasy eyes, a man who might be Reevis and then the girl Ina Grove in her thin shift, phantomed up from years back, the come-hither written all over her face. He tried to reach out, but then there was a shower of stars and the blank blackness again, not even the rippling echo of the Colt or a metallic sting on the tongue.

Then somewhere in the darkness he saw himself at a distance, bending over the forge, his teeth clenched as tight as the tongs that held a new shoe steady on the anvil, the farrier's swage hammer rising and falling onto white-hot metal, sparks flying in every direction, his old bones shivering with each impact of iron ringing iron. The shoe plunged into the bucket, but he was somehow no longer there to hear the hiss and see the steam ghost up. Draft horses were nickering and stomping in a paddock somewhere, and then he saw a strung-out herd of saddle mounts moving in middle distance, some prancing, others merely slinking along. Some in the procession he knew – Vester himself, Dandy, Adair's feisty Marge, his father's old, long-dead Jessup gelding, and others he'd shod or curried, bought at auction, stroked or spoken to on the street, harnessed, chased, dropped with a mercy shot in the dead field beyond Woods Creek. Most seemed oblivious to his presence, but a few turned their heads to stare at him, then gestured with their muzzles, as if summoning. Then for a long spell there was only slick darkness, the close-up ebony depth and simple smell of a worked plow horse cooling down. Then straw, the color of it, brassy and sudden, panther color turning shimmery as he began to regain his senses.

The sunlight pressed upon his eyelids, and it took him a moment to realize this was not yet his first glimpse of the hereafter's famous Fiddler's Green, but the sun just edging over the eastern heights with their sawblade silhouette of pines and not yet obscured by the huge dark mass of clouds directly overhead. His next thought, even before opening his eyes or trying to move, even before registering the dampness and chill, was, "How did I miss it? A brace, a damn mated pair."

He was on his back, cold, stiff on the stony ground, with waves of pain beginning to ripple through him. Left arm throbbing under the numbness, he knew he had been gashed and bruised. The acute coppery tang of blood coated his mouth. Wasn't this the moment to hear angel voices, to see the glimmer of their wings? And then the dreaded Judgment? He took a deep breath and noticed that everything was shining with the thinnest dusting of white. Orion was long gone, but the sky had opened a little just recently, perhaps right on the verge of dawn, and sifted down a tithe of snow. He was lying in a patch of turkey-footed sassafras, and a brace of sparrows was pecking about, so close they must have trusted him to remain a feature of the earth. Looking through the dappled ambers of thinning beech leaves, he could see the red flags of the sweetgum just stirring with a breeze, and that was when he felt the need to survey the damage done all around.

The panthers were rigid, snow-dusted and unreal in their unthreatening stillness. Colt Killer and Silver Eye. They might have been harmless pets, though huge ones, cats built to the scale of ancient wolf dogs. They lay twenty feet apart, the female in a twisted posture, as if she had writhed in anguish and died slowly. It took only seconds for Sherburne to race through the previous evening's events, and when he finally took in a big breath, the resultant stabbing pain signaled broken ribs. He was afraid to check the damage to his arm, and all the old aches he had lugged up the mountain with him began to assert themselves and converge like a straggle of random guilts forming a covey. Touching the stubbly skin along his jaw, he felt a shaggy, wolfish, wounded thing and knew he needed to muster his resources. As he crawled about the copse, scattering sparrows and perched crows as he went, he located his cap, weapons and haversack under the white dust but then grew dizzy and had to lean against a hemlock trunk to collect himself. His breath was coming in stubborn stitches, while a warm feeling in his left forearm told him that, under the ripped sleeves, his wounds were leaking, and though moving about wouldn't help that situation, he would have plenty of movement ahead of him, if he meant to survive.

He purposefully called up the image of his wife and addressed her aloud, "I don't know, Addie honey. I'm hurt, maybe pretty bad, but I'm still here, still casting a shadow, darling, and you were right again. I should have paid heed." For a moment, as he squinted toward the slanting light, he almost thought he could see her, but the figure thinned and thinned until it vanished, leaving him shaken and thinking of the long-perished Carson woman, of the Hostetter girl and then of Ina. As he fought that image off, his sight turned blurry again, and as he slumped over, he dropped into a sleep.

Sherburne woke to a muted sun, dove-colored clouds twisting across the canopy. He fished his father's railroad watch from his coat pocket and, seeing that the glass was cracked, held it to his ear: steady as a heart. Turning it in the light, he could see it was almost half past noon, but he was working on wild time now – no symmetry, no predictability, just instinct and risk.

He might make it, though, an old rawbuckle like him. He'd survived blood loss and bad scrapes before. Broken bones, mean climate, deprivation, remorse and sorrow. It was all subject to luck, grit, how your account with the Almighty stood. The boys and horses were camped seven, eight miles away as the crow flies, but he was one-winged now, and no crow, anyhow. Besides, climbing distance was different. Scenes of the three days' clamber and circle and strain to ascend flashed before him, and gravity would be as much a foe as an ally on the return.

He'd been lost and wounded in the Moreno Heights just after Kettle Hill. Circling a Garlic mule train all noisy with rattle and bray and Spanish voices shrilling, he was keeping his distance, biding his time, looking for a useful target. Every so often, the nervous escorts would volley off into the woods in a random direction for no apparent reason, and when one bullet ripped him in the thigh as he kneeled behind a stump, he had fallen and, as he was about to rise, blacked out. When he came to, he was sweating profusely, worse than could be explained by the merciless weather or the leaves he must have at some point gathered to cover himself. The only noises then were bright birds and monkeys in the canopy – no more mules or maniacs. He thought, "This kind of luck can only be punishment," but then decided not to be judged. He'd poured his rum ration on the wound, bound it and debated what to do, half wishing he had stayed back in Virginia, trading and renting horses, currying and feeding and exercising gentlemen's leisure beasts. He would have settled for hammering hoops and binding carriage wheels or levering the spoke dog, swabbing axles with the skunky-smelling grease. Even back in those days, it had been Adair – his memory and his frustrated desire for her – he locked his mind on, and when he realized he was too weak to walk out, Sherburne weighed his choices and started a signal fire, without knowing if the Volunteers, friendly partisans or the Spanish would see it first. If the Garlics took you, he knew, you'd likely find a meaning to "rough rider" the flag wavers never imagined. But he'd been lucky that time: the fever that gripped him was not malaria, the nearest troops were "Yanks," as the Cubanos called them all, not aware of the history on that word. Scouts from a nearby village had seen the smoke and ran to report to the column. He'd never been so happy to be called a Yankee.

Since there were no enemy troops to consider, it would be a fire again today. Common wisdom said to stay put and assume someone would raise a scouring party, but who would see smoke today and think anything of it other than "hunters" or "freak lightning." He couldn't trust to the slow machinery of the inevitable search, even if he had told everyone "three days, maximum." The clouds seemed to suggest another judgment coming, nothing like the tentative sprinkle of the night before, and the temperature was nowhere near as mild as the past couple of days. If wrath was to be visited upon the mountain from above, he reckoned he was by now a deserving recipient, considering the ever-growing imbalance between his best intentions and his results. That didn't mean he was resigned.

A QUICK INVENTORY REMINDED HIM that provisions were not the issue. He had weapons and ammunition, God's-a-plenty of fresh meat and some natural overhang shelter. His two-quart canteen was half full, but if there was to be snow, the problem would not be water but dry wood. Northward, clouds were gathering. He had to face the real dilemma: the nature and extent of his injuries, the work to be done. Then it struck him. If Susan Nevers and Vic Reevis kept another rendezvous today, despite threatening weather, they were his best hope. Extensive as his trek had been, it had drawn him closest to their hideaway. He knew he lacked the strength to climb the steep thirty or forty feet to the crest, so he'd have to guess their appointment by the previous ones and build his fire behind the promontory. He had maybe four hours to get good smoke rising, and he could attract their attention to it with gunfire. Given the Colt and the Krag, he could S-O-S – three quick pistol shots, three slower, deeper ones from the rifle, then the Colt again. He had always appreciated the symmetry of the message, and if most translated it "Save Our Ship," he had always been of the opinion that the last word in the spell should be "souls," though his late deputy Byron had offered "our shit."

Given the nature of the pair's business at the line shack, there was the possibility they wouldn't respond. Would they make tracks in the other direction to protect themselves? How crucial did they imagine the secrecy was to their own survival? Maybe he was about to find out.

Sherburne was damp from both inside and out, sweat and weather. Some blood. He was feeling woozy with both hunger and the rejection of it, and a wave of nausea frequently shook and stunned him. More inventory: his knife? He rolled Silver Eye over and found the tool's handle still protruding, the buckhorn grip dark with dried blood but intact. He had to push away with a foot against the panther to unwedge it, but it finally slipped out undamaged. That was good. Suddenly, a shiver of panic shot through him, and he began to feel about in his pockets, drawing more air into his lungs as he labored. Flask, tobacco, shells for the Krag, the wallet-fold with a studio print of Adair in profile, cameo-still, her lips and cheeks watercolored pink. His hands fluttered over his clothes, self-frisking, his blood rushing. A whistle, a pen knife, the compass. . . . Then he exhaled with relief. The damaged ribs responded with a blazing pain, but the twine-wrapped flint and steel were in his trouser pocket, so he would at least have sparks.

Knowing this was not the time to save his strength for later, he pulled himself to his feet. This was the infamous "later" he'd often heard of and referred to himself. One of his father's gems was: "When you've walked yourself all the way to the middle of Hell, keep going." He was walking. After an hour of gathering conchy logs and small branches and dragging them, forced to pause with near-alarming frequency, he began to pull together leaves and moss, accumulating them like a field mouse planning a new nest. So much of it was not dry enough to sustain an infant flame. He had to sort and winnow. Twigs, rattle weeds, bark he prized off a strong oak and a pine. Their juices were sucked back for the winter, but they were still more timber than tinder. Then he remembered the checkerback of the evening before and, looking up instead of down, surveyed the tree crowns until he found, just eighty or so feet away, the riddled hickory the bird had been hunting beetles in. Working his knife into it, twisting the blade despite the discomfort in his chest, he was able to free huge slabs of dead wood. In fifteen minutes, the whole thirty feet of it crashed down, breaking into useful sections. For a spell, he couldn't keep standing either.

It was cold enough that he knew it wouldn't be rain, but the clouds promised something. Either snow or sleet. And he still hadn't found good shelter or managed to cut and draw over the pine boughs he'd need for smoke. No hope to get back up to his tree stand. It was getting on toward three, and Sherburne realized he'd come to a fork in the path. He could invest all his industry, until he gave out, in the fire scheme, or he could secure a place to be out of the weather overnight. It was a gamble either way. Fire and no shelter, perhaps no one would see the smoke, and he'd be exposed to the night's offerings, which might include something that sniffed blood. He could bid a final farewell to Orion, visible or not. Shelter and no fire more than maybe a meager stick tepee in front of where he chose to den up, and the sky might storm hard, temperature plummet. They'd just find him in a few days, iced over in a posture somewhere between the womb crouch and prayer. And he couldn't delay and debate; he had to roll the dice.

Maybe this was what he'd really come up from Carolina all those years ago – almost forty now? – to find out. God knows, he'd had plenty of chances to experiment already, but he still didn't know: Am I an eggs-all-in-one-basket man, one toss of the bones, or do I trust to slow good fortune, the chance of little sips of luck adding up? Then he remembered his father by the cow barn looking over at him one evening as Venus sparkled: "Doesn't it seem to you, Blaine, that the heart of boldness is always caution? That a man gathers and plans and works steady as an ant, just so that he can feel strong and ready when the time comes to jump?" Then he'd slung a clot of dried cow dung his son hadn't seen in the gloaming light right at the boy's crotch as he shouted, "Jump!"

Standing again, he was dizzy, and it took a minute to be sure of his stability. Somewhere in the brush a buck snorted and thrashed away. When Sherburne tried to raise his right arm, he couldn't get it higher than the shoulder, and even that achievement extracted a toll. The pain shot through him like barbed wire, and he retched, felt and tasted the bile rising, but he had to hawk hard to clear it out. More pain. He looked around at the incline to the south, the uphill hardwoods and spruce approaching the rim and stubbornly rooted in scree, the slashed carcass of the deer – he noticed it was too cold to draw any curious flies, but the reaper birds were already overhead, six of them circling. They'd probably counted three down and one to go, biding their time, harnessing their glee, feeding on his obvious fatigue. His father had always called their figure "the black rose." It might signal a cow or horse down in the fields, half a possum left by the fox, and back in the wars, his father's and his own, it had meant more. Or perhaps not more, depending on your scale. The Bible's system said only men had souls, and right now he wished to trust its authority in many things. He drew the knife then and tested his right wrist. Still supple, if a little reluctant with the rheumatism and the situation.

A story he'd heard or read reminded him not to plan his signal under any fir bough, as they have a way of holding snow until they can ruin you with it, so he settled on a flat place between two bare and high-limbed hardwoods to build his beacon. Details, he kept thinking. Only details would save his own beloved from widow's weeds.

It was just after four when he strained to hold the steel still with his left fingers. He hadn't calculated that it takes two mobile hands to strike a fire, and he was rapidly becoming a one-wing. His loose twist of tinder was ready, combustibles in graduated sizes nearby, the tepee of sticks ready to take a little flame, whole branches in position to topple when the fire had some zeal to it. Then the greenery, gathered into a heap like desperate Yule ornaments. Guns loaded – the Colt with six beans in the wheel – everything ready, but he couldn't get enough force, enough friction with the glancing strike to shoot out the little stars that could inspire his makeshift sculpture to become a pyre. He remembered knapping quartz arrowheads as a boy, the nicked chips often accompanied by sparks. As his fingers grew stiffer and bruised, he could feel the seep of blood from the cuts on his arm, though he'd bound them even tighter an hour ago. He considered using the pistol flash to start up, but that was no guarantee, and he didn't want to frighten off the lovers. They had to hear the whole code suddenly, with no preface, if this strategy had much chance of success. If it were not hare-brained and doomed from the first. Examination proved his surfaces were clean and dry, the steel rough for friction. Breathe slow, as if taking a shot. Squint and get the rhythm. Now try again.

Twelve strokes later, the loose weave of grasses, leaves and dry vines no bigger than a baseball began to smoke, and he leaned forward, kneeling over it almost worshipfully as he blew softly, steady, more vigorously as an orchid of flame appeared at the center of the ball. When he saw the brightness and smelled it, his eyes dampened, but he was down beneath the wind. Relief, maybe, hope. Knee-walking, almost like a drunk man, he covered the four feet to the lean-to of sticks and reached over, spilling the now-crackling ball into the center of his pile, and the faint smoke rose, flames licked and twisted, cracked like a choir snapping their fingers. As the whole assembly kindled, a squirrel tail of smoke rose and caught the wind, ascended further, as if aiming to join the still-circling carrion birds, some of which had tried their luck already, only to be met by his shouts and tossed chips of shale.

Half an hour, and he was beaten, winded, leaning against the sweetgum, watching the fir smoke billow and waver. The wind was lazy enough to allow the column to tower, and he fetched out the watch again. It was time for the shots, a measured volley. Enough bullets for a firing squad, enough to bring down the biggest animal that walked the earth, even in the Tarzan novel. He had the barrel of the Krag clamped between his feet, aimed where the loads wouldn't strike stone and come back to him. The Peacemaker was at his side. The bruises to his side and shoulder throbbed, and he could imagine the sickening-colored auras radiating outward like the shock waves of an explosion.

Just two more things, he thought, and I know how to do them. Discharge my weapons, and wait. Pray, too, I guess. Three. But I'm unaccustomed to such a peculiar target, aiming to be heard by people I'm beginning to think may have conspired to kill a neighbor for – what? love? lust? profit? And I need to draw them to me. Praying for exactly what, I can't say. Rescue, maybe. Luck or Mercy. Just another round of the passing of the cup – Thy will be done.

If the trysters had struck one of those many varieties of snags, inevitable but unpredictable in matters of the heart, and decided not to venture out, he would have to contrive a long-range plan. The sky had grown still darker, and the kettle of buzzards now numbered nine. Even in this weather, they would have earth-bound rivals, some not content to wait for the meat to spoil. Spindrift began to blow by, snags of new-sheared wool. The snow had started. He dragged a large green bough over the fire to increase the signal's visibility, murmured "deliver us from evil" and fired his sequence – three, three and three – the intervals shaping a telegraphic rhythm. A triple Trinity, he thought. Maybe that was no accident. Sailors are a superstitious lot. Peril will whet your appetite for divine interference. Leaning against a tree, he slid further down, understanding only for a moment the toll of pulling the triggers and working the Krag's action. He wanted to reload and managed only to thumb three new bullets into the revolver's loading gate before his head nodded to the side. This time, the only dream images were a vague storm, dark winds in a dark sky, whorls like the print of a thumb.

TOO WEAK TO OPEN HIS EYES, he could hear the voice but could not separate the words, which came to him as a freshet of gibberish.

Then "painter" and "lucky" registered, though overall it still didn't much signify. He was no longer cold and could not see the sky. He needed to surface and understand, but something gently forceful was pulling him down, and no sooner did he think "not again" than he went limp and surrendered to it.

Next time he woke, Sherburne shuddered to attention, managing to open his heavy eyes – a seam, a chink, then full wide. It was dark around him, blurry and pulsing, but threads of flame rose and quavered, smoke smell, the sharp scent of coffee.

"You gave me a fright that time, Mr. Sheriff. Thought I'd lost you sure."

The pains seemed not to be originating in his side and arm, his neck and knees, but instead appeared to be going to them, radiating from his very center. Feeling wrappings constricting his chest and arm, he rolled to the right a bit to see the man who was kneeling beside him and supporting his weight, in part, on a two-barreled Greener, its butt on the ground, the polished barrels shining. The man's hat bore the pinched crown of a Rough Rider, but it was black, and a shock of fringe stuck out, nearly as red as a woodpecker's crest. The eyes were spruce green and shining.

"Don't strain yourself, my friend. You're weak as water."

The voice was familiar enough, but he couldn't place it. A little husky, but it couldn't be Colonel Roosevelt, Sherburne reasoned, or his father, both throaty voices. Then he said, "Addie." Though he knew that was even farther from the target, it was a soothing word which he uttered like a charm, a benchmark to start from. He had no idea where he was, but he recognized the scratchy feel of his army blanket under his chin, and scanning about, he realized they were both under some sort of cave or canopy. The ground outside was white, and when he noticed the man's shearling jacket, he had a fleeting thought – the snow was coming from that fleece, so it wasn't snow but a shearing yard.

"Everything's sigodlin. I must be drunk."

"It ain't what's got into you so much as what's flowed out. There's blood all over this table of rock. Some whitetail, some devil cat – so there was two of them – and I'd wager more than a drib and drabble is lawman's blood."

Then he understood it was Reevis. He was gaining his bearings, and though uneasy strangers might call him "Law," he had seen to it that most local people addressed him as "Sheriff" or, as his father had been, "Sherburne." "Blaine" to Addie, of course, but more than once, especially after all those years in the proximity of discharging firearms, he had heard it as "blame." In his few contacts with Reevis the term "lawman" had come up a couple of times. The choice, he had once thought, had a shifty feel to it. And there was the defiant-seeming red hair. The tabby cat eyes.

"How did you . . . ?"

"You know the answer to that one." He reached his shotgun – the Nevers's – further under the canopy and lay it there carefully, then swiveled around to fetch something from the fire.

"Coffee?" It was the dented cup from Sherburne's own kit.

"Much obliged."

"It was really smart, Mr. Sheriff, something you must pick up in lawman school – the smoke and the Morse. Wind was right, greenwood smoke was hard to miss. Anyone in range of eye and ear would take the meaning, but how did you figure somebody to be in range out here in the beyonds, or did you just fling out a forlorn hope?"

Sherburne kept the speckleware cup tilted and his eyes turned down toward it while he cleared his head enough to fashion an answer. He didn't want to have this discussion just now, as the man had either just saved his life or was trying to decide whether or not to do so.

"You say your prayers and hope God's got His ears open." When he breathed deeply, his ribs seemed to be shouting out. "I suppose He did this time and sent you, but how in Job's name did He trick you into being in the area. Strays? Hunting?"

"Man's got to get about now and then, see to the edges of things. And what with the big cat raiding so close to farms, it's not a bad idea to ranger out and check for stock, spread your scent along the fenceline. Kind of like a wild thing setting pissing stations: No trespass."

The effort to work through the words and assess motives was too much for Sherburne, and the pain all along his left side was rioting.

"How bad is it, my arm?"

"I hope the baseball ain't the highlight of a church picnic for you. You're a righty, I'd conjecture, so that's good." He reached for the cup, swung back around to the fire and refilled it, then took a long drink himself. "Glad you carry the good stuff, though I appreciate a little cube sugar myself."

This was fencing, and Sherburne's suspicions were increasing.

"How bad exactly?"

Reevis managed a stoic smile. "I'm no shakes at sawboning, but I'd say you've little danger of losing its use. Some thew damage, a couple of streaks ripped out leaving a kerf I don't think doctor science can replace. Be a hell of a scar. No bonebreak, though. Can you raise it?"

He could, a little, and said so.

"You're a tough old owl for a lawman, I'll give you that. Not one of those swivel-seat constables." Sherburne could not mistake the contempt in Reevis' tone, and he seemed at no pains to conceal it.

"You said blood." He was feeling dizzy again but fought back the lure of the depths. "Any idea how much is missing?"

"Hard to say. Again, I'm no nurse. You're pale as a cloud. If I could just build up a shed over you, feed you catamount stew and tend your miseries, in a week or thereabout you could walk out of here whistling "Dixie" without me. But it's been storming, and more to come, so that ain't an option. I don't speck you was planning to winter up here to keep an eye on the valley, though?"

"Then how will you get me down?" The snow was coming harder now, the wind blowing even into the shelter fit to snuff any candles. He watched the erratic fire reflected in Reevis' eyes and tried to remember what stain made the Bible's traveling Samaritan an unlikely deliverer. The man shifted and adjusted a jimmyrigged panel of canvas, pulling it between himself and the weather, and the sheriff could see that his own shelter had provided some of the material, as well as his slicker.

"I sent somebody down to Bluebell. There's a telephone gadget back at the farm. Works most days, and I figured if a body was up here in distress, likely there was more than one man would have the hands for." He turned his head toward the fire, but Sherburne could detect a wry look on his deliverer's face, as if the entire predicament offered some amusement. "And I'm up to these steeps now on the same kind of mare you rode."

It took Sherburne a moment to catch it – "shank's mare." "Yes. Fine. Thank you. Did I thank you yet?"

"Good as." He reached and tossed some sticks onto the fire.

"So you and one of the other boys were scouting the perimeter? That was a stroke of luck for me." He hadn't planned to push the question, but it was second nature to keep going.

"Nearbout. Not exactly." He paused. His normally ruddy face was scarlet in the firelight. "That's what we've got to parley on, Mr. Sheriff. It was Susan I sent back."

"Susan?"

"The widow Nevers."

"I see." He tried to make his face suggest that he didn't, but even in the unstable light Reevis could see his eyes, and the farmhand wasn't anybody's fool.

"You do and you don't. That's what worries me. It would come a surprise to ary a soul, me being a roughcut hand and Susan so fine-sifted, respectable, a schoolteacher before Nevers, you know." His eyes narrowed, and he clasped his palms together before him, squeezing and flexing his fingers, but not really in a warming motion. The wind kicked up again, and the canvas shook, one loose corner snapping like an unmoored sail. A dozen seconds passed like what seemed to Sherburne time enough to harness a team.

"None of my business, I suppose," Sherburne said finally.

"How long you been following that old Indian path along the crest? Couple of days?"

"About. Maybe Tutelos, but Monacan's the best bet. Likely they hunted up this far."

Reevis pointed to the field glasses in their case where it lay close to the sheriff's head. "Powerful-looking scopes there, so I expect you've seen what goes on hereabouts."

No moon, the blowing snow – dark was closing in around the two men, and the fire had subsided, whispered that it needed to be fed. Sherburne flexed his muscles – arm and legs, solar plexus, neck. He was weaker than he could remember in years, perhaps not helpless, but nearly so.

"You and Susan Nevers were riding together yesterday, down by Little Bird Run. I figured it to be about cows."

As Reevis leaned over to grab a handful of stripped branches, he shook his head. "No, you didn't."

They were looking hard into each other's eyes, and Sherburne noted how large and unruly the man's rusty-looking eyebrows here.

"Lawmen don't work that way. They grab up everybody and everything in their mind, then shake them around like gambling cubes. What falls free is let go, the rest squeezed hard, sniffed, tasted, bit open and looked into, always sussing around for secrets.

"I expect you can make the bridge. Susan's husband dead in a unusual work accident, then her and a hired man rough as a cob start to courting. Folks wonder . . . ."

When Sherburne tried to interrupt and say that no innocent person had any reason to fret over his attention, his benefactor held up a palm to halt him and pushed on.

"No, they don't wonder. They opinion. They hold you up to the darkness, pretending it's light, and they scan you up and down, and if you're a plain man like me, a hireling with not much more than his horse and tools and rig to vouch for him, they start the whisper and the glaring." He picked up a stick and began to scratch lightly with it in the leaf litter. "Susan wouldn't abide it well. We drew out a plan – me to collect my earnings and pull up stakes soon, move on, maybe down to Danville, her to follow after a spell, leasing out Bluebell – it's a going concern – then selling it off later. She could teach; I could cow or sawyer. Frame up houses if I had to. Everything slow and easy."

Faltering again, as a rib seemed almost to be stabbing him, the sheriff lay back on his bed of leaves and needles, the colors appropriate to his bruised skin flaring before his eyes. "I've got to sleep, got to go back."

"You do that."

Eyes shut, in three minutes he grew completely still, but for his chest rising and falling with nearly even breaths. He gave all the appearance of sleep, but he was playacting, as awake as when aiming at the big catamount, his pulse pounding in his ears. The thought of renewed jeopardy kept the fire in his mind jumping, and whether due to his injuries, the faint light in the tent or Reevis' own way of circling in, he could not get a fix on his subject, what thorns lurked in the shadows of his talk. This much he knew: Reevis was a red wolf in a sheep's coat. But just how wolfish, he couldn't say. If he lived to see morning, maybe he'd know, but sunrise was a long way off.

FOR QUITE SOME YEARS he'd known the double edge of having your worst suspicions confirmed. On the one hand, it could still cut him to the quick to be reminded how calculating and ruthless people could be, his official and unofficial selves not excluded. On the other, there was always some comfort in knowing your habit of caution put you just a step ahead of the crowd. Not so many surprises. His father had said that the carpenter's code of measuring twice to cut once ought to be observed in dealing with men, but the arithmetic he had to gauge with was a hard one, and it had made him hard.

He was pretty certain now that he had discovered in this matter nothing in the way of simple reserve, but rather a tentativeness born of guilt. It was an old story – a busy husband, the hired man and the bored wife; opportunity and passion or something akin to passion – and though Nevers had been energetic enough in the public eye, his nature didn't quite seem steady, and there was always that something held back, a drifty quality in his eyes. Maybe his secret was just that he was drab and drowsy at home, and his wife was otherwise. There was a peppery side of her, the sheriff was convinced, but he didn't see her arranging an "accident." Grit but not gall. So it would have to be

Reevis, who was strong enough, maybe cagey enough and possibly sufficiently ruthless to set up the little tragedy and get by with it.

Matters of the heart. And had he always been above reproach himself? He couldn't claim the high ground. He had employed bluff and subterfuge to win Adair from Corvis's flashy spell all those years ago, and in that brief and sorry period now over a decade past when he let his eye and then the rest of his physical being follow the siren's whisper – no, it was worse than just following – he had done some shameful stage-managing himself. Listening to the crackle of small logs on the fire, he lay pretending to sleep and thought how often the feigning of unconsciousness now and then had played a role in the charade, in anybody's deceiving their lawful spouse. When Adair had recanted and come home, he'd still carried the taint of it, of Ina. He had wanted to clear the air between them, but he didn't want to confess to his acts any more than he wanted to hear about hers. Likely they lay back-to-back many a night, both pretending slumber. Any minute you're sleeping or successfully pretending to, you don't have to be telling a lie.

The smoke was tickling his nostrils, and he strained not to sneeze, not yet ready to resume his interrogation with Reevis. He didn't know who or what was about to be found out, but he did know how easy it would be for Reevis to finish him – "slay," he thought, for some reason drawn back to the Biblical – and convince doctors and deputies and all the king's men that Silver Eye had done the dirty work, aided by the strain of Sherburne's subsequent labors and despite the foreman's most solicitous ministrations. He could even imagine the doleful look on Reevis's face as he shuffled his feet and delivered the news to Adair. Her whole visage trembling until it collapsed into a scream.

He was gathering his strength, deciding whether to employ guile or try to get a weapon on Reevis, when he felt the man stand and leave the shelter. The fire was guttering a little, and he heard his rescuer shuffling about, moving things, probably branches. Play it by ear, he thought. You don't have to show your cards, even if he has, but why did he? Why was he so sure I was on to them? A sleuthy reputation can be a dangerous thing. He opened his eyes and began to feel around for firearms in the dim light as the man ducked back out of the weather.

"Glad you're back among the living. Thought I should rustle up some more burn logs." With the shotgun still in one hand, he let the wood tumble off his arm into a pile, then tossed on two logs about the size of a man's calf. The fire responded with light and smoke, then increased heat. Reaching into the shadows, he lay down his weapon and produced a spit with some fatty meat strips wound loosely around it.

"Took the liberty to butcher up your little deer and hang it. Clever how you did the whole thing – bait and stand, passing up a lazy, close shot to be sure the cat wouldn't sniff you out. Had to know you could make the hard shot, though. Folks know that about you. Calm and cold under threat. Proper lawman. Hell, I voted for you once."

Sherburne heard every word, but he was pretending a wooziness, hoping Reevis wouldn't get his guard up.

"Shoot the Krag a lot, do you? My daddy had one, but its feed was bad, dinged up, and nobody valued it for more than a souvenir of foolish times. Serving the country!" He snorted in contempt. "Some say the Krags was out of date almost before getting issued."

He'd been watching his patient for signs of further alertness and pushed on as soon as the eyes stopped flickering and opened wide.

"He toted the damn thing all the way to Philippine Island and back but never shot it but for practice. Probably didn't attend to cleaning it much. He was on a howitzer crew, and they had bigger business. Now his is just a kind of keepsake, like Mama's wedding cake knife. We kept it pegged over the mantel with his own daddy's Enfield, which was cut down after the secession war – 'Silver War' he come to call it – so a man could shift easier through the woods with it, but that shortened its reach, or its aim, anyway. Me, I'll go with the Winnie '98 every time or a good shotgun. I'm not a sidearm man at all. I figure that's for a fellow that thinks he might have to shoot at short notice. Not for me. I prefer to hold it to the special occasion shooting, plenty of time to think on it. That Enfield, though, was still a real puncher, and baring down on an antler deer from a stand up in the branches, what with that .55 caliber ball, it was as guaranteed as tomorrow's bacon on the hog farm. Deer, bear, anything. Course that's not what it was bored for."

He stopped suddenly, as if he'd just realized he had an audience.

"Snow's stopped off for now."

"You know guns and sporting, woods. I'm struck that you didn't go off to the Kaiser's war to see the great temples and grog shops of Europe."

"Just mayhem with too many bosses. Killing men you don't know. . . no excuse for it. My brother Lace joined up. Went with the U. S. Marines, a frail boy with a dreamy streak."

He cocked his head back, as if he could see what he meant to say hovering above him.

"Lace liked the field, seeing the corn come up. He wrote back about a different kind of digging – trenches and grave holes – the shells screaming all night, then the green gas and the parley-vous ladies and boiling rats and the officer's whistles telling men to jump up, run into the wire tangles and die. Got to where his letters went on about nothing but hoping to see the hindside of a straight-row mule and feel the reins tight on his shoulders again, watch the mule-colored dirt swale up like ocean waves. And some girl from over to Brownsville named Sally we didn't even know about. He said something about Bellow Woods, and when the letters quit off and the newspaper stories didn't, I knew he wasn't coming back. I was glad then our mama was taken early and never knew, but a man's smart to look out for his own interest; let the flatland people with the money mind the country's business. Up here is just itself."

"That it is."

He didn't intend to warm to the man, rescue or not, but even as he felt the conversation turn ominous, he could appreciate that Reevis had a kind of campfire charm. The sheriff had never heard him talk so much. Maybe this was a feature few people witnessed and Susan Nevers was drawn to. He was aware that the man kept talking through a smile that was almost a smirk, but he couldn't read it. The green eyes, the fox-colored hair. He felt certain that whatever was to transpire between the pair of them was meant to happen and be done before any additional party arrived the next day. If Reevis were telling the truth about that at all.

"The Krag's an old friend."

"You had it in the parrot war?"

"Yes."

"You couldn't of been a youngster, even back then. What would make a married . . . ?"

"I was still alone. Did you bring it in out of the weather? And the revolver."

"I must of missed your sheriff gun. Got dark. Likely it'll get by till morning. The Krag's just to the other side of you. Good luck we heard your first volley. You must of fell into dreamland before you had a chance to reload."

He didn't care for the cat-and-mouse, especially if he couldn't be sure he was the cat. "Mouskerade" he thought. He did have extra rounds in his pocket, but loading the rifle with stealth was out of the question, too complicated, and he might not have the strength for it. Reevis was clenching his hands together again, but this time in the direction of the fire. Their eyes met and locked.

"And how far back does your, let's call it 'affection,' for Susan Nevers go?"

"You're too weak to be sheriffing just now."

"Don't believe it."

He turned full about to face Sherburne and sat Indian style, pulling his sheepskin coat together at the front and tying two sets of straps to close it. As if to clear his thinking, he lifted his hat by the crown, ran the other hand through his bright shock, then replaced the hat. Sherburne had begun observing Reevis' hands and movements closely, though he wasn't certain what he could do if something alarmed him.

"It's been near on a year since we started jawing, doing chores together. She wanted to learn the farm from apples to calving and butchering. Before she married Nevers she ran a little girls' academy up to Winchester, and she said she was used to understanding more about her surround than the kitchen and milking stall and the yard chickens had to offer."

"And you were happy to help her."

"Hell, we all were, but the other boys spent a lot of time out digging posts and feeding the stock afield. I've always been the joiner and the forge man, the one to dose the animals and mend what broke. Handy, you'd say, so I was close about the house and had nobody to hurry home to. All I knew was she wanted to study up on the business of farmsteading. Not the business, I reckon, but the work of it."

"You knew she was a young, pretty woman, what . . . about ten years younger than your bossman. And you knew she was unhappy. She was unhappy, wasn't she?" The wind increased, rippling the canvas and seeming to emphasize the question. This could be a mistake, he knew, opening doors he was in no condition to contend with.

"Who ain't? But it came through slow, it all happened slow. We didn't get past polite till deep into last winter, and wasn't neither of us looking for trouble. We had our own places in the pecking order around Lexington, and we was both safe in lives that could of been much worse. That's what I thought, yeah, but hers turned out more meager, more trial than most anybody figured."

"And unhappy. So how did you get past your shyness, and when?" He was gaining strength as he gained confidence, feeling his line of questioning would lead Reevis to say more than he intended. "Pass me that canteen. You figure to cook up some of that venison?"

Reevis jammed in two forked limbs and set the peeled spit across them, then whittled down a smaller pair of sticks and skinned the ends, as the conversation continued.

The story he told featured simple, accidental escalation – arms brushing together as they pulled an early foal free of its gushing sac, his coat over her shoulders when a surprise rain caught them cleaning up the orchard, banging noggins as they bent to clean up a dropped kitchen crock. They'd talk of their pasts and their hopes, and for weeks Nevers was not mentioned in their confidences. He was just a shadow that came and went, though Susan's moods seemed to vary according to his expressions. The causes behind that remained her own secret.

Throughout the narrative, Sherburne's mind would wander – back to the issue of personal honor breached, his own troubled courtship as a young man, then to the hide-and-seek game Ina had played with him across several weeks when Adair had left him and journeyed to Baltimore. The minx pretended nonchalance, but he had known better all along. He had been married, as Susan Nevers was married, but Ina had not been much more than a girl by then, and he was old enough to be her father. And he was sheriff. That was all part of his burden, no matter what Adair's own distraction had been, and it became evident that the storyteller felt encumbered, as well, though not strong enough to keep him on the straight path. He had no desire to wrong the man who employed him, he said, but he did have desire, and when the dark-haired woman one evening dipped the cup into the milk bucket and lifted it to his lips, the dam had just broken, the backed up waters surging. After he had emptied the tin cup, she wiped the white moustache from his upper lip and licked it off her finger, looking him dead in the eye. It was March and still chilly in the barn, Nevers still in town explaining to some prospering drummer why he could not afford one of those new automobiles and give up cussing the train schedule forever. The other hands had gone back to their homes or boarding houses. The cow tied in the stall lowed "moon, moon" as the pair eased down upon a newly broken bale of hay and, as if little fireworks had gone off inside both of them, began pulling wildly at one another's clothes.

"One thing then another, the way such things go betwixt a man and a woman. But we didn't have a hand in his death. Not one nor the other. After it, Susan said how she didn't believe anyone would so much as suspicion her of deviling, because she'd kept up the pretense of happily married like an actress, and we were just acting crazy, not plotting anything out, no aim at first but to scratch the itch. She ain't a guileful person, not a whit. I wasn't so sure we'd not be looked at hard after the mishap. We erred, yeah, we sneaked and cheated, but we was trying to hide it from ourselves near as much as from him."

The wind lifted the slicker acting as the north side of the tent, and snow swirled in while the smoke reversed its old path and came right at them. They were both coughing, each spasm driving a hook into Sherburne's side, and after Reevis went out and moved around, tightening guy lines, re-setting makeshift pegs, Sherburne could not exorcize his own transgressions. In isolated dells, under lean-tos of fragrant cedar, in the abandoned Stover cabin where he'd brought straw and ticking to make a pallet back in the room that she had straightened and cleaned, even once on an icy night in his own jail. He had made a hell for himself, tossing excuses to his deputies, missing appointments, delegating where he had always dealt first-hand. And when Adair returned, he had moved quickly to smother the embers.

It wasn't that easy, not in the mind and the marrow, and even now he could not prevent the image of the girl – naked in the lamplight, her long fawn-colored hair swaying, her laughter high and taunting – from dancing before him when he felt his life droning. As much energy and concentration as he'd invested in following the straight path through the narrow gate, it galled him that his deepest expedition into the exotic since the lush and garish parrots and plate-sized flowers of Cuba would be that teenage witch of a girl who had likely lied about that bad business up on from Irish Creek and darted in and out of his life for years, always flirty with her eyes. It galled him further that he had kept the secret all that time and played the part of virtue's agent in other folks' affairs. If he met his end up here because he'd discovered how another man's passion had galloped out of hand, it would complete a circle, enact a kind of justice deeper than law.

When Reevis returned, there were stars specking his hat crown, but they faded as soon as they felt the heat.

"Look, before Nevers fell, I was already thinking I'd shat in my own nest on this one and would be looking for work again as soon as the spring birthings was done. Wouldn't be the first time I spoiled steady work with foolishness – scuffles, too many face cards in a deck, breaking temperance – but it wasn't ever a woman before. Not that I hadn't mulled it. And when she looked me back, I thought, 'Hell, who misses a slice off a cut loaf?'"

"So it was just a lucky accident." Sherburne was looking behind Reevis to the low shadows they cast on the canvas – Reevis squatting, lifting the spit away from the fire as deer drippings sizzled, Sherburne propped against a log with his rucksack holding him up. Their postures reminded him of a frog and a lizard, members of the same tribe almost, competitors for the same food, but their different hats made their silhouettes dramatically dissimilar.

"Well, hell no." He was growing agitated and, staring at his hands, seemed to be talking more to himself. "Not lucky for Nevers, not for her neither. Nor me, far as I could see. I figured – I was afeared, anyway – once she was free of him – old dead stick of a man anyway, heavy-handed, judge and jury under his own roof, though he never raised his tone against his workers – she'd look to somebody of her own station. I didn't see the advantage to me, and it – I mean his dying – did put her off me almost all summer. She turned skittish and kept saying how she had to respect the deceased and how we shouldn't've dallied. She was too tore up, partly because she'd wished it, even prayed for something to go amiss with the man, and when it did, she was just, like I said, tore up."

The shadows were still, but the wavering fire gave the two figures the impression of movement. Sherburne decided he should keep his eyes tight on the man. This would be a good moment to turn their talk away toward something else, but he seemed unable to stop himself.

"But you see how it looks." He had to pause for a coughing fit, and the pain ran its knotted cord through him. "You understand why finding the two of you slipping up to Little Bird to convene set some of my curious wheels into motion, and I can't just stop them by saying 'whoa,' not till some things have sorted out."

"I don't see how my story lends itself to proof, one way or the other. I mean, not no more than you and the doctor did right after he took his fall." His voice was turning raspy, as if his breathing had changed.

"I don't either, not straight out, but working that question, following all the threads, that's what makes my job. I never thought murder before because not a one knew of a reason why any soul would stand to prosper from his demise, so there was no possible motive in plain sight, no reason to probe, so to speak. It's different now.

"So let's say you had the chance: How would you set about proving to anybody, in light of all this, that there was nothing underhanded in the death of the bookkeeper?"

He cleared his throat and glanced at the fire, then back to the gaunt-looking man as he leaned on his right elbow, his hand testing his left shoulder for fresh wetness.

"Well, Mr. Sheriff, it seems to me that's your lookout, the proof. Wouldn't I be innocent till somebody proved I'd done something?"

"*Presumed* innocent, which has more to do with opinion than with the fact. Not the same thing. And that's all in a court of law with a Bible oath and the public eye. This is no court. We're out here alone, just us, unofficial, nobody to hear but the fire. How would you? You could start with where you were that evening and just bull on through to why he might have been in the loft, since he had all those hired minions to climb ladders and walk across old flooring and maybe even plunge through rotten timbers and get tined on his behalf, for that matter."

"I don't know much about minions, but it seems to me that court's wherever you're taking breath, probably even if you're squatting in the shit shed or sleeping hard as the departed."

He'd been in court plenty, and he'd interrogated a host of ill-doers, usually with them in a chair, nervous and angry, maybe even manacled, and him pacing the room, pausing to light his pipe or placing one foot on a chair, crossing his arms to lean on the raised knee, his face, with its heavy moustache and tobacco smell and glinting eyes just inches from theirs. Then he mustered his forces and launched into his old habits of speech, whether pressing the point just now was to his advantage or not.

"Then answer just the one: Where you were that evening. It was dusk, wasn't it? The lanterns lit, the missus getting supper on the table, and he went outside. Say there was something he kept up there, or say somebody told him they'd left a thing in the loft, maybe even the hayfork – or was it a pitchfork? – itself. And so he went out and up, and the clock on their wall, the one with the sun face painted on its disc, said a particular hour, and his wife was maybe humming a specific tune, hymn, say a favorite one" – he had to pause and pull in a deep, difficult breath – "and everybody and everything in the world from the brood mare to the sewing scissors to the agate watch fob my wife gave me last Christmas was somewhere, seen or not, doing something or enjoying the not-doing of anything, but in a definite individual location. In which of those specific places at that time – call in leaning toward seven, of a Tuesday – were you?"

"You're jousting at me, Mr. Lawman. Lawing like a crow. You don't want to be wearing yourself out straining so. Like they say, you ain't out of the woods yet."

"A man like me, a law-man, as you put it, has always got to journey to the middle of the woods, and maybe even get lost, in service of discovering. What I'm after is the story in its entire. That's my mission, pursuing the story, and I don't have a stake in what the story turns out to be, long as it all comes to light."

The only available light was the fire, and as he noticed its diminishment he realized he was talking to himself, saying out loud what he often rehearsed in his mind to overcome doubts about his methods or his motives, and it often worked.

"Things come to light, then I'm not lost anymore, and the world can just turn, go on about its business. So where?" Then he felt the energy spilling from him, the light inside him failing, and he settled back, fully supine, staring at the smoke and shadows along the roof of the wind-stirred shelter.

"Like I've said, I'm not sold on this being the best circumstance for you to be doing your pursuing – particular this and particular that – your condition being as it is. But I reckon you got to be willing to die to do this law job."

"To live you've got to be willing to die."

"Well, that's true enough, I reckon, but it ain't much of a charm to live by. This here bucky meat is just about fit to eat, but I wouldn't have it on my conscience if you worried yourself into another bleeding spasm and died right here on the spot, so I'll tell you."

He scraped one ribbon of meat from the stick, skewered it with a twig and passed it over.

"I was in my room at Murchison's over a mile away. I was keeping a bucket of beer company and sanding the rough out of a perched bird I'd carved from a branch of ironwood. I was going to give it to her."

"What manner of bird?" The meat was hot, but his body needed it beyond caution, and he scorched his tongue. As he chewed it, he realized his mouth was dry, and he nearly had to choke it down.

"I can't rightly say, a sturdy one. The shavings made a sweet smell, though. I expect I had a hawk in mind, but the beak was too heavy and the body too middling. The grain got away from me, so I elected to just say it was a bird."

"A shame we can't get it to testify."

"Once you've taken a knife and gouge and the emery sanding paper to something, no reason to expect it would sing up the truth to save you. The wind don't blow that way.

"There you go, Mr. Sheriff. Eat em up."

He speared another tough strip of flank, Sherburne propped up straighter and they ate and passed the coffee cup between them in silence, while a renewed weariness began to weigh on Sherburne. Outside, an owl undaunted by the smoke and sound of human noises voiced its question five times, then again, and Sherburne thought of all the animals out there moving through the night, their intentions only half known to them, any deception they might practice the simple consequence of their natures, not plotted or chosen. When the bird flapped off, both men heard the first subtle wingstroke and turned their eyes, as if they might be able to see beyond their protective canvas.

When they finished, Sherburne said, "That was eatable" and let himself back down. The conversation had been hardest on his ribs, and he was beginning to conclude that his best move would be to get some rest.

"But did anybody see me?" Reevis asked. "That's the lynchpin, right? Well, on that count, I expect there's good news and bad. I walked about. I tromped down the stairs to go out and relieve myself. If he fell round about twilight, I might have been back on the stoop, just before heading to the out shed for some more emery. I remember seeing the sunset like thickish blood on the hay after a calving gone bad, and I thought winter was just starting to say so long till next time. I honest to God hadn't any sliver of an idea Nevers was climbing and falling and dying. I'd been in that loft once or twice a week, and for some time I'd stepped from beam to beam, not trusting it. We all did, the fellows, and I'd said to Nevers that the whole thing was begging repair, wet rot after the roof leaked too long. We'd re-shaked the roof, but he always asked can we get by a bit longer with the loft planking. Everybody who climbed up there regular knew to step lightly, and besides, I don't believe anybody mortal could situate a fork so they could be sure somebody else falling would strike on it in a final way. Be more likely to break your leg or your back and get a stab in your asscheek. Hell, you might have trouble jumping on it a-purpose. Look, I'm no assassin, but if I was to set my cap on sending somebody to the promised land, I wouldn't leave so much to chance. Farm's full of easier ways, and assassins don't leave so much to chance."

"So what's the good news?" He was trying to brush by "assassin" without it setting off little sparks inside him.

"Severn Watkins and Axelrod was both in the house. Plus Miz Murchison. It's a shoddy frame with no plastering. You'd get to know each other's snores and steps and farts. Waking or sleeping, everybody in the place would sense you. You ask them questions about it?"

"I will. When it's time, I will."

"Law, though, it likes an answer, likes to catch somebody. It troubles me to think it, but you might get more hurrah on your own account if you surprise everybody in Rockbridge and work out a murder they didn't even think had been done. Even if it didn't really get done. And your sort has ways of finding things that aren't even things. Election's not too far down the road, remember."

"I don't need votes that bad."

"How do I know to trust you? Trust you to trust me?"

"What other options present themselves? I'm not going to die on my own now, you've seen to that. And you say the mayhem doesn't draw you."

"What if he was hitting her?"

"I don't take your meaning. Like he deserved it? Are you saying maybe you aren't clean in this?"

When Reevis removed his hat and swiped his forearm across his brow, Sherburne saw his opportunity and rolled up and to the left, away from the fire and toward the Greener he could see at the edge of the shadows. It almost consumed him, and it was no smooth trick, but he managed, and by the time Reevis fully understood what had transpired, the sheriff had pulled back the mule-ear hammers to full cock with their serious click, and the farmhand was looking down two barrels so close that, had they been the barrels of a binoculars and it broad daylight, he might have seen far into the next county or the next day. Instead, and despite the fact that he might be looking through those two dark circles into the next world, his face was calm, his mouth closed in a grinning seam.

"I wondered if you had the sand, and when I'd find out. I was hoping we could make us a truce, two of like mind on this truth matter. I didn't want to have to worry about you doing something desperate-like."

"You don't have to worry about anything, if you're an innocent man, but if you plotted Nevers' undoing, even if he was whipping her with hames and willows and barb wire, you'll have to face the music. Fair, mind you, with considerations. And like I say: Innocent, you can sleep easy."

"If you were set on finding a truly innocent man, where would you commence your search? And do you really think you can hold those long barrels up all night? Thirty inches. How many pounds? I expect Susan will be in the party moving toward our smoke tomorrow, and we'll see them mid-morning, but not before, Mr. Lawman, not before."

The prospect of such a vigil was not appealing, and when he braced the barrels across his knee, drew out his watch and tilted it toward the light, he saw it was just after nine.

After nearly an hour of silence and, for Sherburne, deep dark aching in his arm and across his brisket, even with the knee prop, Reevis spoke again.

"I should of figured." He had his hat off again, looking into it like there was an answer inside, then just peering over the brim, his mossy eyes almost mischievous.

"Another man's wife, another man's business. She could of just lit out, pack up and one morning be gone, me not far behind. And I suppose it is a crime to the church and maybe to the law to meddle in such and take her to your bed, so to speak, though it wasn't ever my bed. But for a law, once a man crosses over, it's a doom owed, end of story, and you're a law alright. If he needed punishing, maybe needed killing – and I ain't putting forth an opinion – it was somebody working higher purposes and spying from a higher perch than me seen to it."

The gun seemed long as a ridgepole, and Sherburne managed to pull his heels under his butt to prop the Greener on both knees, while Reevis watched him, almost amused.

"What if I was to rush you? If I get so much as a hand on the muzzles before you squeeze those triggers – and they're no sweetened handgun steel, you got to nearabout snatch them – well, then you'd lose your advantage. I wonder do you have that in you, too, to shoot an unarmed man – a suspect, just – to protect your own hide. I might balk at it myself, and ain't that always the real question, how much one man is akin to another, what any fellow will do when the wolves close in?"

Sherburne tried to tighten his fingers on the weapon, but they scarcely responded.

"I don't even know if I've got the gumption to chance it, and here's the trick: if I launch at you and fail, then that's it, wrong choice, so long to old Reevis; but every minute I don't jump, I can still be thinking about doing it the next and the next and the next, all the while you getting weaker and sleepy. And I can get a nap to store up my powers, but not you, so I'll tell you what, I don't plan on chunking another log on that fire. It's going to get cold and it's going to get dark, that gun not so light as a feather nor, pretty soon, a sledge."

The wind had calmed some, but he could see through the gaps in the shelter sections that the snow was pelting down. Where it accumulated on the canvas, the sections sagged.

Sherburne saw that his predicament was not improving, and it did go through his mind to shoot the man but not give him a mortal wound. Just to even the odds a bit.

"And I suppose you have a different plan, what you'd do if our places were swapped."

"Oh, it's hard to say. Man can't know such things till the occasion opens up, but I hope I might have the good sense to blow you in half."

"And then?"

"Many's the fork down the road after that, and half a day to change things about while the snow comes on and on, if it does. But then you likely don't have the strength to dispose of me so your own rescue party won't discover it all. That's not an outcome you'd be fond of, Mr. Law. You'd have some trouble in your present shape arranging things to stand above suspicion. And anyway, I'm banking on you and me being different as colts and calves."

"But this little island we're on is full of little caves and dens, and nobody would be likely to find the body or, later, the bones. I could say – following your plan – you never even found me, never made it up the steep? Anything could have happened."

"An off-the-path corner like this – high country, rough – it's many a year from being a lure for anybody but the occasional hunter, and awful far to be carting game down, at that."

Sherburne thought again of the Hostetter girl, nine or ten. He'd seen her in the schoolyard, probably, but couldn't say which one she was. Darby and his wife had two others, but they took her disappearance as if she had been their only issue. The wife was in his office every day that first week, and later he'd twice seen Hostetter holding her back in the street, when her clear intent was to march to the sheriff's office again and accuse him of laziness or stupidity or coldness. As if she could read how flawed he was behind his work face and his badge. And he knew showing the hard face was part of the job, his protection and theirs. So this was already a place of bones, and the big cats' remnants would get strewn about and licked clean, eventually added to the secret cache. The little bait buck's, as well. He couldn't allow his own . . . .

"A last time, did you have a part in that man's death?"

"I don't see any answer satisfying you."

"I just want to get to the marrow, to hear it, in case I can't hold out. To have your word."

"The man had spells. It was like something that haunted him come up of its own at times and couldn't be fought off. He hurt her some. She was scared and I got to be scared for her. When he went through that floor, it was providence or some other system of right guiding his fall and the situation of that fork, but not Susan Nevers nor myself did it, I swear by my poor brother Lace's soul."

For the first time since his last sleep, Sherburne felt his body relax, though he had not willed it and did not even welcomed it.

"I'm going to believe you. I intend to believe you, and I'll do what I can to find everything that supports your story, but I don't think I can keep this gun steady much longer. Can we get a pact?"

"First thing, you'll want to break open that gun, just to see if it's as dangerous as you believe."

When he did, he saw neither barrel held a shell, and he sighed, dropped the gun and slumped back.

"I can make it easier for you, if you still want to watchdog?"

"What do you mean?"

He reached under his coat and around behind him, then withdrew the Webley and tossed it onto Sherburne's lap.

"Don't hurt yourself with this one. It's loaded."

Sherburne shook his head and pushed the revolver aside. "You understand, I don't relish being wrong."

"That's the law in you."

And me in the law, he thought, as the waves of pain increased and a new ache appeared in his temples, a swirling heat and hammering that made him lie back again and close his eyes. If Adair hadn't been right last week or last month about it being time, she surely was now. His feet were cold in the wool socks and riding boots, but his brow was hot and wet. His father had long ago recommended he stick to liverying, saying it was a sheriff's business to meddle and make other people's business his own. Before long, he'd get to thinking every mouse that twitched and door that slammed was his lookout. It was no way to be in the world. That first chase, though, much as he had resisted the idea of hunting a man, had taken hold of him, and the seeds were planted. Who wouldn't be drawn to the power of it, representing the right? And every time the responsibility called you out at night or in the cold or off into some forsaken spot like this, you felt yourself the one person able for it, the hero, the knight, and all the stories of the town – joyful or fierce, profit or loss, drought, flood, feast or famine – became your story, because you were the one who knew, the book in which all the stories were stored and simmering where they could talk to each other and make the history of the place. Bitter as it could be, it was a sweetness he had tasted from it, but now maybe that was over, and he could remember one morning last spring when he was dressing for a court session before the fire. Adair still clad in her lavender gown had brought him a second cup of coffee, and as he was pulling at the lapels to snug his new frock coat across his shoulders, she had asked with that molasses tone with a touch of coal oil in it, like medicine, "How many more coats do you plan to mar by running a badge pin through them every morning? How many vests and shirts?"

He smiled and took the blue cup and saucer, then looked at the mantel clock, whose long hand was approaching the twelve. "I'm crucial to the garment industry, the textile barons, all those people down in Southside raising their families on wages drawn at the whistle every Friday down at the Draper mill."

"Blaine, I've married a vain man. Sheriff Vain Sherburne. Lord help us all." She had been smiling, but now he heard the name "Vain

Sherburne" louder and could scarcely summon the sight of her smile or the sparkle in her eyes.

"I'll sleep now," he said, reaching forward, "but I think I'll hold onto the pistol. After while, you get to be what you do."

"I've heard that said." Reevis dropped another hefty limb on the fire, which shot sparks upward and roared to match the wind outside.

And when he slept, he dreamed of a creekside willow stand he called "Shady Grove" after the song. He had first proposed to Adair on that spot, his voice a raw and unsteady thing beside the purl of the water, and though she had not said yes that sunny October afternoon, she had said it later. It was that sound of her confession of love, translated to the sound of clear water over stones and leaves blowing – that was what he dreamed.

AND

Thurston

Shreds of ground fog are still flossed onto the cobwebs in the meadow, but the air is already fierce with heat when the squawking sound summons Thurston Sherburne to the kitchen's north window. He is halfway through the day's first cup of black Maxwell House and stands in what Donyell called his "Joseph coat," a bathrobe from Sears Roebuck with stripes of a dozen colors. Barefooted, untouched by a razor for two weeks, he works a crust of sleep from the edge of an eye. Beyond the parching lawn and the stand of wild plums he can see the remnants of the horse, which went down five weeks ago. Mostly bone now with a few patches of desiccated hide, it has hosted and sustained flying things, crawling things and creatures that come only by night. The noise from it this moment does not issue from the skull bleaching in the July light but from the ribcage, which Sherburne now sees as some undersized boatwright's unfinished project. The empty eye sockets are large enough for billiard balls – "eight ball," he thinks, and "cue." That night he shot cut-throat with Boyd Cole and Jim Feeney at the Rack & Mug starts to run back at him, but it's too much to handle, and he waves it away.

The noise is coming from an immature turkey buzzard, which seems, despite the legendary canniness of its tribe, unable to reckon how one escapes such a cage after his efforts have knocked the bones a-kilter. It has worked its way in for the last scraps and has tried to tear at the softening bones, but now the bird flails its wings and, stretching its neck heron-like, laments its plight.

He remembers seeing the quarter horse, Ree's old mare Hopi, founder and fall one afternoon and even recalls deciding to let her lie there, not eighty feet from the house, and send her death message to a rose of circling black things in the sky, then various other scavengers in their turn. Perhaps something that feasted on the ruins of the animal would know the reason for its demise, but he does not, and he does not care in this new, cruel phase. Rattlesnake, a hunter's stray bullet, old age and the strangles – it hardly matters. "The meat shall inherit," he thinks, then, "no, meek," followed by, "not likely." He has chosen to endure, as penance, the smell and daily depredations wrought by hungry creatures who dragged the entrails out and squabbled over strips and shreds, and he has nearly grown accustomed to the raucous skirmishes, the diminishing carcass and, when the wind is lively, the stench, which is now nearly gone.

The horse had once been a stunning russet color, fully astonishing when she ran and lathered up under the sun, sixteen hands with a strong gait, fast, the hue of the hide so vibrant her form seemed a door to heaven. Ages back, it seems. Ree's horse from before her marriage to Boyd, though she had long ago stopped riding her regularly and sent her out here for, she said, "P and P," peace and pasture. Thurston has seen Hopi feed on sweet grass in a driving rainstorm with lightning cracking the sky and thunder rumbling. He has watched her standing steadfast under the thin blue moon while her last spindly-legged colt suckled, seen her lope behind his own small herd and nicker if they came close. Other than Ree, the aging mare had been the only real beauty in his life since he left the force, and when Ree began to wither in his back room under the medicine and depression, his scrupulous practice of horse-care began to unwind. If he couldn't have both beauties, he didn't want one.

From this window he can not see the plinth stone he has raised over his daughter. The family plot – Donyell, his parents, his sister Rue among the dead from two earlier farm families – crowns the rise just beyond the cow pond, under a stand of catalpas which blossomed only meagerly this year, the popcorn flowers fading and shrinking before fully opening. Likely it was the lack of rainfall, lack of snow, as well. Back in the spring, he and McCall spent a hellish day with mattock, pry bar and spade digging the grave and the stirrup hole for the plinth in stubborn soil. He dragged it from the sloping shale barrens beyond the bull pasture, his own Morgan cross Levi pulling the sled without complaint, despite being unused to such drudge work. The rest of the markers up there are rounded stones, the earliest ones chipped greywacke or limestone, more recent ones granite, but he cannot see them from the house.

The plinth is dark, six of its nine feet showing above the dirt like a rugged finger jutting out of the ground. Green foliage, fall colors, brown or none – he will always be able to see it from the west window over the sink and from his bedroom on the second story. She has been in the ground since early March, and recently the sun ball is setting right behind the dark stone. When the sky has been not too cloudy to preclude it, he perches in his reading chair at the upstairs window and watches the colors unfold behind the figure. "Let ruin have it," he says of everything else, and neither McCall nor Beth Lou can stir him from the conviction that the world is over, and that he has destroyed it. They think it is from simple, heart-riving loss, but more than they need to know is tearing at his insides – questions of vengeance, of justice and duty. The graven letters on the marble footstone read:

REE SHERBURNE
1928-1962
Beloved Daughter, Citizen, Lover of Horses
NEVER FORGOTTEN

Her deputy star is epoxied onto the stone under the profiled horse head chiseled beneath the words, and he has shellacked it over as protection against the weather, but he does not go up there now, nor does he return to the bend of the Buffalo River where no one, not even with dogs, would be likely to discover his secret under the wet stones he was able to move in the dark only with the help of Levi.

It was not, he knew, the cancer in her lungs that killed her. Not even the blistering poisons pumped through her veins in the last ditch effort to save her wasted body. It was Boyd. He had hurt her and weakened her and broken her spirit, and there was no reckoning coming to him from the law, because Ree had kept silent about the damage, partly out of pride and stubbornness, but more, most likely, to protect her father from what he might do.

The first time she came home to recuperate, Thurston bought the same story the others did: It's a rough job. You end up in scuffles with prisoners, chasing fugitives through laurel thickets, over ridges and down treacherous creek beds. Even the force's routine P.T. could be rough on a woman – hand-to-hand, pugil sticks, obstacles more rigorous than Outward Bound just over the county line. And getting tossed by a new horse now and then doesn't help. Bruises and scrapes, an occasional break. He'd been in law. He knew the drill.

Most of the damage she kept private, and it just didn't occur to Thurston that Ree would let a man slap her around, twist her arms and snatch her by the hair, choke her, God knows what else. She was supposed to be armed and dangerous herself, disciplined and cool under fire. "Self-possessed," he'd told people, "able." And she'd gone running to the assistance of too many battered wives and girlfriends up on the ridge farms or down in the Shadows to let a husband abuse her with impunity. That had been his conviction, but it was the bruising about the neck that finally made him skeptical, that unmistakable thumb mark, though standing in the window now, listening to the wing flap and screech of the caged scavenger, he admits that in his gut he had already started to suspect she was lying to him. She didn't practice enough to be good at it, but he didn't want to know, and now that gnaws at him day and night. He is also coming to the conviction that she lost the baby the same way. She was a strong woman, and miscarriage wasn't common to the clan.

Sipping from the cup of coffee, he is suddenly aware again of the day's heat. He can see the air beyond the glass shimmer and feel gravity pulling on his bones the way it does in skillet summer. He can hear the unbalanced vanes of the fan humming in the other room, and for a moment, he can feel Ree standing behind him. The smell of burning tobacco, a hint of Chanel. If he turned around, she would be there, leaning in the doorway, her hair tied back and a cigarette between her fingers. Just a hint of a smile showing the front tooth chipped on a missed jump when she was sixteen. Or she wouldn't be there, just heat and the familiar light filtered through dingy windows, the air smoky with motes and its own strange life. He doesn't turn to see.

Sherburne is still gathering wool, trying to keep his mind off the night down by the river, the night he stepped willfully over the line further than ever before. He's listening to a vireo in the tree line when McCall's truck rounds the barn and throws up a billow of dust as it slides to a stop. His son is trying to smile as he steps out of the door, and Thurston shakes his head. "I taught them so hard to be true, they can hardly fake a thing," he thinks. "McCall, though, I don't know. The quartermaster corps changed him just enough to prime him for commerce – tractors, mowers and balers. He'll never make a killing at it, though, not like the naturals."

"Hey, Daddy. I figured to mosey on out and check on you, see if you're ready for me to crank up the Allis and drag that damn dead horse off. Mostly bones by now, I suppose."

"It's fixing to foal, McCall. Hard birth, though. Might need Doc Lawrence. Look there." It's McCall's kind of joke, he thinks.

"What the hell are you talking about?" He is striding toward the fence, his fresh dungarees and bison buckle bright in the sun, the oxblood boots a compromise between genuine farming gear and showroom costumery. Despite his reddish shock of thinning hair and the complexion that goes with it, neither Thurston nor Beth Lou can convince him to wear a hat, no matter how many they give him. He is smoking a Camel, Ree's brand, and probably not giving it a thought. Not the sight of her with the I.V. tubes, not the grim nurses nor the borrowed Methodist preacher's last "amen." Though Thurston had been doubtful back when his wife said, "Let's adopt a boy" after her surgery, he'd been swayed by the old irresistible light in her eyes, and he's quick to admit McCall has turned out decent. Sherburne has never really regretted it, and he wishes Donyell had lived to see the boy keep afloat in the world. He thinks, "Good to see your name pass on, even without your blood." Then he thinks of Ree's baby again, though it never saw daylight.

"Make scientific history if that buzzard biddy lives," Thurston calls after him, pushing the whim.

"Godamighty, Daddy." After six years of running the dealership, Boyd can slip with ease from slick merchant talk of interest rates and depreciation into his back-slapping feed-lot ways, but it's all tainted by performance now. As soon as he crosses the old cattle grate, day or night, he starts to sound a little like Pa Kettle. "By ding, you done invented what everybody wants, Daddy, a way to catch up the bastards without breaking not a law."

"I try to work within the statutes."

"People with buzzards roosting in their oaks and apple trees and fouling their yards with all that shit and vomit, going after their lap dogs and generally making the place hell, they'll pay high dollar for this idea. You could get a patent, no kidding. Your crews just drag up a bunch of dead horses, and when the birds after the last scraps get befuddled and snared, you go in with gloves and jerk them out. Midwifeing, sort of. You got a plan to haul them off, maybe rocket them up to the moon?"

Thurston has never understood where his son picked up his fondness for such banter. Not at home, he thinks, hopes, or the one short year at VPI. Probably the army. He could remember the kind of mouthy soldiers who found ranking on each other in mock hostility a brand of relief from the foolish military regimen, bad coffee and endless mud. And he'd never really held out much hope of mental excellence from McCall, who was good-hearted but liked his comforts and had a little of his mother's showiness to him. One year with the ranger service was all he could stomach of what Donyell, always smiling, had called "the family business," and at that point Thurston placed all his bets on Ree to rise to the top rung.

When she dropped out after a year of law school – flustered, she said, by the snideness and greed – it nearly broke his heart. She dragged it through the dust even worse with every postcard from Santa Fe, Pueblo or Lewiston during the seven months she drifted, so when she came home, rode hard and put up wet, as they say, he was only too glad to grant his unnecessary permission. When he pinned the star on her jacket at the swearing in, she beamed like the girl he had seen accepting her first ribbon in the hunter-jumper. As Donyell's flashbulbs popped, the tears he felt welling up were from pride in her choice and shame that he hadn't been able to protect her from making it. They wore the same uniform, but they were not steering by the same compass.

"Show's about over, sure enough. We might's well just drag them bones into a hole. Whenever you're ready . . . wait up, though – Beth Lou sent you some stew. Pen-raised rabbit, mighty fine eating. Plenty of homegrowed vegetables, lots of pepper, like you order it. Onions to cut the gamey flavor." He crushed out his smoke and field-stripped the butt.

"I read in the paper that Jim Feeny has sold his acres and decided to relocate down past Roanoke." Sherburne's voice was flat, disinterested.

"Plans to work for the railroad, I've heard tell. Maybe some Draper mill. He's a fair hand with machines. Could be, but who knows? The truth is surely in that old hoss, cause nobody's ever been able to get it out of him." One of McCall's favorite lines.

"I didn't expect his people to ever give up that little scab of land above the river." He scrapes at his shadow with a boot toe. "When he stayed put after that Joelle divorced him, I figured we'd have to look at his ugly face till Judgment."

They are moving back to the house now, McCall carrying the handled tureen, Thurston pitching the last of his coffee onto the dry dirt, the liquid arching like a cat's back. He waits to hear what McCall will say.

"Myself, I don't disbelieve it's about Boyd Cole."

"Talk English, son – you're among friends."

"Well, the whole police clan – state troopers down to the magistrates – seems like they've got some investment in proving he's the hillbilly behind Boyd's disappearing act. They were tailing him hither and yon, stopping him on the street, questioning . . . but hell, you know all that. You're in the club. They probably trotted out all their wild theories to you and asked advice."

"Lately, they seem to know my interest in such matters has dwindled considerably. Let those ridge runners and stump jumpers from over there do to one another what they please. I've got no dog in the fight."

"But you've got your suspicions." At the door McCall turns, his eyes squinting from the sun, "You've always been the one, you know, to swear that hunter taint gets in the blood and won't drain out. 'Once an officer, always one,' you say, 'jump to the belling of the pack.'"

"Not this time, McCall. I've chased my last felon and riddled my last riddle. Ree, she was . . . well, that's where it stopped. That Feeny, though, he'd bear watching."

"I knew it."

In the kitchen, Sherburne lets his cup slip into the sink, where it strikes a pan under the gray water and cracks.

"Shit, that too."

He reaches up to touch the tip of his tongue, where he's been thinking he might have bitten it in his sleep. The dreams were worse than ever, and now he often wakes to find himself sitting on the side of the bed, sweating and breathing hard. For years he's had the one of finding himself naked, facing a felon who is armed or climbing out a window, jumping into the back of a moving truck, but it came most often right before court dates. He'd always preferred the sleuthing, the routine patrols and even the paperwork to testifying on the stand, nervous, wary not to let a slick lawyer work him. Ree, now she could have been better than slick, if she'd just ridden it out.

"Don't," he thinks. "Don't."

But now he remembers this tingling feeling on his tongue from yesterday morning, like a cold sore, but not visible in the mirror, zinging like a shot at the dentist. It isn't likely a bite. Something deeper in the nerves.

Last night's dream was a typical chapter from the recent book. He's in a cell himself, though the office is not one he recognizes. Cold, not much light, no colors in the whole thing. A big schoolhouse clock almost fills one wall, but it has no hands and its ticking is fast, like a downy having a go high on a hollow trunk. Then Boyd and Ree come through a door, spatting, her twisting away from him. At first it seems harmless, husband-wife stuff, but as it escalates, Boyd swells to the size of a wrestler down at the armory, or maybe Ree just shrinks. He is in the cell yelling, but nobody seems to notice him, and then Boyd is smacking Ree with some dark, large object. He can't tell what it is. Then Ree is yelling his name, which she never called him, the short version Donyell had used when they were courting – "Thurst, Thurst!" His hands grip the bars like he's seen a thousand prisoners do, and he tries to shake them, concentrating all his force into his fingers, wrists and arms. And then, when something gives way, like an arm pulling out of its socket, the whole section of bars breaks loose, but Ree is already on the floor, Boyd, or somebody who looks a lot like him, staring Sherburne eye-to-eye, everything, even the clock, gone silent, and he's yelling, but there's no sound, and when he moves toward Boyd with the bars lifted over his head, everything goes dark and light and then grayish, and he is awake on his hands and knees at the foot of the bed, the low gibbous moon out the window a lantern saying "this way, here."

HE HAD NOT BEEN against Boyd from the start, and that knowledge is still sharp inside him, talons hooking up under his ribs and giving him a stitch when he breathes deeply. A big man, Boyd seemed jolly at first and never dangerous. If he drank, he just turned clownier and had to be dumped into his truck and driven home. Because he was from town, he'd been in and out of minor scrapes with authorities – a little post-game vandalism, occasional shooting of pop bottles in the Lexington limits, cherry bombs, open containers, soaping windows – but Sherburne had never had cause to involve himself. Harmless pranks, just signs of dander, and when the boy graduated and went into his daddy's body shop, he bought a cabin out on the Buffalo forks near Irish Mill and joined the sporting crowd. Hunting, fishing, plinking, various sorts of tomcatting and larking. Innocuous, if not wholly innocent. Ree was in school, and then out west. A couple of years later, McCall had met him at a horse race and brought him over to buy the lumber from a stable Thurston was tearing down. He put his back into the work and never flinched, screeching back at the noise of the prised nails like one bird answering another. He had a way about him, Sherburne thought, that suggested some preoccupation, a part of his mind off somewhere. Maybe it was carousing with his running mates, after this uncatchable muskie, the rumor of a panther or some famous one-eyed bear, but he was respectful and offered a fair price for the planks.

He wasn't sure where Boyd and Ree had met, but it didn't take them long to start cutting a figure at cake-walks and picnics, her swinging on the crook of his arm, everybody whispering that, if there was a woman who could bring his mischief down a notch, it was Deputy Sherburne. The women in her line were all strong, strivers and winners. The men were something else, alternately quiet and fierce, most every one of them peace officers who had played a part in taming this pocket of the Blue Ridge where the rough terrain encouraged smuggling, shining and other mischief which threatened to drag it back to the nineteenth century. She was strong stock, all right, and pretty enough to get her way, even the chipped tooth a part of her charm. Her rider's long legs, Donyell's eyes. Let Cole dance; before long, she'd be calling the tune.

That was how it seemed at first. In the span of a season she became Mrs. Boyd Cole, but she went by Deputy Ree Sherburne beyond the threshold of the little bungalow they rented off Jackson Avenue, and it was *Sherburne* on her nametag, *Sherburne* on her paycheck. Thurston figured this would remind anybody, Boyd first among them, that she hadn't stopped being quick and right and everything else stamped into the family name just because she'd worn a veil and sliced a sugary cake.

"DADDY," MCCALL SAYS, "won't you ride back with me and spend the evening? Pitch some horse shoes and hunt up a glass of the Wild Turkey? The baseball game's on the radio later. The world's still here, you know. You need to come on back to it."

"I'm fine, son. I'll throw a rope around that mess and haul it down to the draw, give it a little kerosene and a salute."

McCall winced almost imperceptibly at the "son," for Sherburne was usually content to call him by name.

Carrying the mug's three sharp pieces over to the bin, he could just see into Ree's old room, and though the shade was drawn, he knew what his eyes would fall on if he stepped across the threshold. Even when she came home to die, she had kept her old swallow-tailed drum major uniform on the cedar valet, the blue wool with its gold epaulettes and three rows of brass buttons still clean and moth-free. The white hat with its rabbity-looking cockade. The back, which he seldom saw, read *Rockbridge County Panthers*. She had treasured it more than any relic from the University, more than anything but her riding gear, which he kept soaped and polished in the tack room. She was not fond of the English, but had adopted it for competition. On her own, it was western from the start, and she loved wearing rough gloves, working a quarter horse. She'd ridden all over the county – Pine Top to House Mountain to Goshen – since she was so small she had to learn to pee from the saddle, afraid if she got down, she wouldn't be able to climb back up without a mounting stool.

"Spunky," Sherburne thinks. He almost calls her pet name, "Honeyree," aloud, as he would if she were within arm's reach. "The toughest sweet person God made," he thinks. "Would suffer and grit her teeth and not . . . ."

McCall's voice breaks in on his thoughts: "Stew's in the icebox, but I got to get back and tell some lies. Everybody that's going, get in the goddamn wagon."

SIX WEEKS AFTER she looked him in his tearing eyes, her own dry from resolve or dehydration, and whispered "Daddy" for the last time, he'd taken the pick-up down to Winston's R & M and walked in, looking especially hang-dog on purpose. He'd made up his mind a month ago and let it simmer. They say revenge is best served cold, and he'd allowed the heat to seep out of it, despite the old "crime of passion" defense. By some forms of reckoning, action was allowable; by others, it was his obligation.

It was the first Friday after Easter, and the place was milling with people who'd stayed home and sober during the religious days. He hadn't been through the door himself since he took off his badge three years back, but he wasn't surprised to find it the same – the elbow-shaped bar cluttered and rough with scorch marks and carvings, the sputtering neon beer signs and the big round display with the Clydesdale-drawn grog wagon circling in jerky fashion. He'd liked the white-socked Scottish animals when he was a boy and always thought the beer-haul work beneath their dignity. Even the plastic ones in the smoke-grimed dome reactivated his resentment.

He was looking for Boyd over by the pool tables, but he took in the flashing juke box, yellow neon Miller signs, cues lined up on the wall like weapons in an armory. The cackley country sound he'd never liked filled the room – an old Kitty Wells tune, he thought – punctuated by the smack of colliding balls like breaking bones.

The men nodded to him, saying "Thurston" or "Chief." If they couldn't break the habit, he could live with that, but then they didn't have a hint what had happened inside him.

Glasses clinked, and over at the waitress station a woman laughed high and musical, nervous, sounding no more at home here than he was. Noticing the rodeo shirts on the young people, he thought the place unreal, almost a movie set, and the light refracting against so many surfaces reinforced the impression. But he was looking for Boyd, and nothing else held his attention for long. He felt he was back in one of his dreams, as cigarette smoke billowed and curled in witchy fashion. By the time he reached the corner table, his son-in-law had seen him and offered what resembled a friendly smile.

"Step in, Dad, take a stick. Feeny and me are just about to rack em up – cut- throat okay by you? Let me get you a glass of pop-skull." He talked this way when he was working on a drunk.

"Bottle of beer's fine."

Boyd reached up and placed an unlit cigarette between his lips, where it dangled. Sherburne had seen him hold one there for what seemed hours, tonguing it from side to side, then lighting and smoking it fast. He could see by an exchange of glances that Boyd had a flirtation going with a lean blonde gal moving toward them. Her name was Janette Walls, a teacher's aid, and Boyd was waving her off.

"Glad to see you're getting out."

Sherburne selected a house cue, hefted it for balance and ground its tip into the Silver Cup. The sound of graphite on chalk reminded him of friction between bone and bone.

"Break to me?"

"To celebrate you being back-among-us, right Feeny? Dollar a game?"

Boyd's denim jacket was nearly the color of the chalk, not far off the coats road gangs wore as they whipped their sling blades, counted off and squinted from the light glancing off the gun boss's rifle. Underneath it he wore his orange coveralls from the garage, and they looked no less institutional. Sherburne thought, "The system should take him down. It's not to me." Then he stroked a low ball into the side pocket. "But they won't do it, can't." He knew what he meant to do but had no idea how being here would accomplish it. "Just surveillance. Shoot your game, bide your time."

Money changed hands, at first mostly from his and Feeny's to Boyd's, and the mechanic began to flaunt his advantage, though his shots were less effective as he downed shot after shot of Jim Beam, and the tide turned. By ten, Sherburne was beginning to tire of the make-believe and said he'd need to get home.

The dispute that followed fast after is no less vague to him than it was that night, but Boyd had bet more on his young eyes and bluster than he could afford, and he'd fallen six dollars down to his in-law and a couple of to Feeny. He'd cried foul a couple of times and nearly ripped the baize trying a ridiculous shot. When Sherburne went to the toilet, Boyd followed, jokey, ranking but maybe not meaning it.

"You can't quit a winner, Chief. One more go."

"You're drunk, Boyd." They're alone, and for the first time he eyeballs the bully in cop fashion – aggressive, threatening.

"Drunk, hell. I'mo go down to Buffalo Creek and check my trot lines, then hunt me up somebody special, but first I wanna coup my losses, so don't make me smack you around, you old bastard." He was grinning like a brier-eater.

"Boyd, you couldn't whip a cripple."

"You got no sense of what I could do."

"That's a bet you don't want to back."

When Boyd swings, Sherburne X's his forearms, catches Boyd by the wrist and elbow, then whips the thrown fist behind him, twisting it into a high hammerlock. His left hand grabs a big hank of Boyd's hair, and Sherburne pushes the cussing mouth into the towel dispenser.

"Like I said, you're drunk. If you intend to hurt somebody, Boyd, come at him when you're sober and his back's turned. Or maybe her. That's your best hope. Now I'm going home and put you out of my mind, and you need to fix yourself up before you step outside, son. Be quick about it." A sober man would have been startled at the hiss he puts on "son."

As he strode out, he prayed Boyd would follow instructions and that he'd be too proud to mention the scuffle. If he were to pursue the plan that was forming, it was important their confrontation not be known. Shaking his head, he thought how lucky you have to be once you step outside the rules. If he could catch Boyd at his fishing, that would be luck of the highest order.

Driving home faster than he should on the mountain road, he thought of several men he'd had to arrest because of some mischief that started over a pool table – Jimmy Dinkins, the Mabry boy, Ex Billups, even Gideon Winston himself once. Glass from the pool table lights had spattered under more than one swung stick. Broken cues became clubs, Miller bottles got teeth. Sometimes there was a knife or the quiet mayhem of a razor. Those were the events that had drawn him to the Rack & Mug over the years, on duty, but no one in his recollection had ever been killed over it. Not on his watch, anyway.

A slim moon eased in and out of stacked-up clouds, as he listened to the new Senators lose to the Yankees again on the radio. The boy Maris homered off Cheney in the eighth. It could come in handy to know this. "Location, location," the realtors say, but he knew timing is the key to the world.

In thirty minutes he had the trailer hitched and was leading Levi into it. Ten years ago, he'd have skipped the saddle, but pommel and stirrup had become necessities. Thirty and ten. It was mostly in the numbers, and it was close, risky, even improbable. That was the virtue in it. From bar to barn to the forks of the Buffalo where the man strung his trot lines just under the weir he'd built – illegally, of course. Another of his petty offenses. Sherburne thought, "If I didn't know his routine, his honey holes, I couldn't do this. It's always somebody on the inside, or it's impulse and clumsy and all luck."

He considered stepping inside for his service revolver, but he slid into the truck thinking, "If an idiot's going to shoot me, he'll have to furnish his own." An old joke on the force.

And if he didn't bring it off, just half managed or worse, what would Matthews and Sawyer and the others think, having to cuff and Mirandize him, slide the heavy grill shut and shovel his meals in through a slot? He couldn't let himself think about that. Eyes on the road, careful of the trailer, quiet, over the mountain and down toward the Buffalo.

He tried to distract himself by wondering again if it was named for bison grazing on the banks two hundred years back or if it was *beau fleuvre* from some Frenchman's whim, but the idea that wouldn't free him as the dark fields and farms rushed by was this. Sherburne had long been convinced that law-abiding men decided to cross over in recognizable stages. At first, you were considering it, half fantasy, half logistics problem. Then you began to see a way through it, like an assignment, after which, in a moment of fool's sight, you'd see it all clear, and you would have done it in your mind, the actual crime now almost an afterthought, the true thing already complete in your head. The great mystery had always been: What is the pivot? What kind of shift has to happen inside you to overcome both virtue and inertia? Was it something to do with the challenge? The potential rewards? Or more a matter of some perverse twist in yourself, an appetite you weren't aware of but had to feed as soon as you discovered it, a weak link that strained and snapped? Some men would call it the ripening recognition of an older law, an absolute. His resistance to that convenient logic was pretty much gone.

Little transgressions – illegal search, excess force, unwarranted detention – had always occurred because, for some reason, the circumstances seemed to blur the line or to bend it the way a sustained downpour can alter a current. Some jerk would cuss you or kick out. Once a fat lumberman named Lyle had tried to bite his wrist. When the moment passed, though, the river would be back in its proper channels, the birds singing and the guilty party – previously just beyond the fingertips of the law or in mid-struggle – would be firmly in its grasp. But this was different. The stream had not altered, the justice behind his intent had nothing to do with stretching or re-interpreting or even an over-reaching in the heat of the hunt. With the cooling night air streaming at his face from the windows, he felt a little intoxicated with the thought that he might be leaving the boundaries of rule for "strange and mysterious ways." "Eye for an eye," he said and tried to believe it.

Sherburne had observed the way Boyd's movements in the bar had been a dance, everything from his eyes to his feet, the way he slid his cue stick back and forth, the jerky motion with which he threw back the shot of amber courage. All a self-satisfied dance. Could a scrupulous man ever hear that music, catch that rhythm?

Foolish, and perverse, he knew. He was driving under the influence of his anger, and he needed to settle down, but the feelings rushed through him. He clutched on a curve and slowed in time to prevent the trailer from fish-tailing. "Easy, Levi," he said.

All those years protecting and serving under oath, he had usually been able to hold his emotions in check, as he'd learned from his father, the way of his family for seventy, eighty years, ever since a young hunter and horse trader named Blaine Sherburne had been conscripted to stalk a killer in a snowstorm and nearly died driving his prey off a cliff near Natural Bridge. "The family business," yes, but he had hoped to be the last Sherburne to carry a badge, to sleep in the lean-back chair in a jail office or on surveillance in a misty field, to feel light without a gun, to suspect every person, every word, to bend under the weight of public confidence. But there had been horses in the family for a century and a half, too, and now with Ree dead and McCall more intrigued by diesel engines, there would be no more Sherburnes, no more horses. At least he could tie off one ugly loose end.

By THE TIME he had parked two miles away from the forks in a sheltered lane behind the dump at the Seiver switchback, the ground fog was rising, veiling the quarter moon and stars. Levi's breath was a whiter mist, and he stroked the horse's neck and said, "Okay, fellow, just two miles. We know the way. Likely he won't be there at all."

Tightening the cinch, he swung up and let the reins slack. Levi heard the one click of his tongue and started out, easy at first, then faster, with his choppy gait, once he felt the touch of boot heels. He could never understand how a horse could pick his way in the dark, but they rode briskly through gullies and over deadfalls, weaving amid jabbing stumps and over the cobbles of a dry creek bed. Occasionally Sherburne would rein in and sweep his flashlight across the terrain, then move on, but he wasn't even certain the horse needed it, not because he naturally carried his head low, but for some reason unrelated to sight.

How long had it been since his last night ride like this – rough country, a destination, timing crucial? He couldn't remember, and he was surprised at how calm he felt, as if he had no investment. They jogged and scrambled but never slid badly, and as they approached the stream, he could see the rising embankment beyond the water.

He could hear the shush of the current and then a screech owl's out-of-season shrilling in the distance. What he smelled was the moisture of moss and punkwood, the sweat of the horse and wet dust on the wind. Tying the horse to a snag, he thought it would be too much to wish for rain.

"Boyd!"

The big man was on the bank with a beer bottle in one hand. He had a G.I. flashlight in his other, and when he spun about, its beam jerked up, assuring Sherburne he had managed surprise. For some reason, the limp cigarette visible between his lips made Sherburne's muscles tense.

"What the hell you doing here, old man. If you're messing with me again, I'mo fuck you up something bad." He was leaning down, probably to feel for a stick, when Sherburne's instep caught him in the crotch. It was a forceful kick, meant to be decisive, as he knew Boyd was stronger, and in a tussle along rough, dark ground, strength might play a role he couldn't risk.

Half of Thurston wanted to repeat the technique, catch him under the chin this time and end it, but he had to say his piece, as if an abbreviated trial were required in some fine print deep in the book of revenge.

"Is this too rough for you, Boyd? Rougher than you handled my daughter?"

Boyd was gasping for breath, and under the sound of moving water, his voice was scarcely audible.

"Say again."

Boyd reached forward with his right hand, setting it on the ground before him, perhaps to steady himself, perhaps to seize a stone. Sherburne rested his heel on the back of the hand and pressed.

"Talk to me, Boyd. You beat her, beat her bad sometimes, over and again. She couldn't admit it, but it got so bad she couldn't hide it. This is no time to run from the truth. You beat her when she was carrying the baby, isn't that right . . . son?" He ground his heel a little harder.

"Yeah. . . no, wait. . . ." He was catching his breath but sobbing, probably stalling to weigh his chances. "I mean, we fought. She could be rough, too, you know. Wasn't no frail thing. It got outa hand. She could drink, too, and you know . . . ," weighing again, "you know how it gets for cops, the anger, and they bring it into the domestic, but not with the baby. I never, ever. That was when we was going to fix everything. I swear I was going to get help. . . ."

"And when she was sick. That last day, when she packed up her truck and came back home for keeps. You'd been at her then."

"No. I swear it. I tried to get her calmed. I shook her a little, but nothing bad." Boyd was sobbing hard, straining to get control over his frightened body.

"Boyd, if I can't get the truth out of you, I'm going to kill you tonight. You understand?"

A mistake to warn him, to impress him with the urgency of his situation. The water was flashing by behind Boyd, and there were cicadas intensifying in the pines, their song a separate current. Sherburne's muscles suddenly went slack on him, his breath audible and quick through his nostrils. He was wavering, something inside him was fraying. Find out, that was all he really needed. The confession should be enough. There was still law. He suddenly felt he wasn't going to be up to it after all.

That was when Boyd rose in one gathered, calculated motion and made his rush.

Sherburne let him come, swung his left leg in an arc, letting his body follow. It was almost a matador's move, his hands barely touching the lurching attacker, guiding him into the sycamore as if offering graceful assistance. When Boyd's head struck the trunk, its bark whitish even in the dark, the crack was loud, and Sherburne would have bet the farm right there it was a lethal blow, despite the low, almost sleepy sound that came from Boyd's mouth. His body gave one full spasm, like a hoed snake, then a couple of quiet twitches before it slumped. As the old man knelt by the body to feel the neck for a heartbeat, he could hear only the stream, which was surging, and then Levi snorting up the hill. No pulse, and he drew in a long breath and said, "Well."

The rest was just business, a policeman working his standard procedures in reverse. He needed to get Boyd's truck downstream a piece, his body upstream, then open the weirs to let the trapped water flow over the site of the struggle. With his flashlight, he saw there was almost no blood, so the gambit was simple: create a scene for Boyd's fish business below the killing ground, then get the body into one of the shallow caverns upstream. Weight him and wedge him. He would need to use the horse and lariat to pull some big stones over, then clear up the tracks with water and brush. If he did it with craft and thoroughness, it would just be a mysterious disappearance, foul play suspected but the questions remaining unanswered. Maybe. If he was lucky. Boyd had plenty of enemies, and narrowing the field would be no small task. Now, he would need an hour, hour and a half. And he had the time, so long as nobody happened along, so long as luck stayed on his side.

As he went back for the horse, he realized he was not feeling anything, not about Boyd or Ree or the law, certainly not about the status of his soul. It was a series of tasks to be done by the numbers, and though he was sweating in the cool night, it was just labor, he thought, the body cooling itself. There would be time to reckon the meaning later. He stood the body up, then knelt to swing it over his shoulder. Boyd's wrist where he was holding it was like already cooling. The owl shirred its call, closer this time, and though it sounded like the beginning of his name, he didn't mind.

Covering the horse's trail back to the truck took longer than he'd expected, but by the time he got Levi tied in and the rig turned around on the tarmac, the first taps of rain struck the dusk on the windscreen, and he knew somebody must be looking out for him. As he'd expected, he didn't pass a single vehicle on the way home.

WATCHING MCCALL'S DUST diminish in the distance, he strides over and ducks between two strands of wire, thinking to free the bird from its cell, but his approach agitates the creature so much its flailing wings knock the ribcage further to the side, and it flaps, waddles and shucks free, then rises, hissing what might be either relief or protest as it moves low across the field.

"What is proper penance?" he wonders. All those years, and only one killing in the line of duty, a moonshiner named Suggs, in unquestioned self defense. Not even an inquest, but now he has this shame to bear and no real life to carry it. Nothing but the heat and need for more rain.

Inside again, he gathers his shaving gear and brings it to the bench under the front window. Razor snug in its ivory handle, strop, frayed towel, the basin and ewer of water, tin of soap powder, the wide shard of mirror, which he props on the window sill. Lathered up, he looks hard into the glass, which is losing back-silver. When he locates his eyes clearly between the flecks, he finds them foreign, no more truthful than Boyd's. "Eye for an eye."

He has not dared to look this hard in weeks, and what he sees is less than he had hoped but about what he expected: an old man, cheeks growing hollow, tracks around the eyes as long as an adult crow's splayed feet, lips full. He has not wept since the last day at the grave, and he knows he will shed no tears now. As he brings the razor up, he sees his eyes even more clearly in the stainless blade that has been in the family at least three generations. "Bright as a star," he thinks, and a wave passes through him, a shiver. The sun is on his neck, but he is cold, seeing himself in the two surfaces, two selves that refuse to resolve.

"Hell," he thinks, "I might's well do it. Outside here would be best. Not so much mess to clean up." He should telephone Sawyer down at the office and just tell him, "Something out here you need to see, asap." And McCall could handle it. He's not the sharpest tool in the shed, but he's steady, strong in his way. And he couldn't be sure how people would read it, though simple grief over Ree would provide ample explanation. Likely they'd never uncover Boyd's body, or if somebody did some day, when the creek turns or developers come to throw up vacation bungalows, it would all be ancient history. The consequences he was suffering right now were his sentence, and if it wasn't exactly remorse, it was regret. So where did his duty lie now? To the name, the office, Ree's memory? He could just turn himself in. The boys in the force would arrange for him to enjoy the best treatment possible, and Cree Dunlop would see to it that any trials would drag out, appeals. Plead his record, his sorrow. The quarrel in the toilet would come out, and the struggle at the creek would become another scuffle, another case of self-defense. His only real crime would be the cover-up, and that would not cost him so much, the Sherburne name less deeply stained. Everyone would sympathize.

Make the call, then pull the Sheffield blade across his carotid and watch the first blood spurt at the patchy face in the mirror? Or make the call and get dressed to wait for his old friends to come haul him off?

He can not see the vertical stone on the cemetery rise from here, but he can feel it, and he can remember the day she admitted that Boyd was not kind to her, that he'd gone over the line. She was lying back in the La-z-boy, looking stronger than usual, though she'd just finished her weekly round of poisons. Before the full effect would usually hit her, about midnight, she'd have a few hours of something like her old self.

"I'd kill for a cigarette, Daddy."

"You just about have."

"Yeah, I guess. You must not have smoked them right, unstruck as you are by tobacco. You'd think I'd have inherited that along with the appetite."

He wondered if she meant to make him ashamed, or if this was just twilight banter.

"You got your mother's gumption, Honeyree, and her kindly ways, but I expect her frailness was hidden somewhere down in you, too."

"One more smoke won't kill me."

"I won't kill you either, Ree. You know that. And you know I don't even keep them in the house, so I couldn't give you one if I was weak enough to try." He could feel a sob forming inside him, and he turned to the window where the day's last streak of light lingered.

"Maybe it's my only way out of the Boyd situation, this whole breakdown. These last few years, life has been, I don't know . . . not even the job or the horses. . . . I never thought I'd let it happen to me. Other things, too, things you don't know."

He kneeled beside the chair and extended the glass of Canada Dry in his hands. Instead of looking at her eyes, he looked at the bubbling surface and the fizzing spray above it.

"What exactly? Tell me what he did."

"You know already, Daddy. And you know I appreciate you not taking a hand at it. This was mine, run or stumble, and I botched it. I fell, and it's my fall. It's my doing and my undoing, fair enough. The cancer, it's just a footnote."

"No connection, Honeyree. And you ran faster, stronger than anybody. You are a hell of a woman." He could see the desperation in her eyes until she turned them down to look at the soda, then took the straw between her lips. He knew better than to offer false encouragement. Doctor Phipps had said just the past Friday, "Days, maybe, weeks at best. See to her comfort, and encourage her to order her soul."

"Her soul's not your business, Henry. Nobody's. Best you get your bag and go bother some other ailing . . . soul."

"Might be a pack in the truck's glove box, Daddy. Stale probably, but dry, that's for sure." She managed a smile.

When he returned with the Camels, she was asleep, and he crushed the pack in his hands, listening to the wrap crinkle like a small fire. It was the last real conversation they'd have without morphine playing a major role, and in ten days she was gone. "Run or stumble" was what stuck with him, and "my fall."

But he'd broken the understanding, the "contract," her training would obligate her to say. "Breached." And his contracts with the law and his blood, so there are two kinds of calls he can make, or he can just buck up and live with it, play the hand he's dealt. He thinks, "I've lived with plenty already."

He shaves precisely, carefully, listening to the sandpaper sound of steel on stubble – rasp across cheek, along the jawline, the little wattle under his chin. Squinting and angling to keep the sun out of his eyes, he flicks suds off the blade and into the withered grass, and when he's done, he wipes himself dry and throws the towel and strop over his shoulder, then pitches the contents of the basin. The sudsy water slashes in the sun and slaps the flagstone, and he turns to fold the razor, then carefully draws it across his thumb, where the blood is at first a rosebud, then a seam of scarlet, which he licks, only to discover that the numbness has left his tongue. The man in the mirror is a version of himself, a remnant. He says simply, "Yes. For now, yes. Bear it."

The freed buzzard, or some other – too high now to be certain – is riding a thermal above him, and he thinks, "Rid myself of that horse skeleton before the sun sets, get it where it belongs," as he steps over the threshold and enters the house again, turning to cast a long look across the fence and over the bleak field. Ever so gently, first with his elbow, then his hip, he shuts the door.

Cooper's

He saw it first in the ice, a blur out of nowhere. Reflected in the white river, it came without scale or context, and at first it was as likely a moth as a bird. At least, that's what Oran had thought. He'd been out hunting the colt since just after dawn, and his eyes were tired. He thought he'd walk the steep shore, just in case the knucklehead had ventured in. A Morgan is supposed to be smart, he thought, but this bastard bay takes the cake for pea-brain.

His eyes were tired from the searching and from the cold, and when he saw the hawk in the ice, he thought of the cold slaughterhouse where he'd worked before the German war – what was it now? – maybe twenty years back. All that meat on ice, and he could almost smell the blood again. Down in Carolina, the beeves scrambling on the ramp and the gun slamming its bolt into their brains. The skinning knives, the saws and cleavers, the shit-slick ramps, overhead hooks like inverted question marks. The blood runnel like the answer to all those inquiries. No, you didn't forget that. After that, at least one way, you were never again clean.

And now the new colt he'd had such high hopes for had jumped a slat fence, smashing the top plank, and made east, toward the river. Bold, ballsy. He'd have to change that. The horse was bitey and prone to kick, but all in all a beautiful thing to behold – arching neck, snowflakes burning from inside his hindquarters, the sharp star on his broad forehead, one rear sock black as coal. He was the kind that would never truly be owned.

If the snow had been fresh, Oran would have had no trouble following, but it was patching, receding when the sun had its strong hours. No use for the whistle or calling out "Rango," a name his wife had evidently invented. For hours the horse blundered in and out of mud and melt, over hummocks and through brush and ditches, but other forces – windblown limbs, scavengers out in the warm-up – left equally viable signs. The trail came and went, and the wind in his eyes didn't help. This was not a task for a man with tracking skills or coaxing craft, a former constable and counselman. Nor for a man with farm discipline, good habits and intentions. It wanted a man with his back to the wind and kegs of leftover luck stored in his cellar. It wanted a man with nothing to lose, and he was not that man.

It all unfolded in a Chickasaw minute, and he only had time to think *what? hawk crossing? no, damn it, in full plummet!* before it fell out of a sky like dirty tin and struck the ice, its feathers the colors of late-fall-gone-winter – a slatey blue-gray, the remnant reds and sparse browns. Vein-blue, his brother Hadley would name it, or jute. Shark, pine soot, shingle. That russet shade of a maple leaf fallen maybe eight hours, curling in the cold, its saps all evaporating and fibers fraying. New snow and dirty snow. Hawk color. That's what he'd say, Hadley, who had all the words.

There wasn't time to ponder all that, though, and he didn't think it, just felt it the same way the Morgan felt the chance to clear the fence, the possibility of it bleeding into need in one flash of brain fire. Stout, fast when he wanted to be, nobody's idea of shy, the animal had felt the invitation in his blood and bones. It was his nature to break free.

The bird might have seen something in the ice it thought was prey – chipmunk, grouse – anybody could make that mistake, confusing your self with your similar. Pickings were scarce in this cold. What if it was just like your average yard cardinal seeing its double in a casement plate and attacking out of property pride? Territory. That had spurred the rift between him and his brother, led them to saw the farm right in half. As boys they'd been a team – behind the hounds, stretching fence, bucking hay, even on the force for a couple of years – but since Hadley had returned from his rambles, they'd been like strangers. And it wasn't only territory: the low-splintering, misfelled cedar that had left Hadley with the twisted hip, that was always between them. Now this was Hadley's river, and he had not walked this stretch in three years.

He didn't want the colt to get onto Hadley's acres now and be rescued by that jabbering prodigal. That would lose him his edge. Ever since their father had sworn them to partnership, despite Hadley's wandering years and smugly brisk letters, he had felt betrayed. In the dark room Marge had said, without even sitting up in bed, "Ring him up and say, 'I've got a stray in your fences. When he turns up, just throw a rope on him and phone me back.' What's he gonna do, Oran, refuse you? Call you in, have your Uncle Mac send deputies out to you for not controlling your stock? He's your brother for God's sake." She should have known better than that.

His eyes were tired, and he was squinting, cold. The creature screeched just as it hit the ice, and he thought he felt the collision there on the shore where he leaned against a wishbone sycamore. Then the thing skidded, and there was a little trail of blood. When it stopped and flipped over, he could see it try to shake off the whole mistake, reclaim its dignity. The bird struggled to gain its feet but failed and fell again. He could picture the creature flopping around, actually wing-to-wing and talon-to-talon in contact with its reflection, but of course he couldn't really see that. No image, no shadow. The curve of the beak, though, configuration of the mantle and coverts, coloration of the breast and tail, all designed to fade into such weather as this. Lankier than the sharp-shinned. And the dark cap and owly face – yes, it was definitely a cooper's, an accipiter and an oddly big one, equal to many a crow he'd seen this year. Cooper's, hen hawk, striker, coop. Not the farmer's friend nor the songbird's, but always good for a heart-stopping sweep of beauty or a comforting sentinel pose on a boney post.

It was battling to right itself again, scrambling its claws against the frozen surface, but it couldn't get traction. He figured it must have done something, some bird tactic, to slow itself just before impact, though it couldn't quite pull out of the dive. Why? What drew it to crash into itself? The damage could have been worse, though. Now it was no more than twelve, fifteen feet from where he stood, hackling, and it glared at him with those red eyes. He couldn't move. Blood-colored eyes, and cold. It uttered a shattering, streeling cry.

They had quarreled all through the old man's treatments. When he died, Hadley cussed the typical Sherburne perversity of the will but reluctantly signed on to the forced alliance, saying, "You have to make the livestock decisions yourself. I lack the background, big brother. And old Enoch would have wanted it that way. But I know how a dollar flexes and shrinks or flies. I can learn the market forces and ratios. Futures, juggling, misdirection, presto-chango. I can cut costs and trim fat. I can milk the clouds and cut steaks from the sunset. You were always the fence, I'm the wild-running vine. And what this farm needs is an overall perspective not bound in slipknots or jury-rigged with baling wire and tractor axles just to meet some formula. It needs a vision, and that's what the world has honed me for." Almost every morning they seemed to come out of their corners like bantamweights answering the bell. When the dying evergreen he was chopping with the double-bit had whipsawed at the last second and twisted on its grain, there hadn't even been time to yell out, and Hadley had been laid up for four months, staring out that window at clouds or rain or just the near ridge all stripped of timber, all the while unwilling to admit he was lucky to be alive, unable to accept it as an accident. He would walk with a sway all his remaining days, and when he swung that lame leg forward, he'd be thinking "Cain and Abel," or just "Oran."

They'd broken the covenant with their dead father then, made their division, but the whole slick operation had cost a pretty penny in law fees, and he believed he saw the old man sometimes in his red jacket lurking in the feedlot or under his favorite cigar tree when the popcorn flowers were in full flare or the leaves gone entirely. He could read the scorn in the dead man's face, but the brothers had already filed papers long ago, and now he and Marge had the small cottage but the richest meadow and bottomland. Hadley sat up in the main house and watched his hay go bad in the field, his animals suffer. "Vision." His hired man was little help, and whenever Oran saw him, Had would wave his wolf-head cane at him like some savage with his stabbing spear. It was no good, no good at all.

Then he heard the faint nicker downstream, plaintive and scared. He peered in that direction, knuckled his sore eyes, stared harder. The horse just around the bend would no doubt like to be found about now, the bird would rather die than be touched. His brother appeared to want a war he couldn't figure how to wage, but they were both ice-locked now, shouting at each other even in silence. Nothing to be done.

The distant ridges folding toward West Virginia were not jag-toothed like a ripsaw the way mountains out west were on Hadley's old post cards. They curved, rolled like waves and displayed every shade of blue from heron wing to revolver barrel. Old mountains, they seemed peaceful, even in this hard month, at ease with each other, fortunate in their rootedness. Blue waves under the gray sky, hawk-colored, the whole landscape. Snow and colors to hide in. It should have been a comfort.

The hawk screamed again, more angry than alarmed, and he wondered how solid the ice was, how bad the bird would fight him. Even if it couldn't control its position, even immobile, it had that beak and that warrior heart. If he didn't do something, a fox would. Seeing all this, the coffee club at Gert's in Vesuvius would already be debating which sawdust-stuffed heroic pose would best suit this creature. They'd have opinions about how to position the wings and which glass eyes would be most authentic, most "true."

But what do you do with a wounded cooper's hawk once you've rescued it? Would some raptor center send an expert in a truck to claim it, tend it and train it till it mended? Maybe it had a future as a high school mascot – jesses, hood, bell, the whole outfit. No, it was likely too old to be tamed. Doany McFeeters and her husband were good bird vets and soft on wild things. They would see what was practical, most merciful, repair it if they could. He ungloved, then picked up a glazed limb and pressed on the ice to test its give. In seconds, his hands chilled red. Once he got a solid response, he lifted an apple-sized stone and lobbed it away from the bird. When it struck the ice and skated on across, the report echoed like a rifle shot, but the surface of the frozen river held strong. The bird yelled again, piercing.

The wind was coming stiffer now, the few rays of sun gone to a sky that said "sleet," and "soon." He needed to find the ranky horse, gentle him, blow in his nostrils and halter him with the cotton rope, then walk it back across the cold fields to the barn. He didn't need to be bothering with this fool hawk, so why did he feel responsible? His eyes hurt, his legs were growing weak. It wasn't his to fret with out on the treacherous ice. A fox would get it, a struggle, maybe, but then the end to its misery. Or it would starve, freeze. Would its body heat melt some surface ice, which would then refreeze in the night, clenching feet and feathers in a death grip? There were so many ways to get snared in your errors.

He stepped through the frail whips of a pitiful willow and eased down the bank. Even as he placed his boot on the slick surface, tentative, skeptical, he thought how many would say he was being weak, brooking distraction. But not anybody who had worked at the blood house and heard the dying cries, not anybody who had seen the way a brace of coops could work together like harriers to bring down game on the wing.

The horse in the distance was nickering more now, maybe saying it wanted help and was ready to truckle under, eager for hay, a warm stall and the familiar bray of the jack. The hawk before him was staring defiance, sweeping its wings back and arching its neck, its beak like a gut hook but its eyes somehow softening, asking for something. He should go to the colt. He should bring the hawk in. He should try to soothe his brother's suffering and mend fences or just tear them down.

His eyes were tired, so he rubbed them. He would need them sharp to guide him, if he were going to step out onto the river now out past his own dim reflection distorted but identifiable enough just beyond his feet on solid shore. He pulled on the gloves and limbered the rope, opening the loop, not sure how he would use it. The wind was whistling. Limbs were swaying, and again, just for an instant, he saw something red moving through the trees, then gone.

Under his first step, the ice sank a little, gray water swashing to the surface, darkening the river, a few cracks radiating out, bluish lightning veining the white ice, but not big, not wide yet, not really so bad.

Like a Hawk's Interest in Wind

1

He was kneeling beside moving water, he couldn't tell how big or how fast. Stars overhead were sparse and the moon a shut eyelid. The shards of his reflection triggered no recognition, and he could not read north from south. He was sure there was wind in the trees around him, but he couldn't hear it, and a slash of light on the water was like a silver scar. His hand in the animal's fresh track seemed small, and even in the dark he could tell it was bear or something like bear and was surprised he could not see scat or raked bark nearby nor catch the rank scent. What he smelled were freshly rubbed pine needles. He thought he could feel or hear a horse somewhere nearby, still but heaving like the windbroke saddlebred he'd given Armisted last year. Despite the disparities, the whole atmosphere seemed strangely refreshing, even if the shaggy animal lurked close by in the shadows, its glare locked on his throat. Then the wind came sharper, and he could almost detect the sound and then slight motion in the ferns where he knelt. He brushed a cluster of fiddleheads with his palm just for the sensation. A pointed leaf – gold, poplar – fell on the water before him and glowed there like a star or a spur rowel on the way from the forge to the bucket. His mission was a mystery to him, but he imagined he was in this place to discover, to quench a deep need, though he could not name it. This seemed to be a place where there were no words, but then he heard the horse snorting wetly as it shook its head.

Just as he began to realize he was naked and exposed and started to shiver, a soothing tremolo of sound cut through the night, then grew louder, a bird call finally shrilling, and then he sat bolt upright, shocked awake enough to recognize his cell phone's ringtone. The voice on the other end was gruff and curt but familiar.

"Mr. Sherburne, we got some mischief, serious stuff."

In seconds he had kicked the sheets away, breathed deeply and was sitting up, fully alert but dry-mouthed.

"Not my dog, Polk. Call the real sheriff. You know the drill. I sprung the trap, got the gold badge, talked in the movie. Now I'm the idle rich, and I'm asleep."

Then another voice. "Sherburne, Sheriff Exxum here. I'm looking at the card you gave me, and printed in here between your name and phone number, it says in raised up red letters 'Consultant.' Expensive. Hell, I can feel it with my eyes shut. Well, sad to say, I need to consult you, pronto."

He closed his eyes and could see that moving stream again with the disturbing scar burned onto the water, the spur and the pawprint. It occurred to him that in the dream he had moved effortlessly, still a deft predator, as if neither rusty joints nor the space-age metal ball and socket were part of his current life. Now the aches came rushing back in force.

"I reckon I'm a daylight consultant."

"Doc, we don't cipher this one out quick, it's likely to stay night a long damn time."

He rubbed his eyes and brow. "So what you got . . . just for the sake of argument?"

"Two, uh . . . two officers down – one canine, the other, well, it's Ellen Sensabaugh. Sorry, Doc. Gunshot. She didn't make it. Assailant seemed to know his work, at least the shooting part. Thirty-thirty. An ambush, we're guessing, or surprise." The sheriff paused.

Not Ellen. Goddamn it. He'd hired her, coached her on the range and on crime scenes and watched her make notes like a scholar and blossom into an efficient and imaginative deputy. A quick study, often she'd been two steps ahead of him. She had cop senses, hunter instincts, a future, even her own Wednesday "Is that the Law?" Q & A spot on local radio. Startling green eyes that didn't miss a thing and, eventually, radiated and inspired confidence. He didn't want to believe Exxum's words. Computers, hand-to-hand – nothing Ellen couldn't master. She would have been, what . . , twenty-eight in less than a month? He clenched his right fist and kept listening, eyes shut.

"We're down at the old McClung warehouses on the Maury, near Grant Pearlman's stables, nigh to where the Alone Mill Bridge crosses . . . ."

"I know it, Buck, back of my hand." He opened his eyes again and saw the green numerals on the clock. 2:32. He hadn't slept much more than an hour, and his muscles knew it. He'd been working the roan Rubicon in the afternoon, forking hay, then stacking cordwood when the sun bled down. And, despite the flaring arthritis, he'd moved the living room furniture around again before he poured his glass of Turkey and worried what kind of devilment Forrest might be up to these days. That boy. Doc couldn't get past the conviction that he'd raised his son wrong at every turn, stick or carrot, but that would indict Mina, too, as she had a strong hand in it, and she'd been almost flawless. What that woman had seen in Sheriff Doc Sherburne had to be something beyond anything conversation might disclose. Right up to her last hour, it remained her secret, which she bore with a smile. Then his other regrets began to flood in, shortcomings professional and personal, and he sighed and twisted his neck till it popped. This was not exactly what he'd thought retirement would feel like, but the word "tire" was in there all right.

"I figure you for fifteen minutes away. And Sandy, he was involved, too, but he'll be fine."

"Hurt?"

"Wouldn't earn him no purple heart. Pride, though."

"Crime van?"

"Halfway here, the only number I called before yours. I've learned a thing or two, but they's something twisted here, Doc, something big we don't know yet, and on top of the recent brouhaha over that NFL asshole, it's all just a mite too mommicked up. We're just not this kind of place. I'm starting to grasp at straws."

"Well, it's a real kick to be needed, hoss." But Ellen. He remembered the first time he'd laid eyes on her, in the college weight room working out in those purple sweats and Skins ball cap. For sanity's sake, he had been glad he was twenty years past foolishness. Not just a thinker and a looker, but quick to grasp a situation and make her move. She was no more likely than a Doberman to drop her guard on duty. So, what? Goddamn.

"Doc, I thought you'd want to know from the get-go. They's a horse missing, a million-dollar-plus Arabian or something."

"Now the water starts to come clear."

There was a pause. "Tell it to the Marines, which is me. You're the animal expert." This was Polk's voice again, stone scraping grist, trying for a joke. He'd served in the Corps, and no one was allowed to forget it. What was it they said? Difference between Marines and Boy Scouts is the latter's adult leadership? He couldn't dispute it.

"Shitfire. I'm on my way."

WHEN THE PIPES RATTLED and the well finally sputtered water up, it wasn't like the liquid he'd dreamed, not wet enough. Beside it, the mirage water was quicksilver, but the source of this gushing stuff was plenty deep, and it was cold. Splashing his face and shoulders, he realized he'd been sweating, though the house was not warm after the showery evening. He turned to stare into the curly maple chiffarobe's mirror – long jaw, hawk nose, hard eyes – a Sherburne all right. His personal scar through the salt-and-pepper eyebrow. One gold tooth showing. He ran his hand over his cheek. Emery, but there wasn't time for the razor, and the owls and bats and coroner's crew wouldn't object. Besides, the complaints about his handling of the cult had painted him almost an outlaw.

There's no end to it, he thought, and then his mind strayed to Chris and right on past her back to Mina, three years dead now, despite the medical wizards in Charlottesville with all their chemistry, the herbals and meditation. Did strokes run in the women of the family? No, that was stupid, because Mina was a Kline before she signed up for the Sherburne life – "she-burden life" his grandmother had called it – so no relation to the others – his mother, his niece. Still, nearly all Rockbridge women were prone to something, it seemed, the vaster family. A pang of guilt shot through him. It was troublesome how most any thought of Chris brought forth Mina's ghost. They weren't that much alike – Chris the keen, even prickly civil liberties attorney who chucked it all for food bank administration; Mina, whose soothing gaze and quick wrists could mold any desk pilot into a dignified rider, gentle any jughead horse into a boon companion, quietly calm her husband's frequent rage. Grace personified, but clever and usually right. And it was all too fresh, her fast decline, his desperation to be recovered.

Likely he'd hurried things with Chris, he thought, and with himself, probably uneasy in the quiet house, even after Mina's personal things were mostly gone, but it might not be too late to rein in a little without much damage, get his heart straight. Chris was patient and too whip-smart to overreact to any of his addled stop-go. "And associations," he said aloud, "they're natural as spit. Grief doesn't blow away in a day or even a year, things still going off inside you like a string of firecrackers. But it'll pass." The adage didn't muster much comfort, and he thought of the warmth between the boy and his mother, then the cold shoulder, the boy's refusal to even be civil to Chris. They'd come to words over that. As Forrest's smirking face, not all that different from his own, gradually seemed to usurp the mirror, he shook his head and swore. Cop's kid syndrome, and spite was one habit the boy had likely inherited from him. But Forrest was no longer a boy, not by a long shot.

He twisted the spigot and drew a dipper of water to wash down the Aleve. Surely not this limestone-fretted stuff to blame for so much illness – the asthma, the strokes and the cancers – but the local air was good, few fumes in a town that lived off tourists, college kids and retirees. Two quarries, a timbering outfit, the Blue Ridge Equestrian Center. Environmental culprit? Not here. Industry? No coal, no dyeing or asphalt plant, no more tanneries or tin outfits. Little box manufacturer and tire plant over in B.V., farms, managed care centers. All clean, but he'd been raised by cops and been a cop himself too long to believe in coincidence.

Suddenly aware he was delaying, he sloshed the water around in his mouth and spat.

"This," he said, "is not going according to plan."

Dressing, he had trouble with the right boot and shook his head. Everybody and his dog had said you're good as gold a year after the hip replacement, but the hitch was still there, the instinctive sense of wrong mending, though X-rays disputed his conviction. At least his left leg could take the stirrup and bear the weight. He flexed his fingers and listened to the joints popping painlessly.

Already he was conjuring scenarios. What would even a greenhorn thief think he'd do with the kind of trophy horse that couldn't be disguised or sold or rented to stud? Especially one of those cantankerous Arabs. You'd almost have to believe in a whole underground horse market, and if such existed, wouldn't he have been about the first to know? In the foyer, he wondered if Exxum would give two hoots if he strapped on his full rig, but that wouldn't make sense, no need this trip for cuffs or pepper, the big revolver. Tonight's real action was likely past, and he now held no actual power, beyond the carry permit. This would just be brainwork. Clues, photographs, dead ends, tossing a lariat in the dark, shaking the usual suspects down. As a "consultant," he'd be operating in the shadows and hoped there was still some heat in the trail. And he was glad it would fall to somebody else to drive up Collierstown way in a few hours and interrupt June Sensabaugh at her shearing and stapling upholstery to say, "I'm sorry for your loss." June had deep eyes and a history of bearing grief, but this might be one too many.

He knew from the shuffling leaves on the locust beyond the glass that it would be brisk outside, so he pulled on his plaid woolen and took the slate safari hat off its peg, lifted the sap from the window sill and jammed it into his belt. Then he reached into the darkness of the boot bench and grasped a little S & W 9 mm, which he slid into his slash pocket, confident it held a full clip. Always keep them loaded, his father had demanded, so nobody will ever be shot with that "empty weapon" so often referred to on the late news. "And God bless the Virginia Legislature. Even somebody who actually knows how to use a gun is allowed to carry one." "The Sherburne wit," he thought. The old man had been gone nearly six years, dropped from a cardiac in his garden, just as he'd always hoped, bird-head Colt still jammed into his coverall pocket. The old man. . . but that was for some other time.

Outside, he shrugged more snugly into the jacket but leaned back to expose his face to what wind was moving. Southwest, by his reckoning. Likely there would be no more snow, but the season had not fully turned the corner. Blackberry winter. The moon was a bent coin, low enough to highlight the eastern ridge where the pines sawtoothed black against the deep blue. The damp grass glistened. When he swung his left leg into the Jeep, he felt a stitch in the hip and grabbed the wheel to distribute his weight. "Just like old times, Sheriff Sherburne." Then, "No, not 'sheriff,' just 'mister.' Shitfire. And old to boot." In the back of his mind, the dream river shimmered, promise of a better pursuit, and he could see his face distorted, smeared across the curved windscreen, ghost-like. He twisted the key, threw the Cherokee into gear and scattered gravel in his wake.

2

ALONG MOUNT ATLAS ROAD and Smokey Row, the familiar trees fields and fences slid by in their nighttime guise. This whole area close to the land he'd lived on most of his life was more familiar in dark than in the sun. For professional reasons, he knew every farm light, shadow-walled barn and deer corridor, the dead ends and fence lines, ravines, creeks and brambles. The morels and 'sang, too. The familiarity soothed him and allowed the tumblers in his mind to click and mesh.

"We're not this kind of place." How could anybody, least of all Buck Exxum, say that after the business with the renegade Mormons called Terrible Swift Sword, a gang of heavily armed bastards quoting scripture as they prowled about in their holy skivvies and abducted young women for righteous harems. Reeled them in off the streets and playgrounds for nearly a year, cruised the neighborhoods of Buena Vista in vans and date-doped them in bars. Even had a go at a couple of Washington and Lee co-eds, which was one of their most reckless moves. Those zealots, he thought, must have hated scouting the night spots for their victims, mixing with all those Gen-Zero drinkers of spirits, Tweeters and cursers of God who populated the bars and the so-called margins of respectability. With Ellen for bait but closely watched and wired, he employed every trick in the book, and out of it, to lure them up and snatch them out of the Shallows, and when he got them into his interrogation room, he'd showed them the dogs of war up close. One by one, they broke, spouting scripture and mocking the laws. He hoped they found the state pen a perfect hell.

All that hullabaloo, the sting and arraignment, the trial and then the "Dateline" documentary had scarcely died down, the ink on his retirement forms hardly dry, when the playboy wide receiver, Marcus Watson (aka "The Hurt)," had started showing up in a condo outside Lexington and, if Doc read the evidence right, screwed his way through the college girls and townies till he finally found one damaged or brave enough to cry rape. Doc still expected others to step forth, but despite Ellen Sensabaugh's thorough investigation, that case now seemed hobbled by outside influences, from the scuttlebutt he heard. What the local News Gazoo only half revealed were leads which any respectable cub reporter with a lick of sense would have sniffed, bayed and plunged after at full speed. Anyway, the episode already had everybody on edge, and the national media was still swarming about town like ants on a dead snake. Whatever kind of place this crease of the Blue Ridge called Rockbridge was, it was no longer just colleges and retirees, farmers and small-time pot growers whose bumper stickers read GONE GREEN with a marijuana leaf as an exclamation mark. No longer anybody's haven, it had suddenly become "that kind of place."

In another month or so they'd be up to their eyebrows in routine graduation ruckus, shock and awe fireworks, trustee fanfare, all manner of sly pretense that drinking was not part of the national college culture, that W&L didn't have its share of bingers and gropers who thought affluence conferred license. For once, though, everybody with the sense God gave a nematode just might be wary of anything resembling sexual assault. The rogue Mormon to-do ensured a new vigilance, or so he wanted to believe. But then there was the ballplayer. Much of that collegiate mischief had always gone down inside the town limits, anyway, and was not his problem, though sure to muddle any on-going investigations. Hell, none of it was his problem now. "Not my dog," he thought, "not my wormy, mangy, rip-eared, three-legged, retired dog," but then he crested the rise and saw the blue lights flashing off the trees and the river, and he thought of Ellen, seeing her frustrated in those brief months back when she and Forrest were keeping company, and he had thought, "Atagirl, civilize the little jerk." But his son was so far crossed over to the other side – liquor and pot and petty mischief – that not even having his own private cop could rein him in any more than Mina's shrewd tenderness had managed. His own father would have had an answer, but not the right one.

And now, he thought, to flummox things further the local scofflaws had contrived to turn the clock back to horse stealing.

HALF A DOZEN CIVILIAN cars in the weedy parking lot were spilling their passengers, and one network news van from Roanoke was already on the scene, so he knew the sanctity of the yellow-taped cordon was unlikely to be honored. Two decades ago, he'd have been there already, yelling on the bullhorn, and if necessary, he'd have discharged his weapon in Orion's general direction. But those days were gone, the reception and pressure resulting from his tactics with the un-Mormons proof of that. Now he mostly minded his own business, chored and read about horses, called up Chris or drank himself toward that river of sleep. While one of Supervisor Girton's soft municipal hands shook his in thanks, the file folder in the other had held a petition from the council, the implied message being "retire with honor or prepare for uncomfortable consequences." Results be damned, once the smoke had faded. "Doing the needful," "spirit of the law" and "procedure my ass" were expressions of the past, "rough justice" no longer preferable to cold cases and felons at large. The new day had dawned, so he took the deal.

HE WASN'T AT ALL elated to be again washed by the strobe-swirl of blue lights, shaking hands all around and mumbling the standard witticisms, checking for sugar in the coffee he was handed and confirming that the green light on his digital recorder was on. Nodding to everybody, uniformed or not. At least Polk and Exxum knew to give him space, though Exxum managed to slip a temporary deputy star into his coat pocket, where it clacked against his Smith. He started toward Ellen's unit, then thought better of it and reversed himself. When he saw the black bag on the other side, the blue lights brushing across it put him in mind of a beached mussel shell, and he turned away, pivoting on his game leg and paying for it.

Polk caught his eye and pointed toward the corner of the warehouse where the young deputy, still whippet-lean and pocked with acne, was slumped on a stack of rotting beams in the midst of much scurrying, his head bandaged and even in the erratic light some blood showing through the edge of the gauze. Sandy's eyes were not quite right, but functional. Someone had draped a khaki blanket over his shoulders, and he clutched it together with one hand like a flood or fire victim. Doc got right to it.

"Okay, son? Doc Sherburne here. Start with the chase. We'll go back in a minute to your finding her, but I want the pursuit phase first. Full narrative. Shoot."

"Wellsir, here goes." He pinched his upper lip, as if to free the words. "Uh, yeah, I called for more backup soon as I realized. You know that part, but I was alert that the rear face of the building he'd run into, out there in the dark, even if nailed up and hasped, had old ramps and gates onto the river where the barges used to dock up. You know, where they used to load horses to float to the equestrian arena, and since I couldn't see all that from the front, I was afraid he might, you know, pry up some boards and slip out through a window, so I figured it best to get Solly on in there and tree him. You know Solly. He was always eager on the hunt, about to stretch his leash. You can hear the braid tightening when they lean their weight full, you know."

"I do."

"Solly, ninety pounds if he's an ounce, and he's all go. I made the mistake of reaching for the light switch by the door, double mistake I reckon cause they must of been off at the breaker somewhere in the dark, and secondmost cause I couldn't hold a scent-keened, uncut shepherd with one hand, not then, so he pulled loose and tore off, claws clicking on the old pine floor, and it wasn't a minute till I heard the shot back in the darkness, old Solly yelping. They found the brass. I can still hear the echo ringing. Poor fella." He was fighting back tears. "Then it was just a banging about. Crates maybe. So now I knew he had a weapon and he'd use it, which made me sure it was the right suspect, so you see, it wasn't like I just broke procedures and ran in like the pup. I had to try to corner him inside, I figured. I was sweeping the area with my flashlight, but nothing moved."

Sandy was shaking his head slightly, and Doc could see in the reflected light that he had a sizeable bruise across his cheek and brow. "Badge of courage" he thought.

"Say you'd called it in?"

"I had, and getting out again, he could go anywhere if he – or they, for all I knew – got by me or over the river. Clyde is out with a flu, howcome I was alone. I didn't know how long it would be for a respondent vehicle, so I gave it my best, I mean, I had a plan, but that's when the other shots commenced. I hollered out, 'Stop, Rockbridge Sheriff's Office. You're surrounded.' Standard stuff, and when I went to dive under that table or whatever, something smacked my head. I believe I had a second when I thought I'd been shot, but then I's out. I's gone. Happens I just struck on that damn plankwood jabbing out by the door there. Fool of me. Dark, for sure, but I wasn't just rushing about. I had me a plan. I was, you know, I was aiming. . . ."

His voice trailed off, and Doc could see he was growing woozy again. He reached a hand onto Sandy's shoulder to steady him, and the gesture felt foreign. He could feel his phone vibrating in his pocket, and looked long enough to see it was Chris. He'd just as soon about face, walk off the scene and drive to her, hold her and twine his ailing body with hers, but she'd have to wait. Ellen took precedence now.

"It's okay, son, it's like just prize fighting: everybody's got a plan . . . till he gets hit. Too bad you couldn't stick to the notion of tracking, Solly's job, but shots fired changes the game. Look. Follow along my beam there. Dust so thick you can read the whole story – where he went in, where you went in, the dog, where the perp came out right beside you. The prints – hiking or work boots, looks like – around where you were, where there's a left missing, suggest he stepped right on you as he skedaddled. He might of shot you, Sandy, might of kicked in your head, but he gave you mercy or just didn't give a shit, which means we don't rightly know what kind we've got here. Maybe it's a smart-ass sense of humor, maybe haste, panic. We just don't know."

"Poor Solly. Jesus, poor Ellen."

"Polk says the pup didn't suffer. Likely the same for Ellen. Bastard shoots calm, knows his way about. We'll understand more when the forensics geniuses begin to piece the puzzle. We will get this fucker."

He could see the boy was beginning to shake, tears welling in his eyes.

"You sit tight, Sandy. You're likely concussed. I'll get the rest of your statement from Ex. Maybe what you need now is this." He handed over the coffee. "And Polk will have a flask. You did good, just didn't know what you were up against. Hard to know that. Sometimes it's all shadows. Me, I'd of maybe done it different when I was your age." He gave his Sam Eliot grin.

"Howso, Sheriff?" He was blinking fast.

"Tangled on the leash, fallen, shot my toe off or the dog or some downstream night fisherman on the ricochet, hit a gas can and sent us all to Bejinctum. A full-fledged half-wit. But you, knowing the drill, following procedures, trying to box the shooter, yessir, you did just fine."

The boy still didn't know about the missing horse, but Doc figured he had enough to carry for now. And Sandy hardly knew a mule from a Shetland. Didn't need to with Doc about. Though many assumed Harmon Sherburne had gotten his nickname when he came back from college the first time, a smug comment on his return, the old-timers knew it was from working for Ralph Faile at the vet clinic, and that was why he had long been the horse cop, that and his wife's steadily-growing corral. His career change had divided his parents, but the service played a role, as he'd ended up an M.P. in Okinawa and didn't see a horse up close for two years. Sherburne harbored no nostalgia for those days, but his mother would never call him Doc after he chose enforcement over healing.

Then he caught himself drawing air through his mouth in a soft reverse whistle, tasting it. For the first time in nearly a month he wanted tobacco, just a little packet in the cheek to sweeten the facts. "As if that ever. . . ." And he walked back toward the high sheriff and his cadre, whose feelings about him were, he knew, mixed.

3

THE DAY HAD BROKEN breezy, the gray sky agitated, new leaves twirling, and Doc Sherburne was still short on sleep, blinking a bit as the river like an enticement, gleamed, vanished and gleamed again through the foliage on the west side of 11. He wore a corduroy sport jacket now, the dingy deputy star on his lapel, and a battered brimmed headgear he always argued could not rightly be called a cowboy hat. His face smarted with Aqua Velva, and he resisted touching the gauzed razor nick on his jaw. But his hands wanted something to do to relieve his irritation at riding shotgun while Polk drove, though this was the old gunny's unit, and he held the lawful authority here. What was it they said about second in command? *You're not the lead husky, the view never changes.* He fished a foot of thinly braided rawhide from his pocket and started tying knots.

As a cluster of crows scattered without comment from a blighted roadside locust, the deputy cleared his throat, adjusted his tan cap and broached the topic that had been hanging between them like stale smoke for miles.

"You mind if I do most of the jawing, sheriff."

That last word Polk pronounced in inverted commas, but Doc agreed, while discouraging the use of the title. Both statements soured in his mouth. Polk had always come across as blustery with civilians, able to condescend to anyone from a nun to a judge. He was not much better with officers, but Doc refused to attribute it to his inherited woodpecker hair and close-set eyes. His daddy, also a carrot top, had worked himself from scrabbleass poor to managing an antique mall and been good company, a smiler who meant it.

"Anyway . . . ." The deputy removed an unlit Pall Mall from the sun visor and pinched it between his lips, his compromise with Department policy. "Anyway, the less you say, the less wary, so to speak, he'll be about your presence. Any of them. And it's some that still recollect you wildcatting on that Mormon business. They don't know what to foresee from you. Secret weapon, you know. "

Where they turned off the road the fancy gate sign said, "The Larches."

THAT WAS NOT HOW it went down. Grant Pearlman and Sherburne, who had met only once before, sized each other up, shaking hands vigorously, while both sets of eyes said, "Looks like we're stuck with Deputy Fife here." There was something about the horse farmer, blonde-going-silver and stern-faced – maybe military, more likely military school. He was nearly six three, which meant he and Sherburne were pretty much talking over Polk. He was carefully tanned, sported a horseshoe moustache and wore both a heavy gold signet ring and a fresh haircut. Smoker's teeth, drinker's eyes. Doc knew his primary dwelling to be an heirloom estate on a wooded edge of the Beltway but decided to accept the pretense of "local." A lean liver-colored hound sauntered up, sniffed a bit and ambled off at the first sharp snap of Pearlman's fingers.

"You seen old Duvall this week?" the breeder asked.

"Not to speak at, but his truck's been around town, and a squad of the paparazzi. This kind of event would lure him."

"He knows his stock and is always casting a movie. He would surely have gone starry-eyed over that horse."

"Tell us about it."

Polk, seeming to understand the equation, was busying himself making notes in his billfold pad. Pearlman, who was a clenched-down version of the actor who had played Jock Ewing and carried himself with a blend of force and grace, rocked back in his Tony Lamas and launched into a near-smitten salesman's pitch, the gist of which was that "Sheik's Pride" was a 6-year-old Barbary blacker than a licorice river with a confirmation to put Pegasus to shame, big shoulders for his kind, intelligent lean face and eyes you'd swear belonged in a philosopher. Not a wasted ounce or angle.

Sherburne seized the occasion to survey the terrain – hills to the west, stone-pocked ground sloping toward the water on the east, vast pastures fenced along the river. The sweet smell of feed and droppings was in the air, leather and horse lather, and he could see eight grown horses and a colt in the far meadow, three men working a couple quietly on a string, business as usual. There were songbirds – dees most prominent – in the woods, and just once he thought he heard a tom gobble and flap wings across the Maury. The remnants from the investigative team seemed the only unusual features of the place, and none of the recent drama showed in Pearlman's face. Just as Sherburne was getting bored, the tawny-maned wife in a plush blue robe came down the steps with a mug of coffee, handed it to her spouse and half-heartedly offered to bring more for the officers, but when they declined, she strutted back to the house in showy fashion. Sherburne watched Polk watching her go.

"Trained up like a dream, smooth in his low gears, quick to the whip, saddle-savvy from the get-go. And run! Man, that horse was some Bedouin's wet dream. When he put his ears back and stretched out, you could just see dunes and palms and a moon like a peach, his tracks disappearing behind him in sand." His eyes glazed over, and he forced a grin. "I've never seen a Barb that could out-Arab the Arabs, but this is the one. Maybe nothing like the legends of Eclipse and Herod, of course, but reminiscent. He could rack for a hundred miles and then fight a tiger. Honest to God the best fifteen hands of horseflesh I've ever eyed or stroked or saddled. Once in a lifetime. The damn jackpot."

The enthusiasm from a reputedly shrewd trader deepened Sherburne's forehead furrows, but his hat brim pretty much hid that, and he held his tongue. After all, he wasn't in the market to purchase a horse, especially one that had recently become invisible. The spiel had sounded almost memorized and lacked the flavor of anger you'd expect from a man with emotional ties to either the horse or its worth. Jesus, the thought, he's showing that slick, empty look Forrest can get. Sherburne looked harder into the owner's eyes.

"A damn noble horse, great draw for this week's all-breed show, just his presence. We got our full fee, and then some half-wit who'll have no idea how to ride him or sell him had to sneak in here at night. And with guns, goddamn it. I was sorry to hear about, you know.... Well, I hadn't met her myself but heard she'd been one of yours."

Sherburne was, in fact, saying little more than Polk, but this new turn in the conversation slowed Pearlman down, and he paused and squatted, picked up some straw from the ground and sniffed, then let the wind take it, as if to signal his sensitivity.

"I hope to hell they know how to tend him, anyway. I'm sure you all will do what's humanly possible. And the girl. That's just shit. They need to be flogged. Hell, they need to be strung up like back in the day."

"A man who knows how to bend with the wind," Sherburne thought. "Or something."

"Race him?" asked Polk.

"Hell, no. Just enough show for the horsey press to get their tongues lolling and cameras snapping, then back into the shadows. That old boy is going to fetch a Saudi prince's ransom in the end and spend his life poking mares and eating sweet grass. That was the plan. No need to even risk those legs."

"Ransom." Sherburne looked around at the trim fencing and elegant stables, the antebellum with its three-story dorics and white gliders, and asked, almost winking, "How much bounty would he draw?"

"Wouldn't care to say offhand, not being a horsenapper."

"Insurance value?"

"Have to look it up. It's more the long-term possibilities, and the principle."

"Or the interest," thought Sherburne.

Polk paused in his scribbling. "I'm glad to save you the trouble, Mr. Pearlman. Laptop in the cruiser." He was trying to reassert himself, but he had to feel the other two men looking into each other, maneuvering in subtle fashion, his input insignificant.

Pearlman shot Sherburne a look and said, "Much obliged." What Doc saw in the man's dark eyes was an understanding. Pearlman must have known who he had to deal with here, and despite his affable mask, he wasn't sure he was pleased. Doc was beginning to suspect he knew some things himself, but he didn't want to rush conclusions.

Now that the ball was rolling, the owner quickly ran down what he knew of the previous night's drama. Horses bedded and given a final check, grooms bussed back to their mobile home park, trainers sipping brew in front of the TVs in their caravans. Pearlman and his trophy wife Serena snuggled into sleep by designer single malts, the whole spread was left to the hound who slept like the newly dead under the porch and a pair of screech owls who had recently taken to whinnying in the hillside hardwoods.

Shots woke them at 11:50 – Pearlman had looked at the bedside clock – and in a sentry's minute he was trousered and sprinting toward the river with a Winchester, feeding it as he ran. He was maybe five years younger than Sherburne and, Doc guessed, similarly fit, though on a leaner frame. Likely no titanium rammed up his femur. Sherburne formed the mental picture of the scene and wondered if the fellow had lingered to don the fancy boots.

Polk blurted, "Didn't you think of the stables first?"

"Shots didn't come from the stables."

"*Shots* you say?   How many?"

"I can't honestly recall, Sheriff Sherburne. At least two."

"And now, Mr. Pearlman, for the sixty-million-dollar question?" Polk flipped a page in his notebook. "How long before you to know the horse was gone?"

It turned out that Pearlman had not even gotten down to the water before his head man, Tolly, yelled out that the stall was open, the animal missing. From the porch Serena yelled she would call 9-11, and everyone on the spread was up and scouting about, lanterns or big Mag lights in their hands. The time sequence wasn't clear at this point, but that was understandable. Would Serena Pearlman's be the call that brought Officer Sensabaugh: shots in the night in sparsely held territory. "Jacklighters," Ellen would likely have thought. Trying to wipe the image of her face from his mind, he decided, "No. Those first shots were at her. She was onto something already." He'd been told that examination of her cruiser had revealed no surprises: cold coffee, computer asleep, riot gun still racked. And she had gone down with a light in her hand and her weapon still holstered, the snap undone.

"Your help all present and accounted for, I expect."

"Right, deputy. Just the three overnighters, Serena, me."

Polk and Pearlman ducked under the yellow ribbon and started walking the site, careful not to disturb anything the lab team had tagged or chalked, while the owner unwrapped a slender cigar, lit it with a butane and described the nightly routine, as he led the deputy to the muddy area outside the paddock where Lily Jansen and her intern had made plaster molds of tire tracks. Sherburne said he would catch up and only later learned that there had been "lots of comers and goers" about during the week of the show, mostly part-timers Pearlman called "Mex boys from the horse center." They were, he said, "not shirkers but sly, sticky-fingered, but nothing big." Serena had a trainer out, but she vouched for him, somebody she's known.

While Polk took the statement, Sherburne circled the perimeter – exercise ring, training post, troughs and jumping gates, greenery in pots, a dingy surrey under a shed – but found nothing out of the ordinary, except some scuffs of moss near the trailer ramp. This valley had gotten little rain in the night, but enough for some things to cling. The green clots were off a waffle-bottom shoe, could be anybody's who didn't wear riding boots. He guessed tens or so. Still, he felt something cut through him, that old feeling saying "this is more than it appears," and he waited for the catch of breath that came when stray slices meshed and showed the whole pie. His father used to call it "the dawn."

As he scrutinized his find, he felt the single shiver in his pocket meant to remind him on the hour that he had an unchecked message. Shit, might as well bring Chris out of the dark, he thought, should have done so already. He got the busy recording and wound up saying into the flip phone that he'd been called in to consult on the shootout and rustling of the night before. "Sure you've heard the basics. I'm working, still pert and curious," he ended, "but sleep-deprived. I do look forward to speaking to you without the magic of Verizon."

While Pearlman fed Polk his story, leading here, pointing there, Doc ambled over to where a stocky Latino in a straw cowboy hat was tying up a gray gelding. It was a little Arabian, somewhat in need of the curry but all muscle and gristle and spirit. In exchange for a little harmless update on the local adventures of the skirt-chasing NFLer called The Hurt – he'd been interviewed and released, investigation pending, back in D.C. or St. Kitts: all gleaned from the TV – Sherburne learned from Manuel Tofoya that the missing horse had not impressed him so much, and he preferred this "grullo," which was short on looks but long on performance and personality.

"Jefe," he said, "Sabe los caballos. You would see pronto. That

Pride, that fart horse, he some windsucker, eat air like it was oats. But muy hermoso. Dios mio, he probably wear out on a mare horse fast as when he is the one ridden. Strong pedigree, maravilloso on the book, but an emptiness. Whatever loco stole that horse will have cause to regret."

Sherburne's eyes were already on the silvery river rippling through the shade as he walked away, but he was again feeling the lack of sleep and only waved over his head when he heard, "You see the movie cowboy, you tell him Manuel can vaquero for any camera they got. Verdad. I am waiting him to call."

He wanted to be back near those night rapids, in the spell of some mystery that would help unlock his own nature or just let him drift. River of forgetfulness would do just fine. And this little caper was becoming too easy. No, not little and not a caper, once you factored in the shooting, which he could see was never intended to happen. But some fool had brought a weapon. And did Pearlman take them all for hicks, having his own expired star of a horse abducted to hide his error or collect a big insurance check? With the stable workers likely all aware of the ruse with the Barb, the trumped-up praise for an animal that didn't compete, how far did he think this could go before the jack jumped out of the box? He had to be missing something, not shooting a tight group, but he was getting close.

Then the phone buzzed again, and he spent five minutes exchanging pleasantries and summarizing for Chris. She was hot on the trail of a possible donor of some weight, but she hoped to meet Doc at The Palms for a steak when the sun went down. When she signed off with "love you soon," he thought, "I ought not screw this up, no matter how much voltage the past carries. This is a good woman and here right now. I need to focus, and Forrest will just have to adjust his shorts or find the locks changed."

Back in the Interceptor, while Pearlman and the re-emerged Serena – now in boots, jodhpurs and a fringed blouse made for a less buxom woman – grew smaller in the mirror, waving extravagantly, arm in arm, as if a dinner party had just concluded, Polk jammed the cigarette back into the corner of his mouth and whistled. "Woman's a lioness, no lie . . . but two things you might be more interested in. Pearlman recently noted a 'suspicious character,' who he identifies as 'not one of the ethnics and not one of mine.' I don't know it's a lead, though. And he also knows your boy, who was a mighty big help with the stock in the days leading up to the exhibition. I've met him on occasion myself. Smart as paint and your spitting image."

The wind picked up again, and Serena Pearlman's dyed blond hair flared out like a pennant in the side view. She was almost familiar, but he'd seen hundreds of the type, former buckle bunnies grown shrewd and greedy, maybe easier to profile than her husband. Forrest, though, seemed out of place here. He was a stellar hand with horses and would be one of the go-to guys if someone had a stallion he wanted to show off to good advantage. From curry brushes to hoof pick and right down to shoeing, you couldn't do much better than Forrest, but this was not his crowd, more the clique he had contempt for. And even Pearlman could probably peg him in five minutes' conversation . . . but no, that was wrong, he thought, as trees and again the meandering river slipped by. Forrest had his cunning side and knew what to conceal and when. He could work a stranger and make a good show. And if there was trouble, it drew him like honey. A bad thought was beginning to come to Sherburne, like the first scent of fresh buck piss in the rut.

He sighed deeply, leaned back and pulled his hat brim over his eyes.

"I've got to steal some sleep here, sarge. We do have some pondering to do, but what you say we just let it drift till we hear about the plaster casts and prints and such. I appreciate you tending me this morning, but now us geezer types have got to rest."

"Sure thing, boss." Doc could hear all the undertones in that.

4

THE NEXT EVENING and no closer to seeing Chris, whose newest work emergency had cancelled their steak rendezvous, Doc was heading to Glen Maury Park in Buena Vista, where a little picking and grinning festival was scheduled. He knew the boy didn't saw fiddle much anymore, but he was still a moth to the flame of hot bowing, the campsite gossip, beer and a conviction that it was you, rather than opportunity, that did the knocking. The people he thought of as his tribe, with whom he cooked up business and swapped stories, were likely to be there and with them Forrest working some angle. Sherburne hoped to find him and hear him out before his name came up in a dispatch, so he was rehearsing a way to thread the needle between inquisitive and patient without seeming to interrogate.

For Doc, lawmen bringing the family their anger and their habits of force wasn't just an unsound practice to be forbidden, then reprimanded. It was criminal. More than once his own glad-handing father had hammerlocked him or cuffed him for just long enough to "give him a taste" of the power of the law and a man with the law behind him. It had reached a new low when he was seventeen, pumped up to fullback proportions but already learning to grit his teeth and avoid confrontation in most circumstances. The rift between them had never healed.

One Sunday evening just before "Bonanza," the last dinner dishes rattling in his mother's hands, his father was supervising, telling her stories. Doc had bushhogged some and tended the horses, so was excused from kitchen duty. While his father smoked, sipped bourbon and talked with his mother, Doc – still Harmon at home – had been on the bran-colored sofa trying to show Lizzie how to find lowest common denominators. Anything mathematical left her anxious and bird-eyed, and when he corrected the same mistake a second time, she'd done something – he never knew quite what – with the mechanism of her ring binder till it snapped shut like a varmint trap on the webbing between her thumb and forefinger. Her scream was straight out of the slaughter pen, and as Doc moved to extricate her skin, his father had rounded the corner, quickly misconstrued the situation and with a hand on Doc's throat shoved him away, shouting, "You asshole."

Once he regained his balance, he stepped forward, trying to explain, but his father's fist caught him in the jaw, snapping his head to the side. Doc reeled but did not go down, and his counterpunch to his father's eye was almost involuntary, with substantial weight behind it, and his father stumbled backward, stunned, sending a lamp crashing to the floor.

In seconds the old man had recovered and was shouting "not under my own damned roof" and saying something about "gun," and then Doc clearly made out, "I'll shoot you, you little son of a bitch." The old man headed for the stairs and the bedroom where his service revolver would be on the telephone table.

Doc's mother grabbed her son by the shoulders and guided him to the door, saying, "Get out. To the barn, out to the woods, Harmon, anywhere. Go. I'll try to gentle him," and then she turned her thin body to block the door from her husband, who appeared on the stairs, his face redder than rhubarb. Backpedaling fast, Doc could see the cylinder of the .38 special open and turning as J. W. Sherburne checked the rounds. His mother's voice was almost shrieking, "Jack, no. Stop, stop and think."

Doc never knew what passed between his parents in the following hours, but he spent the night in the back barn's loft, wide awake, as afraid as he was angry, for he had never seen a handgun look so large as the Smith and Wesson nor a man with such rage in his face. After decades of dealing with people whose anger and horror contorted their expressions to gargoyles, that face could still surface in his dreams and wake him. The next morning his father's cruiser was gone before he awoke, but after ball practice he went home with Robbie Finlay and stayed over. Across the next few days he gradually returned to the household, keeping to his room in the basement, receiving mostly cold stares from his father and strained smiles from his mother. Lizzie said she was sorry she'd screamed and hugged him, breathing shallowly as he tousled her hair, but he knew this was only a side bet, the bigger issue undecided and not about her.

Things never returned to the old truce again. Wrestling season, track. He spent the next summer on the road working at Faile's second clinic up in Staunton, and when fall approached he shipped off to Charlottesville in time for pre-season practice. Though his first run at college lasted only two years, he did not sleep under their roof again until he was well into his thirties. He could remain every bit as angry and spite-driven as his father or, for that matter, Forrest, but some spring or ratchet in him had been turned different that long-ago Sunday, and he repeatedly told himself that rites of passage were always hard and tried not to linger on it. He kept his mind on his goals and aimed to find the right current to drive him along in a balanced fashion, always working extra hard, just to prove his worth, to show the old man wrong, even when Jack Sherburne had long stopped looking.

For this reason, he had kept an even temper and a civil tongue in disputes with his only youngster. And Forrest had been a happy enough child, smallish, less affable than secretive, as if he drifted in uneasy waters his father could only guess. Not until high school did he start to practice his lying at home, keeping it petty. He had become something of a flim-flam with teachers and down at the Southern Inn, where he bussed tables in the summer, cleaned up and evidently ran a penny-ante crap game after hours, drinks and smokes included. Once he dropped out of VMI after a year of majoring in demerits and general studies, he began to move easily in the rough crowd of townies, the drop-outs and fly-by-nights who collected rumors, tattoos and misdemeanors. Even when his boasts got back to Doc, the confrontation was mild, the ultimatum matter-of-fact. What Forrest had told his running mates was that he could outwit his father, whose interrogation techniques were widely praised and studied among his peers statewide.

"The boss hardly ever has to interview anybody more than once or twice," the nineteen-year-old had said. "But I'm used to his pattern, his little stories and concerned looks. I can see his 'surprises' around the corner, and when it comes to worst, I know how to plea bargain. He's got a soft spot and's always wanting to believe I've done something less – not stealing a pick-up bed full of pumpkins to sell, but just lifting a couple for jack-o-lanterns for the fun of it. All it takes is knowing the rules behind the rules."

Doc had hoped a measured exile, which he had never meant to

be permanent, would have a scalding, an instructive effect, but it held for years. Even when Mina took sick, the boy would only visit for an hour or two and avoided his father when possible. Without ever waving a firearm or applying any corporal punishment, he had inadvertently managed to repeat his father's error and banish the son who, Mina said, was his spit and image, his very double in the saddle, but a decidedly better fiddle player.

And Forrest was not really mean, had never seemed interested in bullying or fighting but preferred hunting or fishing for specklers in the Little Cowpasture. Unlike some of his associates, he hadn't made a study of violence or revenge, but he was easy enough to flatter, and that could lead to trouble. First one off the high dive because a buddy boasted he had "perfect form," first to take on a hard horse because some winking lot hand had said, "That Sherburne boy could ride a diamondback." Probably first of his age group to shoplift or roll a joint, and all along he was learning the patter, becoming, Sherburne thought, "slick as owl oil." It was likely he'd been brought in and egged on into much mischief, but talked his way into more. As Doc pulled his Jeep up to the pavilion at twilight where a series of old-time sessions were in full swing, he thought, "I'll know soon enough." When he opened the door, smelling the woodsmoke and burgers on a grill, tobacco and a hint of marijuana, he smiled at the memories, but then the side glass flashed something, and he realized the badge belonged in his pocket just now.

THE "INTERVIEW" DID NOT go well. Forrest and two old hands from the rowdy crowd, Franklin Clegg and the Pretty Boy Butch O'Dell – neither of them strangers to the Miranda recitation nor lacking a rap sheet in the computer – were laughing and drinking longnecks on the perimeter of a fire where eight musicians were driving "Fox on the Run" to its crescendo, a laddering of "fox" into five syllables rising to a shrill falsetto. He caught James Leva's eye as his bow rocked rapidly across the strings, and they nodded. Clegg caught the fiddler's movement and turned, showing his spade beard and long face. He had for a while been known as a crank cook, but not in Rockbridge, and Doc guessed from his eyes and bone-lean look that he'd not given up that avocation.

Instead of a hat, Forrest wore his sunglasses propped on his head, and the collar of his green Levi jacket was turned up against the dropping temperature. He too was lean, but broad-shouldered and beginning to fill out like his father. He hadn't shaved in several days and had a bit of a foxy look himself. With his hand lightly on Forrest's shoulder Doc said, "Son, can you spare me a few minutes."

"Why not." There was nothing in his voice to suggest surprise or even resistance, and his face was too shadowed to reveal much, but the way he slumped as they walked across the ball field told Doc his speculations might not be too far off. He heard "long harm of the law" and "Dochead" aimed at their backs in Clegg's twangy accent, along with a snaky laughter.

They were near second base now, the campsites and RVs at some distance, but all around them banjos were ringing behind fidgety mandolins, guitars and bull fiddles keeping it all honest, a dozen tunes rising to meet in the air under a clear sky and a coppery moon. Buena Vista's signature rounded peaks looked black but soothing against the muted blue. Somebody was slapping a gut bucket bass. A few couples by one Winnebago were flatfooting and yee-hawing. In two months such a concert would begin with whip-poor-wills and give way to jarflies, who would work the whole night shift, as if stitching the world together, but for this cool spell the only music was human and incidental. The atmosphere was one of the things that had summoned Doc back to Rockbridge and kept him there all these years. In the field lights he could study Forrest's face as he concentrated on draining his Miller bottle, and what Doc saw there was not bucolic so much as tense.

"Leva's in fine form."

"When's he not. They say he teethed on fiddle wood."

"Likely. But I don't see your guitar-strumming Redskin friend."

"Don't start in. That dude stopped being my friend soon as the Lilburn girl said it was forced. She's not known to lie. He's nobody's buddy now."

"Good to hear." Sherburne knew he'd stepped on hot ground, and unnecessarily. "Guess I should have known."

"Yeah."

He looked into Forrest's lonesome chestnut eyes, saw his late wife's signature there and felt the pangs of her absence. They talked haltingly, asking after a couple of mutual acquaintances, but it didn't take long to get to the subject at hand, as everyone knew some version of the story by now, and when Ellen's name came up, Forrest was unable to conceal his emotion. His jaw set, and his breathing came deep and labored. He had treated her badly in the end, and his mother had slapped him and said he should be ashamed.

"I know she meant more to you . . . ."

"You'd be surprised."

"I'm all surprised out, Forrest."

"So did somebody just decide to off a cop or what?"

Doc caught the strain and knew the question itself was wrong.

"It looks related to the horse thieving. Timing, proximity. Has to be." He removed his hat and ran a hand through his thinning hair to give something a moment to happen.

"I was there, out at The Larches just two days before, but you'd know that. Am I some kind of 'person of interest'?"

"More like an ace in the hole. Mostly Pearlman uses semi-skilled, beyond his regulars. What did he call you in for?"

"That black needed some special handling. He'd turned rangy, nipped at Pearlman, started cribbing his stall. Man said the horse had taken a foolish mood and needed some fresh ideas."

"But . . . ?"

"He's was swallowing his own breath, and it wasn't just for the occasion. A bored horse, addicted to those endorphins sucking can trigger. It's going to take some trainer with serious vet moves a good while to break him of that habit, probably a Miracle Collar for the long haul, but Pearlman wanted it camouflaged for the time the bastard would be on show. The horse and I took to each other, and I know a couple of tricks. You too."

"Maybe. Makes it clear why the horse doesn't race. But things went well, I mean, in the public eye?"

"If anybody suspected, tongues were held." He spat onto the ground and then rubbed his boot toe over it.

"Any scuttlebutt about what went down between the show and the crime?"

"I don't know. And why are you asking me?" Gesturing broadly with his empty bottle, he brought some long-dead actor to Doc's mind, but he couldn't call the name. It was clearly meant to camouflage an uneasiness. "Hell, half the people here fretting strings or tapping their silly feet around this field know at least as much as I do about what goes on out there at the horse circus. Did it ever occur to you that I'm not some 'embedded agent'? Looks like you've taken an interest in all this."

"Like a hawk's interest in wind."

"But what the hell are you nosing into it for? After the way they treated you, I thought you wanted to be free of serving the people of this fair community." The spin he put on "fair" was vintage Forrest.

"Fair question. For them, I'm in it because I'm supposed to know horses and horse mischief. For me, it's a little about having to keep living here breathing this air and a lot about Ellen. I thought we might have that motive in common, son."

Doc could see that Forrest felt the sting. He had long been too good at such ambushes, and it was probably still out of line to use professional tactics on his own family. Mina had said that more than once. That was why he winced but kept silent at Forrest's retort. That, and because this was business, no matter how much he wanted to deny it.

"Maybe they bring you in to take the gloves off. Rough justice, right? Who better?"

"When you're topping timber, son, don't strap your belt above the cut."

"Yeah, I reckon." He studied the tops of his boots again.

The whole conversation was headed downhill, and Sherburne heard fear interceding, creeping into the rhythm of Forrest's speech. He needed just a couple more answers out of the boy before he shut down entirely with his signature "whatever."

"Pearlman. Exactly how did you hook up with him to start with? And do you trust him?"

Forrest's voice was tentative, slightly high. "Butch had been working with his wife on a kind of consultant basis. She competes in barrels, the fancy western and such and wanted to weave a few sweet moves into that latter guaranteed to snow the local judges. If you've been out there, you've probably seen her prize quarter horses and thoroughbreds. Being close to the event, Butch knew the judges' preferences and tendencies, so he coached her up. He's a champion on the sweet moves. Not really cheating, just what you'd call 'resourceful.' They got to talking about the balky horse, I suppose, and somebody asked him, and he said me, near as I can tell. Coincidence as much as anything."

Doc was nodding, not just registering, but pantomiming agreement, as Forrest kept rubbing the ground with the toe of his boot.

"Pearlman's a little fancy himself, but he pays good wage and on time and keeps his temper, far as I've seen. It was a good enough gig. That answer your question?" Sherburne wondered why his son was afraid of the wealthy horseman, but the fact was there, and it didn't add to Forrest's credentials as innocent bystander.

"Anything else that would help me, help Sheriff Exxum . . . "

"Who you hate."

"'Dislike' is all I can afford on retirement. Anything else that would help us run down whoever did this?" He removed his hat again, scratched the back of his head. It was designed to maintain his control of the pace, suggest he was pondering. He spat into the dirt. "Horse be damned, Forrest. Anybody involved in the killing of Ellen Sensabaugh is going to wish he could hide in the heart of a stampede."

"No mercy, then, Dad?"

"None within the law's limits. Anything you know, you believe, even a hunch?"

Forrest looked him straight in the eye for the first time, locked gazes and lied. "No. No, but I wish there was."

Doc couldn't remember the first time he'd caught that pitch in his son's voice, but it always signaled some kind of dodge, never an incidental one. It was as if the boy had a special tone he saved up in the belief that it provided cover. Doc thought of it as off key, about a half step above true notes. This time he was sure it meant the ground was not solid underfoot.

"Thanks for your cooperation, Forrest. You come round and see me soon, you hear. See how Rubicon's grown into an impressive working horse. Some Tuesday or Thursday, one of Chandra's days. I'll have her whip us up some cheese grits and shrimp. I've got some beer from a micro up in C'ville, dark ale I think you'll like."

"Sure thing."

Sherburne tried to keep his parting handshake almost official, untranslatable, but then he added an affectionate pressure at the end, just to be sure the boy might realize he was not so cunning as he meant to be. Forrest would not quite meet his eyes again.

"Just call first."

"Yep."

It was Leva's red fiddle that led him out. He had just finished whining a verse of "Orange Blossom Special" in Vassar's style, and then he let the horsehair, sheep gut and mysterious fiddlewood complete his testimony. Doc was inclined to look over and wave his appreciation to the musician, but he wanted Forrest to see him striding away as if fully absorbed by the task at hand. He wished the fireflies were out already or that it was light enough to see the first color on the redbuds and the pinwheels on the blackberry canes. He hoped he could still catch Chris tonight. His watch's radium signaled it was nearly nine, and he said, almost involuntarily, "Clegg's hard-boiled but no thinker. Butch of the slick smile, though. Concealed weapon. '05? Or '06? Sex assault twice, but both charges dropped. Always in the vicinity of mischief. They'd better not be dragging Forrest in."

WHEN EXXUM ANSWERED HIS cell Doc said, "If Butch O'Dell

didn't steal that horse, a speckled trout is a blue spruce. But he might have had permission, might have just been sneak-assisting more than stealing. He's at Glen Maury right now, but you might have a welcome committee at his cabin when he gets home. Just for routine questioning. If the horse is there or has been there, signs will show. One question for him would be: Are you going to enjoy taking the fall for that rich son of a bitch?"

"You know some of this as fact?"

"I do not." In the glove box he found a tin of no-spit tobacco pouches and inserted one behind his cheek.

"So why are you not hard-roading it there yourself?"

"Trespassing, Sheriff. I'm nothing but a consultant."

"Not to mention a pain, but you think this will wrap it up?"

"I'd not make that bet."

5

NOT CONFIDENT IN MUCH of his crew, Exxum told Pete Goodloe and Gentry Wallace he'd meet them at O'Dell's cabin on the bend of Jacob's Ladder out toward Vesuvius. He evidently wanted to catch the bear in its den, so they converged just before midnight, the moon gone and a rain spattering. Crossing the yard, they had to wade through weeds and creeper, discarded satellite disks and engine parts. Goodloe stumbled and almost fell over a headless stone angel that clearly belonged on someone's final resting place. Approaching the front door, they quickly determined that a trailer had come and gone, breaking branches and leaving deep tracks that resembled the photos from Pearlman's, and there were enough horse apples beside the garage to suggest an actual horse, a cribber, in fact, as one corner of the building was freshly gnawed. What they had not expected to find when O'Dell opened the door in his skivvies, was a female voice shaping the dark behind him. As Exxum told Doc, "I knew it straight away for Serena Pearlman's, and I must of grinned like a possum. She was dressed in a bedsheet she didn't quite know how to wear. I felt like a safecracker who'd hit the combination."

"They do love the wicked boys," Doc added.

"Who would of thought her behind it? I wonder if she used the same bait on all three?"

"Three?" The question had practically seeped out.

"Franklin, he'll likely be showing the buyers to Yankee Mule Ridge . . . ."

"You're shitting me."

"Nope. That's where they picked, up by the waterfall."

"And?"

"Sorry to be the messenger, Doc. Butch says the details were all Forrest's design, especially not bringing the out-of-state rig any closer to town but parley-vooing up there where there's no human lights. The trailer's been waiting over in Amherst, two characters Butch says have country club written all over them and a satchel of cash, the whole thing clandestine as a B movie, even a little old-fangled."

Sherburne watched the dark landscape glide by, dream-like, inviting him to close his eyes and tune it all out. He gripped the wheel harder. His worst fears were beginning to materialize.

"So they're coming south and Forrest is hauling the trailer up the Parkway from Vesuvius? Whacky plan."

"Gets a bit worse." Sherburne could hear Exxum's radio squawking in the background, but he was focused on the words, blinking a little at the fir tips as they curved across his windscreen.

"He's going to ride it. Daybreak. He had this notion to overland with the animal and make the transfer quick and quiet. "Sneaky," Butch says. Course, Butch's got his own agenda and might have agreed if we'd asked where Forrest has hidden Blackbeard's gold or Stonewall's arm. Meet me at the station?"

6

SATURDAY MORNING HAD OPENED soft, showery up on Timber Ridge, but it had found Doc already in his Levis and downing two Aleve caplets with his coffee. As the shower passed and the first edge of amber showed in the east window, he perched on the side of the sleigh bed and stared appreciatively at Chris's brown hair with one gray streak, her olive skin and smooth shoulders. He wanted to seize the moment and preserve it, to drink her in for hours, to pull back the diamond-eye quilt and stroke her warm skin from brow to soles, but he leaned forward and nibbled her on the ear, then blew into it softly.

She rolled over, languorous, eyes still shut, automatically reaching for his body but not finding him where she expected. After they had made love just hours before and lay quietly in the lamplight, she'd joked that the scar along his flank resembled an old bent sickle like those ornamenting Cracker Barrel walls. He'd smiled and thought, "Rather go back into the forge than serve somebody as be a souvenir over bad cornbread."

Now he whispered, "Time. Sorry, Sugar." As he extended the coffee to her, she shook her head as if to chase out some nightmare remnants or refuse the stoneware mug, but then she accepted it.

"That was the shortest night on record, Doc Sherburne. I'll be glad when this thing is over and you and I can 'consult' again, no holds barred, followed by blueberry pancakes and a whole day ahead."

"You read my thoughts, Sugar. As usual. I'd as soon never see a horse again as do this day."

"Look." She was pointing to the west-facing window where the season's first luna moth, drawn to the lamp, was trembling against the glass.

ALTHOUGH FRANKLIN'S RAM AND the trailer had been seen around town that evening, no one knew it was being sought till after Sherburne had slung O'Dell against the holding cell wall and he started to break down. He also gave up Clegg as the shooter on the river and then, when he saw that pinning the scheme on Forrest was not winning him constituents, named Serena as the bright spark behind the whole idea. Her motives would probably remain secret as long as there seemed to be holes in what the lawmen knew and her lawyer liked the cards he was holding. Polk guessed it was just run money. Russell Pooley figured it was some kind of revenge, and Sandy just shrugged. Exxum himself ventured, "Gentlemen, I am damned if I understand any of it beyond the fact that a horny May gal with a rich December hubby has fallen in with some studs who happen to like to steal." Opinions about the value of the horse and the random way crimes evolve were offered. Arguments over the virtues and vices of the fairer sex started and sputtered. Nobody mentioned the deep misfortune of Ellen's straying from her routine checkpoints, but Sherburne sipped his coffee in a corner, staring at a framed photo of the three rookies in her class, none of them now left on the force. The picture was one of the few remnants from his tenure, and though he'd been in the office for only twenty minutes, he figured he'd about reached his limit.

The outlaws' plan had been as simple as it was stupid: to count on Serena to keep Pearlman distracted while they stealthed in and absconded, then to meet the buyers with their own trailer on the Parkway, swap the Barb for a knapsack of cash and swing on back to Lexington for a nightcap and a good laugh. Franklin, youngest and least civil of the Cleggs, would collect Forrest behind the Tapp Inn, then the horse at O'Dell's, and off the two of them would go. Plan B, which had stalled with the knowledge of the shooting by the river but which had swung into action as soon as Doc left the fiddlefest, was to drive the horse from O'Dell's garage to Vesuvius, where Forrest would saddle up and slip off, then at first light follow a path, now used mostly by deer, where few riders had ventured in half a century. Overgrown, the trail had during the Civil War been a regular route for non-partisan raiders and later by those in the white whiskey trade. Over rough, usually mossy terrain, it twisted through laurel hells and across limestone fields and scraggy brambles more forbidding than moonscape, and it swerved around caves black bear and snakes favored when the snow was down. Occasional swards of broomsedge or wildflowers offered easy footing, but the path's main feature was its scabby ascent from 1200 feet to 3500 in five crow-route miles. It was much longer for anything wingless, and it began in Vesuvius near the railroad bed not far from Gert's Store and Game Check. That was where Sandy and Bill Corcoran had found the trailer, and when they called it in, using their car radio in the absence of cell reception,

Exxum's immediate question was, "You telling me both those idiots climbed on that horse and tried to go up the ridge in the dark where there's nothing but a corpse of a path?"

It took Sandy ten minutes to scout around and report back. "Only one man got out of this truck, and he left an empty box of 30-30 cartridges on the cab floor, a couple of rounds in the crease of the seat."

"Sounds like Mr. Clegg. I won't say some such hasn't been coming."

But when Exxum told Doc he shook his head. "I've hunted that surround, the first ridge and the holler right after, before it goes steep. Almost twenty years ago. Forrest was just a chap but had a Ruger .22 bolt action. I can't say about his more recent trekking in the area, but he knows it. If that horse is trying to escape Pearlman by stumbling up Rangle mountain to a caravan, he's taken Forrest for company."

"Surely not even Forrest is fool enough to start that jaunt in the dark."

"Exxum, there's fool enough to go around, so don't go painting my boy to me. He'll be holding up somewhere with a cold camp, resting the money horse, feeding him and brushing him calm, waiting till dawn. He'll expect somebody will see the rig not long after that, but he'll count on time and his trail sense and the secrecy he doesn't yet know has broken up to give him the edge. Maybe he'll count some on the lack of a cell tower out that way to work for him, but he won't be able to reach out and touch either. He won't realize the whole conspiracy has collapsed or that Sandy has already found the trailer or who's going to be on his trail on that mountain about sunrise."

"And who's that?"

"The one man who can catch him before he gets up there and possibly talk him into seeing the lay of things clearly."

"And if he can't listen or see his way to admit he's beat?"

"If Forrest can't throw in the towel, I'll do whatever's necessary."

The sheriff paused, then said, "Sheriff, it takes a hard-barked man to hunt his own kin."

Sherburne crossed the room and took his hat from the rack. "I don't want somebody else catching him when it's too late to turn back or getting trigger itch just because trackdown is exciting. It's no secret that Forrest himself can shoot, and he's now pretty spooked. Stupid as it sounds, I might be everybody's best hope for a result that doesn't involve a second coffin. If O'Dell lured him in, I can maybe lure him out."

He stared at the raggedy horse thief in the holding cell.

"You want to shake him up again?"

"Hell, Exxum, I didn't want to the first time."

"Let's look this over, Sheriff. You're not what you were, hip and all. Are you sure you're up to this? You know I've got some volunteer riders I could send with you, at least. Old hands. Or why not let us just locate the trailer up on the scenic route and trawl them all in when Forrest gets there? Polk could back you up. He's got shortcomings, but he's a good horsebacker, and you know, Doc, if this goes wrong, it's not just your ass that's in a sling. I could be the next ex-sheriff, even without fake Mormon maniacs."

"Polk. I'd as soon sleep with rattlesnakes. And the boy will have some glasses. If he senses something off kilter, he'll just keep riding and getting more desperate. No good outcome to follow that. He won't ride into a trap, but if he sees it's me dogging him, it will set him to thinking. I do know him. A gang of riders, and he'll not think so much as react." He settled the hat on his head and started buttoning his jacket. "I know this is no plan anybody would have invented, but now it's got to serve. And remember, I serve your interest here when I serve mine, which I intend."

"Anything you need?"

"To talk with my spiritual advisor."

"Gear, firearms, armor vest? Forrest aside, we don't know where Clegg is, and he'll have no family reasons to hesitate."

"He'll likely be taking the Parkway to the meet, wanting his share of the payoff but safe from being seen with a stolen horse in tow. Or he'll have taken the chickenshit highway toward Florida, believing distance to be his ally. Either way, you'll reel him in."

"I'll get out a call on his Ram."

"I'll head home, tell Ruby we're going to a morning trek and catch a few winks. See you at Gert's."

ON THE WAY DOWN eleven, Chris, who had agreed to drive his trailer back to the house, wanted to know what he thought would happen to Forrest if things didn't complicate further. The light was beginning to gather itself, but some clouds to the north looked surly. The redbuds along the highway were showing their colors, and the landscape that had seemed stern and forbidding for months was becoming more inviting. The spring wheat was showing and great battalions of starlings whirled their strange geometry like some computer-designed pattern of birdshot. Deer too hungry to sense their danger browsed on the shoulder, and he kept his speed down.

"He'll serve some time, maybe make his way to a roadside crew, if he's lucky. It won't be long enough to ruin his life, but might be he's on that path already. I almost wish he'd head for the flatlands when he gets out, just leave Rockbridge to his past. He'll be harder then and will make his own life harder because of it. If I can't straighten him, I don't care to be a spectator."

"You don't think he'll see it as a life lesson and try to reform?" She swiveled a bit to try to catch any message in Sherburne's eyes. "I mean, maybe this is naïve, but courses can be altered. The strayed sheep can be saved. He's a bright young man, and by God he's got good genetics."

This was the way she usually complimented him, just obliquely enough to pass unacknowledged, and when Doc turned to look at her, he saw her fresh-brushed hair framing a face that could still make juries gawk, but also the right side view mirror, in which the landscape was rushing past like a river of stirring and budding things that would in an instant be gone forever. Right now he figured a man ought to hold his focus on what was immediately before his sights, to lower his threshold of attention to the one thing the world had come down to for now.

"Well, he had one good set, but the other's in question. Jury's still out." He forced a smile. "I begin to suspect every skill I taught him came tainted."

"Why would that be?" She placed her left hand on his shoulder.

"There are rules between the rules, and I've gotten them all tangled up."

"Oh, look at that red-tail on the power lines." She pointed, but his gaze did not follow her lead.

"I hope we don't find Polk down there at Gert's. I've had all of him I can stomach for one consult."

"You know I'll worry about you up there. My one hope for the world right now is that you'll still be casting a shadow tomorrow." She cradled his cheek in her hand.

"Forrest, too."

"Yes, you and yours, Doc, you and yours."

In five minutes they had put behind them the snakeback macadam of Bright Road and were pulling into the circular drive at Gert's, which was already open for strong coffee and yesterday's Krispy Kreme. Thankfully, Exxum had kept his deputies from whirling their circus lights, and as he swung out of the truck, Sherburne was absorbed for a moment with the stiffness in his back and the torque in his hip like a rope being twisted tight. The silhouettes of ridges were distinct from the sky, their line meandering like a river, and a covey of stars were still showing in the west. He tried to stare the foothills before the heights into clarity and thought, "Forrest, I know you're out there. Be your smartest self today, boy, for everybody's sake."

"Best get this horse rigged and get him moving while the bees are still in the butter." He winked at Chris and dropped the ramp.

7

IT HAD STARTED EASILY, the morning chill an ally, the first ground familiar, blackberries with their white petals and early prickers the worst barrier. Amble, canter, once a dead run through a rye grass meadow when Ruby was ready. Cloud by cloud the sky was opening up, as if someone were brushing dense limbs aside, but the mist from the hollers and ravines gave the woods an eerie feel, the dogwood flowers seeming to float in mid-air. At Brinder's Run, where the signs of Forrest and the Barb were all over the place – tracks and scuffs, a gum wrapper amid the lady-slippers – the pursuers had drunk their fill. Doc doubted the horse was aware of his muzzle reflected in the shaded water. When he saw his own face, though, he spied a tired, stern man, his own father as much as himself, and alerted by the sight he could smell the lichen, iron in the water and somewhere fresh scat, probably a coon or fox. Before he spat a mouthful of water into the still pool, he reached into his pocket and pinned the borrowed star onto his coat. If he were going to act on behalf of some authority beyond self-interest and paternal impulse, he might as well bear the brand. Chickadees complained in the hardwoods, and occasionally he saw the quick-cautious forms of winter-coated deer, curious but keeping their distance.

Shortly afterwards they had gone by Auten's orchard and his bee yard, two smashed hives amid the ground fog already testifying to the stirring of bears. The blossoms were just beginning to open and release their fragrance. Much as Sherburne enjoyed the idea of keeping a colony, what had always held him back rushed to his mind in images: once a black bear has had a taste of honey in one place, nothing a bee farmer can do will discourage him till all the sweetness has been exhausted and the gums demolished and scattered like a village subjected to artillery fire. These hives were mostly empty in this season, but he could see where his son had stopped to rob the still-sleepy insects of the winter's dregs. Moving slowly now along the ridge above the apple trees, he reminded himself that men were far more like bears than like the selfless bees. Women, too, he added, and some people go into the human combs for money, intoxicated by it, just driven wild and unwise. Money and pride. Why else would Serena, O'Dell and Clegg have opened such a foolish play? And lust. Shouldn't overlook that. With Forrest, things were more complicated, as he couldn't pass on a chance to show the law foolish, since he saw the system as pretty much his father. Did that make him more guilty or less? And was Sherburne himself somehow an accomplice? Mina would have said not, would have promised that he'd done all a man could. He had to duck suddenly to keep a wild cherry limb from unhorsing him, and the sudden motion activated every ornery joint in his body.

Maybe Chris might have been more circumspect and asked if we didn't all share guilt in so many ways that clemency and forgiveness just had to come with it, over time. He thought of her sleepy green eyes just opening again, and her pulling the quilt across her face like a mask, teasing. If he had a future, he knew it was with Chris, though he had to make peace with his ghosts, too. Ellen's death and the knowledge of how thin the bonds were between his son and himself had made it clear that the solitude he'd been falling toward in the past year, over a year, was an intermission that life doesn't allow. He'd been aware of that fact since boyhood, so how had he forgotten?

The path grew faint again due to deadfall limbs and punky logs with their mushrooms, red roots jutting up like the bones of men and animals, and he had to work the reins to help the horse choose the better footing, while he made sure that the fresh trail and the path didn't diverge. This trail had secrets, he knew, that would never come to light, tales of rancor and maybe even romance, pursuits not unlike this one, family matters, matters of justice. Doubtless there were real bones shallowly concealed at every turn. Staring ahead at the little cedars and anonymous vines, he heard a hawk, likely a red-tail by his rising-then-falling scream. Scanning the sky and high trees, he could not see it or any other birds. Had Forrest heard the same cry and wondered what had triggered it? It could be a bond between them, that cry across the heights and wild spaces. An omen. That freedom and discipline were not contraries was what he needed to explain to the boy, to show him, persuade without pressing, if such a dialogue were at all possible now. "Damn fool," he said, of no one in particular, then clicked his tongue and slapped the red horse's butt with the reins. "Good Ruby. We need to make better time."

At another time, this path, despite its rigors, would have been worth a pleasure jaunt to see where the sycamores and willows gave way to poplar, sumac and poke, then to densities of white oak, ironwood, hickory and fir. A few jacks were showing in their pulpits on soaky ground, orchis were up and flagging. A ruddock blurred by like a scarlet bullet, followed by his dull-colored mate. But there were roughs, as well. More than once he had to dismount and lead the horse, who was usually as sure-footed as a scotch ram, over stubborn terrain where the limestone was loose and mossy with the week's meager rains. It was easy to pick up sign on those stretches, but by now he was convinced he had only to keep to the ghost of the path and he would find . . . what? The culprit? The rider? The young man who might be the last of the Sherburne line? Two hours after he had kissed Chris and shaken Sandy's hand, tightened the girth and swung into the creaking McClellan, he was making decent progress but weary of the rocking motion of the saddle which taunted his back and both hips. When he flexed his fingers, they sounded like kindling snapping. He downed two more Aleve gels and resorted to a tobacco packet to sharpen his attention. Between gum and cheek the sachet was not really sweet, but he soon felt the stimulant in his system and swore again that he would give it up, as he sucked his palate to enhance the effect. Checking his compass, he wondered if this path didn't veer off toward Whetstone Ridge, instead of Yankee Mule. He couldn't recall, and all he had to go on was a scared snitching crook's word, though he did have his true bearings as the sun kept climbing. The waxing moon would soon be up in the east but concealed by the Windy range, and the fourth time he had to lead Ruby over scabby patches and sweet talk her, he toyed with the idea of letting Exxum's team do the damn work, just throw it in and say "too steep, too dense with new cedars and scrub," but he knew there was no cell phone reception till you neared the crest and the Parkway, no way to recant, so he soldiered on, trying not to think about Abraham and Isaac, a parallel too close for comfort, too strained for consideration. That was when the horse lost its footing and began a sideways slide.

"Whoa now, whoa." He clenched the animal's sides with his knees and hauled back on the leathers, and the pain that shot from his hip both down the leg and up to his neck made his eyes widen and breath suck in audibly. It was the worst jolt in months, but he was able to swing out of the saddle at the right moment and stop the horse on solider ground. For ten minutes he led Rubicon, talking gently about the nature of the law and of human instincts, any babble he could summon, so long as it sounded confident and mellow. They both needed more composure. When he saw partial prints of Forrest's boots, he knew the Barb had been troubled by this stretch of rough. He wasn't falling farther behind, but he needed to be closing. When the ground gave better traction, he mounted again and drove the horse less cautiously, not even granting a second glance to an impressive antler shed just off the trail or a low-slung hornet's nest not much bigger than his fist.

Before long they had come through the Blue Needles, though the spruce there were not properly blue except caught in a stormy light when the mist twisted among them like the spectral bodies of the dead. And soon, on this trajectory, they would cross the Parkway, where there might be a truck and trailer waiting, along with men to whom Doc would present no more than a target. He knew Franklin Clegg had no love for him and had sold, or at least delivered, weapons to the Latter Day Knights, though the proof wasn't quite there. Given another couple of months, he'd have unearthed it, though. Now, if Buck's story held any water, Clegg knew he'd get no clemency over the shooting of Ellen. Sherburne tried not to think of whether the other officers (or Mina, could she be here) would see in all this even more travesty than he did. How deep did the blame cut into him? It didn't matter. It was his to bear, and he quickened the pace.

Already Forrest and the Barb were ridging toward Augusta County where even with his temporary deputy badge, Doc was only a civilian, but that wouldn't free either of them. This had to be ended before they came in range of the rendezvous, had to be solved before Forrest got clustered up with his worst influences. So long as the boy hadn't killed anybody it was maybe salvageable. He'd been duped, and maybe a good lawyer could make the case that he was, for all he knew, essentially helping Serena Pearlman relocate a horse that was legally her own. When he heard Ellen had been killed, he just panicked and tried to hide it. A valuable witness for the prosecution? Unlikely, but if Doc could talk him in with no more harm done, it might go light, lighter. There might be a cleansing and no need for further blood to spill. That's what he was hoping as he reined in the horse to check his compass and make his periodic survey of the terrain. Some hard time, but not enough to ruin the boy's life. He had to make this work. As Mina would have said, "This is where your gift lies, Doc, finding the basic justice lurking inside the law." Time, though – that was the key. Far behind him he could see the sun silvering off the river, which was beckoning to him like the place of rest. A boar's snort seemed to come from both the north and the west, but he saw nothing and heard no leaves scuffled. He had climbed a long way, but not cautiously, not the way he would have man-tracked an armed felon who might plan to waylay him. You had to trust to something, he thought.

He knew from occasional lens reflections the boy was trying to glass him up, calculating space and time and options, using all the art his father had given him over the years. Forrest knew exactly what was happening and might start to sweep his trail some, lead the horse through running water for a spell, the coves and ridges, drink from his canteen at the canter, might even make certain he had chambered a round in his Remington. That was likely, no matter how much he knew or didn't. Just precautious in his recklessness. A Sherburne.

Though the air was humid, the stolen Barbary, aware of another of his kind, was likely snorting and pawing the ground up on the heights. His own mount was already schooled not to announce what he knew in such circumstances. Whicker of horse, a bough moving in the valley, a skirl of dust or covey of quail flushing – now that he was closing, anything might give Doc's progress away. Forrest had known for an hour who they'd sent, but knowing and seeing were not stopping, and his son would realize his own skill was not enough, any ruse futile, close ambush too risky and foolish and rockbed wrong, that all he could conjure was a warning shot or delay, and not much of that, unless his rendezvous and exit strategy were planned for close by.

They crossed a knob with blueberry brush on the far side, and he noted that the redbuds up here were showing no hint of flower. How much stomach did the boy have for all this? He couldn't strangle back the faint suspicion that this pursuit was part of Forrest's scheme from the starter's pistol. Mano a mano on the brushy ridges, a race at least, a test. That was crazy, he thought, downright demented, but still maybe there, unconscious. Doc's dream on the night of the phone call came back to him – the shining river, quarry not far ahead, his own appetite for the chase. And his nakedness. But here the main object was more akin to gentling a stubborn colt, to soothe and settle, talk sense. The real question did not hinge on his intention or his strategy, but how far into the dark country the boy had gone. There was trilly on the ground, squabbly crows disputing his right to be there. The slab rock was not easy to negotiate, but Ruby had heart and was learning more about balance with every step.

Then he could see just enough movement on the next ridge to know that Forrest had wheeled the Sheik and given him the heel. Limbs shook and dust rose. Doc touched one flank with a spur, just as a whisper, and Ruby moved like a hound that had sniffed the fox. The ground directly ahead of them was easy, a sward of grass, bird's-foot violet and new pines. "Git," he said, and Sherburne was coming on now, faster than most would attempt, every touch of the trail hot under his eyes, his jaw set and the hammer strap of his holster loosed from habit and jouncing with the motion of the horse. He did not feel the morning heat or his lungs working hard. The metal joint in his hip was a steady ache, but he could summon the strength he needed, and the horse wouldn't know he was weak-thighed. And strength wasn't ever the crux for a seasoned rider, just habit and ease in his seat. He leaned forward, and then he gave the flanks another graze.

The strawberry roan put his ears back and took the gallop. He appeared to see it all as a lark and almost lunged with every stride, not even close to a lather yet. Leaning further over Ruby's neck, Doc had the impression the animal was in an ecstasy and would like to laugh with his own dark power like the horse in the Bible. They were in such concord, he grew confident he could overtake Forrest in time to prevent further mischief, as if the horse gave him dream powers. Weaving through paw-paw trees and outcrops as natural as a river follows its bed, he was coming on. The sounds of hooves on the stones and then the solid earth and the breathing of the horse were all he heard, the swoosh of a pine limb as they brushed it aside and moved, he thought, "like the wind."

Following the trail's diagonal up haggard slopes, he registered the thinning-out understory and saw that the rocks and trees gave way to blue just above the stark arrowing points of acid-killed pines. He was nearing the Parkway, and if he didn't emerge close enough behind to see or hear Forrest and the stolen animal, he'd have to guess whether they took the asphalt south or north. He paused on a swag of green ground to read sign, and just as he leaned forward to urge the horse on, he heard the bullet snap the air nearby, the crack of the rifle followed by the flat impact of lead on mossed stone. The recognizable voice said, "You've come too far, old man." He thought he could smell cordite on the wind, but that might be a phantom sense, just due to the unmistakable sound of the shot. God knew he had phantoms enough. He realized he should dismount and pull his Winchester free, but instead he just held the reins steady, let the horse paw the ground and snort in frustration. If his father could see this, he'd have shaken his head and yelled, "You should have stayed an animal doctor."

Scanning the treeline ahead, above, he spotted on a knob amid a stand of young cedars a green that was not needles and not quite still. Forrest's jacket, and beneath that a black darker than the night they'd left behind. It was moving from side to side, and he reckoned the boy's control of the prize horse a little sloppy. Not accustomed to shooting from the saddle. And sunlight on metal – he could see that as well and thought he picked up a whiff of diesel fumes.

"I see you've got the better of me, son. My rifle's in its scabbard and I'm putting my hands up in view." He had to breathe deeply to amplify his voice. "You need to listen to me outline how things stand and see that there's hope for a bargain here. Clegg shooting Ellen, that's at the heart of it, and the D.A. will need witnesses who did no killing to corroborate O'Dell's story about the Pearlman woman and how things went down." He took another deep breath, tasting the piney wildness of the place.

"I came up here hopeful."

The boy rode around the trees, his rifle level and ready. Seeing the Sheik for the first time, Doc had to restrain the impulse to let out a whistle. The gloss of the horse was astonishing, and the lather he'd worked up just served to highlight the unfoamed patches. To the eye, he was everything everyone had promised – confirmation and intelligence, a poise you'd have to call noble, and energy to spare yet – but Sherburne quickly pushed on with this chance to make his case.

"I wanted to help you take this gift. Exxum will see to it you don't get the handling Clegg's headed for. Do you hear me? Accessory turned state's witness, you'll get off light. Happens all the time. You know it does."

He waited, knowing he had to get the boy talking, too, had to make him say human words.

"Well, isn't that the way of it, Daddy. You all get people, friends, to turn on one another, turn snitch, then you pick us off one by one. You know I've been busted before, and they're not going to treat me like some sunny angel."

"Minor stuff, junk charges. This is no game, Forrest, but it does have smart ways to go and other ways to go. You and me wait it out for the sheriff's crew to get the bracelets on your buyers and such, then we ride in, all the guns with me, but you freely directing that fine looking horse. Just that picture will burn into them, more like cooperation than any surrender. Worth a thousand words."

"Why do I feel like Geronimo here? And how'd he end up?"

"Different times, different circumstances. Think about what your mother would want you to do now. She'd say to show your grit and face up to the music."

The horse appeared to recognize he was at the center of this exchange, and he reared up, pawing air. It was Doc's chance to go for the sidearm, but he didn't take it, not because the horse recalled that coal-slick river of his dream, though it did, but because he had confidence that there was enough of Mina's sand and decency in

Forrest to keep things from taking a tragic turn.

He rose in the stirrups, then cocked his left leg in front of the saddle and crossed his wrists on the pommel. Leaning forward, he was letting his body confirm what he was about to say.

"Son, this is in your hands. I didn't follow you up here to stop you or to bring you down. I just came to let you know the path still forks, and you could go either direction. My way . . . ," he paused, thinking "whoever controls the breathing," then added, "and we work on this together, see what we can do to bring the whole thing to a close. Everybody still standing."

The boy wasn't answering, but he wasn't moving, and Doc didn't know whether or not he'd levered another round into the chamber.

"I know how you felt about Ellen, no matter what you showed. She got too close, and it was the best and scariest thing in years, but this whole shebang went beyond pranking or just stealing when she went down. Now we've got to make it right for her sake. I'm sure we can."

Forrest eased the black horse forward, his ears twitching, his breathing loud. Then the boy lowered the rifle across the saddle and slowly let down the hammer. He rose in his stirrups with the poise of a lifetime horseman and in one motion alighted on the uneven ground.

Sherburne nodded and started a grin that reached up and squinted his eyes. He nodded again, but just as he turned his head to spit out the tobacco, he saw the motion among laurel leaves on a knoll just east and slightly down ridge of Forrest. The light was in his eyes, but as he reached back for the pistol, he was able to discern only the brightness of sun striking a barrel, and neither the sound of the rifle firing nor the passage of the bullet were in his world, which was suddenly blacker than any river polished by dream or the daylight realm. Maybe he heard a sound inside him like a hawk's cry sheared in half. Maybe he saw the face of his wife or his father or his son's, but he pitched backward off Ruby, who spooked and ran off up the ledge as Doc Sherburne's body struck a limestone boulder and rolled down a little slope, scattering scree which rattled and clicked under the reverberation of the shot, coming to rest on a ledge where the year's phlox was just beginning to blossom. Then the only sounds were the stones sliding under Forrest's feet as he plunged downhill, the branches he rattled as he brushed them aside and the long echoing syllable of his "Nooooo."

R.T. SMITH is Writer-in-Residence at Washington and Lee University, where he also edits *Shenandoah*. His previous collections of stories are *Faith*, *Uke Rivers Delivers* and *The Calaboose Epistles*. His books of poetry include two winners of the Library of Virginia Poetry Book of the Year Award: *Messenger* and *Outlaw Style*. Other work has appeared in *Best American Short Stories, Best American Poetry, The Pushcart Prize Anthology* and *New Stories from the South*. Smith has received the Governor's Arts Award from both the state of Alabama (1988) and the Commonwealth of Virginia (2008). He lives in Rockbridge County, Virginia, with his wife, the poet Sarah Kennedy.